HAROLD ROBBINS
AND JUNIUS PODRUG

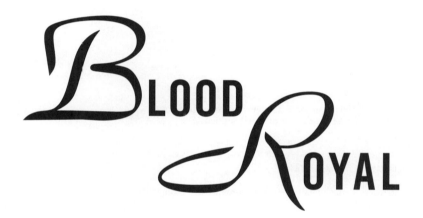

A TOM DOHERTY ASSOCIATES BOOK
NEW YORK

BLOOD ROYAL

A Forge Book
Published by Tom Doherty Associates, LLC
175 Fifth Avenue
New York, NY 10010

www.tor.com

Forge® is a registered trademark of Tom Doherty Associates, LLC.

ISBN 0-765-30811-8 (hardcover)
EAN 978-0-765-30811-5 (hardcover)
ISBN 0-765-31509-2 (first international trade paperback edition)
EAN 978-0-765-31509-0 (first international trade paperback edition)

First Edition: September 2005

Printed in the United States of America

0 9 8 7 6 5 4 3 2 1

Harold Robbins
left behind a rich heritage of novel ideas
and works in progress when he passed away in 1997.
Harold Robbins's estate and his editor worked with
a carefully selected writer to organize and complete
Harold Robbins's ideas to create this novel,
inspired by his storytelling brilliance,
in a manner faithful to
the Robbins style.

❖

For
Adréana Robbins and *Jeff Greenberg,*
with love

(Trotsky, too)

Acknowledgments

*I want to thank the people who assisted in getting this book through
the creation, editing, and publication process:
Jann Robbins, Hildegarde Krische, Carol McCleary,
Elizabeth Winick, Bob Gleason, Eric Raab,
Irene Gallo, and Kevin Sweeney.*

❖

1

❖

Once upon a time, in a kingdom far away . . .

I was nineteen years old when I was asked to become the next queen.

I rode through the streets in a glass coach to the cheers of thousands on my wedding day.

And it's true that I have two older sisters, a wretched stepmother, and that I was scrubbing the floor in the kitchen when the call came from the prince.

People called it a fairy tale when a teenage girl with a poor education, whose only work experience had been babysitting, became the Princess of Wales and would someday become, by the Grace of God, Queen of the United Kingdom of Great Britain and Northern Ireland and of her other realms and territories, Head of the Commonwealth, and Defender of the Faith.

Six months after that ride in the glass coach and a wedding televised to the entire planet, I threw myself down a stairway soon after I became pregnant with the future king.

I had fallen through that thin line between dreams and nightmares.

Now as I stared at myself in the dressing mirror, a mature woman with pale features drawn by tension, my knees shook as I took a gun and put it in the small bag that hung from my wrist.

❖

I didn't hear the maid enter as I was fumbling the gun into the little bag.

"Your Royal Highness, I beg your pardon—"

"What?" I said, startled. I held the gun close to me, concealing it with my dress.

"The—the cream you sent me for—" she stammered.

"Put it on the counter and leave."

The woman put the jar of makeup on the dressing table. Her face was flushed.

I stopped her before she went out the door. "Please remember what I told you. My husband is not to be told I've arrived. Nor is anyone else. Do you understand?"

"Yes, ma'am."

She flew out the door. I knew what she was thinking, that the princess was acting erratic again. "Hot and Cold," I once overheard a staff member call me while talking to another employee, because of those mood shifts the tabloids all say I have. That's where I find out about myself, not from family and friends, but from what's been reported in the tabloids.

I wondered if the snotty little bitch of a maid lied about not telling the prince that I was here. I'd always known that the staff has worked against me. I made many mistakes and one of them was trying to be friendly to the help. The servants respected His Royal Highness and the toadies who hung around him and treated them like footstools—but they were appalled at me for popping into the kitchen to grab a sandwich and chat with them. It had never happened before. Familiarity does breed contempt.

After the door swung shut, I ran for the bathroom, dropping the gun on the floor. I didn't make the loo but threw up in the sink. It wasn't the bulimia this time, I hardly had anything in my stomach. It was my raw nerves. My skin was clammy. As I leaned over the sink I got a rush of cold chills, then a hot sensation crawled up my legs and back. I held on to the sink for support as the burning nausea spread from my toes to my brain and I teetered on the edge of passing out. I slowly slid down to the floor and sat with my back against the wall. The tears came, as they always do when these attacks come. In the haze, I thought about the gun lying on the floor of the other room.

❖

Good work, they find you passed out with a gun nearby and they really will lock you up.

As I talked to myself, my thoughts went to my two boys. Tears came that I couldn't stop. What would they think? What would people tell them about their mother? They needed to understand that I wasn't crazy, that it was the situation that was insane, that things were so confusing for me, sometimes my thoughts spun like a merry-go-round.

How could I explain that there are horrors that are far worse than murder?

I had to go on. I got to my feet. My knees were still wobbly, but I stood up straight and leaned on the counter for support. I took deep breaths until the room stopped moving and stared at the face in the mirror, pale, drawn from worry, eyes puffy from crying. "The fairy-tale princess isn't doing too well," I told the reflection.

I blew my nose and rinsed my face with water, but there was no way I would be able to get rid of the redness around my eyes. I got my feet moving and went back into the dressing room. I knelt to pick up the gun, not daring to bend over for fear the nausea would hit again.

As I went back to the mirror to put the finishing touches on my face and my costume, I heard my husband's hunting dogs baying outside. I knew it was just the pack giving out their last volley before they were placed in the kennels for the night, but the sound reminded me of stories I'd heard about dogs howling over the body of their dead master. People say animals can sense things beyond human experience. I shuddered.

I hurried with my costume, wishing I could have the maid help me, but I could not take the risk. I was not expected to attend the prince's annual costume ball after the fox hunt at Cragthorpe. Everyone knew—at least everyone who read the tabloids, and that was just about everyone—that I hated fox hunts. What does a poor little fox feel when the dogs get to it, when they rip its guts and throat—*what does a man feel when a bullet rips through his heart—*

Terrible upheaval in my stomach rose again and I rushed back to the sink and dry-heaved. I had been alternating between dry-heaving and vomiting all day, eating only a little food in order to have some-

❖

thing to throw up because it hurt so bad when it seemed like only my insides were going to be wretched out.

When I came out I sat down on the vanity stool and thought about what I had to do. What would people think? How would the world judge me? Would they understand that the fairy tale became a nightmare, that love turned to hate, that everyone has a breaking point?

Thinking about my husband brought a poem from Byron to mind.

> When we two parted,
> In silence and tears,
> Half broken-hearted
> To sever for years,
> Pale grew thy cheek and cold,
> Colder thy kiss . . .

Colder thy kiss.

Isn't that the truth. I used to joke that my sleeping companion on trips with my husband was a vibrator. That's how it went, the other woman, all over my husband like a bad rash while I held a vibrator.

Frankly, I was tired of being the discarded wife who had to look on while her husband told another woman he wished he were a tampon so he could always be inside her. Imagine my horror when I found out that my fairy-tale prince was recorded saying that over the phone to a married woman.

I was not Mother Teresa. I am a *woman,* with the same needs, desires, and even lusts as other women. Men may need to just get it off, but women need cuddling and romance. Living in a palace and being married to a prince didn't mean I don't sometimes need my ego stroked and my clit caressed. It didn't mean that I don't need to let my hair down and let the slut come out of me once in a while. You could not put me on a shelf in a room full of medieval armor and Ming vases and expect that I will curtsy to queen and country every time you take me off the shelf and wind me up.

People have wondered about my romantic frustrations, but you know, royalty has a protocol for everything, even making love. A word of caution for women out there who fantasize about marrying a prince—

❖

never marry a man you have to call "sir" until your wedding day, and thereafter having to walk down the hallway to his room on those nights scheduled for coitus, pretending to the spying servants that you're not horny, but just have a need to talk about matters of state.

And never engage in "coitus"—it just isn't as satisfying as good, old-fashioned lovemaking.

Do you know what separate bedrooms do to romance? They said I'm a silly girl who read romantic drivel, those Barbara Cartland stories of women and men who come together in passionate embrace. Maybe I did read romances rather than philosophical tomes, but none of the lovers in those books have separate bedrooms—*and they live happily ever after*. Maybe if—

No, it was too late for all that, there were no more "ifs." I was so tired of wishing and wanting, of hoping things would change. And tired of protocol, sick to my marrow of being a fixture in the institution of royalty. . . . I wished I could have puked out that part of my life and flushed it down the loo, too.

All I ever asked was to be treated like a woman, not a piece of palace furniture.

Now there was only one way out.

I completed my outfit, a pirate's costume, Blackbeard, or Bluebeard, or whoever the old-time buccaneer was. I selected the pirate's garb because the antique pistol I took from my husband's collection went nicely with it.

It was a pretty little gun, small and clever like a toy, but what made it real was the weight and grip. It wasn't really an antique; it fired a regular bullet rather than black powder and a ball. But it was an historic piece—the mistress of the Duke of Orleans had shot the duke with it when she learned the duke had taken another mistress. I had chosen the weapon carefully, certain that the tabloid press would easily find an analogy to the situation that I faced with the other woman crowding my marriage.

I'd fired a gun before. All of the royals were given training by the Royal Protection Service, firing the same sleek and modern weapons that police and terrorists use. The idea is to be able to pick up a gun that's fallen on the ground during a terrorist attack and use it. All I really got out of the lessons was which way to point the gun and where the trigger was, but that was all you really needed because they taught me not to aim but simply to point and pull the trigger.

That was all I had to do tonight, I told myself, just point and pull the trigger—the weapon would do whatever else was necessary.

I slipped the gun into the waistband and surveyed myself in the mirror. I didn't look like a very terrifying pirate, but like a tall, slender blonde, a young thirty-something, mother of two, features drawn, emotions ready to burst, a woman undergoing physical and mental distress. And I saw something else, a look in my eyes, I thought, a bit of the feminine feral, that wild, preternatural glint a woman gets when she can't take any more.

Thoughts started crowding my head again about my two boys, the oldest a young teen. What would they think? How would they handle it?

Tears welled in my eyes and I took deep breaths. *One step at a time,* I told myself. *Just take one step at a time and you can conquer the world.* I kept that silly thought in my mind as I left the dressing area and went into the bedroom.

I hated rooms like this, twenty-foot-high ceilings, gilt molding, elaborate murals, furniture made before King George was fighting the American colonies. It wasn't *like* living in a museum, it *was* living in a museum. Modern heating was hidden in the walls, but it was still a cold place. It would be cold to me even in the middle of a heat wave because the coldness came from the institutional nature of the place. Royalty was an institution. Royal marriages were an institution. There was nothing personal and passionate about institutions. I wasn't attached to anything in the room—nor to the furniture in any of "my rooms" at any of "my homes." That's why the prince carried his childhood teddy bear with him—even when he traveled or seasonally changed homes. He had never known anything but the institutional life of royalty, and that little stuffed toy represented a tiny speck of normalcy.

Cragthorpe was a duke's country estate, one of those extensive properties that came with the title Prince of Wales. When we were in residence, this was *my* bedroom. Not *our* bedroom. I know, this bedroom thing was really caught in my craw. None of those toady courtiers who hung around my husband had bothered to tell me before we were mar-

ried that we would have *separate* bedrooms. And nothing I had imagined prepared me for it—certainly nothing in my "literary" education
based upon romance novels. As a teenager, and then as a young woman
barely more than a girl as I rode in a glittering carriage to St. Paul's
Cathedral, I had fantasized about love, about having my own "Prince
Charming." In those daydreams my nights were warm and intimate as
I lay in the arms of my lover, naked unto each other, soul mates, his
heat firing mine, our love becoming volcanic . . . nowhere in those
magic moments did I ever imagine *separate* bedrooms. I often wondered
if the servants kept track of the number of nights my husband traipsed
down the hall to my bedroom—and vice versa. Did they have betting
pools about how many times a month we did it?

I pushed myself to the bedroom door one step at a time, and opened
it. The air in the hallway felt cold against my feverish skin. I heard
sounds from the party below where eight hundred guests were gathered for an old-fashioned "hunt" dinner while cameras beamed the
event to millions. Even without the gun tucked in my waistband, I
would be tense. Few people realized how frightened I was of the public
appearances I had to make, how strange and terrifying it still was
when I appeared in public with thousands shouting my name, to have a
hundred hands reaching for me, dozens of camera flashes hitting me. I
was really not sure what sparked the public outburst of enthusiasm
wherever I went, but I suspected that it was because people believed I
was living a life that they'd only dreamed of. Of course, those people
had little understanding of my life, they didn't know how utterly boring
and stifling life was as an exhibit piece in a museum.

This time it was going to be even more frightening to face an audience. This time I had a gun.

The grand stairway that no manor house would be without was at
the end of the corridor, a sweeping path with a gnarled oak banister
down to the Great Hall. I loved hardwood banisters, so warm and
strong, so enduring. Walking down the stairs, my hand running along
the banister, feeling its strength, was one of the small pleasures I found
in living in museums. I was once accused of sliding down a banister in
Buckingham Palace. It was the same stairway I used the first time I
hurt myself when I was crying out for understanding.

❖

I went along the corridor in a daze. A servant was posted at the top of the stairs to make sure that guests did not make their way up to the royal rooms, but I didn't notice him until he greeted me. I was sick, terribly ill, with an almost overwhelming desire to run back to the loo and vomit.

I had to stop and hang on to the banister for a moment when my mind took flight and my knees turned to jelly. Thoughts of my boys kept popping into my head and I had to fight them back because I knew I would collapse if I let my emotions escape the tight rein I had on them. The boys were at school. And they would be well cared for. The queen would take them into seclusion. Their grandmother was the wealthiest and most powerful woman on earth. The boys would want for nothing. *Except love.*

"May I announce Your Royal Highness?"

I stared blurry-eyed at the servant posted at the bottom of the stairway. It took a moment for him to come into focus. "No, no, I want to surprise my husband."

I kept myself going, one step at a time, but the dread was making my feet drag. Music came from the balcony, a Melbourne symphony on tour of the "old country" and roped in for a free royal command performance that they would probably later use in their advertising. Being a Royal was much about promoting the country's products. No one told me before I married a Royal that Cinderella had to be concerned about where her glass slippers were manufactured.

As I got closer to the balcony doors and the party noise and music got louder, a merry-go-round of thoughts spun in my head—I saw my husband at our wedding in his magnificent uniform, saw him across the table from me at so many dinners when he was reproachful and unsympathetic about my "condition," saw him surrounded by those cronies who curried royal favor and were always all over him like a bad rash, saw him in the arms of that woman. . . .

Is it right? Am I the crazy one? I fought back my fears and doubts and kept moving forward, forcing my feet along. A blur of people were on the patio, with the orchestra off to my right. I kept my eyes straight ahead.

He was standing next to the balcony railing, looking down at the

❖

boars that were being barbecued over a huge bed of coals. His costume was black, from boots to hat, with a black mask over his face. Black Bart, the English highwayman. It was the costume my dresser told me he'd be wearing. Even with the mask, his ears made him recognizable.

One of the toadies next to him was pouring champagne off the balcony and onto the boars roasting. Cheers came from the guests spread out on the lawn as $1,000-a-bottle champagne splashed on the cooking meat. When you are rich enough, you don't think about the inappropriateness of showing off with expensive champagne at a charity ball.

Bright light from the television crew momentarily blinded me. I squinted and kept my eyes locked on him. One of his friends nudged him and gestured in my direction and my husband turned, starting at my approach.

I heard my name and realized it was the TV announcer off to my left speaking into his mic, telling the audience that there was a surprise appearance by the Princess of Wales. I didn't need a lip reader or crystal ball to know what thought jumped into the head of the prince's cronies the moment they saw me: *There she is again, being erratic, saying she wasn't attending and then suddenly showing up.*

I stared at my husband. There are moments in life in which it seems like time stands still—the moment I was married, the first time I made love, the birth of my children. I suppose it has something to do with an adrenaline rush that captures your mind, your whole existence, at that moment.

My heart thumped in my chest and my ears filled with a roar as panic and terror shot adrenaline through me. I fumbled getting the gun out of my wrist purse and nearly dropped it.

One of his friends, that toady bastard who had been leading the campaign to discredit me, laughed and said something to him. I heard a little of what he said through the roar in my head, something about "Maybe she's going to kill you," and my husband laughed with his friends.

I was ten feet away when I stuck the gun out, not aiming but pointing it as I'd been taught.

He grinned at the gun and spoke to me.

I don't know exactly what he said, something about how real the

❖

gun looked. I pulled the trigger and the world exploded. The bullet knocked him backward, his champagne glass flying out of his hand, his body twisting as he fell to the floor.

As my world spun out of control someone was beside me, grabbing my gun hand, propping me up as my knees collapsed.

Behind me I heard the television announcer's shocked voice.

"The princess has shot the Prince of Wales!"

❖

2

❖

Old Bailey, London

Anthony Trent, Q.C., lead defense barrister in the case of *Regina vs. Princess of Wales,* came out of the courthouse and paused at the top of the steps in the glare of TV and news camera lights. Beside Trent was another member of the defense team, a grizzled elder rock of justice, Lord Douglas Finfall, Lord Chief Justice, retired.

Standing behind the princess's barrister, awaiting his turn to face the worldwide news media coverage of a legal case that would have driven a World War off the front pages, was the Crown Prosecutor. Above all the commotion at street level, on the dome high atop Old Bailey, the home of London's central criminal courts, stood the golden statue of Justice, armed with sword and scales.

Trent, tall, distinguished, in the wig and robe required of the English trial lawyers called barristers, wore an "old school tie" beneath the black robe. Black-haired with a sprinkle of gray showing at the temple, at fifty he was fit, successful, and conveyed just a hint of the smugness that sometimes glowed from members of the British "Establishment."

Nothing in his long career or even his imagination had prepared

❖

him for the day he would represent a royal defendant in a murder case that held the attention of the world. But being very reserved in the uniquely British manner, he did not convey to the outside world his elation at having his image and name broadcast daily to just about everywhere on the planet.

He knew Lord Finfall hated having to be his standby as the media feeding frenzy focused on a mere barrister, and it gave him secret delight to be one up on the gray-haired, rock-jawed justice who had more than once interrogated him in the past when he had appeared before the high court for oral arguments.

Trent paused, letting his eyes adjust to the lights that glared in the gloom of a gray London late afternoon. Questions would be shouted at him from any number of newspeople, but his public relations person had already posted several up front and those were the ones he would respond to.

"Is it true that the princess is planning to enter an insanity plea to save the nation the trauma of a trial?" was the first question.

"The princess's options are still being assessed," Trent said.

Both the question—and Trent's response—had been arranged. Trent's spiel was that the princess was aware that the case constituted a matter of grave national concern. His reply was intentionally noncommittal, neither answering the question nor shutting the door on the issue.

As Trent gave the response the defense team had worked out, a BBC reporter awaiting her turn to ask a question pressed her earphone closer. "What?" she asked, her question relayed back through the mini-mic clipped to the top of her blouse. Hearing the same information again, she shook her head. "My God!"

The BBC reporter stepped forward, interrupting the planned sequence of questions that Trent's defense team had arranged. "Is it true that the princess has hired an American lawyer to assist in her defense?"

The question had the effect of a pistol shot. A moment of stunned silence. Trent, a practiced trial lawyer who was used to thinking on his feet, was caught completely by surprise. "Nonsense," he said. He

❖

couldn't think of anything to say and the denial simply fell out of his mouth.

The BBC reporter pressed the earphone against her ear again.

"It's coming over the wires," she told Trent. "The princess has hired the Burning Bed lawyer to represent her."

❖

3

❖

A knight in shining armor and panty hose . . .

Marlowe James, Esq. was seated in the first-class section of a London flight, with Greenland looking like a colossal iceberg forty thousand feet below, when she caught the action in the seats across the aisle from her. It was late, the wee hours before dawn, the cabin lights were dimmed, but there was no doubt about it—the man and woman across the way were getting it off.

A thirty-nine-year-old trial attorney with a reputation for winning, Marlowe wasn't shocked by the idea that the two people were enjoying each other on a plane seat. To the contrary, it grabbed her attention. Ordinarily she would have had three words to describe sex play on an airplane: *tacky tacky tacky*. But this time it stirred something in her—a prurient interest. And memories of her own explosions of desire. Her husband and she had enjoyed each other more than once as subtly—and dangerously—as this couple were, but that happened long ago, at a time before their marriage and lives crashed and burned.

She snuggled under her blanket with her earphones on and pretended to sleep while she watched the action out of the corner of her eye. They were being very discreet. *No one but an old pro at dangerous liaisons would recognize it,* she thought.

❖

The couple looked a few years younger than her, maybe in their mid-thirties, she thought. Could be they were lawyers, too, or doctors? They both had a professional look to them, as opposed to business-people or the idle rich. The man had the window seat and the woman the aisle, within a few feet of Marlowe. Like her, both had their airline blankets pulled up to their necks. They were married—the woman had a wedding ring and a not-too-ostentatious diamond engagement ring.

It was both the movements under the blankets and their body language that tipped her off that they were masturbating each other. She had seen his hand sneak across to the woman earlier. While pretending she wasn't looking, Marlowe could see the slight movement in the blanket in the woman's lap area that exposed the fact he had his hand between her legs. Her pumping movement in his lap area was slightly more noticeable.

But it was really their faces that gave it away. His face was rigid as he tried to suppress a grin, hers was flushed, her cheeks warm, eyes closed, her breathing slow and deliberate as she struggled to pretend she wasn't experiencing erotic pleasure.

Marlowe found herself getting aroused. She also shared a seat with a man. She sat in the aisle seat and to her right was a conservatively dressed gentleman with short-cropped salt-and-pepper hair. She had always wondered if a man's pubic hair turned gray when the hair on his head did, but didn't think it would be polite to ask. Instead, she thought about what it might be like to have the man make love to her. He wasn't a Cary Grant type, the unrealistic standard by which she judged older men. And there was no doubt in her mind of how she would have reacted if the king of sophistication had approached her— gray pubic hair or not, she would simply have torn off her clothes and spread herself out for him.

Giving a sideways glance at the man beside her again, she decided he wasn't her type. Not an iota of Cary Grant there. He wasn't a sensuous man, but very much a businessman, his mind and soul into matters of commerce rather than the heart. And if Marlowe was anything, she was a romantic, though a practical one—her love life had been a rocky road.

She found herself more emotionally connected to the couple caress-

❖

ing each other across the aisle than to the man beside her. She lowered the music on her headset and snuggled back under her blanket again. Closing her eyes, she imagined herself across the aisle, in between the married couple.

His hand came to her under the blanket, warm and firm, impatiently clutching at the belt to her slacks. She undid her belt for him and unzipped her slacks, lifting up off of the seat a little so she could pull down her slacks and make it easier for his hand to slide in.

Her body trembled as his hand went between her legs and cupped her. As he began to gently stroke, her legs opened wider and her feminine juices awakened.

She sneaked her own hand across his lap and rubbed the bulge in his pants. She remembered how, when she was married, she liked to catch her husband unawares, guiding his penis out and before it became erect, feeling it grow in her mouth until it was full and hard.

Now she unzipped the man's pants and used her fingers to open his shorts and release his organ. It sprang out of his pants, a beast of a thing, pulsating excitedly as it slipped out.

She grasped the hard stalk, surprised that he wasn't circumcised. She had never had sex with a man who wasn't, but it was a nice difference. A female friend had told her that the head of the penis of an uncircumcised man was extra-sensitive because it was ordinarily covered by the foreskin. Remembering that comment, she was careful as she pumped, sliding the foreskin over the head of his penis and back down again. She had an insane impulse to lean over and take his cock in her mouth and almost giggled aloud at the thought of what the flight attendant would think as she came by and saw a head job.

Enjoying the feel of his maleness in her hand, flowing with the rhythm of his fingers caressing her, she leaned back, breathing shallowly. She gasped as a hand touched her breast.

She had forgotten about the man's wife! She was wedged in between the two of them, could feel their warm thighs pressing on the sides of her own thighs. The woman's hand had traveled over and found her breast.

Still hidden beneath the blanket, Marlowe unbuttoned her blouse and unclipped her bra. As the bra came undone, the woman's warm

❖

hand grasped her breast and delicately petted it. Her finger came over Marlowe's nipple and rubbed it.

As she pumped the man's firm stalk, squeezing the muscular tube with its load of hot blood, her own nipples grew hard under the sensation of the woman's touch. Between her legs, a fire had erupted. Trying not to make it obvious that the woman's husband was masturbating her while the woman caressed her breast, she began to flow with the action, her crescendo soaring.

Having sex with two people at the same time, being touched by a woman sexually, were forbidden passions. Now she rode the sensation, creaming her pants at the erotic pleasure. She turned to look at the woman and the woman smiled and leaned toward her with full red lips and—

"Ms. James."

Marlowe almost ejected from her seat.

The flight attendant bent down and whispered, "The captain asked me to advise you that there will be a large number of newspeople waiting when we get to the gate." She bent a little lower. "All the girls on the flight are for the princess. He done her wrong, as they say in the old movies."

Marlowe murmured her thanks. She didn't say anything to the flight attendant because she knew from past experience that statements from loose lips end up on the evening news.

She took a deep breath and pushed the blanket down. She was sweating.

The man seated next to her paused in putting away papers in his briefcase. "I thought I recognized you," he said. "You're Marlowe James, the American attorney hired to defend the princess."

"One attorney of many," she said. "The rest of the team is British."

"You're the specialist on husband killings. They call you the Burning Bed lawyer, don't they?"

"They call me many things, especially if the sources of news are tabloids."

She could have told the man she never actually represented a woman who burned her husband in bed, that it was just one of the appendages that had been stuck on her by a clever reporter. The "Burning Bed" expression arose from a 1970s legal case in which a wife, after suffering years of battering from her husband, poured gas on him when he was passed out and tossed a match on the heap.

Somewhere along the line, during seven high-profile trials in which she successfully defended six women and one man, all abused spouses who had finally struck back and killed, a tabloid had pinned the "Burning Bed" label on her. But the man beside her probably knew from news accounts that there was something in her own past that made her connection to the princess's murder case even more sensational.

She would have been more comfortable being called the "Heat-of-Passion lawyer" because that was how the law defined a killing done in a moment of anger after provocation.

"What the princess did was very bad for the country," the man said. He spoke with a soft English accent. "Very bad indeed." He appeared to be in his late fifties, a well-to-do businessman, perhaps upper management with a London financial institution: He had the smug look of a person used to handling other people's money—never risking his own, of course.

She mulled over his comments and tone as she removed her work materials from the tray in front of her and put them into her briefcase. He had voiced by word and inflection disapproval both for her as a lawyer and for the princess as a defendant. She had generally found that men make better jurors than women in cases involving women abused mentally or physically. Men have their sense of chivalry outraged, and are generally repulsed by a man striking a woman, considering it cowardly. On the other hand, women tended to be harder on the abused woman, sympathetic for her pain but unforgiving because she had put up with it for so long. *How come she stayed and took it? Why didn't she walk out? Why didn't she just get a divorce?* women asked. When it came down to selecting a juror, she almost always was inclined to believe that men were the best pick when it came to judging a battered woman who had resorted to a "Texas *dee*-vorce"—ending the marriage with a gun or kitchen knife as opposed to legal papers.

But she had never defended anyone like the princess before. The Princess of Wales was admired by women throughout the world, many of whom no doubt were rallying behind their "wronged sister" in this time of crisis. She had to consider whether this time women, especially younger women, would make the best jurors.

So far she had heard from one woman, the flight attendant, who was emotionally for the princess, and one man, the businessman, who thought they should hang her for the good of the country.

The fact that she was on her way to London to defend the Princess of Wales in the most provocative murder trial in history had still not settled comfortably in her mind. Why she had gotten the call was just one of many mysteries about her being hired—certainly there were exceptional lawyers in Britain capable of defending the princess.

The couple across the way were now relaxed. *Satisfied,* Marlowe thought, not without envy. She could have told them that she wasn't a stranger to sex on an airplane. Her now-deceased husband and she had been sexually daring, even dangerous in terms of the potential to get caught. Once, on a flight from L.A. to Chicago, they had gotten worked up just sitting next to each other, just the rubbing and touching that comes with closeness on a flight. They had ended up together in the plane's tiny toilet compartment, he sitting on the toilet and she pulling down her pants and spreading herself backward onto his erection, doggy-style—

The flight attendant was suddenly back at her side. "The captain has received a request from airport security that you be the last passenger to deplane. There are quite a large number of newspeople waiting for you at the gate, a whole army of them."

"Are you sure it isn't a lynch mob?" Marlowe asked. She had had press coverage before, but never "army"-sized. But the size of the coverage was to be expected in a legal case that made other "trials of the century" seem as unimportant as a traffic ticket. Worse than ordinary print and TV coverage would be the in-your-face tabloids. She hated and feared them, knowing it was ridiculous, but she was hurt and humiliated and often just plain angry at their unprofessional, often lying coverage. And the reputation of British tabloids was worse than that of pit bulls.

She was thrilled that her image was being beamed around the world. She had instantly gone from having a modest national reputation, mostly in the legal community, to being a celebrity. To be asked to defend the princess had been a stunning surprise. What lawyer wouldn't have been drop-dead thrilled at the prospect of handling the trial of the century? And the trial of the century itself got an extra dose of sensationalism when she was hired.

The whole country, the whole world, had to be wondering why the princess had reached across the Atlantic and hired an attorney whose most famous case was defending herself on a charge of murdering her own husband.

Marlowe James was wondering, too.

4

❖

It was a dark and stormy night . . .

fuckfuckfuck. He was so damn stupid, breaking into Westminster Abbey
to find a bloody damn body—only to find out *he wasn't alone.*

Tony Dutton saw the movement when he crept out of his hiding
place in Henry III's tomb after midnight. He had spent a cramped and
uncomfortable half dozen hours waiting for the cleaning crew to finish
and leave. Westminster wasn't just a cathedral where they crowned
kings and queens, it was a damn indoor cemetery, with tombs and
crypts and wherever else they stick dead people. No, those had not been
pleasant hours, lying there, side by side with *God knows who.* There
was a bronze likeness of the king, but Dutton didn't know if that was
old Harry himself dipped in bronze like a baby shoe or if it was an effigy
of him. If nothing else he had just spent hours within kissing distance
of King Henry's death mask only to climb down and spot someone moving in the shadows.

It was just a shadow—but a *shadow that moved.* Someone else was
creeping around the Abbey at the witching hour and it scared the hell
out of him. His heart and lungs suspended with pure shock as he stared
into the darkness and tried to find the shadow that had moved.

Was it a trap? Was I lured here to be killed? fuckfuckfuck How stu-

❖

pid can I be, creeping around a place full of dead people for a story? Fuck my arse—I might end up the handiwork of a killer just to get a goddamn story.

No self-respecting tabloid reporter expected to get hurt covering a story—it was part and parcel of a dishonorable profession that cowardice went along with the lying ink and personality assassination the reporters specialized in.

That bastard Howler had told him he would find "the body of a crime" in the Abbey. He didn't know exactly what the hell that meant, some sort of legal phrase, *corpus delicti* or some other Latin mumbo jumbo used by attorneys. It hadn't occurred to him that "body" might mean there was a killer—*and that he himself might be the victim.*

When he'd seen the movement, Dutton put his back to the wall and froze. He had been making his way along the aisle that ran along Edward the Confessor's chapel. That was creepy, too. Edward might have been a saint who died in bed, but didn't Shakespeare claim that Richard II was murdered in the chapel by an assassin, one hired by the next in line to the throne?

He didn't know where the "body of a crime" was—hell, he didn't know *who* the body was or even *what* Howler had meant by his cryptic statement. Not that it would be unusual to have bodies in a graveyard. That's what Westminster was, a big church with an indoor graveyard where Britain had dumped the remains of the high and mighty since before the Magna Carta.

He stared into the darkness, but the other side of the cathedral was just a black pool. *Did I see something?* His heart had come alive, pounding against his chest wall, as pure fright made room for adrenaline.

It had to be a fuckin' graveyard that bastard lured me to.

He hated graveyards. Even though he was well past the forty mark, he still held his breath every time he drove by one, still playing that game about not breathing in ghosts he learned as a kid. He didn't really think he would breathe in ghosts, but . . . what the hell, he *hated* graveyards.

Nothing moved in the dark pool. But he couldn't have seen a movement if there had been one, it was too dark. In a moment the moon would pop out from behind clouds and bring a little light to the mid-

❖

night interior. It had been a wet and nasty late afternoon, London gray and drizzling, when he came into the Abbey with the last of the tourists and stayed behind and hid. Now the rain had stopped but the north wind was pushing dark clouds past the moon, letting it peek out every couple minutes. Intermittent moon glow was the only light in the crown jewel of England's religious past, the enormous Church of England cathedral where British sovereigns were still crowned. When the moon slipped out from under the cloud cover, it shone faintly through the cathedral's mullion and colored glass windows high in the vaulted ceiling.

Something moved.

Or had it?

He couldn't see a damn thing. *Just my imagination,* he thought. *The only thing moving in this place are the creatures instilled in my head when I was a kid and learned about the bogeyman.* That was his damn problem, too much imagination. He should have been writing fiction instead of news stories. Maybe that's what made him a good tabloid reporter—most of what he wrote was *fiction,* junk fiction at that. And, as he boasted over a pint or two—or three or four or more—it took a truly junk mind to write stories that were so outrageous, they had to be true. But tabloid reporting wasn't just all about farm girls giving birth to two-headed lambs after being raped by aliens. Sometimes there was real news to be reported.

He hadn't always been a tabloid reporter, using his imagination to give stories a slant that appealed to the reading public's lust for serial killers and the sex lives of the rich and famous. There was a time when he had been a respected journalist, a prizewinning investigative reporter who had his own byline and dug deep into the ills and sins of society. Those days were years past, that life was trashed because he had made a mistake that cost the life of someone he loved. Now, like the never-ending revenge Zeus took on Prometheus, chaining him to a mountain and sending an eagle to eat his immortal liver, Dutton was doomed to assault his liver with booze while he cranked out imaginative tabloid trash.

It was his damn imagination that got him into invading the Abbey in the first place. He tended to believe his source, Howler, a onetime famous plastic surgeon, long prohibited from practicing after he gave one poor bastard a Boris Karloff face. The fact that he had been under the influence of a controlled substance at the time was a given. Howler now supported his drug habit doing part-time work for the coroner's office, reconstructing stiffs who were no longer recognizable so they could be identified.

Howler was a crazy, but he had that sly perception of some addicts that seems to remain behind after the druggies have burned out trillions of brain cells and begin to look like cast members of *Night of the Living Dead.*

His heart stopped again—something in the place—or in his imagination—moved in the darkness.

Somebody there? he almost croaked, but choked back the question.

He was between the proverbial rock and hard place. There weren't any guards inside the Abbey, though he assumed they had to be somewhere nearby. If he stood up and started screaming, maybe they'd come running—and maybe, when they found him, he'd get five-to-ten at Dartmoor Prison for invading a national treasure. He had already done a few months in jail, back in those heady days before he fell from grace as a reporter for a prestigious newspaper and turned to shoveling muck for the muckiest tabloid in the country. And he wasn't anxious to return. There were people in jail a lot crazier and meaner than even the ones he dealt with for the tabloid.

He also wasn't anxious to make news in a more gruesome way. He was beginning to wonder if he would end up as the lead story in his own paper—*Crazed Killer Skins Reporter Alive as Elvis Watches* was how a good tabloid headline editor would run the story on the front page.

Before he risked prison or tabloid immortality, he had to find out what—*who*—was in the shadows. And hope it wasn't an ax murderer.

Com'on, moon. The place was creepy enough without shadows that moved. It was supposed to be a church, but somewhere along the line they starting planting people inside like the pharaohs of old Egypt. Most of the bodies were in granite-looking tombs standing four or five feet high with the form of a body lying on top. As in the case of Henry III, Dutton didn't know if the bodies decked out on top of the tombs were bronze statues of the dead person or were actual bodies bronzed. Whatever they were, all the bodies lying around made the place ghoulish in the darkness even if they were a bunch of kings and queens, poets and statesmen. A ghost was a ghost.

His phone rang. It was in his breast pocket, a palm-sized cellular. Well, it didn't actually ring—he had the ringing turned off and the vibration mode on. He felt the vibration against his heart. It kept going off and he grabbed it.

"What?" he whispered.

"Did you find the body of the crime?"

Dutton groaned, tempted to throw the phone down and jump up and down on it. "There's someone in here with me," he whispered hoarsely to Cohn, his editor.

"In the Abbey?"

"Where the fuck do you think I'm at? I dropped by to be fuckin' crowned."

"Good Lord! It's probably a serial killer, someone Howler learned about at the coroner's office. A killer in there with you, what a story."

"I'm going to be fuckin' murdered."

"*Grrreat* story. What—what does he look like?"

"How would I know? Don't you give a shit that I'll be murdered?"

"Of course I care, Tony." Cohn's voice was honey.

The last time Dutton had heard the man's voice purr like that was when he had called in a story that one of the Royals was caught on camera having her toes sucked on the Riviera by her accountant—while people in Rwanda were eating children to stay alive.

Dutton shut off the phone and put it back in his pocket, cutting off Cohn. Lousy bastard. A tabloid editor's heart was harder than that of a Soho whore.

The moon was coming out again, giving the window a faint gloomy glow as cheerful as a granite headstone. As the hazy glow spread, shadows formed in the cathedral and appeared to move.

Was that all I saw? A play of shadows?

He let out a deep breath of relief that he had cooped up somewhere.

You're just a schoolgirl, Tony Dutton. No guts. Now get your ass in gear.

❖

———

ACROSS THE HOLY OF holies cathedral, a rat scurried across the floor. It was no ordinary rat but the breed of a big, brutal creature known as a wharf rat that had invaded the public buildings near the Thames since Britannia first ruled the waves and ships returned home from faraway lands with more than cargo.

The rodent went up the tomb of Queen Elizabeth I, the Virgin Queen, coming to rest on top of the queen's effigy atop the tomb. In the opposite wing was Mary, Queen of Scots, whom Elizabeth impolitely had had beheaded because of a disagreement over whose church wore the biggest boots.

The rat stopped and sniffed the air. Lacking Tony Dutton's imagination, it was not at all concerned about the metal statues it ran over. The rat was a carnivore and the blood it sensed was fresher than the centuries-old corpse entombed beneath it.

The rat had followed the scent of blood across the Abbey. Now its nervous system caught on fire and it froze, ready to dash away as its own dark eyes locked on to a pair of startling blue ones.

❖

5

❖

Dutton crept down the center aisle, keeping to the right side. He was certain that what he had seen was nothing more than shadows that moved as clouds swept the light of the moon coming through windows, but . . . he wasn't *that* sure.

He hummed a little, almost noiselessly, a little air passing his lips to keep him company, to give a little *life* to the oversized crypt of a church. He'd had to memorize Tennyson's "Charge of the Light Brigade" as a kid and some of the lines never left him. Now he hummed a bit of it. *Half a league, half a league, half a league onward, into the valley of death rode the six hundred, cannon right and left, brave six hundred, do and die . . .* He wondered if Tennyson was buried in Westminster.

He wondered what he had seen in the darkness.

His phone vibrated in his breast pocket again and he ignored it. It was probably Cohn calling to see if he could get an exclusive interview with the killer while the maniac chopped up Dutton's body. Tabloid editors had the moral fiber of used-car salesmen and child pornographers.

He reached the entrance to Henry VII's chapel and paused, crouching down to make a smaller target. The whole damn place was dark, but the blackest pool was the left side of the chamber. He had to get

❖

across that murky sea and into the tombs beyond. When he got out of this mess—*if he got out in one piece*—he was going to pay Howler a visit. The guy had fed him dirt for years without ever raising doubt as to his credibility, but this was a corker.

Howler was no ordinary tipster about bodies—he knew a lot about the dead. Howler had started on the slippery slope of addiction two decades ago when he found that he got no satisfaction from cocaine—and graduated to heroin. In between trips to hospitals when he overdosed and jail cells when he got caught buying and selling, besides his work at the morgue to re-create people, he got occasional work from Madame Tussaud's Wax Museum—reconstructing victims of infamous crimes for the Chamber of Horrors section.

The coroner and the Chamber of Horrors, not very pleasant work either way. Gruesome, was how Dutton thought of the man, gruesome in appearance and in the workings of his mind. If he wasn't cast as part of the living dead, he'd have done well in the role of the psycho motel manager in Hitchcock's most famous thriller. Dutton had heard that of late Howler had developed another quirk—weenie-waving. He liked to stand at the glass doors of tube trains and open his raincoat, exposing his dick as the train rolled into a crowded station.

Howler had sold him information about morgue cases for years. His gruesome, inside details on the Little Red Riding Hood Murders got Dutton's lurid stories on the front page of the tabloid for ten editions. His information was always as accurate as it was macabre.

This time Howler called and told him that he had evidence of an even bigger royal scandal than the princess shooting the Prince of Wales.

Dutton had laughed when Howler said it. Nothing less than bona fide proof of the end of the world would be bigger than the princess blowing away the heir to the throne on national TV. But what the hell, Howler probably had something big even if it couldn't be *that* big.

He had refused to say what Dutton would find in the Abbey other than his cryptic hints about the body of the crime. A royal cover-up, was how Dutton took Howler's innuendos and inferences. But a cover-up about what? And what could Westminster, England's holy of holies, have to do with it?

❖

Now I've fallen to burglarizing churches, he thought. *How the mighty have fallen.* He was once a highly regarded journalist, a gonzo newspaperman—outlaw reporting, writing unrestrained stories about the dark streets of London, the ones tourists—and the police—rarely tread. His stories were full of unusual characters, street people, and often carried a social impact. In those high-flying days, he'd won the British Press Award and What the Papers Say Award. But he fell from grace with respectable reporting after a news source, a woman, was murdered due to his negligence. Racked with the pain of guilt, like Howler, he didn't tumble from his perch in life, but had belly-flopped into the gutter, clutching a bottle of cheap booze with him. It had taken six years to dry out enough for him to write hack articles for a tabloid.

The moon came and went again and did little to illuminate any of the demons Tony Dutton's endless imagination could conjure. There was only one way he could get across that black pool—get up and walk across it. He hadn't brought a flashlight because it would risk having him discovered, but right about now he was willing to risk a little discovery over bumping into *God knows what* in the dark.

He stood up, took a deep breath, and briskly walked into the chapel. He took ten steps when he stumbled over something and went crashing to the ground.

Music suddenly erupted. Dutton's heart almost jumped out of his chest.

Organ music filled the hollow guts of the Abbey, somber, soul-shaking tones of a powerful, cathedral-sized organ. Stage lighting went on around the large instrument.

He realized he had stumbled over a control box for God's Voice, the German organ on display from Cologne. He had seen the damn box earlier when he was playing tourist. Now the sounds of Beethoven's "Funeral March" boomed in the cathedral like a big foghorn on a small puddle, making enough noise to wake the dead and alert every guard station for miles.

He ran for the tombs in the chapel, crouching down beside the Virgin Queen's crypt, peeping back out the wooden bars for the guards that he expected at any moment. He backed away from the grille, on his hands and knees. His foot hit something—*holy shit, he'd bumped into someone.*

❖

He let out a yell and spun around, fist cocked, ready to swing. Enough light came from the organ spotlights to reveal someone sitting in the throne chair on display in the crypt. He saw the legs and clothing first, a man in a Tudor-era dress.

It appeared to be a life-sized wax dummy, the sort of thing he'd seen at Madame Tussaud's. As his eyes focused he realized that there was something on the man's lap.

A head. The head of a woman.

He heard a drip.

Dark liquid was dripping off the chair the figure was sitting on.

Blood.

6

❖

Westminster Abbey

Rotten luck, Dutton thought. He would have preferred getting chopped up by a serial killer than falling into the hands of Inspector Bram Archer of the Metropolitan Police—Scotland Yard—Homicide Division.

Archer was in the crypt examining the body—and the head in its lap—and had posted Dutton on a bench in an anteroom with one of the Abbey guards who had come running when Dutton began screaming. It was past two in the morning and the guard, an elderly pensioner doing light duty after retiring from a clerical job with the Ministry of Housing, was nodding off beside Dutton.

Dutton tried to think of all the reasons Archer hated him and it really boiled down to one: a story Dutton wrote when he was still a respectable award-winning journalist, an exposé on excessive force in arrests involving minorities. He reported a case in which Archer had broken both arms of a nineteen-year-old small-time Jamaican drug dealer. Something to do with the guy spitting on Archer.

Dutton was trying to think of other reasons the homicide detective would have to hate him when Archer's partner came out of the crypt area.

Dutton smiled with false cheer at Sergeant Lois Kramer. Kramer was a well-nourished blonde with a healthy bust line and a lovely well-rounded ass. "Good to see you, Lois. How are things?"

"We're going to hang you on this one, you rotten, slimy son-of-a-bitch."

"Lois—"

"I'm surprised you can remember my name. You kissed up to me to get information, then dumped me."

"I—"

"I turned down a date with a real man to meet you, only to spend the evening twiddling my thumbs in a pub because you never showed up." She leaned down so they were face-to-face. "And what really pisses me off is the guy I stood up won the lottery and married some tart I can't stand."

"That was two years ago."

"And how many times have you called me since then? Archer's going to burn your ass on this one and I want to be around to throw jet fuel on the fire."

Archer came out of the room, looking smugger than Dutton had ever seen him. The police inspector was short, about five-seven, but he was barrel-shaped and had about the same girth as height. Built like an artillery shell, he was probably the meanest little bastard on the school grounds when he was a kid. He had grown up to be a mean big bastard.

Archer wanted to get in his face, too, and came close enough to breathe down at him. Dutton kept his features neutral, still wondering if there was any way he would be able to weasel out of charges of illegally entering the Abbey. Not to mention finding a dead body—or two.

"I'm going to squeeze your balls," Archer said, grinning and cracking his knuckles as he spoke. "I'm going to put them in the opening of a cell and slam the door shut. Permanently."

The sound of the big fists having their knuckles popped gave Dutton an uneasy feeling in his groin and gut.

"Archer . . . Archer"—he wanted so badly to tell the jerk what he thought of him, but worked to keep a civil tongue—"you know I didn't have anything to do with—"

❖

Archer cracked a knuckle and the sound echoed in Dutton's empty stomach.

"Dartmoor." Archer grinned, his fat lips smacking with pleasure at the thought of Dutton being locked up in the prison. The man's face was almost cherubic, with its flushed cheeks and red-wine bulbous nose. "What d'you think?" he asked his partner. "You think this smart-ass reporter for the filthiest rag in London will like Dartmoor? How long do you think it'll take before he's some ape's sex toy?"

Lois leered down at Dutton. "I'll send you some vaginal cream. You're going need it."

"Fuck you. Both of you."

The guard stirred enough to look up at Dutton with tired eyes and shake his head. "Not smart."

Dutton shrugged, cocky. "My editor will have me out of custody in an hour." *In a pig's eye,* he thought.

"No, not this time." Archer's voice went lower and Dutton could feel the heat of his rage and his foul dragon's breath. "There's a reprimand in my personnel jacket because of you. I'll retire a grade lower, and every month when I get five hundred less than I deserve, I'll think about you, getting your ass poked at Dartmoor—if you live long enough. I'll put out the word that you have a snitch jacket."

"You have nothing on me, it's not against the law to chase a story."

"I've got a dead body back there dressed up for a costume ball. And someone else separated from their head. Two people have been murdered," he almost whispered, "and all I hear from you is that you were following a lead and fell into the lap of a corpse. But I don't hear the name of the person you claim gave you the tip."

Dutton had been agonizing over that dilemma. If he coughed up Howler's name, he would betray a source. He had been down that road before. Not that Howler's life wasn't in jeopardy already—when he got his hands on Howler, he'd strangle him. Besides, no matter what he did, Archer would burn him. If he was going to get himself untangled from this mess, he would need some leverage. The identity of his source was leverage. When the news media got wind of the gruesome twosome at Westminster Abbey, he hoped there would be enough pressure on Scot-

❖

land Yard to find the killer that Archer would be forced to deal with him for information.

"I can't give you the source. You'll just have to trust me."

Archer howled with laughter until he started choking. When he got his breath back, he said, "What's the matter, Dutton, afraid you'll get someone else killed because of your stupidity?"

"Archer, to me you're nothing more than a pile of air in this world, heavy air, a *stinking* pile of heavy air."

Archer cracked a knuckle with a big pop. "That'll be your neck someday," he whispered. Then, in a louder voice, "Your refusal to cooperate in a murder investigation leads me to believe you are lying about the reason you came here and that you are involved in the murders of two people. I'm going to—"

"Inspector, Sergeant, can I see you for a moment?" It was Nulty, the scene-of-crime tech in charge of gathering evidence.

"Watch him," Archer told the night watchman. Archer and Kramer followed the forensics tech back to where the body was. Other crime scene technicians were checking the area for prints and using a microscanner to check for tiny bits of evidence. A medical technician was examining the head on the tomb when they entered the crypt. The body was sitting passively on the throne chair, the woman's head still in its lap.

"It's a man, late fifties maybe, a woman about the same age," the medical tech told him.

Archer snorted. "You don't need a medical license to figure that out. You have an estimate as to time of death?"

"That's for the pathologist. This is what I wanted you to check out. Put this on." The medical tech handed Archer a plastic surgeon's glove used in handling evidence. Archer stretched the glove over his fat fingers.

"Feel here," the tech told him, touching the dead man, "under the chin."

"Why?"

"You want to know time of death? This will give you a clue."

Archer grimaced. He hated corpses. Not a poetic sort of aversion, life lost, love lost, but hated them because they reminded him of his

❖

own mortality. But he didn't like to show a weakness to anyone for anything and he dutifully pressed under the man's chin. "It's hard."

"It's *frozen,*" the tech corrected.

Archer felt farther under the chin. "What do you mean, frozen?"

"Frozen as in meat freezer, frozen like your mother stored kippers in July."

It wasn't registering with Archer and he swung around and glared at Kramer. "What the hell's he talking about?"

"You're telling us that this guy's been iced?" Kramer asked.

"Been and still partly is. Same with his lap mate."

"It's not cold enough outside or inside to freeze someone," Archer said.

"You need a detective's license to tell that?" the medical tech chortled.

"Bodies that have been frozen? What the hell did Dutton do? Kill them by sticking them in a freezer?"

"This will play hell on time of death," the medical tech said. "You may end up being given the *month* of death rather than an hour or day."

"What about the rest of the bloke's body?"

"Thawing."

"Why would someone keep a bloody body frozen?"

No one had an answer.

On the way out of the room, Kramer said, "You know there's no way that Dutton—"

"He's caught red-handed."

"He was covering a story."

"That's what he said, but where's his source?"

"You know why he won't give up his source."

"He's been caught with two frozen stiffs and won't tell us who did it. As far as I'm concerned, that makes him the number one suspect." Archer cracked three knuckles on his left hand in quick sequence. It registered like machine gun fire in the little room. "I'll make the bastard tell us how this bloke got iced."

❖

ARCHER AND KRAMER CAME into the anteroom where they had left Dutton and the elderly guard. Archer's hands were clenched into big fists as if he meant to use them.

The pensioner was sitting alone on the bench.

"Where the bloody hell is Dutton?" Archer asked.

The old man nodded sleepily at a door marked MEN across the corridor. "He's spending a penny."

Archer stared at the restroom door, an ugly suspicion forming in his mind.

"Is there a window in there?"

7

❖

Heathrow Airport

As Marlowe waited on the exit ramp, a tall, very thin young man about thirty or so was admitted into the area. He offered a handshake.

"Philip Hall, Miss James, I'm an associate of Anthony Trent."

Hall gave a warm, firm handshake. If Marlowe had had to guess Philip Hall's occupation prior to his introduction, with his pin-striped, dark-vested wool suit, old-fashioned bowler hat, and long black umbrella, she would have guessed he was a young Foreign Office official fresh from the Crimea with Churchill . . . apparently he was a young attorney who wasn't afraid to capture the grace of another era in his dress and manners. Or maybe that was how attorneys dressed in London.

"I've been permitted back by airport security to give you moral support as you wade through the news hounds from hell. For reasons that are inexplicable, Britain produces the most vicious newspeople on the planet. Right now there are probably fifty or sixty of the wild animals waiting to attack."

"I've faced reporters before, but never an army of them. I was considering borrowing a flight attendant's uniform and sneaking out with the crew."

"Never get by our tabloid reporters, they have X-ray vision. Trent's suggestion is that you simply smile and say absolutely nothing. Even a 'no comment' reply is interpreted by the press in any manner they want to use it."

"Fine." Marlowe suspected Hall had been sent to make sure she didn't give a news conference. She wasn't the type to try her cases in the media, but she didn't blame Trent. He didn't know her and the case being defended truly was the shot heard around the world.

"We'll get your luggage and be on our way. I have a car waiting outside. Trent has called an emergency meeting of the team at his chambers. Would you mind terribly if we dropped by before I left you at the hotel? Not jet-lagged after the Concorde flight, are you? Rather sensational crossing the puddle in a couple of hours, isn't it?"

She had started the trip in Los Angeles on a regular jet, and no, she wasn't jet-lagged, she was too excited to be groggy. She sensed Hall was gentlemanly enough to be uncomfortable at whisking her off to an "emergency meeting" before she even had a chance to freshen up at her hotel. "I take it Mr. Trent wants to see what sort of horror the princess has hired before I'm let off a leash in London."

Hall blushed with guilt and Marlowe instantly felt bad that she had exposed the truth. She took his arm. "Shall we meet the Fourth Estate?"

As they stepped into the terminal Marlowe blinked under the assault of camera lights and a barrage of shouted questions. Security officers flanked her and Hall as they walked down a center aisle roped off from the newspeople. Being the focus of the attention of literally a mob armed with cameras, microphones, and questions was disconcerting. She had never faced a news conference of more than five or six reporters, most of whom were reasonably well mannered. These truly were hounds from news hell.

She started to whisper to Hall about how intimidating it was but instantly shut her trap, realizing that some of the microphones might have a long range.

Someone suddenly shot in front of her, startling her, a shabbily dressed man with long greasy hair and a scraggly three-day beard. He shoved a mic in her face.

"You and the princess both killed husbands—will you use the tactics from your own murder trial to defend the princess?" he shouted.

❖

Her mouth dropped and she almost stumbled into him. Hall grabbed her arm and pulled her past the intruder as a security officer shouldered the man aside.

They were separated from the newspeople and going down the escalator before either spoke.

"I must apologize for that rudeness. Elliot Smithers of *Burn,* one of the trashiest tabloids in Britain."

Marlowe pushed a lock of hair off of her forehead. Her knees were wobbly, but she kept her face stoic. "I've heard it before." Her voice was hard, but her insides were mush. She'd heard it before but never as a brutal attack.

Safe behind tinted glass in the limo, Marlowe relaxed back in the car seat and scratched the tip of her nose. "I've been dying to do that since I stepped off the plane. What a nightmare it must be for celebrities, to constantly be in a fishbowl with every move monitored by the news media."

"Absolutely horrid. One would have to really be enthralled with a need for attention to appreciate such an invasion of privacy. There is some belief that the princess's mental processes were affected by the constant hounding of the press, especially tabloid reporters like Smithers who can be very vicious about it."

"You mentioned going to Mr. Trent's chambers. I take it that's his offices? We use the word *chambers* in reference to a judge's office."

"Quite right, chambers are a barrister's office. There has been a meeting set up with members of the defense team."

"I hope the papers aren't calling it a 'dream team.'"

Hall smiled. "Not yet, but I suppose they will turn to that phrase when there are less monumental details to report. The hiring of you by the princess is the current feeding frenzy."

Hall blushed a little at his comment. A very nice young man, she thought, and at the same time feeling old at thinking of a man only seven or eight years younger than her as "young."

"Philip, are you a solicitor or a barrister?"

He smiled. "American lawyers are always so curious about the distinction. Your attorneys are licensed in all matters."

"True, but other than small-town lawyers who tend to do everything, American lawyers separate somewhat along the same lines. We have lawyers who do transactional-type work, contracts, wills, that sort of thing, and trial attorneys whose arena is the courtroom."

"I am a barrister. Trent, of course, as lead counsel, is also a barrister. As you probably know, he's one of the most respected attorneys in Britain."

She had never spoken to Trent, nor heard of him until the story about the killing hit the news and stayed there. That the princess had hired one of the leading attorneys in her own country wasn't a surprise. Marlowe had been hired directly by the princess, though an American friend of the princess made all of the arrangements. Other than a telephone conversation in which the princess confirmed that she wished to employ her as part of the defense team, Marlowe had not spoken to anyone directly connected to the case.

It was strange that she was hired by the princess when the woman already had attorneys working for her—but that was just one card in a crazy deck. The facts that the princess reached across the Atlantic to hire an American lawyer when Britain had outstanding attorneys, and had chosen one who had some notoriety in her own right, were also wild cards.

"Our office is taking care of the arrangements to have you appear *ad hoc* in the matter," Hall said.

Ad hoc was a legal principle that gave judges the right to permit attorneys not licensed in their jurisdiction to appear before their courts. Thus a California judge could permit a New York attorney to practice before a California court for the limited purpose of representing a particular client. Usually, the out-of-state lawyer had to associate a local attorney in the matter. In this case, an attorney licensed in one country was requesting the right to appear as trial counsel in an entirely different country.

"It's a bit unusual," Hall said, "but since you are an attorney from a common-law country with similar procedures and rules of evidence, we believe no serious obstacle will be raised. The fact that Anthony Trent will be lead counsel will clinch it, of course."

Marlowe let the "lead counsel" remark pass. She intended to cooperate fully with Trent and the princess's other British lawyers, but she

❖

had made it clear in her brief conversation with the princess that she would only come aboard if she had the last say on the defense. Marlowe was not a team player. Teams were committees and her feelings about committees was summed up by someone's observation that a giraffe was a horse designed by a committee—or was it a camel?

She would cooperate with Hall, Trent, and whoever, that was a necessity, but when it came down to making a major decision on defense strategy, she would follow her own lead.

A newspaper from a stack that sat on the bottom shelf of a liquor cabinet wiggled out enough from the motion of the car so she could read the screaming headline: *NEW GUNFIGHTER IN TOWN.*

The subheading was *Slow Trigger James Rides In.*

That was another name they had for her, "Slow Trigger" referring to the fact that she had convinced juries that the reasonable provocation needed for a heat-of-passion defense could be abuse stretched out over a period of years rather than a sudden incident.

Hall shoved the paper back inside. "Sorry, but we really need to keep up on all the news, don't we?"

"I was just thinking of the way trial lawyers in California would harangue the other side's expert witnesses. They call them hired gunfighters who have come to town just to viciously destroy the poor victim's case. Then there would be snide inferences that the expert was a member of the world's oldest profession."

Hall raised his eyebrows. "Very undignified, isn't it?"

"Very effective. If you want to leave a negative impression in the mind of jurors, branding someone as a hired killer is rather a good way to do it."

MARLOWE JAMES SURPRISED HALL—her appearance, voice, and body language were not what he had been expecting. He had had very definite ideas about what the American lawyer would look like. Around Trent's chambers it was assumed that she would be a "ball-breaker," a woman who "castrates the men around her to make sure that they pay for ten thousand years of feminine servitude," Norton, a junior clerk, had hypothesized.

❖

Hall didn't think in those terms, but the TV shows and movies cranked out by Hollywood featuring women lawyers had at least made him expect her to be excessively aggressive and assertive. At the least, he thought she would be so brisk and efficient, one would have the inclination to stand up and salute when she walked into the room, her stride quick and sure, the steel of her spiked heels ricocheting off marble walls. One had to consider who she was, after all. You wouldn't expect a woman who had been tried for murdering her own husband to act like an ordinary person.

It was an erroneous assumption, he knew, because the husband-killer Marlowe came to represent was not anything like that—the princess was known to be charming rather than assertive.

Still, Marlowe James was a lawyer in the tough big-city American arenas and one would expect her to be, well, different from the refined princess.

For certain, she wasn't the proverbial ball-breaker, he thought. Not that there was anything soft about her. She left no doubt that she was a woman who knew her own mind, but she hadn't displayed a tendency to flex her muscles with him. Rather, she came across as very professional, very businesslike, though perhaps a bit more of a mover and shaker than he personally felt comfortable with. She had a bit of that annoying bluntness Americans tend to display, but none of her dynamic traits made him feel any less that she was *woman*. He had become overly sensitive about female lawyers after he had been verbally chastised by one, a dynamic London barrister who offended his sense of dignity by referring to his private body parts, calling him a "prick" outside the courtroom during an argument over a case.

Another factor in the good impression Marlowe made upon him was the fact she was appropriately dressed for a flight. He hated men and women who flew across oceans and continents in jogging outfits. He never boarded a plane dressed less formally than how he would show up at the office, and that meant a proper suit and tie. Marlowe was wearing a pants suit with comfortable shoes. Rather wisely she had a very small purse because she also carried a briefcase. He had seen female lawyers whose purses were almost as big as their briefcases and he wondered what they carried in them. He was not married

❖

and there were parts of womanhood that were as inexplicable as Stonehenge to him.

Good tone to her body, he thought, not buffed like a telly star Trent represented, but a woman who kept her body in decent shape. He personally hated all forms of exercise, especially anything that would require him to go outdoors, and he kept his body trim by pushing away from the dinner table, grateful that his mother had raised him to stop eating before he got that full feeling.

There was a tiny scar on her lip, on the right side, giving her lip a little bit of an unbalanced look, and he couldn't keep his eyes off of it. He wondered if she had gotten it from her husband—ex-husband, that is, very *ex* indeed, Hall thought.

It puzzled him and everyone else in the office as to why the princess had gone "outside," *far outside,* to hire an American woman to help defend her.

What was in the princess's mind?

For that matter, what could have driven her to kill the Prince of Wales in front of millions of home viewers?

Perhaps the royal lady was as bonkers as many people claimed.

❖

The Inns of Court

8

❖

The limo carrying Marlowe and Philip Hall took them to Legal London, the area between the Thames and Holborn where the main courthouses and most attorney offices were located. Hall explained on the way that Trent's "chambers" were in the oldest and most famous of the "inns of court," those privileged old establishments where barristers gathered to share office space. The limo negotiated its way through a throng of reporters and into a private driveway. During the short walk from the car to the office building, bewigged, robed barristers going to and from court stared at her. She realized that she was on her way to being one of the most famous women on the planet.

She exchanged a smile with a female barrister. "They wear wigs and robes, too," she told Hall.

"Really?" he said.

The hardly audible, dry reply was the closest thing she'd experienced so far in terms of him having a sense of humor.

Anthony Trent's offices were mahogany and brass from another era, a time when Britannia had half the world under the Union Jack, and the cream from its colonies found its way to the table of the "Estab-

❖

lishment," that small core of wealthy British who owned just about everything in the country.

The office furniture was aged, heavy hardwood, cut in colonial jungles during the time Britannica ruled the sea and the sun never set on the British Empire. The bookcases were filled with elderly volumes that conveyed a sense that they were both old and authoritative. It was hard for Marlowe to imagine any modern judge overturning the precedents in legal texts as venerable as those she saw in Trent's office.

Passing by furnishings that took her to a grander age, she was disappointed to see through an open door a modern computer bay with a data-entry clerk fast at work. Scribes with quills and ink pots would have fit the ambience more.

Hall led her to a conference room. Several things struck her the moment she walked in—the scent of fine cigar smoke, a fainter wisp of brandy, a mahogany conference table solid enough to be used as the bowsprit on a battleship . . . and six people who were careful to keep their disapproval behind fragile masks of civility.

Five men and a woman were seated at the table. The men stood as she entered the room. Hall started the introductions.

"Marlowe James, may I present Anthony Trent."

Trent had thick, combed-back black hair that came also to a point at the front of his head, heavy eyebrows, and a patrician nose. His suit was as conservative as Philip Hall's, but the wool was of the finest, a smooth, almost slick midnight blue with a barely visible black stripe. His shirt was starched white, French-cuffed with gold links, and his tie was blue-and-gold-striped, displaying the colors of one of the snooty British public schools.

Marlowe had expected a Type A personality, the character trait almost universally expected of trial attorneys, but her first impression was of a man who commanded by force of personality rather than snapping jaws. Her second impression was that subtle arrogance that sometimes comes along with wealth and success. Trent was commander in chief in his chambers—his countenance was appraising, his smile and handshake were professional but lacked warmth.

"May I present Lord Finfall."

❖

Lord Finfall was a white-haired elder statesman in a medium-gray heavy worsted suit that was woven to last the ages.

Trent said, "His Lordship is the Honorable Lord Chief Justice, retired. He brings to our team a half a century of judicial experience and leadership."

Lord Finfall shook hands, giving a rough heavy paw that Marlowe guessed from the calluses she felt had seen some gardening recently. He appeared to be in his seventies. His jowls had begun to droop and liver spots blotted the delicate pale skin on his hands and face. She assumed that a Lord Chief Justice was something akin to Chief Justice of the United States Supreme Court. And that the "Lord" part made him a peer of the realm. She wondered if he had been brought out of retirement to throw his great prestige behind the defense. He was definitely Yesterday, while Trent was Today.

"Helen Catters. Helen is a barrister by profession and is on the Board of the London Family Council. She brings to us her experience and reputation in handling family matters in court, a very important skill, since our client, the princess, is well known for her concern for the two princes."

"A pleasure," Helen Catters said. Catters did not stand up, nor offer to shake hands.

A divorce lawyer with a social worker background, Marlowe guessed, or something akin to it. Catters looked to be in her early fifties, Marlowe thought, a rather plain, large-busted, thick-waisted woman with dark brown hair who probably tended to blend into the background at social events except when her opinion was solicited on family matters.

Dr. Duncan McMann introduced himself with a Scottish growl. Mc-Mann was a big man, bull-necked, with a flat, broad face and sandy hair that was already turning gray even though Marlowe guessed his age at around the same as hers.

"Dr. McMann is a psychiatrist and teaches at the University of Edinburgh," Trent said. "He is one of the most distinguished forensic psychiatrists in Britain. He is also able to give us the northern view on the matter."

Marlowe nodded, trying to look suitably impressed. She instantly evaluated him in terms of his jury appeal as an expert witness and didn't like his demeanor—he had that casual arrogance of doctors who let you know that someday you'll be dying and will need them. "Northern view," she guessed, was the Scottish view, a not-too-difficult presumption since Scotland was to the north.

Lawrence Dewey introduced himself and shook hands.

"Larry is with Bartlett's, the best public relations firm in Britain," Trent said. "He's also a solicitor, and has taken leave to join our team."

Dewey appeared to be in his fifties, a slender man with narrow, pinched features, creating the impression of an inquisitive bird.

"And this distinguished gentleman is Sir Fredic Nelson. Sir Fredic is the princess's solicitor and he is the instructing solicitor in this matter."

Sir Fredic looked very much the wealthy, successful corporate attorney Marlowe took him to be. Corporate attorneys worked on the business side of law, representing major entities, battles of titans against each other and battles of titans against little people. It was not an area of law practice she, as a street lawyer, could relate to.

Anthony Trent said, "And of course you have already met Philip, who will be assisting me in the trial. Won't you have a seat, Miss James?"

Trent showed her to a seat at the opposite head of the table from where he had been seated.

"Please call me Marlowe."

"Of course. We are all on a first-name basis here," Trent said. "And with Lord Finfall and Sir Fredic, we use *both* their first names."

There was a polite laugh around the table. Trent took his seat at the end of the table opposite Marlowe and Philip took a seat at his right side.

There was a silence as the seven people stared at her.

She smiled and raised her eyebrows. "I take it I have the hot seat."

There were polite chuckles from Dewey and McMann. Helen Catters coughed with what was probably a bit of a laugh.

Anthony Trent smiled, exposing thousands of dollars' worth of caps and a bleached-white smile. "Well, we are a bit curious about you, I must admit. As you know, Her Highness did not consult with us prior to hiring you. Frankly, we found out about it from the evening news." He didn't have to spell out what a breach of protocol *that* was.

"I was a bit surprised myself, to say the least. I understand that a friend of hers married to an American had read about the cases I've handled and recommended me."

"We understand you recently tried a case in Savannah, Georgia, in which you applied your defense theory. Something called the slow trigger," Sir Fredic said. Despite what he probably thought was a neutral tone, Marlowe easily picked up a negative attitude underlining it.

"Slow trigger is what the American news media has come to call it. I don't have a name for it, but it seems to commonly pop up in the cases I've handled where abused women killed their husbands. Rather than a legal theory, it's a fact pattern that arises from the cases."

"You'll have to familiarize us with the theory," Trent said. "I'm afraid those of us in the justice business in the old country are not as progressive as you Americans are."

Trent's tone again was neutral, but she knew he was being both condescending and deceitful. He was a good attorney, handling one of the most famous legal cases in history—and his client had reached across the ocean to hire another attorney. He had to be shitting bricks since the news broke that the princess had hired an infamous American trial attorney. What did the princess tell him? Did she make it clear that Marlowe was lead counsel? Marlowe didn't need a crystal ball to realize that the princess had certainly not told Trent that he was to be second chair. If she had, Philip Hall would not have referred to Trent as lead counsel.

She also didn't need a fortune-teller to realize that from the moment the news broke that the princess had hired her, Trent and his team had been frantically researching her, that they already knew everything about her, from her bra size to the color of her toenail paint. They not only already knew her trial strategy, but no doubt had been playing a game of devil's advocate to see how many holes they could punch in it.

She played along with the charade, knowing also that she had been hustled from the airport so they could talk to her before she had a chance to express her theories to the press: Trent and his cohorts wanted

❖

to make sure they censored out anything that did not please them.

"I understand Britain and America have similar laws concerning homicide defenses and mitigation," she said.

Lord Finfall snorted. "Of course we do. You Americans got your legal system from Britain. Most of the present foundation of the laws on homicide are centuries old, many even go back to Roman times."

Marlowe smiled and nodded. What an old ass he was. "And as you all know, I'm sure better than me, a mitigating defense for murder, to reduce it to manslaughter, is what we call heat of passion, not really in reference to romantic passion, but used in the sense of a sudden, violent anger. The law understands that some people are reasonably provoked into reacting violently to an emotional situation. One issue always present is the reasonableness of the provocation—was the victim's actions such that we can understand the defendant's reaction to it? Traditionally, the real key to the defense is not whether the provocation itself was of a nature to justify—juries often find the provocation justified when it involves emotional responses to situations like spousal abuse, infidelity, cruel insults, and the like."

As she spoke, it occurred to her that not only were the judge and attorneys already well briefed on the defense—it had to be on their minds from the moment they were hired—but that even the two members of the team who were not attorneys had to be knowledgeable about mitigating premeditated murder down to the lesser charge of manslaughter. Marriages were hotbeds of emotion and it would be a rare spousal killing where mitigating murder down to manslaughter was not at least considered. Often, instead of mitigation, juries had found the abused defendant not guilty. So why the pretense at ignorance and the hostility not only toward her but the concept that the princess was an abused spouse? She went on.

"We all understand that if you step into your bedroom and find your spouse in bed with another person, a jury would probably find that a reasonable person could fly into a murderous rage, grab a gun, and pull the trigger. Back home, we call this a Texas divorce."

Hall was the only one who smiled. He looked the stuffiest, but Marlowe decided he was definitely the nicest.

"In my experience, the real key to the defense is the time between the provocation and the lethal blow. The law says that the deadly blow must be delivered in close time proximity to the provocation, hence the expression a *sudden* heat of passion. There are no precise time limits, each case is judged on its own merits, but the courts have universally tried to limit the time between the provocation and the killing, with many courts getting offended if it's more than a matter of a few minutes. The easy cases are those with provocation and almost instantaneous reaction—you walk into the bedroom, find your spouse in bed with someone, and you grab a gun, or you're in a bar and someone says something insulting to your companion and you swing a beer bottle.

"The tough cases are those in which there is a greater length of time between the provocation and the killing. You find your spouse in bed with another person, you leave the house, go to a gun shop, buy a gun, and come back and start shooting. To find heat of passion, the courts prefer that you react at the moment of the provocation. If you run into the kitchen and grab a knife, or to the den for a shotgun, those cases are also often winnable. But if you go for a drive to think about it, if you have time to cool off, or leave to buy a weapon, the courts say you are no longer reacting under heat of passion.

"So the *amount of time* between the provocation and pulling the trigger—or the stabbing, bludgeoning, choking, or however the lethal blow is delivered—is crucial. That's where the cases that even have adequate provocation are commonly lost—you have to be provoked, you have to pull the trigger while you're still in the grip of powerful emotions from the incident."

All seven faces were blank. She had no doubt at all that the subject of provocation for a heat of passion defense had been discussed by the group until each of them had it down pat and could repeat it by rote.

"As I'm sure you all know, if there is time to premeditate, it's murder and not manslaughter. Murder in general requires malice, and malice usually comes from premeditation in which the killer has thought about the crime. Thus to mitigate the crime down to manslaughter, there must first be provocation and second, delivery of the fatal blow immediately thereafter. The phrase 'slow trigger' has arisen in my cases because I've managed to stretch out the time period from the provocation to the reaction."

❖

"How much time have you managed to stretch?" Trent asked.

"Years."

"My God!"

The exclamation came from Lord Finfall. And Marlowe recognized immediately that it was not astonishment at her amazing feats, but something akin to horror that anyone had perverted a legal theory that probably went back to antiquity.

"Years between the provocation and the killing. For a killing in a *sudden* heat of passion." The hair on the back of the neck of Lord Finfall's fifty years of legal training was standing straight up.

Marlowe smothered a grin. "The killing still remains a sudden event, though I've stretched the decision to kill from minutes to hours," she said smoothly. "What has been stretched out is how long the provocation has existed. To understand why provocation can take place over a period of years, we have to look at the unique relationship between husband and wife, and the differences between men and women.

"Spouses are not feuding neighbors who come into occasional contact with each other, dancing with someone else's wife at the local bar, a couple guys rubbing each other the wrong way on the street, or a hundred other possible situations. People in a marriage are bound together—and sometimes a marriage can be turned into a *prison*. I don't want this to come across as sexist, but in most marriages that have turned into prisons, the man is the jailer and the wife the inmate because the man commonly controls the family finances and has greater physical strength."

"You will not find that that theory plays as well here as it does across the pond," Helen Catters, the divorce lawyer, said. "Britain is behind many countries in terms of the advances of women in society. Male jurors are apt to get offended if you start characterizing them as prison wardens. You need to know, too, that the battered-woman theory has not yet been accepted as a separate diagnosis by either our courts or our medical profession."

Marlowe smiled. *Dumb bitch.* "The idea isn't to antagonize male jurors, but to get them on the defendant's side by showing the bad things other men do, things that they wouldn't do in their own marriage and would offend them."

❖

"Do you find male or female jurors more sympathetic to your theories?" McMann, the psychiatrist, asked.

"Generally men are more sympathetic to a woman's plight, female jurors are more critical. But it's an issue that will have to be studied when we start considering the unique social and political elements of this case."

"I'd like to hear more about your theory," Trent said.

Marlowe nodded. "This may sound like a simplistic model in a society in which so many women work outside the home, but statistics show the aggressive dictators of family life are more likely to be the husbands than the wives. And that a large number of the heat of passion killings by women of their husbands arise out of marriages in which the woman is a financial and physical prisoner. Most of the killings also involve the woman having suffered physical abuse from her boyfriend or husband. Mental abuse can come from either side, but again, the cases turning violent are much more likely to involve physical abuse of the female by the male, if for no other reason than men are physically stronger and more likely to inflict serious injuries on the other person. Thus most killings by women commonly arise out of situations in which the women are trapped in relationships with physically abusive and financially dominant men. It seems to be the nature of human beings that with power comes the abuse of power."

"So your strategy rather vilifies the male," McMann said.

"No, my strategy is to get the jurors to understand what the perpetrator went through that caused them to lash out violently. If it's a wife who was beaten and humiliated, and if it makes the deceased husband look bad, then the man had vilified himself without any help from me."

"But there is a focus on showing bad acts by the deceased?" Trent asked.

"Yes. Obviously, most heat-of-passion cases arising from marital relationships involve wives who have suffered physical and mental abuse over a period of years, and who are—or feel they are—trapped in a relationship with a physically and financially stronger male. At some point the trapped, beaten animal strikes back."

Lord Finfall scoffed. "Such tripe."

Marlowe smiled, but her eyes were stone cold as she turned to the

❖

retired jurist. "Perhaps if you were beaten and raped repeatedly by a dominant male in a prison setting, you might have more understanding and empathy for what a battered spouse endures."

Lord Finfall turned red and Trent hastily interjected, "I'm sure Miss Marlowe is just trying to give us an example. Not necessarily one I would agree with, of course. Perhaps you can enlighten us on how you've, uh, slowed down the process, this so-called slow-trigger theory."

"To lay a little more groundwork, again, as we know, the easy cases are those in which there is a lethal blow delivered during provocation. A blow is struck, one not giving rise to a self-defense plea, when a spouse is discovered in another's arms. The cases that I've handled that give rise to the slow-trigger theory are those in which the killing was planned as opposed to arising in the heat of the moment."

Lord Finfall shook his head in disgust. "Madam, it is fundamentally impossible to plan a killing and have it arise in a heat of passion. If you had come before me with your theory when I sat on the bench—"

"You would have found in my favor after you had given careful consideration to the law and facts," Marlowe said, giving him a smooth smile. "What it comes down to is that judges and juries have to revisit the concept of *time*. It's easy for us to understand that some things happen in a flash—an insult is given, a face slapped, a loved one is engaged in sex with another—these are all short-fused situations. There is sudden provocation and instant reaction. But there are situations that are provocative but don't arise suddenly. Let's go back to the prison analogy I used a moment ago—it's one I frequently use so men can get a better idea of what a woman endures in an abusive relationship. If a male prisoner was abused, humiliated, and raped repeatedly over a period of time by a cell mate and one night, while the tormentor was asleep, the battered prisoner stabbed him—or burned him in his bunk—we would probably judge the battered prisoner the same way we would judge a whipped dog who one day bit the master who beat it.

"There are people trapped in marriages that are every bit as abusive as the situation I described and almost as confined as in a prison cell. In cases where people are trapped in a marriage with an abusive spouse, the battering and humiliation are rarely sudden provocations. Instead, they arise over time, getting more and more brutal over the years.

❖

"And that is why the 'sudden' heat of passion doesn't fit the situation. It's not a sudden event, a fight or observed infidelity, it's a slow, spiraling, long-term series of many events, in which a person's dignity is taken from them and they are beaten and degraded like the proverbial whipped dog."

Lord Finfall made a strangling noise. Obviously, he was having a hard time swallowing her remarks.

"Madam, there are laws of homicide to cover the whipped dog, that is why we have degrees of murder. But it is not a situation to which we can extend the concept of a heat of passion. It is an elementary, centuries-old casebook law that the perpetrator will be judged by the reasonable-man standard, and that standard says that the blow must be struck in close proximity to, if not at the same moment, the time the provocation erupts. An insult is delivered, a reasonable man strikes back."

Marlowe smiled broadly. "I couldn't agree with you more, Judge. And what is wrong with that theory in regard to the abused woman is precisely how you explained it—the actions of the perpetrator is judged as a reasonable *man* would have acted."

"Certainly you are not proposing that we have one set of laws for men and one set for women." His lordship spoke through clenched teeth. "We all know that the reasonable-man standard refers to the actions of a reasonable *person,* man or woman."

"I disagree with you, Judge." She would give him the respect due his position as a judge, but refused to use the lordship bit with the old fart. "As you pointed out, the law is centuries old. For those centuries, right up to the present, over ninety percent of the violent crimes committed each year are done by men. Women represent half the population but commit only a fraction of the violent crimes. Because men have always dominated the courtroom—until recently almost all judges and lawyers were men and nine out of ten defendants were men—*the law developed based upon the emotional response of men, not women.*"

Lord Finfall slammed his palm on the table—hard. "Poppycock! The law is applied equally to the sexes. I can guarantee that your ideas will be thrown out of the courtroom before they ever reach a jury. There are no judicial opinions in this country or yours supporting your position."

❖

Ah, an admission they had researched her. "There are many judges who would agree with you, but my theory is a question of *fact* for a jury, not one of *law* for a judge. There aren't appellate decisions on the slow-trigger concept because a prosecutor can't appeal a not-guilty verdict. And I've had seven juries not find it to be poppycock. Talking to jurors afterwards, what impressed them most was that it appealed to their common sense. And while I have been in your country for less than two hours, I suspect that this case is a hot political potato besides being a criminal case. If your judges plan to arbitrarily take away a jury's right to decide a case on its facts, it's not going to play well with the public."

Trent said, "His lordship is simply giving you a practical considera-tion. We would not permit the judicial system to deny the princess her right to a fair trial by jury. Can you elaborate a bit on how you deal with the differences between men and women?"

"When it's pointed out to them, juries readily accept and under-stand that the two sexes have a different emotional base. The fact that men and women are sexually aroused at different speeds is probably the best-known example. The use of physical violence is another. When women get angry, they're less likely to resort to physical violence. Men are more aggressive, perhaps because of their traditional role as the hunter, women instinctively more gentle, perhaps because of their role as the caregiver. But the law of manslaughter, the sudden reaction to provocation, *is based upon how a man would react, not a woman.* Two men bump shoulders on a street, an argument erupts, one hits the other, the victim falls down and hits his head. That's typical *male* heat of passion, a physical reaction to provocation. But for most women, you would have to provoke them for a much greater time before they would react physically, months or even years.

"And because they are physically weaker than the male, they may have to plan out their reaction in order to obtain a weapon, rather than just striking back at the moment of provocation."

"So that is the basis of your slow-trigger defense, that jurors are to judge a woman's response differently than a man's?" Trent asked.

"In a nutshell, yes. Men have a different reaction to provocation than women. Women react slower. But the law is based upon the male reaction."

❖

"Perhaps you can give us an example of how you've been successful with your theory. You had a recent case in Savannah, didn't you?"

"The Savannah wife had suffered years of mental abuse by a husband who played the most vicious kind of tricks on her. He never hit her, but he humiliated her and degraded her in front of their children and friends for years. He was the physically and financially dominant spouse. The wife was a frightened submissive person who tried to protect their two children."

"I sometimes find myself lacking sympathy toward women who have more than one child in an abusive relationship," Helen Catters, the family-law lawyer, said. "I give them the benefit of the doubt for the first one, but the second child? And so often you hear about a third and fourth child in a bad marriage."

"I agree," Marlowe said, "but if these women were strong personalities, they would not have gotten into the relationship in the first place. And once in, they are stuck—especially if there are children in the picture. Some women run away from the relationship like scared rabbits, by themselves or taking the children with them, but others, like my Savannah client, didn't know how to run and hide. To make matters worse, her husband joined a religious group that had attitudes toward women similar to those found in the Middle East and Africa."

"Women are work animals," Lawrence Dewey said, "that sort of thing?"

"And sex objects," McMann, the psychiatrist, threw in. "I don't suppose he instituted the *purdah* in Savannah."

"As a matter of fact, he did. Not to the point of her wearing veils, but in the way she was to treat him and address him. She was to obey his commands without question. He even demanded she call him 'sir.'"

Lord Finfall guffawed. "Nothing wrong with that."

"But he didn't earn his knighthood, Your Lordship," Trent said.

"What did your client do to this . . . ah, abusive spouse?" Helen Catters asked.

"She sat in her car in the parking lot where he worked. When he got off work and started walking to his car, she ran him down. Then she backed up and drove over him again. And again."

❖

"Sounds like he drove her insane," Trent said.

"An insanity defense, even one of temporary insanity, really didn't fit the situation. She didn't have a developmental or other mental defect. She knew the difference between right and wrong, she had freedom of choice and the ability to decide on a course of action that led to the homicide."

"Doesn't sound like a strong case for a heat of passion defense in Britain. Your Savannah jury must have had their brains a little dulled by the humidity," Dr. McMann said.

"The jury no doubt had its emotions aroused by the facts," Marlowe said. "Not many women have had to endure the type of mental torture this woman did. The final humiliation came when he told her that unless she was willing to fully accept the rites of his religion, he was forcing her out of the house and would see to it that she didn't have any contact with the children."

McMann sneered. "I imagine his rites were one of those group sex things."

Marlowe's cheeks reddened. She did not like the psychiatrist at all. And she didn't like doctors—or lawyers—who jumped to conclusions before they had heard all of the evidence.

"Not at all. As a matter of fact, the religious sect the husband belonged to tended to be puritanical. What they required from their women, in addition to being baby factories and work animals, is that they be mutilated."

"Mutilated?" Lawrence Dewey asked.

"She was circumcised."

9

❖

Marlowe left the meeting with Philip Hall. They were in the back seat of the Rolls before Marlowe spoke.

"I'm glad none of your team was on any of my juries," Marlowe told him. "They're a hanging jury, for sure."

Hall smiled. "I believe you held your own. There are a great many complications with this case."

"If it wasn't a tough case, the princess wouldn't be reaching around the world for more help. Honestly, what do you think? About selling a battered woman theory to a London jury?"

"Has the princess told you she was abused by her husband?"

"We haven't gone into the specifics because we both feared the police would listen in to our telephone conversation, but she inferred it, she said she needed to hire me because of my success in defending abused women. How did she describe her relationship with the prince to you?"

"I have not spoken to her about it. Trent and Sir Fredic are the only ones who have been privy."

"They don't share the information with the other members of the defense team?"

❖

"This is a very sensitive case."

That didn't answer my question, Marlowe thought. She suspected Hall knew the princess's version.

He pursed his lips. "I don't believe I know enough about your theory to stand in judgment. You've explained it, you have been successful at it. But your success has come in American courtrooms, where you sold facts to a jury rather than legal theory to a judge. Our legal system is not as sensitive to women's issues as yours. Political correctness isn't as adhered to here. Our judiciary has been accused of being an old boys' club and there's reasons for it. How long would a judge last in America who states that a wife contributed to the rape of her fourteen-year-old daughter by her husband, the girl's stepfather, because she denied him sex?"

"It would have made headlines and been the subject of talk shows. The judge would be hounded off the bench."

"It caused a flap, but not the sensation that it would have caused in America. People may be just as offended about the remark, may seek to have the judge redressed for stating it, but the judge wouldn't be electronically lynched by a massive media campaign."

Marlowe said, "The cases I've won were achieved in the courtroom, not in the media. And the way I succeeded with them is no different than the way most attorneys try to handle criminal cases. I humanize the defendant until the jurors can stand in the defendant's shoes and understand the pain and suffering, the feeling of being trapped and terrified, with no way out except to strike back."

"You're right." Hall nodded. "But then the issue revolves around how a defendant is humanized, as you put it. Trent, Lord Finfall, and the others think of American courtroom tactics as somewhat, um, shall we say, *cinematic.*"

"In other words, they believe that my tactics are theatrical, and that a British jury won't go for it."

"I suppose that's a fair statement."

"Do you ever watch movies?" Marlowe asked.

"Movies? Why—yes, I suppose I do, once in a while."

"Are you aware that despite the fact most movies are made in America, in terms of the actors, directors, and so forth, there are many

Brits, Australians, Canadians, and New Zealanders involved in the production? Considering their smaller populations, as compared to the States, there are probably as many of them as there are Americans in films."

"I don't really follow movie lore, but I'm aware that many top stars are from Britain and other English-speaking countries. What is your point?"

"Barrister Hall, since we all share the same cinema, and much the same TV, what makes you think that a British jury is going to be any less receptive to courtroom drama than an American one? *Hamlet, Macbeth, Romeo and Juliet, King Lear,* murder, lust, insanity, I don't recall any of that being invented by Hollywood. If we're going to talk about theatrics, England has been exporting it for centuries. Most people in London may be more conservative than most people in Los Angeles, but you're talking about the way people walk and talk and dress. I would find it hard to believe that Londoners have different attitudes toward battered women than people in L.A., Paris, Rome, or the Tonga Islands."

She gave a long sigh and put her head back against the headrest. "I feel like I've been run through a ringer."

"I'm sorry, it was really inexcusable to hustle you directly into a meeting after a transatlantic flight. You said earlier you were anxious to see the princess. But if you wish, I can pick you up in a couple of hours and take you to see her after you've had time to freshen up."

"No, let's go now. I'm afraid that if I go to the hotel, I'll crawl into bed and crash for the next three days. Which jail is she held at?"

"The oldest in England. The Tower of London."

❖

10

❖

London Police Morgue

"Why frozen?" Archer asked the question aloud to himself as he went down the hallway of the medical examiner's facility. His head was spinning with unanswered questions.

First the Princess of Wales blows away the heir to the throne. Then a body dressed in a Tudor-era costume with a woman's head on its lap turns up at Westminster Abbey. Fresh out of the freezer. Why would a killer want to freeze a body and then move it to a national shrine?

What was the significance of freezing the body? To make the time of death difficult to calculate? The significance of Westminster as the dumping site was a real puzzle. And dumping it in the Henry VII Chapel in the Abbey? With the head chopped off and sewn back on? Dressed in the fashion of the Henrys and Elizabethan eras?

The whole thing made no sense, though one thing struck him about the location: The wing where the body was placed was the bloodiest in the Abbey. It held Henry VII, the father of crazy old Henry VIII who chopped off the head of a couple of his wives. Henry VII was also the grandfather of another Westminster resident, Queen Elizabeth I, a woman who was not opposed to having a head or two severed if she

❖

thought it helped the country. Also in attendance in the wing was Mary, Queen of Scots, whose head Elizabeth had whacked.

"Gone nuts," Archer declared. "Whole bleedin' world." Or at least that part of it situated on the British Isles that he knew. It certainly was a different world from the one he had been born into close to a half century before. More complicated. Faster. Crazier. He defined the difference from the good old days to the present time with one word: *Drugs*. Not technology, not faster planes and cars and electronics, but narcotics, the stuff that nightmares are made of. The stuff had been with mankind from the beginning but came out of the closet during the 1960s and infected the world like a plague, a worldwide pandemic. Technology only moved people and things faster, drugs made people crazy.

He stuck two sticks of gum in his mouth as soon as he entered the building and pulled the peppermint taste into his lungs and nose. He hated the morgue, *really* hated it. Not with a poet's grasp of death, but with a personal grudge.

It was an old building, sitting there forever, built of strong Devonshire brick and made to last a millennium. Like the Abbey it was bone-chillingly cold, but it was a different type of cold than the Abbey, a cold that made Archer shiver whenever he entered the building. The place was not haunted by the ghosts of greatness past, but by horrors—a daily regimen of murder and accident victims from one of the world's largest metropolises being wheeled down the dank corridors.

The outer building was respectable, a dark gray stone tarnished by the ages and the dampness carried from the Thames. But the ivy on the walls was dark, ugly with burnt edges, as if the living plants were being poisoned by the horrors the building had seen.

Inside the hallways were nicotine-shaded white walls and dark granite floors scarred from the rollers of the gurneys that wheeled the institute's guests to the autopsy rooms.

Archer hated the place because it had scared the crap out of him. Three years ago his brother, only a couple years older than him, had been brought in, dead from a heart attack. When he came to identify the body, it was laid out on an examining table, mouth gaped open, fea-

❖

tures locked in frozen pain. Death had not come easily or peacefully—the Archers were a stubborn breed and his brother had locked his jaws on living.

As he stood looking over his brother, affected by his death but not succumbing to the morose—the Archers were a stoic lot and didn't cry over spilled milk—Archer had glanced up at the ceiling mirror above the examining table. He saw the reflection of his brother, dead on the table, and saw himself at the same time, his own broad features so similar to his brother's . . . he realized with a shock what he would look like when it was his turn on the gurney.

He had told no one about having looked death in the eye. And it didn't keep him from entering the facility. He just chewed gum to temper his taste and smell and kept his hands in his pocket as much as possible, reacting to a fear that he might touch or breath in something that would kill him.

DR. HANE WAS EXAMINING THE body in Room 12C. Archer leaned up against the wall and popped his gum as he watched the pathologist bending over the grisly finds at Westminster Abbey. He had always wondered about autopsy pathologists, again not with the soul of a poet but just out of the morbid curiosity his family was noted for. It was true that most doctors dealt with death, dying was a part of living, but morgue pathologists dealt *only* with death, like morticians. He wondered how they felt cutting up dead bodies, how a pathologist could chop up a dead body, slicing it open with an electric saw, and then sit down to a steak dinner, cooked blood-rare. . . .

Archer shivered. Was that what the pathologist who sliced him up was going to do—cut him open, run his hands through his intestines, then go home and have liver and onions for dinner?

Hane pulled off his gloves, dumped them in a hazardous materials container, and stepped out into the anteroom.

"They're dead," he told Archer. The doctor had a sardonic grin.

The remark threw him. "Of course they're dead. A man and a woman, two stiffs."

"Them and the others."

❖

"Others? What do mean, others?"

"I'm talking about what you found."

"Have you been sniffing that stuff you use to kill germs in here? We had a man's body and a woman's head brought in from Westminster Abbey. Two decedents, not an army."

"You had *body parts* brought in from the Abbey."

"Body parts? What are you talking about?"

"Ears were placed backwards on the head, they're from someone else's body."

"What?"

The pathologist grinned. "I don't have the lab results back yet, but it's obvious, from skin tone and the cut left from taking ears off one body and sewing them back on another, the ears and head don't match."

"They're from two victims? We have three stiffs, counting the woman's head?"

"It gets worse. I'm sure the lab will tell us that the man's head doesn't match the body."

"Doesn't match the—?"

Dr. Hane grinned with delight. "Someone created a Frankenstein monster, taking body parts and sewing them crudely together."

"A serial killer."

"Probably. I'm sure the male body is from three different persons and you have a woman's head."

"Cause of deaths?"

"Don't know yet, none of the parts have mortal wounds, except the cut made separating the parts from the bodies. Unless something comes back with toxicology, we may use a Ouija board to determine cause of death. And there are more surprises."

"Tell me."

"The body, the part from the head down, has an abdominal cut that looks the same as an autopsy cut. The internal organs are missing. And the cuts made to separate the parts from the bodies—all made with surgical precision. I'd say that your killer used a surgeon's saw to cut off the head, the ears, so forth."

"Mother of God—we're dealing with a Jack the Ripper copycat. That bloody bastard used to do surgical cuts like that."

"It looks professional, that's for sure, as good a cut as I could make myself. So why did the killer do such an obviously crude job of sewing the parts together? And where are the missing parts? Are they going to show up in St. Paul's or Parliament? There's a message there, somewhere, that's what my gut is telling me."

"Time of death?"

"Deaths," Hane corrected. "Remember, we're dealing with at least four people. We've sent samples to the lab, they'll tell us something, but the parts were frozen, so it'll be tough to get it down pat. We may not get it down to hours or even days unless we have information to fill in the blanks with. Identification would help. We've sent the prints to the crime lab." Hane's face screwed up. "How does one get a body into Westminster without being seen?"

"Not as hard as it might seem," Archer said. "Back in the fifties some Scottish radicals stole the coronation throne with the Stone of Scone from the Abbey, all three hundred and some-odd pounds of it. I'm less puzzled by how the body got there than I am *why* the body got there."

Archer left Hane. On his way out, he met Detective Lois Kramer in the corridor and filled her in on what the pathologist had told him.

"Four bodies, maybe more. Cut up, pieced together, even dissected just like the Ripper used to do it."

"We have to find this nut," Kramer said.

"We'll get him. Dutton can't disappear off the face of the earth."

"C'mon, you don't really think—"

"I don't think, I know. That son-of-a-bitch is on a murder rampage and I'm going to take him down before he kills again."

11

❖

Tony Dutton opened the door, slipped quietly into the dark apartment, and fumbled for the light switch. And then there was light.

"Freakkkkk!"

"Shut up, you ugly birdbrain."

The African Gray glared at him from its cage across the room. The feathers on its head were ruffled.

"Freakkkkk!"

"Featherbrained bastard. Keep your voice down or I'm going to pluck out that black heart of yours."

He headed for the kitchenette and grabbed a beer. He leaned back against the sink counter and exchanged glares with the bird. It wasn't his beer, his flat, or his bird. He was certain his own apartment would be where Archer of the Yard looked for him first.

The beer was okay, but he wouldn't have given a chipped quid for the flat or the bird. Both belonged to Meg, a photographer who had gone off to Rwanda to cover a war crimes tribunal. Meg's next-door neighbor was given a key to feed the bird and Dutton got the key when the neighbor took her vacation on the Costa del Sol. Knowing the animosity between Dutton and Dr. Livingstone, the African Gray, Meg had made

❖

Dutton solemnly promise that he would not roast the bastard bird over an open fire when it became his turn to feed the creature.

The problems between him and the bird started when the creature got bird fever a couple of years ago. The treatment was to take a hypodermic needle, a needle big enough to excite the passions of a drug addict, and jam it into the bird's chest. Meg got queasy jamming the big needle in, especially when it made a little popping noise each time the needle was plunged through the bird's taut paper-thin skin. Dutton had the dirty task of pushing in the needle while Meg held Livingstone. The bird had never forgiven him for it—or forgotten.

The apartment was industrial modern, a loft in a converted factory, the kind of place that artsy-fartsy types drool over while reading designer magazines. Dutton was unable to get into fashion statements that included exposed ducts, pipes, and electrical conduit. His own tastes ran toward the more conventional, rooms that had ceilings he could jump up and touch, flat square walls—four to a room—toilets hidden in rooms behind doors, furniture with four legs on the floor, that sort of thing. As far as he was concerned, Meg's apartment was designed in hell. Just one room, a small square space with a large wide steel-meshed stairway against the back wall. At the top of the industrial stairway was a small landing where Meg had one of those Japanese beds that resembled a throw rug and was as comfortable as a bed of nails. The rest of the living space was what was left over by the big stairway—off to the left a compact sink, fridge, hot plate, and microwave, to the right the toilet and a claw foot tub separated from the rest of the room only by hospital curtains on rollers.

Hanging from a chain in the open area beneath the stairway landing was a couch. Behind the couch, suspended from a metal bar under the stairway, were her hanging clothes. Going up the stairway were her "dressers"—wicker baskets on almost every step, a basket for underwear, for sweaters, tops, socks, and the rest.

Nothing in the loft was normal or to Dutton's taste, least of all the artwork. Meg had a fetish in her private photography—male nudes. They were everywhere and exposed *everything* from every possible angle. The blowup shots were on the walls and ceiling. Everywhere you turned in the place you came face-to-face with male anatomy. Maybe he

❖

was prejudiced, but he was of the opinion that men looked better with their clothes on.

Ignoring Dr. Livingstone's squawking, he took his beer across the room and collapsed on the couch, keeping it from swinging by putting down his feet. Meg's glass coffee table top was held up by a stone figure of a nude man with his male member pointed straight up. Dutton laid magazines on top of the glass so he didn't have to stare at the guy's plumbing.

He was over four decades old and had managed not to be on the run from the police most of that time—present situation excluded, although he did do some jail time, a month in the local clink back in the heady days when he was a top journalist and going to jail was a matter of principle.

Besides the fact that there were no grand principles in the Abbey killing, at least none that jumped out and grabbed him, he was fresh out of ideas and had no intention of going to jail for Howler, who was not only a drug addict and street scum, but had probably set him up.

It was entirely possible—hell, *probable*—that Howler freaked out on bad dope, killed someone, and dressed him up like a Madame Tussaud's wax figure—actually, there were two "someones" who were killed, counting the head in the lap.

But he couldn't shake the notion that Howler might actually be on to something. As a former idealistic star reporter and current hack writing tabloid trash, Dutton had developed a talent for spotting a story. Like a water witch who dowses for wells with a couple of sticks, he had an instinct for dowsing for stories. It was an itch in his right ear. He scratched the itch now, thinking about Howler and the bloody surprise at the Abbey. The Abbey horrors were insane, but he wasn't ready just yet to throw Howler to Archer.

Not just a bigger story than the princess shooting the heir to the throne, but a colossal scoop on the subject, was what Howler had baited him with. "She didn't kill the prince because she was jealous . . . it's all in the letter," had been Howler's statement on the phone that lured Dutton to the Abbey on a dark and stormy night.

What letter? The bastard wouldn't tell him, but it was the mention of a letter more than anything else that had hooked him. There had

❖

been rumors about a princess vs. prince letter floating around the news business for months, a letter the princess had sent to a friend that was supposed to have revealed some dark, deep secret about the Royals. There were different rumors as to what the letter contained and the one Dutton liked the best was that the princess had become convinced that the prince and his hangers-on had decided she was a nuisance who needed to be put away—in a grave if she wouldn't voluntarily commit herself to a mental institution.

The notion of a royal murder plot atop a royal murder made a tabloid reporter's heart beat faster than a pimp visiting a girl's school.

"What if it was self-defense?" he asked Dr. Livingstone.

"Freakkkk!"

"What if the princess had killed the prince not because of jealousy, but because she believed that he and his cronies were going to do her in?"

The bird had no answer for that one, but he twisted his neck and cocked an eye up at Dutton.

"You can smell it, too, can't you, featherbrain? It stinks worse than Hamlet's Denmark."

Dutton opened another beer and gave the matter as much serious thought as a tabloid reporter was capable. The story wouldn't be as big as the Princess of Wales blowing the Prince of Wales away, but it would rank as the second greatest story in a millennium. And better than the actual killing, which was caught on videotape and witnessed by millions, it would be an exclusive that he would make Cohn and *Burn* pay the proverbial arm and leg for.

It wasn't impossible that Howler had gotten wind of something that important. He could have stumbled on to something when he was called in to the medical examiner's office for a job. Maybe the purse of an accident victim sitting nearby as the owner of the purse was being chopped up by a pathologist. The victim could have been a friend and confidante of the princess. Howler sticks his hand into the purse, looking for the price of his next fix, pulls out a letter, it's in the princess's own hand, it says that the Palace Gang plans to—

"Probably not," he spoke to the bird, "but there are all kinds of possibilities." And *if* there was such a letter, and *if* he could get his hands on it, it would be a giant scoop, a regular "Royalgate."

❖

Howler said he wanted ten million pounds for his information. A nice round figure that rolled off the tongue. But there'd be millions for each of them if that crazy bastard really did have a death-threat letter.

He needed to talk to Cohn. The man would be on top of the Abbey investigation by the police—he had paid sources everywhere. But he couldn't tell Cohn about the Howler angle. There simply wasn't any honor in the tabloid business. And Cohn was very good at his job, earning his nickname of Cohn the Barbarian for the hordes he had massacred with printer's ink. The editor had a colder heart than the guy with the exposed plumbing under the coffee table. It went with the business of turning out a tabloid—editors, reporters, even the secretaries and mailroom boys had it. Cohn often criticized Dutton, who had gone to tabloid reporting only after his fall from grace with actual journalism, for not having the killer instinct of a true tabloid reporter. The criticism came during those times Dutton tried to insist on some semblance of the truth in a story.

He used his cellular to call Cohn, figuring it might be harder to trace than the apartment phone. He wouldn't put it past the man to have his call traced and turn him over to the police—as long as Archer agreed to have a *Burn* photographer catching the anguished and terrified and surprised look on Dutton's face as he was hauled out of the loft by the yard.

"Tony, where are you?" Mangus Cohn asked.

"Why do you want to know? Has a reward been posted for me?"

"The police are looking for you. Bram Archer thinks you're a suspect in the four bodies found at the Abbey."

"*Four?* How could there be four?"

"The head didn't belong to the shoulders down, and other such discrepancies. You didn't know this?"

"Of course not. I chop up people so fast, I lose count of how many I kill."

"I know you're only joking, Tony, but has it occurred to you what a fabulous story we are sitting on? Every rag in the country is headlining the royal murder case and here we are with one of our star reporters suspected of being a serial killer in the nation's holy of holies. Wonderful stuff."

❖

"Jesus, Mangus, I'm glad I made your day, but while you've been putting together the latest edition of that disgusting rag you dare to call a newspaper, don't forget that I went into that bloody church to get a story for *you*. Tell me about the damn bodies."

"I don't know that much—yet. My source says that someone has put together a body from pieces of other bodies, that sort of thing. The ears were sewn on backwards, didn't belong to the head, head sewn on the shoulders, that sort of thing. Very bloody, very newsworthy."

"Jesus. Are you saying that someone's gone on a murder rampage and is cutting up bodies and piecing them together like a jigsaw puzzle?"

"Isn't it wonderful?"

"Not if it's your head the killer wants. Bizarre. Pieces to four bodies, seven in one blow."

"Seven? I haven't heard about seven."

"It's a fairy tale—you know, one of those fantasies that predates the fantasies your paper turns out. A meek and mild tailor killed seven flies with one blow, people thought is was men instead of flies, and—"

He set the phone on his lap for a moment while Cohn raved on about how they would try to fit the "seven with one blow" into their lead on the story. Implying, of course, that the four deaths already were just a drop in the buckets of blood that Tony Dutton, Abbey Killer, left behind.

The man had the loyalty of a rabid dog.

He interrupted Cohn. "Fuck your story. Tell me more about the Abbey thing. The body was dressed in some sort of costume."

"Tudor-era dress, Elizabethan, that sort of thing. Police are checking costume rental companies. The stuff was frozen."

"What stuff?"

"Head, body. The theory is that the killer kept the body in deep freeze."

"That's weird, but it would play hell on setting time of death, wouldn't it? But why would he dump them in Westminster Abbey? How'd he get them into the place?"

"Police theory is that it was carted in, maybe even in baby carriages. Or through a rear delivery door in a box on a hand truck. The

❖

Abbey's open to the public most of the time. Could have come in many ways."

"Frozen." Dutton nodded to the bird, soliciting any comments it might have on the subject. "Besides making it hard to pin down time of death, thus making it unnecessary for the killer to have an alibi for when the victims were killed, it makes it all easier to transport. Easier to move because the stiffs are stiff. No messy blood splashing around. And parts are easier to cart than a whole body, they'd stack nicer. But why Westminster, and why piece together the body parts? And where's the rest of the stiffs' stuff? St. Paul's? Buckingham? Nelson's statue?"

"Tony, my boy," Cohn purred.

Dutton's hand tightened on the phone. Cohn had no interest in sex, money, or liquor. He only purred for stories.

"We need to give deep thought to the situation with you and the police."

Oh-oh. The last thing Cohn gave deep thought about was an Elvis sighting. "*What* situation with me and the police? I've got a loose-cannon cop trying to trump up charges against me. You make some phone calls and get the bastard off my back."

"Archer has put out a nationwide armed-and-dangerous alert for you in connection with the killings."

"Mangus, why don't you get down to the bottom line? I'm getting the idea in the pit of my stomach that you're trying to make me an Aunt Sally so you can sell papers. I'm not going to play an Aunt Sally for you."

"Tony," he purred, "think of what a great story we're sitting on. A *Burn* writer actually suspected as a serial killer. Murder in the Abbey. It's the stuff of . . . of fairy tales—"

"The kind written by Stephen King, a fuckin' horror story."

"We at *Burn* understand and sympathize with what you are going through. Hell, you know I personally think of you as a son."

"Lying bastard."

"What we had in mind was in the way of a confession."

"*What?*"

"*Freakkkk!*"

"What was that?"

❖

"You want a confession from me? Are you crazy?"

"Not a full confession, just something that implies that you've gone amuck. We'll run it for a couple weeks and then come out with the true story."

"What true story?"

"The man whose head was found at the Abbey reminded you of the priest who molested you when you were—"

"Freakkkk!"

Dutton hung up. "For once I agree with you, birdbrain," he told Dr. Livingstone. "I deserve it. I've been out crucifying people with rumors and innuendos, now it's my turn to be chased by the jackals I run with."

What a pisser. Frozen body parts at Westminster. Pasted together as one man. Dressed in a period costume. With a woman's head as a lapdog.

He called Howler's home number. "Piss off," the recording said.

After the beep, Dutton said, "If you're there, pick up, I have money for you."

Nothing. Howler either wasn't home or was dead. Those were the only two reasons he wouldn't have responded to an offer of money.

He tried the coroner's office next. Howler only got occasional assignments from the coroner, but it was possible he was there working on one. He wasn't. "Haven't seen him in days," someone named Mrs. Stewart told him.

Dutton had Howler's mother's number, too. He called it, though the odds of the man being there were slim—Howler only showed up once a month at his mother's the day she got her social welfare check. The phone was answered by an elderly woman.

"Good day, Mrs. Howler."

"Is this the police?" the woman asked.

"Yes," Dutton said. You don't become a top reporter for a shabby tabloid without knowing when to lie.

"Is there any news about Walter?"

Walter. Dutton had forgotten that the man had a first name.

Any news. That would make Howler missing.

"That's what I wanted to talk to you about. Now, Mrs. Howler, you, uh, let me see . . . ?" He made a paper noise shuffling a *Stud* magazine on the coffee table.

"I'm the one who made the missing persons report. I knew something was wrong when he didn't show up on my check day."

"Yes, that was very intuitive of you, but a mother always knows, doesn't she? What I need is to confirm the information, so let's start from the beginning. Last time you saw your son?"

"About a month ago. The last time I got a check."

I should have thought of that myself, Dutton thought.

"He said he was off to the countryside, been invited to the prince's ball, he had."

"Prince's ball?"

"The Prince of Wales. Terrible what happened to him. That's why I'm so worried about Walter. Maybe someone shot him, too. They say the princess is quite insane, don't they?"

Dutton stared at Dr. Livingstone across the way. The bird was strangely quiet. Dutton himself was speechless. Invited to the prince's ball? Howler had less chance of being invited to a royal party as he did of addressing the United Nations General Assembly on medical ethics.

"Wasn't that the information I gave before?" she asked. "My memory isn't as good as it used to be. I don't always—"

"What exactly did he say to you when you saw him last? About the prince's ball."

"That he was off to the country with the prince for that hunt and ball that's been in all the news. Before he left, he dropped by to pick up clothes he had stored here. He was really quite proud that he was shouldering with royalty, you know. But I always knew my Walter was special."

Her Walter was special, all right, and he had about as much chance of rubbing elbows with royalty as a wallowing pig did.

"That's the last time you've heard from him?"

"Yes, I expected him to call me after that terrible thing happened to the prince."

"What did the police tell you?"

"You're the police."

❖

I should have thought of that myself. "I mean the other officers who spoke to you."

"The ones that came to my apartment? They told me not to worry, that Walter was on a special assignment for the police. They also told me not to discuss Walter with anyone but them. But I call them every day because I know he needs to come by and get money for his medicine. You know that he takes medicine, don't you?"

Yeah, Dutton knew what kind of "medicine" Howler used, it was bought on the streets and went into a hypodermic needle that was injected anyplace on Howler's body that didn't already have more holes than a pincushion.

Dutton had her give him the police telephone number, "Just to make sure you're calling the right one," he told her. After he jotted it down, he asked, "Uh, did Walter have any close friends? Someone he might have confided in? A girl?" *Someone he shared needles with?* he was tempted to ask.

"No, he broke up with Betty over a year ago, when she went back to jail. Walter was very particular about his women friends, you know. He couldn't afford to have his reputation tarnished."

He signed off and hung up after assuring Mrs. Howler that Walter was being well taken care of and swearing her to secrecy about his call. He wondered what it was about mothers that made them blind to the fact their Johnny was a serial killer, rapist, or druggie.

He got another beer from the fridge and sat on the couch with pen and paper. He outlined what he knew.

Bodies or the parts thereto were found at Westminster Abbey.

Howler had tipped him that a body would be there and that there was a royal connection. How did Howler know the body would be there? Did he put it there? And what about the letter Howler mentioned. Where was it?

The Prince of Wales was dead.

Before he died, the prince invited a notorious drug addict to his hunt and charity ball.

No way! The last "fact" was nonsense. There was no possibility Howler was invited to the ball. He obviously made up that story to cover something else he was doing.

❖

But . . .

The police told Howler's mother that her son was on a special assignment. Okay, Howler did special assignments for the coroner's office, reconstructing bodies. That's police-connected activity. But what kind of assignment could the man have that was *secret?* And that included an invitation to the prince's ball?

Dutton underlined *special assignment*. It stank of more of that Danish stink Hamlet complained about.

The body parts were dressed in a Tudor-era costume—the era of Henry VII, Henry VIII, Queen Mary, and the Virgin Queen, Elizabeth I. The present royal family weren't Tudors, but would be related because the crown kept going to cousins and such after the main houses ran out of heirs. But why historical royal garb? What was the message?

They had been frozen.

Why? To make it hard to tell time of death? To make them easy to transport? Those were the easy answers. But were they also frozen to preserve them until they could be placed at Westminster?

Why Westminster? One thing he had learned about covering the crime beat was that serial killers are crazy . . . but that there was always a method to their madness. That's why they were called "serial" killers—they had a game plan they usually stuck to. And they not uncommonly operated off of messages—ones from God, Satan, voices in their head, telepathy with their victims.

The killer didn't dress up the body, body parts, whatever they were, and leave it in the Abbey as a matter of caprice. The stuff had been frozen and transported into a national shrine.

There was a message involved, maybe a series of information that added up to a single statement. He had to find out what it was before a loose-cannon cop and an avaricious tabloid editor got him hanged.

He telephoned the number Howler's mother had been using to call the police.

"Royal Protection Service," a male voice answered.

Now, that was mind-blowing. The RPS unit was composed of top officers recruited from other police branches to provide protection for the Royals. They had essentially the same function as the Secret Service officers who protected the U.S. President and Vice President. That they

❖

could have business with Howler made as much sense as Howler rubbing shoulders with the prince.

He turned on the telly to see what the evening news had to say about the break-in at the Abbey. And caught Archer grinning for the camera.

"Is this tabloid reporter, the man you have identified as Tony Dutton, suspected of being the killer?" a TV reporter asked Archer.

"Dutton is a very dangerous character, a man who broke into a national shrine and was caught red-handed with bodies—actually, they were body parts."

"Bastard. Hanging me with rumor and innuendo," Dutton told the television set.

But not even the sensational break-in at Westminster could crowd the royal murder case off as the top story. Still thinking about Howler and the prince, he watched the arrival of the American lawyer whom the princess had hired and saw Smithers ambush her in the terminal. Smithers was the worse kind of creep, a tabloid reporter who would make up a story if he couldn't find one. Dutton himself refused to completely make up a story. Someone had to tell him that he or she had actually seen Elvis or had been raped by an alien.

Of course, after the basics were established, it was up to him to give the rest of the story.

What Smithers pulled on the lawyer was a shabby trick, but Dutton had to admit that it was effective. The TV news carried the lawyer's look of surprise at the ambush. Dutton would bet that the woman's gaping mouth would highlight the front page of *Burn* tomorrow.

As Dutton watched Marlowe James on the tube, it occurred to him that he might have something in common with the American lawyer. It would be in the interest of her client if there was any dirt out there on the Prince of Wales that could help the princess. And Dutton needed information about Howler and his "invitation" to the royal ball. Not to mention a copy of the letter, if one existed.

He wondered if the princess's defense team knew about the letter. Wouldn't it be something she would tell them? They would have to have the letter; it only made sense. It would be part of her defense, probably her main defense. Though killing the crown prince because she thought he was going to have her killed might be a little premature.

"Is it legal if you kill someone because you thought they were going to kill you?" he asked the bird.

"*Freakkkk!*"

She had a child-like confidence . . . that one day a man whom she could love and who loved her would come into her life.

She had always imagined him coming to her like a crusading knight riding a fiery half-tamed horse over the green steppes and nothing would matter but their ecstatic love for each other.

—BARBARA CARTLAND,
THE PROUD PRINCESS

Life is 70 percent slog and 30 percent fantastic.

—DIANA,
PRINCESS OF WALES

12

❖

Tower of London

"It was originally a fortress, dating back to Roman times," Hall told Marlowe as the Rolls arrived at the infamous tower. "It's housed the nation's gold and the crown jewels, it's survived attacks by terrorists, revolutionaries, and Nazi bombs, but the Tower of London is probably most famous as a prison and for its escapes."

"Didn't Mary, Queen of Scots, lose her head here?"

"Actually, she was held prisoner here, I believe, but her head was removed at Fotheringhay Castle near Peterborough. But many other famous heads and souls were severed here, Anne Boleyn, one of Henry the VIII's doomed wives, Sir Walter Raleigh, the conspirator Guy Fawkes, Sir Thomas More, who refused to recognize old Henry as head of the Church of England and whom the Pope later canonized. I'm sure there's a list posted somewhere for tourists. Also, there are the ghosts."

"Of course, there is always one in a haunted castle."

"This one has several dozen, I'm afraid. The most notorious is Catherine Howard, the fifth wife of Henry VIII. Catherine was only about twenty when she married the king. After just over a year, he found out she had had premarital relations with other men. He had her and two of her former lovers beheaded."

❖

"He had her executed for having lovers *before* marriage?"

"He probably got tired of her and having her head chopped off was an easy way out. There is a tradition that she haunts both Hampton Court, a palace where she tried to escape her captors, and the Tower of London, where she was executed." He pointed at one of the twelve towers of the castle. "That one is known as the Bloody Tower. It's said that the boy-king Edward V and his brother, Richard, the Duke of York, were murdered there."

"Why?"

"Edward was twelve or thirteen and had inherited the throne. No one knows for sure who had him and his brother killed, probably Richard III or Henry VII, who defeated Richard and grabbed the throne. Anyway, the boy-king is occasionally seen wandering around, looking for his murderer. He probably bumps into Anne Boleyn, another of Henry's wives who lost her head here. And Lady Jane Grey, who at sixteen years old was to be queen for all of nine days before Henry VIII's daughter, Mary Tudor, had her head whacked."

"Charming family history, isn't it? Anyone ever escape from the Tower?"

"Quite a number, actually. Two or three men in female clothes smuggled in by their wives slipped passed the guards, who thought they were visitors leaving."

Hall pointed at an imposing building. "The princess is being held in Queen's House on Tower Green. It's usually the residence of the governor who administers the yeoman warders we call beefeaters, much to their chagrin. It's been furnished and guarded for her stay," Hall said. "You can imagine the quandary of the police and the Royals in regard to holding her for trial. They couldn't just stick her in the regular jail. The security problems would have been overwhelming. And despite any ill feeling the queen has for her, she wouldn't want to set a precedent of having a Royal locked up like the rest of us."

"Us unwashed masses."

"Exactly."

They passed guards wearing the colorful traditional uniform of beefeaters, but Marlowe noticed there were numerous armed uniformed guards and men hanging around whom she took to be plainclothes officers.

"Royal Protection officers," Hall said. "As you probably know, most London police officers are not armed. Special Branch and the officers assigned to protect the Royals are. There's a unit of commandos stationed here, too. The killing of the prince has whipped emotions in the country to a frenzy. Some people say off with her head—and about every day the Yard discovers another plot by her admirers to break her out of the Tower."

"I suspect she's the most popular woman on earth. At least she was up to the shooting."

They passed a man feeding a flock of large black birds. "The raven master. Ravens with clipped wings are kept on the Tower grounds. We have a traditional belief that if the ravens ever leave the Tower, the fortress would crumble and the nation fall."

While they showed identification and waited to be processed, Marlowe brought up what she knew would create a riff with Hall.

"After introductions are made, I will need to speak to the princess alone."

The young barrister was startled. "That can't be done. Sir Fredic must be there. He'll be here in a few minutes."

"Why does he have to be there?"

"He's the instructing solicitor, the attorney who hired Trent. It's not ethical for a barrister to meet with a client except in the presence of the instructing solicitor."

"Who's in charge of the case, Trent or Sir Fredic?"

"Trent is in charge of the trial, but you need to understand the relationship between a solicitor and a barrister."

"You can fill me in later. Right now I have to see the princess and I'm going to see her alone."

"I told you that it's not—"

"Philip, I'm not a barrister, I'm an American trial lawyer, I was hired privately by the princess, I don't answer to an instructing solicitor or a managing barrister or anyone else. I realize Mr. Trent doesn't think my leash should extend beyond his reach, but I was hired by the princess and there are matters that have to be discussed privately with her. It's not arguable, it's simply how it will be handled. I will speak to her alone."

"That's your prerogative," Hall said rather stiffly.

She grabbed his arm and squeezed it as a gesture to create a friendly connection through touch. "I'm sorry, the leash remark was uncalled-for, I forget how reserved and polite you British are. But you and I know that there was a reason the princess hired me directly rather than going through her own attorneys."

"And that reason is?"

Marlowe smiled. "I don't know, but I won't find out if I can't speak to her alone, can I? I'm not trying to cause trouble, but I have to insist."

"No problem, I will excuse myself and wait outside for Sir Fredic, to advise him of your wishes."

"Thanks. Again, I don't mean to be ornery."

"It's no more than what I would expect from a pushy American lawyer." He said it with a smile.

"But, of course, we Americans are pushy and loud and you British are all so reserved and polite," she said, "but that's nonsense, isn't it? You people have ruled half of the world with an iron fist and you've had sex scandals that have rocked your whole nation. Not to mention the present matter."

They were led into a sitting room by a woman who had identified herself as a secretary to the princess, but whom Marlowe took to be a jail matron.

"Her Royal Highness will be with you shortly."

The Princess of Wales came in a moment later. She was blond, tall, about five-nine, slender, but rather large-boned. Attractive, not unlike an American's concept of the prototype blond, clean-cut, ruby-cheeked Iowa farm girl, but the princess was not a great beauty, not a Princess Grace. As Marlowe had heard a British friend once say about herself, she was no oil painting.

She smiled at Hall. "Good afternoon, Mr. Hall."

He gave her more of a polite nod than a bow. "Your Royal Highness. May I present Marlowe James."

She held out her hand to Marlowe. "So kind of you to come."

❖

"It was, uh, kind of you to ask," Marlowe fumbled. Was she supposed to curtsy or something?

They exchanged firm handshakes. Marlowe's father had taught her to grip a person's hand firmly when shaking it, and not offer the limp fish that so many people do. Someone had taught the Princess of Wales the same thing, she thought.

"May I offer tea or coffee?" the princess asked.

"Is it all right if I be pardoned?" Hall asked. "I have an urgent telephone call to make."

Hall fled and Marlowe and the princess exchanged small talk about Marlowe's flight and the weather as a servant brought in drinks and sweetcakes. The refreshment was served in fine china on exquisite linen. The princess drank coffee while Marlowe took tea with cream. Marlowe suppressed a grin at the irony of a prisoner and her attorney in a murder case being served tea and crumpets—she usually considered herself lucky when she could speak to her clients face-to-face across a steel table in a concrete room rather than with phones through a Plexiglas window.

"Yes, it is strange, isn't it?" the princess said, reading her thoughts. "But they're not really doing it for me. I suspect the queen would rather like to see my head chopped off, but she has to maintain protocol. That's what royalty is all about, a set of rules, a code of behavior, what the queen would call our traditions. And that's what people of my background are all about, too, people with noble titles and named estates who desire to maintain traditions."

"By keeping the status quo you keep your privileges," Marlowe said.

"That's true, but don't we all try to maintain our positions?"

"Not if you're one of the have-nots. And I'm not trying to be facetious or argumentative, it's something we have to consider in your defense. People are creatures of prejudice, all of us, we just hate or have contempt for different reasons. Lawyers who represent wealthy clients know that there will be someone on the jury who resents the rich. In your case, people can even have political bias."

"People who want to get rid of the Royals and nobility." It was a statement, not a question. Marlowe inferred from the princess's tone that it was a subject the princess had mulled over.

❖

"Yes, and people who believe you should be punished for attacking a Royal."

"So that's what a jury is? A group of people with prejudices?"

"That's what people are like . . . and juries are made up of people. Fortunately, most people don't have steel-trap minds, they can be persuaded to put aside minor bigotry, but some prejudices—religion, race, and resentment against the rich—are difficult for people to set aside. There are people who are blindly loyal to your husband because of his position, but that mind-set might be easier to set aside than the prejudice some jurors will have because you came from a privileged background."

"I see. In their minds, are privileged and happy the same thing? Let me assure you, there have been many times in my life, including the present moment, when I would have given my titles and material possessions to be in a happy marriage with a man who loved me."

Would you? Marlowe wondered. Was there a woman in the world who would not have sacrificed a little happiness to marry a prince and someday become queen? But it wasn't time to challenge her on her story.

"That's a point we'll get across to the jury, that there's more to happiness than material possessions and titles." Marlowe met her eye. "I've met the rest of your defense team. They appear to be a well-rounded group of professionals. Why did you reach across the ocean and hire me? You had to know it would throw jet fuel on an already raging fire."

The princess stared at her a little openmouthed, started to say something, and broke into a laugh. "You Americans, always so blunt. Do you have an ax in your briefcase you'll bludgeon me with if you don't like my answers?"

"I'm sorry, but I defend my clients with all my heart and all my energy. To win cases, I need to explain my client so well that the jury walks in my client's shoes. To do that, I need to first walk in the shoes myself. Before we start building a defense about the shooting of your husband, I need to start with one of the most perplexing things about the case—why you hired me."

"You called my defense team well-rounded. What did you think of Anthony Trent?"

Marlowe thought for a moment. "Intelligent, perceptive, probably a very able negotiator—all together, a sharp attorney. Well groomed, successful, distinguished, a leader in the courtroom and outside it. Not a typical criminal defense attorney, at least by American standards, where I've heard the best defense attorneys described as pit bulls with snapping jaws. In the States, I'd see him as more of a high-powered corporate attorney, perhaps even one who defends CEOs accused of white-collar crimes."

"Would you say he's ambitious?"

"Ambitious? I don't know him well enough to answer that, but most successful people are. Including me."

"I would imagine that the ambitions of most American attorneys are to succeed at their profession, win cases, and make money. Having the admiration of your peers or the public and financial rewards are universal motives that I can also imagine. But in Britain, we have an added mark of success. Knighthood. And above that, a life peer."

"Life peer?"

"One is granted a noble title for life, but unlike hereditary titles, the title expires with the person. Lord Finfall is a life peer, awarded the title for public service. Do you know who creates knighthoods and peerages?"

Marlowe nodded. "The queen. I see what you're getting at. Sir Fredic is a knight, Lord Finfall is nobility."

"And Sir Fredic would like to be Baron Fredic. And I can't tell you how much it would warm Anthony Trent's heart to be called Sir Anthony."

"You think they'd sell you out for a knighthood or peerage?"

"Selling me out, as you put it, would be too strong. They are honorable men and women, the people on the defense team. I don't believe any of them can be bought or sold like common merchandise. It's something much more subtle."

"What do you mean?"

"Our legal system is very tight knit. The people at the top of it went to the same schools, socialize together, and no doubt think pretty much alike. That's most of the reason I wanted an outsider as part of it, to bring in fresh thinking. And the other part is this knighthood thing. I trust Trent, he is a good and honorable professional. I don't doubt his

❖

ability or his loyalty. But I can't help wondering if somewhere in the back of his mind there might be a nagging thought that if he defended me too aggressively, he would never be Sir Anthony. I can't help wondering if that nagging thought might inadvertently tip the scales against me in a critical moment."

"You're right, we don't have anything like knighthood in the States, unless it's membership to a snooty country club."

The princess took a sip of her coffee. "I rather suspect that Americans don't understand the role of the Royals in British life. You have royalty, too, you treat your movie and music stars not just as celebrities, but in many ways with the pomp and adulation we treat the Royals. In Britain, the Royals are not just people who enter your life when you see a movie or play a song, but are a part of your life from the day you are born. And surrounding the Royals are families like mine, people in the upper echelon of the social, political, and financial strata, and the Royals possess a powerful social hammer. The richest people in the country don't feel fulfilled until they hear the titillating sound of 'Yes, Your Lordship,' or 'How are you today, Lady Jane?'"

She eyed Marlowe. "I suppose this thing about royalty and nobility is difficult for an American to appreciate."

"Not as much as you might think. Because we read and speak English, it's British literature, British law, British culture that most Americans relate to. Your queen in a sense is our queen, too."

The princess lowered her eyes a moment, wondering how to approach Marlowe with a touchy subject. "I understand that, uh, your financial background is much different than mine, at least when you were young. Will that make it difficult for you to understand me? To fight for me? Or do you fight the same for all your clients?"

"I fight for all my clients, that's what my profession demands. I'd like to say that it doesn't matter if the client is wealthy or not, but the truth is that rich people can pay for the teams of experts that can make a difference in a case."

"Do lawyers work harder if they're paid more?"

"I can only speak for myself and I'd like to say no, that I don't work harder for the rich than I do the poor, but that would be a lie. I won't turn down a case that I believe in just because of money, but I have to

❖

pay rent, buy food, and cover office expenses like anyone else. Someone has to pay for that, and it won't be the poor."

The princess spread her fingers on the table and stared down at them. Her fingernails had been chewed on. Embarrassed, she hid them as she realized Marlowe had noticed.

"In a sense, I see you as a counterbalance. Asking you to represent me was not a spur-of-the-moment decision. I actually had you thoroughly checked out. I learned that in America, successful criminal defense lawyers gain something of celebrity status—"

"Or notoriety." *It wouldn't have taken much for the princess's friends to have checked my background,* Marlowe thought. There had been plenty of stories about her over the years.

"Or that. Naturally, I was impressed by your string of victories. But also with how you managed them. The person who investigated you on my behalf called you a master of empathy. You were able to explain your clients to the jury in a way that they truly understood what the clients went through. You could only do that if you had a great reserve of empathy. And if there's anything I need, it's for people to understand from my point of view what drove me to pick up a gun and pull the trigger. I think you can understand that better than anyone else."

Marlowe got an intuitive flash as to why the princess had hired her. She wasn't just looking for empathy. Marlowe's attraction to her was that both of them had taken abuse and humiliation and struck back at their husbands the same way.

"I don't want to be locked up in prison. Or a mental ward, which is the place they'd most like to put me. You see, that would explain everything to their satisfaction, wouldn't it? If I was crazy, it's not his fault and it's not really even my fault, either, because I had no control over my actions. But that would mean not only that I would be written off as a crazy, but that I would be locked up forever.

"My main concern is for my children. I could never explain to them why I killed their father. They've asked me why I did it and I simply shook my head and cried. I need to leave them a legacy about me that doesn't simply label me a crazy. There are things about a relationship between a man and a woman no mother could ever explain to her child, things that are so personal or painful that the words can't be said to children. But I hope I can give you those words and let you explain me to the world."

She met Marlowe's eyes. Marlowe saw sadness and world-weariness in the princess's moist eyes.

"I want you to be my champion, Marlowe. To be my advocate and fight my battles. But most of all, I want you to understand me, so you can explain me to the world. I can only hope to God that my sons learn things about me and my marriage that makes them understand that I was driven to a heinous act. I took their father from them, but I did so only after years of mental abuse that robbed me of my dignity and very nearly my sanity."

The princess locked eyes with Marlowe again. "They made me do it, drove me to it. That's what I told the police investigators—and that is the truth. The biggest problem with my marriage and my position as the future queen was that I never really belonged. My husband's family and his circle of friends never accepted me. They lined up against me when they found out that I would not simply stand back and take it."

"Why don't we start at the beginning?" Marlowe took a tape recorder out of her briefcase.

"I'd prefer not to be taped, just in case it fell into the wrong hands."

"Okay, but I'll have to take notes." She substituted a notepad for the recorder. She actually knew quite a bit about the princess—her legal assistant was a compulsive reader of tabloids and magazines that revealed the private lives of celebrities. She had given Marlowe an hour-long dissertation on the princess and other Royals. But how much of it was truth and how much was made-up lust and disgust and other exaggerated nonsense was yet to be seen.

"I first dated my husband—"

"No, I mean really at the beginning. Let's go back. I need to understand you, not just the woman who married a prince, but the person you were before you entered the spotlight."

The princess sighed. "I have been trying to understand how I came to be held a prisoner in the Tower myself. I suppose you're right, the cause goes back farther than my marriage. But I need to have you understand one thing about me that probably dominated my life, at least after I reached puberty and began dreaming about who I would spend

❖

my married life with. You see, I never thought of marriage as arranged like a business transaction, but as something created in heaven. And I'm afraid that neither my parents nor my husband and his family thought of it the way I did." She lifted her hands palm up in a gesture of confusion. "Where do you want me to start?"

"Let's do it the way the king told a witness at the trial in *Alice in Wonderland*: Begin at the beginning and go on till you come to the end, then stop. So let's start with day one, your birth, your childhood, and move forward."

13

❖

"She what?"

Philip Hall smothered a grin. He, too, was offended by Marlowe's insistence that she interview the princess alone, but Sir Fredic's expression was a mixture of shock and outrage that bordered on the comical.

"She insisted on going in alone. I informed her that was not our ethical practice, but she—"

"The bitch. I knew we would have problems the moment the news broke that she had brought in this American." Sir Fredic shot a glance around to make sure they were not being overheard. "It makes one wonder about the princess's sanity, doesn't it?"

Hall raised his eyebrows. "She wouldn't have killed her husband unless she was a bit bonkers, would she?"

THE PRINCESS SPOKE WITH her coffee cup to her lips, her eyes staring past Marlowe, looking back over the years. "My birth. Well, I suppose you can say I was disappointing people from the moment I came into the world."

"How can a baby disappoint anyone?"

❖

"When the baby's a girl and a boy is needed to inherit a title that's been in the family for centuries, it's a crushing disappointment. My parents had been trying to have a boy. Before I was born they had two daughters and a son, but the boy died in infancy. When my mother became pregnant with me, there was great pressure on her from my father and his own father, the seventh earl, to produce a boy who could ultimately inherit the title and estate.

"My parents were so counting on a boy, they had not even chosen a girl's name. So I came into the world, a naked, crying little thing without a name and as a big disappointment."

"Did your parents ultimately get their male heir?"

"My brother came along several years later, but the damage was done to the marriage. My father is not a particularly easy man to get along with. He blamed my mother for producing girls—"

"That's nonsense."

"When you're dealing with centuries of tradition and only a male can inherit the title of an earl, the difference between a boy and a girl can be earth-shattering."

"An earl, that's a significant noble title?"

"Yes, below a duke, above a baron, what they call a count in many European countries. While my grandfather was alive, my father was a viscount. After my grandfather passed when I was a young teen, my father became the eighth earl, my brother the viscount, and I became a lady."

"That's heady stuff for a young teen."

"Not when you are raised in an atmosphere where it's just part of everyday life. I was born in and spent most of my preteen years in a manor house on the queen's estate at Sandringham. Being so close physically and agewise to the queen's two younger sons, my siblings and I often had the two royal princes as playmates not the man who became my husband, of course. My husband was thirteen years older than me, but his younger brothers are close to the age of my brother and I.

"We had been a significant family in England for nearly half a millennium, dating back to the fifteenth century when my family had been wealthy sheep traders. Charles I awarded one of my ancestors an earldom and a family crest, no doubt in return for a substantial contribu-

❖

tion to the royal coffers. I suppose it did Charles himself little good because he soon became the first of our kings to lose his head—literally—in a dispute with Parliament.

"There is nobility on both sides of my family tree. My mother was the daughter of a baron, a family with roots in Ireland and England. It was my mother's family, actually, that had acquired the rights to our house on the queen's estate. King George V had granted my grandfather, the fourth baron, the lease of the house. It had initially been used for the overflow of guests and staff from nearby Sandringham House, the queen's winter residence."

"So you were raised rubbing shoulders with royalty."

"Yes and no. My husband was not part of my growing up. As I said, he was much older and he was heir to the throne. The queen and the Prince of Wales are not just Royals, she is *the* Royal and he is the heir to the throne. They both function at a much higher level than the other Royals. I had little interaction with either of them before my late teens. And I was engaged to marry him by the time I was nineteen."

"You said something about the damage was done, after your birth."

"I suppose the pressure my father put my mother under to produce a male heir caused irreparable harm to their marriage. There was also an age difference, almost the same as with my husband, my father was thirty and my mother eighteen when they married. I have learned that while a twelve- or thirteen-year age difference between a man and wife is not significant later in life, an eighteen- and thirty-year-old are worlds apart.

"Emotional trauma erupted in my life as I became one of the pawns in the parental-blame game that inevitably follows contentious divorces. My father would show silent disapproval when it was my mother's turn to have me, and my mother would cry when we parted after visitation, making me feel that it was my fault my parents had broken up.

"One of the blame-game tactics was to shower us children with gifts, but it was done without any real feeling. At Christmas or a birthday, my father gave me a toy catalog and told me to choose something. But expensive gifts without feeling behind them didn't take the place of hugs and kisses.

❖

"I always wondered whether that was why I seem to have an unful-filled yearning to be loved. It seemed to be the story of my life that I would constantly be seeking love. At home I had stuffed animals, dozens of them, they crowded my little room so much there was hardly space for me. I hugged and kissed them so much the poor little things were always needing stitching and patching."

"They gave you unconditional love. Did you also have a dog or cat?"

"Of course not, pets might damage the furniture or carpets that had been gathered for centuries and were meant to be handed down for more generations of my family during the next millennium. I did man-age to sneak my horse upstairs one day," she laughed. "I got hell for that one."

"You wouldn't describe your childhood as happy?"

"I had food and shelter and even servants in a world where millions of children go to bed hungry every night. Or even starve to death. But I was not an emotionally content little girl. One of the big scars of my emotional makeup was the breakup of my parents. No one ever said it to me, but as I grew up, I pretty well understood that my birth was the proverbial straw that broke the camel's back. But like so many other things, their marital problems were never discussed or explained to me.

"The actual split came when I was six. It had a terrible traumatic impact on me. There was a nasty custody battle that everyone knew from the beginning my father would win. He was much more aggressive than my mother and it didn't help that he trumpeted the story that my mother had abandoned her four children for a man. It also didn't help that my mother had been named as the other woman in the divorce of the man she would later marry. Even her own mother criticized her for not staying in the marriage for the sake of us children. I lost my mother except for occasional visitation and I was basically placed in the hands of a succession of nannies to be raised."

"I take it your father wasn't the house-dad type?"

The princess exploded with a howl of laughter. "If you showed my father a baby's nappy, he probably would have thought it was a hand-kerchief to wipe a horse's nose. No, he was not maternal, nor particu-larly paternal, either. My father wasn't comfortable with his children. He raised us the way he was raised, with the same formalities and restraints that existed between him and his parents. He was more jolly and relaxed with his hounds than with his children.

"The worst thing my father did to me was fail to explain why he and my mother were divorcing. It was a terrible trauma for a six-year-old with horrible guilt feelings and I still bear those scars. He did not believe that he owed his children an explanation. And I suppose my mother felt the same way, but since I lived mostly with him, my father became more of a dominant influence in my life than my mother."

The princess said that when she was in her early teens, her father was named as "the other man" in the divorce of her soon-to-be stepmother. "At first I rather disliked my new stepmother, perhaps out of the jealousy children feel when their parent remarries, but I got past all that. But in one of those quirky things that happen in life, my stepmother was the daughter of a world-famous writer of romance novels and I loved the books. Do you read romance books?"

"No, I don't, though I know people who do. I don't have the time for reading anything but law." Marlowe smiled. "That makes me a bore, I'm afraid."

"They say that the books are part of the reason for my problems."

"They?"

"That pack of hangers-on and cronies that are always all over my husband like a bad rash. They talked behind my back, to my husband and the queen, and even the tabloids. They spread stories that my mind had been ruined by reading romances, that I was caught up with romantic fantasies that my husband could never have lived up to. I know many people thought the romance novels were foolish, virginal heroines being swept off their feet by dashing heroes and all that, but there was always great passion and fiery sex." She laughed and her eyes sparkled for the first time since Marlowe sat down with her. "Of course, the sex itself was never on the printed page, it was only experienced in one's imagination, but that's the best kind, isn't it? Best of all, there was always a happy ending."

"Do you believe he did love you? Your father."

"Oh, yes, he loved me. With formality and restraint. If you are going to understand me, my husband, and the whole British Establishment, for that matter, you must keep those two words in mind. Formality and

❖

restraint are what characterized the family and social environments both my husband and myself were raised in." She shook her head. "How I have come to hate those words. I ran afoul of them constantly, banging my head against their sharp points.

"But to give the devil his due, as my father would say, while we were privileged, we were taught not to be snobbish. It was considered a sign of good breeding to be well mannered on all occasions and to treat everyone with respect, whether it was a servant, a stranger, or the man who hauled away the trash. Some people would say that it was all bunk, wouldn't they? It's certainly true that there are people of all walks of life who are snobs. Regardless of those people, I find that there are about the same percentage of titled people who are snobs and twits as there are servants and shop clerks with the same attitudes. But you know, no matter how we treated others, we knew that we were different from the madding crowd. And part of that difference was to show the formality and restraint that typified people of our class, and to a some-what lesser extent, most of the people in the country."

"This was how you were to show yourself to the public? Reserved, conservative?"

"Not just the public, but within your own family. You could literally only let down your hair in the loo. You have to wear two masks, be ca-sual and laid back in private and formal and restrained in public, but even in private you are not expected to go beyond the limits of the pro-priety of your class. You are what you were raised to be, what you were molded as. People of my class are expected to walk like we have a ram-rod in our back and keep a stiff upper lip, no matter what is coming down. Don't have a cry, for goodness' sake, but if you really have to do it, go into the loo and lock the door so no one will know."

She took several deep breaths before she could go on. Marlowe made scribbled notes on her pad, key words to jog her memory when she sat down later to memorialize their meeting in greater detail.

"Sometimes I felt like I was part of the family furnishings, first of my parents and then of my husband, more like an expensive piece of fine furniture that is to be kept polished, rather than a girl and then young woman with fears and hormones. The house we moved into after my father became earl is a good example. The family manor is stuffy and depressing, with dark hallways draped with portraits of long-dead ancestors, and dark creepy places that made the unimaginable real. My grandfather had loved the place. I'm told he used to follow visitors around with a duster and once even pulled a cigar out of Winston Churchill's mouth. But it was like living in a sterile museum, not a warm loving home."

"Doesn't sound warm and inviting, for sure."

She looked away as she sipped her coffee, then put her cup down and raised her eyebrows to Marlowe. "That's what it's like to be brought up in a manor house with nobility and the Royals. Formality and restraint dominate personal and public personas, home has the ambience of an exhibit hall at the Albert and Victoria Museum, and family life has the warmth of institutional living. Dinners were with the nanny, not my father. I don't recall having dinner with my father until I was a teenager."

"That's incredible." Marlowe found it jaw-dropping. That one fact brought home everything the princess had been saying about her upbringing.

"You find that bizarre—I guess I do, too, now—but when you're raised in that atmosphere, it's the norm. There was always a separation between parent and child. My father never threw us into the back of the car and headed for the beach or a drive-in movie. When we went to the beach, it was the nanny who sat in the back seat with me and a picnic basket while the chauffeur drove and my father went off somewhere with his friends. I was soon packed off to boarding schools despite my tears and protests that he wouldn't send me away if he loved me."

She stopped. She was trembling, her face flushed. "I can't tell you what a disheartening experience it was to be nine years old and have your parent send you off to live in a dormitory with other unwanted children."

"An orphanage."

"It was a boarding school."

"It was an orphanage for rich children, that's what I'd call a place where children are sent to live in a dormitory away from the warmth and love of home and family. *Boarding school* is just a fancy name for it."

The princess sucked in her breath and stared wide-eyed at Marlowe. "I never thought of it that way. You're right, it was just a fancy orphanage. Nobody wanted us children, eight-, nine-, ten-year-olds, we were sent off so we wouldn't be in the way. It's a horrid thing to do to children."

She took deep breaths, getting her breathing under control.

Marlowe sat quietly and listened as the princess talked. She knew from experience that it was a cathartic experience for the client to open up and talk out the steps that led to tragedy and despair.

"I suppose my unhappiness had an affect on my grades, too. Scholarship certainly was not my forte. I received D grades in the classroom, but I did excel at community service, visiting the elderly, the sick, and the handicapped. I had a natural ability to talk to people at all levels and tended only to be quiet in class, out of fear that I would expose my ignorance. I also won prizes at swimming and diving and was pleased with ballet, but was too tall to make a real go at it. Nevertheless, ballet was important to me. I used to sneak out of the dorm at night and do my ballet in the hallway for hours on end. It released the tension in my head."

The princess sipped her coffee and looked at Marlowe over the rim. "I suppose you were an outstanding student, scholarships, awards, that sort of thing."

"You couldn't be more wrong. I was a poor student, like you I seemed to excel more at dealing with people than with facts and figures. But there's an interesting maxim that says much about lawyers and scholarship. I call it the ABC's of lawyering—A students become law school professors, B students become judges, C students get rich . . . and D students get very rich."

The princess laughed and clapped. "I love it, you must let me use it when Anthony and Sir Fredic come. May I ask you about your interesting name? Your parents were admirers of Christopher Marlowe, Shakespeare's muse?"

"Actually, my father was a fan of Philip Marlowe, a tough private eye in novels written by Raymond Chandler, who I believe was British-American."

"Good for you, your private eye is a more interesting namesake than a centuries-old playwright."

❖

"You were telling me about your schooling."

"As you might well imagine, I left boarding school without a sense of accomplishment, feeling rather like a dud. I saw myself pretty much as a failure, though as young as thirteen, I had a premonition that I would marry someone in the public eye."

"What do you mean by that?"

"I don't know, I suppose it's the sort of thing many girls of my class would imagine. After my less-than-illustrious academic career at boarding school, I was sent to a Swiss finishing school."

Marlowe said, "I've always found that term, *finishing school,* interesting. Sounds like it's intended to polish a fine gem."

"Turning a rough stone into a diamond is their objective. Finishing schools are intended to turn girls of good family into young women possessing charm, good social graces, and the ability to discuss the arts and other cultural matters at the dinner table. In other words, I was sent off to get buffed and polished."

"Why the polish job?"

"So I could be placed on the high-society marriage market. What other path was open to me? University was out of the question. Besides the fact my scholarship was a disaster and I hadn't completed the necessary schooling, I lacked the desire. And I wasn't ready for a nunnery."

As Marlowe jotted down a note, she asked, "Besides marriage and raising a family, where did you feel your talents lay?"

She thought a moment. "I enjoyed working with people."

"Especially people in need?"

"Yes, I suppose so. Why do you think I'm that way?"

"Perhaps you're seeking the loving reinforcement that you never got from your parents."

She nodded. "I rather suspect that's the case. You get unconditional love from the sick and dying. And stuffed animals. But, as I was saying, I was sent off to finishing school, but the very expensive school didn't succeed in rubbing off my rough edges. We were supposed to speak French all the time and enmesh ourselves in the arts. Naturally, I spoke English and worked on my skiing. I was unhappy at the school, feeling very much a failure. I was shy and overweight. And lonely. I finally managed to convince my father to let me return from Swiss exile."

❖

"You were what, sixteen or seventeen when you left school? What were you like then? How did you think of yourself?"

"Not very highly, I'm afraid. I suppose I was something of a prig. I didn't smoke or drink, I liked watching TV, glitzy soaps like *Dynasty* and *Dallas,* chatting with friends and my flat mates, dinner out."

"You were essentially, what, a school dropout? Waiting for an offer of marriage?"

"It's horrid to put it that way—but it sounds like the awful truth."

"Were you happy with yourself?"

"Happy? I was happy day to day, not depressed. If you mean satisfied, no. I thought of myself as dumpy and overweight. I was eating too much and putting on too many excess pounds. But I did try to keep busy. Back in London, I was too young to set up housekeeping on my own, so I spent time living with a family whose children I took care of, and later my mother let me stay in her city apartment. When I was eighteen, my parents bought me a three-bedroom flat in a mansion block as a growing-up present. I got a part-time job teaching kindergarten at a fashionable school in Pimlico. Along with working with children, I also had babysitting and housecleaning jobs from friends."

She splayed the fingers of both hands on the table. "I guess you can say I did my Cinderella chores as I waited for Prince Charming to ride up on his white charger and carry me off into the sunset."

A long moment passed as the princess stared down at her hands, looking into the past. Finally, she looked up and met Marlowe's eye.

"My husband was raised by a nanny, too. In more of an institution than I was. I'm certain that's why he was so cold to my needs. The absence of love in the way my husband and I were raised was the reason I was determined to show my love for my children. More than anything else, what I yearned for as I grew up was to marry and have a family and household that was full of love and sharing. I hated the upper-class, stiff-upper-lip upbringing, with parents who treated their children as if they were part of the furnishings."

"Your husband had more formality and restraint?"

"My husband was the epitome of proper British formality and restraint. Once when we were on a native dugout in the tropics being rowed by half-naked islanders wearing loincloths, he was dressed in a dark blue business suit, starched white shirt, with French cuffs and yellow tie. He insisted I wear a Bond Street dress and hat that was suitable for afternoon tea in an air-conditioned room."

"It must have been hotter than hell."

"Now that I think back about it, I don't recall him ever sweating. Now, that's restraint!" She exploded with another one of her nervous laughs.

Marlowe looked at her watch. "I've kept you long enough, and frankly, I need to get to my hotel and take care of some jet lag."

"Did you know he was held only twenty or thirty minutes a day by his mother?"

"Your father?" Marlowe asked.

"My husband." She shook her head. "It's all an accident of birth, isn't it?"

"You mean life?"

"Rich and poor, sick and healthy, it's all potluck, isn't it? As one of my friends says, it's the luck of the draw." The princess shook her head. "You are so lucky."

"Lucky?"

"You were born poor."

14

❖

St. Andrews Hotel

A pack of newspeople, no fewer than the number who had ambushed her at the airport, was lying in wait in front of her hotel. Marlowe made it through the front door with Philip Hall and a doorman running interference.

Inside, Hall told her, "Trent has already arranged for your registration."

She felt like asking if he had already had the room bugged, too, but restrained herself. She liked Hall. She thanked him before he left her at the elevators.

It had been a long day. She was beat but kept her head up as she stepped inside the elevator. When the doors closed, she leaned back and gave a sigh of relief. When the doors opened at her floor, she straightened her shoulders and stepped out, half expecting to be ambushed by a crazed reporter. As she walked down the deserted corridor, she had the feeling she was being watched, but put it down to paranoia.

In her room, she immediately tossed her clothes and climbed into the shower. She leaned against the shower wall, letting the hot water flow down her body. She was exhausted, mentally, partly from the media circus that had erupted in the wake of being hired by the princess,

❖

but she had to face something else, too. From the moment the news was leaked that she was going to represent the princess, her own past had been shoved into her face from blaring headlines and a media blitz. The husband-killer defending the husband-killer had become the stuff of late-night talk show jokes.

Later, wrapped in a big terry-cloth robe and a towel around her head, she drank hot tea and stood at the window, staring out at the foggy night, listening to the horns of boats on the Thames and the sound of Old Ben heralding the time. Remembering.

❖

MARLOWE

15

❖

Modesto, California

Sixteen-year-old Marlowe and her brother Robbie, who was two years older, were walking to school when he shocked her with a family secret.

"Dad hits Mom. He beats her at night when they're alone in their bedroom."

Marlowe stared at her brother Robbie with disbelief. "Bull, you're lying."

"No, I'm not. I heard them last week through the heater vent on the floor of my room. He hit her and she kept crying." He spoke in a monotone, controlling his voice.

She stared at him, unable to accept the truth of what he said. Her brother's face was grim and she could see that he was ready to cry.

"So you only heard them once?"

"No, I've heard sounds before come from their bedroom, but it's not loud enough to make out what they're saying. Remember they had a new venting system installed a couple weeks ago, so I hear things now if I get down real close to the vent. I was doing my push-ups on the floor."

"Why'd he hit her?"

❖

Robbie turned and looked at her. "He does it all the time. Apparently, he's been doing it for years."

"No!"

"That's what I heard through the vent last week, that she's been putting up with it for years."

"Did you hear her fight back?"

"No, she just cried kind of softly."

"I don't believe you. You heard wrong. Maybe it was the TV in their room."

He shrugged. "I know what I heard. I don't think he beats her with his fists. It's not like guys fighting. I think he hits her with his open hand, that sort of thing."

"That's crazy." She didn't want to believe him, but there was a ring of truth to it. Her mother suffered bruises frequently, but claimed it was because she bruised so easily. Sometimes she had big bruises, not the kind of thing you got just from bumping into things. She even had a black eye once, but she claimed she slipped in the shower.

"Dad's rough on her, you know that, he's always bullying her, putting her down. She just sits and takes it."

She glanced at her brother. "He's hard on you, too, Robbie. And you just take it. I've told you a hundred times to stand up to him."

"I don't want to argue."

She opened her mouth to give him a lecture about dealing with bullies, but stopped. He was too disturbed about what he had found out about their parents. So was she, but she was still in the shock and disbelief state, the response she went into when she didn't want to believe something. And while Robbie would have sat back and said nothing, she was going to confront the issue the moment she got home from school.

"You can't say anything," Robbie said.

"I'm going to find out if it's true."

"Don't, please, Dad will jump all over me for it."

"You mean he'll hit you?"

"I don't know what I mean. Just don't say anything. Maybe you're right, maybe I heard the TV. Look, if you promise not to say anything, next time I hear something, you can listen."

"You'll come get me?"

"Yes."

"Okay, then I promise not to say anything."

They were the only two children of the family and were close emotionally, but had far different personalities. In many ways, Marlowe was more like her father, while her brother was more like her mother. Marlowe was precociously mature and sure of herself. At sixteen she thought she knew everything about everything and was usually willing to argue the point if anyone said she was wrong. While she was assertive and outspoken, rarely thin-skinned about anything except the number of freckles on her face and cracks that she should use Band-Aids instead of a bra, Robbie on the other hand was sensitive and introspective. He had an intense interest in learning and was an A student, while she barely tolerated school and was satisfied with C's.

Even though Robbie was older, she often played the role of big sister, lecturing him on standing up for himself when he wasn't assertive enough by her standards.

Her father drove a truck that made deliveries of mechanical parts for farm equipment, with his main customers being the farmers in the delta. He was a very precise man, neat and orderly to a fault. Robbie claimed that just watching their father change a set of spark plugs in the family car drove him crazy. "The way he meticulously changes the plugs like he's a brain surgeon doing an operation, not getting a speck of grease on him afterwards, drives me nuts. Just once I'd like to see him with egg on his face."

Robbie bought him a bumper sticker and pinned it on the door to the garage that their father used as his woodworking shop: A CLEAN DESK IS THE SIGN OF A MESSY MIND. He was not amused.

Her father was domineering and it often brought him into conflict with both Marlowe and her brother. He was constantly critical of Robbie. Nothing the boy did seemed to please him or pacify him. He didn't ride Marlowe that much, partly because she screwed up in his eyes much less than her brother and partly because she wouldn't take guff from him without lashing back.

Robbie wasn't athletic and was built more like his mother, tall but slender and small-boned. Almost from the time he could walk, his father had been verbally deriding him about his inabilities at sports—he

❖

threw a ball like a girl, couldn't catch or bat, couldn't make a basket, got pinned almost immediately in wrestling, and broke out crying when his father put boxing gloves on him and started punching.

For the past couple of years the criticisms of Robbie had been getting more and more pointed as his father made snide remarks about his son's manhood. The words *queer* and *faggot* increasingly crept into their conversations. And brought Marlowe increasingly into conflict with her father as she tried to protect her brother.

The person who should have protected Robbie, his mother, was too much like him to be of much help. Like her son, she was delicate and sensitive. A homemaker during most of her married life, she had taught first grade early in the marriage but stopped when Robbie was born. She was a quiet, passive woman. Because she lacked confidence in herself, when confronted with criticism from her husband she was apt to take the blame for things that weren't her fault.

As Marlowe walked with Robbie, she thought about the accusation that he had made about their father. She had never seen him physically strike their mother. Even though he was the dominant one in the house and tended to bully his wife, he was not a macho, physically aggressive male outside the home, although he could be sarcastic to people. He seemed to reserve his domineering character for his small family.

When there were serious disagreements, her parents resolved them behind closed doors. But that was essentially what Robbie was saying, that their father was being abusive in the bedroom.

Her father wasn't the warmest person in the world, that was a given, but he didn't go into rages and physically abuse anyone in the family. He did tend to belittle her mother and Robbie, and that was always done by sarcasm, not beatings. He had no close friends that Marlowe knew about, no drinking buddies, no getting together with the men in the neighborhood for a beer while watching a ball game. In fact, her parents never seemed to go anywhere. When they weren't in front of the TV, her mother was fussing in the kitchen or in the yard and her father was doing woodworking in the garage.

The woodworking was the only distinguishable thing she knew about her father. He worked for endless hours in the garage making decoys—wooden ducks used in hunting. He would start with a block of wood about a foot square and give it a rough shape with saws. Then he'd put the wood on his lathe and other machines and work it until it took the shape of a duck. After carving in the fine details, he'd paint it.

If he had a claim to fame, it was the ducks. They were even sold in gun shops. He didn't make any real money off the decoys, they were too much work, but he had a passion for making them. To Robbie, it was redundant, monotonous work, making the same ducks over and over.

Her thoughts were interrupted with a shout from across the street.

"There's Marlowe and her sister Roberta!"

The jeer came from Billy Yeager, a boy in Robbie's high school class. The group of boys with him on the corner broke out laughing. One of them made a snickering catcall.

Robbie kept walking and didn't look in the direction of the heckling kids.

"What's going on? Why is he calling you Roberta?" Marlowe stopped. "Robbie, why is that asshole calling you a girl's name?"

"Let's just keep going. *Please.*"

Marlowe reluctantly kept walking with him.

"You can't let that jerk bully you," she said.

"What do you want me to do? Get down to his level? He's bigger than me, can kick my ass without trying. That's what he wants. He knows he can't start fights because he'll be expelled. He wants someone else to start it."

"But you can't let him bully you."

"That's easy for you to say, you're a girl. What do you want me to do? Get beat up so I can be humiliated even more?"

"Maybe you should lift weights, take boxing lessons—"

"Get lost." He hurried away from her.

She knew he was probably right. If he looked cross-eyed at Yeager, the bully would punch him out. Challenging Yeager physically wasn't the answer—Robbie wouldn't and couldn't do it. Besides, there were lots of Yeagers in Modesto, farm boys who grew big muscles tossing hay bales. Unfortunately, too many of them developed muscles between their ears, too.

Robbie hated the town. He was constantly talking about running off to San Francisco, about a hundred miles west of the quiet San

❖

Joaquin Valley farm community. She was down on the town, too, probably because of Robbie's attitude toward it. Even though the two of them
had different approaches to life, she idolized him in terms of his smarts.
She was proud that her brother was brainy and artistic. He called
Modesto a "cow town" even though the economy was based more on ir-
rigated crops than cattle ranching. "San Francisco has everything," he
told her more than once, "It has *culture*. The only culture in this cow
town has *agri* before it."

Life in Modesto was not exactly on the fast track. The only movers
and shakers around were the farm machines that shook the fruit put of
trees. Not even the name was a standout—*Modesto* was Spanish for
"modest." It got the name when a railroad tycoon refused to have the
town named after him.

The biggest news, other than pileups from tully fog on Highway 99,
was an occasional local boy killed in Vietnam, although it did have a
couple famous home-grown boys. In later years, the world would know
the town as the boyhood home of movie king George Lucas. But even
Star Wars George was probably embarrassed about the dusty town in
the Golden State's central valley—it was supposed to be the small town
in *American Graffiti,* but he filmed much of the movie in other places.

Also giving the town claims to fame was swimming great Mark
Spitz, the first athlete who won seven gold medals at a single Olympics.
A more tentative claim was country singer Merle Haggard. Although he
was born in a boxcar near Bakersfield, a bit farther down Highway 99,
Haggard, who had a poverty-stricken youth and rode the rails, entered
a music talent contest in Modesto before he took time off from his fledg-
ling career to do time at San Quentin for burglary.

Marlowe ran and caught up with Robbie before they had to go in
different directions for their classes. "If it's true that Dad is hitting
Mom, why would he do that?"

Robbie shrugged. "Maybe because he can."

❖

16

❖

Robbie stood in the shower in the boy's locker room after PE and let the hot water run down his body. It was a communal shower, with enough spray nozzles to handle an entire class at a time. He had deliberately chosen a shower head in a corner. He wasn't entirely sure why he felt uncomfortable in the showers. Maybe some of it had to do with the horseplay and grab-ass that took place—he felt more vulnerable when he was naked and the other boys started throwing bars of soap or slapping with wet towels. But there was another feeling he had been experiencing, a feeling he didn't quite understand but that had been with him for a long time. He found himself sexually aroused at the sight of the other boys' naked bodies.

Out of the corner of his eye, he watched Jimmy Dent rinsing off a few feet away. Like himself, Jimmy had little body hair. Robbie found the other boy's body sensuous, even seductive. His only sexual experiences of any kind had been self-administered, mostly in the bathroom and under covers at night. Ever since he was eleven, he had been experiencing more frequent erections and they always came at the sight or thought of another boy. Without any overt acts on his part, without discussing his secret passions, somehow other boys had picked up on his feelings. Maybe it was a look he had given them. He didn't know how it happened, but the bully Yeager had become the most vocal about it.

He had not talked to anyone about his feelings. To talk to his father about his passion toward boys would have been only slightly less painful than poking needles in his eye. His mother would not have understood. She probably would have blamed herself for his "perversion" and started crying. Marlowe was the only one he considered actually talking to, but he didn't want to expose himself to possible ridicule from her. He knew his sister well enough to know that she would not deliberately humiliate him, nor would she expose his secret, but she never really understood her strengths and his weaknesses. Few people thought of homosexuality as natural—it was almost universally condemned as an illness and perversion.

Marlowe would be horrified at first, then she would want him to see a doctor for a pill or a shot to make him "well," and finally, she would put up her fists and be ready to fight her father if he tried to punish Robbie for his "perversions."

As he watched the glistening water flow down Jimmy Dent's buttocks, Robbie started to get an erection. He quickly turned on the cold water. When he stepped out of the shower and turned to grab a towel off the shelf, he got a sharp pain to his rear. He yelled and spun around. Yeager, naked, had wet his own towel and cracked Robbie with it.

Yeager howled with laughter.

"You son-of-a-bitch!" Robbie said. He hurt like hell.

Yeager stopped laughing and stepped up close to him. "You called my mother a name, shitface."

"I didn't call—"

"Yeah, you did, you called my mother a bitch." Yeager gave him a shove, sending him back. "I'm going to kick your ass, *Roberta*."

"Leave me alone."

"Ohhh, did you hear that, guys? *Roberta* wants me to leave him alone."

The other boys in the locker room started making catcalls. "Give the faggot what he really wants."

Yeager grabbed his cock and pushed up against Robbie. "This what you want, *Roberta*? Get down and eat it, you little cocksucker."

❖

Robbie's knees trembled. He started crying.

"Knock it off!"

The reprimand came from Mr. Ramirez, their gym teacher. "Get your clothes on," he told Yeager. He glared at Robbie, disgust in his face. "Wipe those tears off or I'll send you over to the girls' gym."

❖

17

❖

"You bastard!"

Yeager whipped around. He was barely out of the schoolyard, on his way home after school, when he heard the curse.

Marlowe James came at him, red in the face.

"What'd you call me?"

"I called you a fuckin' asshole, you prick. You ever touch my brother again and I'll see you pay for it."

"Oh, I'm so scared. What are you gonna do, shitface? You gonna hit me with that flat chest of yours?"

She got up close to him. Other kids had gathered at the commotion.

"I'm going to tell everybody you tried to fuck my brother."

"That's a lie."

"Is it? I'm going to tell everyone that I caught you trying to do it doggy style to him, that's why you pick on him, because you're horny for him."

"You lying bitch, nobody'll believe you."

"Your old man will. Everybody knows what he did to you when he caught you fucking a goat. And I'll keep spreading it, letting everybody know."

❖

Yeager shook with rage and fear. Bullies operated in a hierarchy of muscle and his old man was the meanest, cruelest father in town. He wouldn't just believe it, he'd make the story his own just for the pleasure he'd get in beating his son.

"Fucking bitch," Yeager said as she walked away. But the defiant tone was gone and he spoke almost in a whisper.

Marlowe burst into tears before she'd gone a hundred yards.

"Poor Robbie," she said.

There was no one around to hear her.

Her girlfriend, Betsy, caught up with her.

"I heard you just reamed Yeager," Betsy said, breathless.

"That asshole."

"It's all over the school," Betsy said.

Marlowe glanced at her. "What d'you mean? I just did it."

"No, I mean about Robbie being a queer."

Marlowe stopped and faced her. "Don't you call him that."

"C'mon, you know what I mean, homo, fag, whatever, jeez, don't blame me, I'm talking about what happened at the Sadie Hawkins."

"What do you mean, what happened?"

Sadie Hawkins was a once-a-year event in which roles were shifted and girls invited boys to the dance. The concept became popular back in the thirties after a *Li'l Abner* cartoon featured a hillbilly girl named Sadie Hawkins who was in dire need of a husband.

"Nancy Karr invited Robbie to the dance, she thinks he's cute. What I heard is that when he took her home, they parked outside her house to make out. Nancy wanted him to feel her up—"

"Nancy's a slut, every guy in school's been in her pants, she'll never make it to senior before she has to drop out with a kid."

"Tell me . . . she lives two doors down from us. Every time she gets into trouble over some guy, my parents give me a lecture and ground me like I'm going to catch being a slut like you get a cold."

"So what if Robbie didn't feel her up? Robbie's got good taste."

"C'mon, Marlowe, guys don't think like that, they'd feel up a cow's tits if they got a chance."

"I'm going to kick her ass if she keeps saying things about Robbie."

Betsy gaped. "Girls don't fight."

❖

"Why not? If she says something about my brother, I'll punch her. I will, too. Haven't you ever heard of the girl gangs in San Francisco? The girls all wear blue jeans and carry switchblades."

"No way, José, that's just bull."

"Let me tell you something that isn't bull, and you can pass it on to that slut neighbor of yours. She better stop mouthing off about my brother or else."

"Jeez, Marlowe, how did you get so tough? Definitely not from your mother."

"You have to stand up for yourself and your family because no one else will."

They parted company at the corner. Marlowe didn't get ten feet before her knees started shaking and tears welled in her eyes.

"I'll protect you, Robbie," she said quietly.

18

❖

Marlowe was flopped belly down across her bed, sleeping with her head buried in her algebra book, when Robbie came in and woke her up.

"They're in their room, I think it'll happen tonight."

"Whaat?" she answered sleepily.

"I think he'll hit her tonight."

Marlowe twisted off the bed and got to her feet. "How do you know?" It had been three months since Robbie first claimed that their father hit their mother. After a few days of intense anticipation and anxiety, the notion had gone cold and faded from her mind.

"Didn't you notice them at dinner? He was on her about buying that new tire at the gas station, he said he could have gotten it cheaper at Monkey Wards."

"He isn't going to hit her over a tire."

"Shhh, they might hear us." He closed Marlowe's bedroom door.

The family had a modest, fourteen-hundred-square-foot California ranch-style home, a rectangular house with the kitchen-family room at one end, a step up to a living room, then the "bedroom wing," three bedrooms and two bathrooms crowded together at the end of the house opposite the kitchen.

❖

Robbie and his parents shared a common wall with an aluminum air-and-heat duct serving both bedrooms.

"You don't get it, do you? He doesn't hit her because something she does makes him mad. He looks for an excuse to hit her. Mr. Crowell told me that."

"He's your swim coach. You told him that Dad was hitting Mom?"

"He's a good guy, he isn't going to tell anyone. I told him because he's the only person I can talk to."

"You can talk to me."

"You're too damn old," he told her. "Sixteen going on sixty. C'mon."

They went quietly down to his room. He closed the door after they came in and put on the Beatles song "Yesterday." "Have you heard this song?" he asked as they sat with their backs to the vent, one on each side.

"Yeah, they're okay, I'm not crazy about those guys like you are."

"There's a new group out of San Francisco I like better, the Grateful Dead."

"What a stupid name. They'll never make it."

"It isn't stupid, you're just not hip."

"Yeah, and you are. Look at you, you hippie."

It was the mid-sixties and new words had entered the vocabulary—*hippie, LSD, Beatlemania.* Words like *gay* and *cool,* which had been around a long time but not been widely used, were suddenly popular. There was a neighborhood in San Francisco called Haight-Ashbury where guys wore their hair long like girls and college dropouts gathered in rooms and took off their clothes, smoked pot, and played folk music while they had communal sex.

Most of her information came from Robbie, who talked about San Francisco like it was a new rock band that played seductive music. He had let his hair grow long and had started wearing a turquoise necklace. When she called it Indian jewelry, he corrected her and said it was made by "Native Americans." Marlowe wasn't attracted to the San Francisco counterculture scene, but her body was suddenly developing curves that seemed to form overnight and there was a lot of talk about something called the Pill that young women were taking to keep from getting pregnant.

❖

Besides his outrage at the idea of young people having sex, her father took particular umbrage against a former Harvard psychologist named Leary who was trying to get everyone high on a hallucinogen called lysergic acid diethylamide, LSD for short.

Sometimes her mother would stare at Robbie and Marlowe and complain that the world seemed to be constantly changing under her feet. To add to the turmoil of a drug-sex-rock-and-roll scene that kids were being inducted into was a war brewing halfway around the world—President Johnson had sent over a hundred thousand young Americans to fight in the jungles of Southeast Asia, women were demanding equal rights with men, and Americans of African descent were demanding to be treated as equals. There were even a few voices who said it was all right to be gay or lesbian, but those were whispers and not shouts.

Marlowe had watched changes coming over Robbie that she didn't understand and couldn't relate to. Yeager, the school bully, had gone on to fresher meat, but Robbie brought on jeers from other boys because of his long hair and jewelry. While her parents' problems had faded into the woodwork over the past few months, her concern for Robbie had increased. That she was increasingly coming to realize that he was not sexually orientated like everyone else around her, like everything she had been taught to expect about sex, had made her conclude that he was sick and she needed to find him a cure.

Men who loved other men rarely showed any inclination toward their sexual preference in public. If they did, they were subjected to scorn, ridicule, and beatings from straight guys. Homosexuals were not just banned from the army, many companies would fire them if they made their sexual orientation known. As her father was quick to point out when he saw Liberace on *The Ed Sullivan Show,* homosexuality was illegal. "That sodomite bastard belongs in prison," he said.

She couldn't imagine what two men would find attractive about each other, being hairy and muscular and all that.

She hit a stack of books next to her with her elbow and one fell off the pile. A scrap of paper used as a bookmarker slipped out. She read it as she started to put it back in the book. "'The love that dared not speak its name.' What does that mean?"

❖

"It's something that was said during Oscar Wilde's time."

"Who's he?" The picture on the cover showed a strange-looking young man of great height with girlishly long curly hair and a velvet suit with a lace collar. "He looks like a giant version of Little Lord Fauntleroy."

"He is," Robbie said. "Oscar Wilde was the model for the Little Lord Fauntleroy painting. He was a poet and playwright back in the Gay 1890s."

"Was he queer?"

"He was a homosexual, if that's what you mean."

"Robbie, are you queer?"

"Fuck you."

"Don't talk to me that way."

"Then don't talk to me *that* way."

"Shhh," he said, as she started to verbally pounce on him. "Listen."

Marlowe heard the voices coming through the vent from the other room.

A sound came through, causing Marlowe to flinch—a slap. A sob from her mother followed.

"He hit her!"

She was on her feet before Robbie could stop her. She flew through his door and tried the handle on her parents' bedroom door. It was locked. She banged on the door. "Let me in! You son-of-a-bitch! Stop hitting her! Stop it! Let me in!"

She pounded until her hand hurt. When she stopped, she heard her mother crying. Her knees went weak and she slipped to the floor. "I'm here for you, Mom, I'm here for you," she sobbed.

❖

19

❖

Marlowe stayed in bed and didn't get up for school the next morning. She heard her father leave as usual at six and Robbie left for school nearly two hours later. It was ten o'clock before she got up. Usually her mother would have bugged her by now. When she walked in the kitchen, her mother was making dough for a pie.

Her mother didn't turn to look at her when Marlowe entered. She continue to knead the dough, pushing it harder and harder with her hands. Marlowe could see her mother was tense.

She fought back tears as she came up behind her mother. "Mom, why do you let him hurt you?"

Her mother swung around and slapped her. The blow sent Marlowe staggering back.

"Mind your own business!" Her features were raw and ugly. She was trembling. Marlowe had never seen her angry or explode before.

"What happens between your father and me is our business." Her mother shoved the toaster off the counter. It flew over the edge and dropped until the still-plugged-in cord stopped it. "I don't want you ever spying on us!" her mother screamed as the toaster flopped against the cupboard door.

❖

Marlowe left the room in a state of shock. She cleaned the flour and dough off her face and left the house. Her mind was swirling. She needed to talk to Robbie. She didn't understand why her mother had hit her, why her mother had not accepted her as an ally in the terrible treatment that she was getting.

Nothing made any sense, her father hitting her mother, her mother not fighting back, her brother dressing like a hippie queer.

At sixteen years old, it felt as if the whole world had gone crazy.

❖

20

❖

"You can never tell what goes on between a husband and wife in their bedroom," Tom Crowell told Robbie.

They were seated in the enclosed patio at the back of the Crowell home. Tom was the high school swim coach. Robbie sometimes came to his coach's house to practice and receive instructions from the coach as Robbie swam in a long, narrow lap pool in the backyard.

Robbie was seated on a wicker couch with his right leg extended out to a footstool. His leg had cramped up as he swam laps. Tom sat on another footstool and rubbed Robbie's upper leg to release the tension.

"Nerves," Tom said, massaging the leg. "You're carrying the weight of the world on your shoulders."

Robbie liked his swim coach. He was the only teacher he really could relate to and the only sports coach he could even stomach. Tom was not like the full-time phys ed instructors—they were all macho guys with locker-room humor that most of the boys liked and Robbie hated and dreaded because he was often the butt of the rough humor. Tom was different, more intellectual, more worldly than the dumb-jock coaches. Robbie figured it was because the swim-coaching job wasn't a full-time one. Most of his school duties was teaching history.

❖

"Did you ever read *The Catcher in the Rye?*" Robbie asked.

"Of course I did, everybody has to read it in high school or college, it would be un-American not to."

"Really?"

"That's a joke. You are uptight, aren't you?"

Tom's wife, Cathy, came through the door from their family room with a pitcher and two glasses. "Lemonade. Do we have an injury?"

"Robbie cramped up during practice. Painful, but we probably won't have to amputate till later."

"Good, I hate the bloody messes you make when you cut off the legs of your students. I'm running over to my mother's with the kids. I'll be back in a couple hours."

She gave her husband a peck on the forehead and left.

"What about *The Catcher in the Rye?*" Tom asked.

"Sometimes I feel like Holden Caulfield, like I'm stuck in a phony adult world and I have to keep running from place to place to find the truth."

"I think all boys and maybe even girls feel like Holden Caulfield. You young people see the hypocrisy of the people who run the world. That's one of the great charms of being young—until you grow up and become a hypocrite like the rest of us, you have the innocence of the little boy who saw that the emperor's new clothes were a fraud."

"What did you mean, when you said you can never tell what goes on in the bedroom between a married couple?"

The coach shrugged. "Exactly that. Married people don't act all the same. It's different strokes for different folks. I imagine my minister and his wife sleep in bedclothes and have sex with the lights off. There's a couple two doors down that are into wife-swapping. They've invited me and Cathy to a party where house keys get thrown into a hat and you go home with the person who drew your key."

"No way. Did you do it, too?"

"Of course not, but the point is, husbands and wives don't live by a single set of universal rules. Sometimes a man even abuses a woman."

"And she lets him get away with it. That's what's driving my sister nuts. She can accept the fact that he's a bully and gets off hitting our

❖

mom. But it drives her crazy that my mother doesn't do anything about it."

Tom shrugged again. "Maybe they feed off each other, maybe she's afraid, there's a lot of other maybes. Whatever it is, it's nothing you can control. It's between your mother and father. You'll find out when you get married that you and your wife may not have the same bedroom habits as what you imagined they would be like.

"What your sister did embarrassed your mother. It was her bedroom secret and your sister brought it out into the open, exposing your mother's humiliation. That's why she exploded at Marlowe. Your sister had inadvertently made matters worse by trying to help."

As Tom talked, he guided his hand up and down the boy's leg.

Robbie started to say something and then hesitated. Finally he got it out. "What if I didn't get married? Ever."

"Why do you say that?"

"Just what if? What if I just didn't want to, you know? Does everybody have to get married and have kids? Can't some people have a different sort of life?"

"What sort of life do you want?"

Robbie shook his head. "I don't know, I just don't know. I'm so confused. That's why sometimes I feel like the guy in *The Catcher in the Rye*. He thought about killing himself. Sometimes I think it would be a relief just to do it, like kill myself so I wouldn't have to deal with all this crap."

"I don't think it's unusual for someone your age to wonder about suicide. I did, too, and I wondered about marriage, too."

"You did? Did you ever consider not getting married?"

"In our society, it's what men do. They get a wife, a family, a house, a car, and a job."

"What if . . . what if a person, a guy, just wasn't attracted to, you know, married life?"

"You mean not attracted to women."

Robbie nodded. "Yeah, I mean that, too."

As his coach's hands gently caressed his upper leg, gliding up closer and closer to the crotch of his bathing suit, Robbie had the urge to grab

❖

the man's hand and push it hard against his groin. It wasn't the first time that he felt aroused being near him.

"I don't think it's unnatural not to be attracted to women. Not all of us are."

"You are," Robbie said. "You have a pretty wife, two kids."

Tom Crowell smiled a little sadly. "I told you that you can never tell what goes on in the bedroom with a married couple. I love my wife and my children, but that's not my entire life. There's another part of me, a piece of me that I've never been able to share with my wife, that she would never understand if she found out."

As he spoke, the coach's hand slipped up Robbie's leg and in under his bathing suit. He grasped the boy's throbbing penis.

"We are a lot alike, Robbie. More than you probably realize."

21

❖

Marlowe was in her English literature class when she was called out by the school principal's secretary. She was seventeen, going on eighteen. She basically hated school—it was February and she had less than four months to go to graduate. When she did, she knew she was getting out of Modesto. She had been treading water, carrying a C-plus average, just getting by until she could bail out of hell—Modesto High School—and move to San Francisco.

There had been a time when moving to San Francisco had the lure of a mecca, but that had been when Robbie lived there. He was no longer in San Francisco. He had been there for about a year, fleeing the valley as soon as he graduated from high school, but he had come back to his home town in a box hauled by Giovanni Brothers Mortuary.

Poor Robbie.

Overdose, had been the diagnosis.

He had made a quantum leap from smoking grass to shooting heroin without stopping in between. Fresh from small-town Americana, he had arrived green in Baghdad-by-the-Bay and got into a clique of bright young men, most of whom had fled small-town Americana and come to the Bay Area to experience "a different way of life."

But Robbie had not found love in the arms of another man. The love that he had been actually searching for was love of himself. He tried to fill the hollowness within him with drugs.

Robbie's death had splintered the James household. Marlowe blamed her parents for her brother's death, her father for being insensitive—and even cruel—when Robbie wanted to march to a different drummer, and her mother for not being strong enough to deal with the fact that her son had chosen a controversial lifestyle.

They hadn't been there for Robbie. They had abandoned him emotionally when he found himself confused about his sexuality. Marlowe had accepted his decision to go to San Francisco and find his place in life. But she had been unforgiving toward her parents since the day a San Francisco police officer called to tell her parents their son had overdosed and flatlined from heroin.

She remained in the house, but got a job at the beginning of her last year of high school, soon after Robbie's body had arrived back to be buried in the town he had fled. She worked part-time at a Foster Freeze, saving every cent she made. She had a game plan—she felt that she had to finish something. For Robbie's sake, she had to get out of Modesto and make it in San Francisco.

"There's been an accident," Mrs. Gomez, the principal's secretary, said. "You—you need to get to the hospital."

"An accident?"

"It's your mother."

"Is she okay?"

"I don't know. I'll drive you to the hospital."

She was lying, Marlowe knew it immediately, there was something in her tone of voice. But Marlowe didn't want to push it, didn't want to know. It would take fifteen minutes to get to the hospital. She could wait. The phrase "no news is good news" flew through her mind.

As they walked to the car, Marlowe could tell by the woman's body language that it was bad. Really bad. The woman kept giving her sideway glances and seemed about to say something, then would close her mouth and stare straight ahead. "The doctor will tell you," the women said. The woman wanted to tell her, wanted to blurt out the tragedy and share the moment of traumatic drama with her.

Marlowe didn't insist on an answer—she didn't want to know.

It had been hard to concentrate at school for the past couple months. Nothing had seemed real to her. But Robbie's death was real. She saw his face in the coffin. And his death stayed in the house, his ghost a depressing element. Her mother had taken it the worst, talking little since Robbie died. "It's my fault," her mother had said. "I killed him." Her father had started berating her mother for taking the blame, but Marlowe had gotten in between and shouted at him, "Touch her, you bastard, and I'll call the cops!"

Since that time her mother had grown thinner, paler, her face a mask of depression. Marlowe tried to be supportive, but didn't have her heart in it. Where was her mother when it counted?

Marlowe was about to ask the woman driving her to the hospital whether she could smoke, but instead just lit up without saying a word. No objection came from the woman.

That's when Marlowe really understood her mother was dead.

HER MOTHER HAD BEEN killed in a one-car accident, hitting a concrete freeway buttress at high speed. Her father wanted Marlowe to believe she went out of control after she was cut off by another car.

"She killed herself," Marlowe told him.

In a six-month period, Marlowe had been to two funerals. She was seventeen and a half years old and only a dozen weeks from graduating from high school. But she couldn't stay in the house or the town any longer—there were too many bad memories, too many ghosts. And too many tears.

She stood in her bedroom and looked around. It had been her bedroom her entire life. But she couldn't stand it anymore, or anything else in the house. She left the bedroom and paused in the kitchen by the open door to the two-car garage that was her father's shop. He was at the lathe making a wooden duck.

❖

As she watched him, she suddenly realized what had antagonized Robbie about her father's hobby of making wood ducks.

Wood ducks were decoys used to lure real ducks to be killed.

It was a cruel thing to do.

She didn't say goodbye.

22

❖

Marlowe had $612 in her purse when she arrived in San Francisco and bought a newspaper to hunt for an apartment and a job. The first shock she got from reading the classifieds was that she had a significant amount of money for Modesto, where she could rent a one-bedroom apartment for $100 a month—but in the city it was more than twice that for a studio apartment and it would take much of her nest egg to pay first, last, and security deposit. The manager at the first building she went to gave her more bad news. "You have no job, no credit history, no one is going to rent you an apartment. It's supply and demand, hon, people beg for apartments in this town."

She checked into the YWCA and spoke to a counselor about getting a job and apartment. One problem she didn't share with the counselor— she was still nearly three months short of eighteen. She would have to lie about her age to get a job and hope she wasn't asked for ID. And what kind of job could she get? She had no training, no vocational skills from school. She was supposed to have developed secretarial skills, but had dropped out of shorthand the first day and could hardly even type— she had long fingernails in her junior year when she took the class and had barely passed.

❖

Technically, she was a runaway, but she knew her father wouldn't report her missing or even come looking for her. There had been no angry words, no recriminations. Instead a silent indifference had settled between them. They had barely exchanged words since her mother had died. She rode to the funeral with a neighbor rather than be in the same car with him. After the funeral, when he had stopped by the open door to her room and saw her filling a suitcase on the bed, he left without saying a word and went to the garage to make decoys.

She recently heard a Jewish expression in a movie that fit her feelings about her father: "I've said kaddish for him," the actress had said about a husband she was divorcing. She didn't know exactly what the word meant, but she realized the woman was erasing the man from her life. And that was how she felt about her father. She didn't love him or hate him, he just didn't exist anymore.

The counselor told her, "You might be able to rent a room and get kitchen privileges, but the only places available will be in neighborhoods you won't want to live in. The only jobs available will be minimum wage. Your best bet is to get a live-in job taking care of a working mother or couple's children. You'll get room and board and can save whatever you're paid."

The counselor gave her a list of three people who wanted live-ins. "Be careful of the men, some of them expect more than cleaning and changing diapers."

The first man she spoke to had that kind of expectation. "My wife travels with her job," he told her. "Our son's six and pretty much takes care of himself. You'll have very light duties."

The house was a pigpen, the kid was a snotty-nosed little shit, and the man gave her a once-over—from bust line to butt line—and offered her the job.

She told him she'd think about it.

"I can sweeten the offer," he said.

"I'd rather stick a needle in my eye," she said to herself when she was a block away.

She liked the next house much better. "Cool," she said when she got off the bus and trampled up Nob Hill to a building that reminded her of the Manhattan brownstones she'd seen in movies.

Dr. Sean Williams and Dr. Valerie Gilbert were the first interracial couple she had ever met. She couldn't remember seeing a mixed-marriage couple in Modesto and had only seen one other such couple during the three days she'd been in San Francisco. A tall, slender man with short-cropped hair, large dark brown eyes, and smooth ebony skin, Dr. Williams—"Call me Sean," he said—taught psychology. He wore a heavy gold necklace and had a tiny gold earring in his left ear. Dr. Gilbert—Val—was of medium build, about the same as Marlowe's five-six and 128 pounds. She had pale white skin, faint freckles, red hair, and green eyes. She was also a psychologist, a family and marriage counselor with a private practice.

Marlowe had not encountered many female professionals and the Gilbert-Williams couple was the first she'd met who used their separate names.

It was all mind-blowing to a girl from Modesto. Everything about the couple was gold in Marlowe's eyes.

Their apartment was a cultural—and counterculture—showplace, two stories decorated with artsy pieces from Africa and Asia, some of them risqué—a wood statue of an African warrior had an elephant-trunk penis.

Sean and Val were friendly and hip, and their son, Adam, was easy to care for because he was only six months old. Their previous nanny had married and moved to Seattle.

"We have a woman who comes once a week to do heavy cleaning," Val told her. "You will be expected only to do straightening up, no cooking except for breakfast and lunch for yourself and Adam, mostly your weekends will be free. We'll pay you extra when we need you to babysit Saturday nights."

Perhaps the best thing of all was that the couple were worldly and sophisticated. Marlowe felt like a country bumpkin in comparison to them. She was a quick study when something interested her. She wanted to peel off her small-town cornhusk skin, and hanging around the Gilbert-Williams couple would be a perfect orientation to

❖

the world of intelligent chic. Marlowe felt as if she had died and gone to heaven.

She moved into a room on the first floor. The couple had a few friends over the first night. The mystic sound of South American flutes and the smell of high-quality cannabis came from the living room as Marlowe lay on her bed and read a fashion magazine. She had smoked pot once before, just a couple puffs off a joint that was passed among a group of kids hanging out back of the school gym during a dance, but it didn't have any effect on her. After she bragged to Robbie about it, he told her the kids were so stupid, they probably were smoking alfalfa instead of marijuana.

The door to her room was at one end of the living room, next to the stairs that went up to the second floor. The guest bathroom, which was the one she used, was next to her room.

The baby had a crib in Marlowe's room and also one in a room at the top of the stairs.

She got a glimpse of the two guests in the living room as she came down from replenishing her supply of diapers in the baby's room upstairs. Like her employers, they were thirtyish, university types, dressed hip, both the man and woman wearing stylish jewelry. But she did a double-take when the woman opened her blouse to show the others her naked breasts. From the gist of their conversation, Marlowe picked up that the woman had just recently gotten breast enhancements.

What Marlowe found even more unusual was that Val had reached over and felt each breast. *Nothing wrong with that,* Marlowe thought. She'd heard that breasts felt different after they've been augmented, harder or firmer. And it was just a woman feeling another woman. That wouldn't be proper in Modesto, but she was in Frisco now, Baghdad-by-the-Bay, these people were cool and hip, they weren't constrained by all that hypocritical, puritan bullshit people in the valley mouthed all the time.

She put it out of her mind until she got up later to go into the kitchen and get a soda. The music had stopped and when she stepped out of her room, the living room was empty. She assumed the guests had gone home, but then she heard feet running and laughter coming from the bedroom area upstairs, and it sounded like there were more

❖

than two people involved. She assumed their guests were staying the night.

Nothing wrong with that, she thought. But a nagging question stayed with her.

Just how hip and cool was the Gilbert-Williams couple?

❖

23

❖

Marlowe had been with the couple for nearly three months when Sean made an unusual proposition to her. They hired a babysitter and took her to the Tiki Room at the Fairmont Hotel, her choice for an eighteenth birthday dinner, to discuss the proposal.

She had gotten to know—and like—both of them, but had to admit that the two were not only strange animals by Modesto standards, they were not quite typical for the city, either. They had mostly a "don't ask" relationship with Marlowe. She didn't raise her eyebrows when guests disappeared upstairs with her employers and wild party noises flowed down, no explanations were offered when Sean was out of town and one of their friends stayed the night with Val upstairs—and it wasn't always a male friend.

They didn't bother Marlowe. While they never asked her to join them with guests, or serve food or drinks when they had guests over, they were very laid back and she knew they would welcome her if she decided to sit down and light up one of the joints that were neatly laid out on the coffee table when guests arrived.

There had been a couple of incidents when she went upstairs and had gotten a quick glimpse of Sean in his birthday suit as he wandered

❖

from his study to their bedroom, but it appeared innocent on his part and she simply averted her eyes and went into the baby's room. Neither of them seemed to have much of an affinity for clothes once they reached the upper limits of their apartment—Val had walked butt-naked into the baby's room once to ask Marlowe a question.

Marlowe's imagination worked overtime wondering about the two, mostly about their sexual activities. From what she heard and read about group sex and the wild things going on at college campuses, everybody seemed to be doing it—except her. In Modesto, her sole sexual experience other than minor petting and making out was letting Billy Meter finger-fuck her in the back seat of his car at a drive-in. She had experienced pain and her panties had some blood on them afterward. Her girlfriend Betsy told her that his fingers had broken her hymen and that she wasn't a virgin anymore. Like other girls her age, she hadn't resisted going all the way because she lacked the urge, but out of the fear of getting pregnant.

She suddenly wondered what it would be like to have sex with Sean. The fact that he was of a different race made it a taboo subject for a girl from Modesto, but the forbidden thought kept sneaking into her head. Sometimes in bed at night she would fantasize walking into their bedroom and catching Val and Sean doing it, their skin glistening from sweat, a stark contrast between the white and black of their naked skin.

Pot seemed to be the drug of choice with them. Although Marlowe suspected that cocaine was occasionally used by guests, Val and Sean didn't seem to be into it. Cocaine was an excited high, while they were looking for a different feeling, a lush low—pot went with the laid-back mystical music they liked, their Bohemian lifestyle.

She had learned a lot being around them, not the least of which was how diverse the world was. It wasn't unusual in their living room for Buddhists to drop by and chant, an African drummer to pound a frantic beat, or a folksinger to drum a guitar while bemoaning the sounds of war coming from Southeast Asia. It was all interesting and sometimes exciting, but it wasn't for her. As Sean jokingly put it when Marlowe had turned her nose up at raw fish at a Japanese restaurant, "You've come to us meat and potatoes, but we're going to turn you into escargot."

❖

She turned her nose up at snails, too. "How can you eat those nasty, slimy, wiggly things? Without even gutting them? You eat their poop and all."

"They're fed cornmeal or something similar to clean their intestines before they're cooked," Val said.

"So you're eating cornmeal-flavored shit?"

Marlowe noticed Val didn't eat any more snails that night.

Sean broached his proposal when they were having dessert. "If you're looking for extra money, there's a project at school you might be interested in joining. Keep an open mind as I explain it."

What they didn't know was that she was looking for extra money to move out. She was tired of being a glorified babysitter and wanted the privacy of her own place. She was over eighteen, an employable age, and knew enough about the city to realize some jobs—being a waitress, clerking in a store—were low pay, but she could work hard and rise to better things. And after listening to the Gilbert-Williams couple talk about the benefits of an education, for the first time in her life she thought about college.

"Have you ever heard of psychedelic drugs?" Sean asked.

"I'm not sure, it sounds familiar."

"You've heard of mushrooms that Indians eat and a drug called LSD?"

"Sure, they get hallucinations."

"We don't call them hallucinations, that's what people who don't understand them call the experiences. A hallucination would be a false image, something you've imagined but isn't real. There are a number of groups who have studied the effects of the drugs, the most famous being a Harvard study headed by a professor named Timothy Leary."

"I think I've heard of him. Are you doing it, too?"

"Our psych department has a grant to study the effects. Both Val and I have also experimented personally with some of the substances, mostly psilocybin, which is obtained from mushrooms grown in Mexico. The Aztecs used the drug both spiritually and medically as part of their pharmacology. Some people say they have mystic experiences after taking it. A much more common reaction is an OBE—an out-of-body experience in which they can see themselves interacting with other people."

"Wow, that's wild."

Val said, "I had a much greater sense of awareness, experiencing a cosmic consciousness. Everything around me became clearer, more vivid. I was able to see things that I never even realized existed."

"It's seeing life through a microscope," Sean said. "Not a speck on a petri dish, but everything around you. With ordinary consciousness we see sunshine and a field of grass. When our consciousness is expanded, we see all the colors of the spectrum."

"How does it happen?" Marlowe asked.

"That's what the experiments hope to determine. We believe the drug focuses our perceptions dramatically, slowing down our senses, permitting us to study a meadow and see the individual blades of grass as opposed to our eyes and mind simply skimming the surface."

Val said, "It made me supersensitive—I became acutely aware of everything around me. While I did nothing more than physically lie on my bed, my mind traveled around the room, seeing things I'd never noticed, like the dust on the top of a door, a place we never look. After a while my mind left the room and went around the apartment, seeing Sean and the baby in ways that I had never experienced before. I was able to study them and the whole place, I had an awareness of everything, even a little spider under the refrigerator weaving a web."

"Wow."

"My experiences were similar," Sean said, "but I had a broader consciousness—it seemed to make me one with the universe. One thing is clear: We all have individual visions, there are no common threads except the expansion of consciousness. Where our minds take us is unique to each of us."

"You don't want me to take this stuff, do you?"

Sean chuckled. "You're always one step ahead of me. We have funds to hire a subject and I wanted to run it by you first."

Marlowe shook her head. "My brother died of an overdose of drugs."

"You told us he died of a heroin overdose. Heroin in and of itself is not evil, it's basically a powerful painkiller, a form of morphine. The problem is that it's so strong and its side effects are so dangerous, it's risky if it's not administered under strict medical supervision. The drug we use is not addictive like heroin, and is being administered as part of a program similar to the one Harvard had."

"Sean is just trying to do you a favor, Marlowe. We know you need money and it's a way to make five hundred dollars for just relaxing for a few hours and later being interviewed about your experiences."

"It's not dangerous?"

"Not a bit," Sean said. "You can trust me on that."

"Don't you have students who want to do it?"

"I want someone who has had no prior experience with the drug and no preconceptions about how it will affect them. Many of the students are affected by the results they hear from other kids. But I don't want you to participate if you're not a hundred percent—"

"Just as long as it won't hurt me."

"I guarantee it won't hurt you."

❖

24

❖

The experiment was set to take place in her bedroom. Sean set up a tape recorder on the end table next to her bed.

"Our research indicates that the dose you're getting should start having an effect in about twenty minutes and the period of increased consciousness, the time during which your mind expands, will last several hours."

"I'm not going to see monsters, am I? Like in the movies?"

Sean smiled. "I don't know what you're going to see. Everyone goes into a dreamlike state—"

"A trance?"

"No, more like how you'd feel if you took a sedative to relax, one not strong enough to put you to sleep, but that puts you into that twilight between sleep and being awake. But we haven't had anyone see monsters and freak out. Most people find the experience very pleasant."

"Okay. But if I start seeing the Blob, you better warn the neighbors, because I'm going to scream my head off."

Val came in with a glass of water. She set it on the end table. Sean set a pill next to it.

"Get yourself comfortable, in your bedclothes. Turn off your light,

❖

lie back, and relax. When you feel like it, take the pill. Then close your eyes and make your mind blank. If you feel like communicating, just speak out loud, the tape will be running."

"Where will you guys be?"

"Upstairs. We're going to bed, but I set the alarm so one of us will come down and check on you periodically."

They left the room. Marlowe slipped off all her clothes and pulled a simple cotton nightie on.

She was a little nervous, but she trusted Sean and Val. They were a little too cool for her in terms of their lifestyle, but she didn't sense any malice in them toward her. Besides, she needed the money to get out and get her own life going.

She slipped inside the bed, took the pill, and turned off the light. She stared up at the darkness. There was no window in the room and the only light that entered was a faint glow at the bottom of the door. Her first sensory impression was that her heart beat rapidly and her breathing came fast. *Nerves.* Sean told her that might happen. She started relaxing, telling herself that she had nothing to fear but fear itself.

She lost track of time, but she soon realized she felt light-headed. The feeling slowly spread through her and she experienced a feeling of her body weight fading, a feeling that she could rise up from the bed and float to the ceiling.

The sense of weightlessness grew. She strained to see the ceiling, but it was a black void. She imagined herself floating, lightly floating up to the ceiling and looking down, seeing herself on the bed.

The image faded and everything went dark.

She didn't know how long she had slept, wasn't sure she had slept at all, but she had the sense that time had passed. She was hot, sweating under the covers. She kicked off the blankets and pulled off her nightie. She lay back on the bed, naked.

Her eyes closed, she imagined again that her mind had left her body, that she was overhead looking down at the glow of her pale body on the bed. An image of Sean naked, his smooth ebony body glistening, appeared. She saw him slowly come toward the bed. As he came toward her, she felt her own hands touch her nipples, then slip down between

❖

her legs and caress the fleshy mound there. She was wet and ready for him. She pushed her breasts up at him as he hovered over her.

Then he was gone. She was alone again, on the bed.

I'm hallucinating, she thought. Or maybe she said it aloud for the recorder, she wasn't sure. She was in a warm, wet, lush, dreamy state. "I'm horny," she said.

She got up from the bed and walked across the dark room. She opened the door and stepped into the living room. She would never have left her room naked, she wasn't like Val and Sean, who walked around without clothes on.

Being uninhibited in the warm, safe cocoon of a hallucination was titillating. *It's fun,* she thought.

She went up the stairs, slowly, reaching the top of the landing. It all seemed so real to her, almost as if she were awake.

Light spread out into the hallway from the open door to their room. She went to the light, seeing herself barefoot and naked. She came to the doorway and paused in it. No one was in sight. The door to their bathroom was open and she heard the shower going. As she stood in the doorway, Val came out of the bathroom with a towel wrapped around her head. The shower was still going, which meant Sean was in it.

In her dreamy state, Marlowe stood silently as Val came to her. Val reached out and touched her cheek. "Hello, sweetie," the woman said.

She cupped Marlowe's chin in the palm of her hand and leaned toward her, brushing Marlowe's lips with her own. The kiss felt real to Marlowe, real from head to toes.

Val put her arm around Marlowe and led her to the bed. While Marlowe lay on her back, Val kissed her again, softly at first, then harder, her tongue pushing between Marlowe's lips as her hands explored Marlowe's body.

The woman's titillating fingers traced the outline of Marlowe's breasts and gently caressed the tips of Marlowe's nipples. Her lips slid down to Marlowe's neck, making small sucking noises on her neck, then she encircled her naked breasts with her tongue, and sucked each one of Marlowe's erect nipples.

Marlowe felt dazed, in a state of wonderful abandonment. She put

❖

her hands on the woman's ample breasts and squeezed as they kissed. She slipped down and took one breast in her mouth, sucked it, then moved to the other breast, enjoying the strange feeling of having another woman's breasts in her hands and mouth.

Val's hand slipped between her legs for just a moment, feeling the soft, wet flesh, and she rolled Marlowe over on her stomach and started kissing her at the back of her neck, working her way down her spine, sending a tingling sensation through Marlowe, before she massaged each of Marlowe's buttocks, giving them a playful little bite.

Marlowe had never experienced anything as sensual as this before. Her body tingled with excitement, sexual arousal mounting in her.

Val positioned Marlowe so that the girl's legs were split above Val's face. She pulled the girl onto her face, parting her pubic hair with her fingers while the tip of her tongue found the sensuous nodule between the fleshy lips. Marlowe squirmed and wiggled as the older woman's tongue licked her sensitive clit. Marlowe's arousal ignited as flashes of pure ecstasy vibrated from her head to her toes, and she gasped in delight. She rolled off Val and spread herself on the bed, wet with sweat, still shuddering from her climax.

She opened her eyes and saw Sean was standing next to the bed, a towel wrapped around his waist. He let the towel slip off and she stared at his long black stalk. Val moved her into a half-sitting position so that Marlowe's head and shoulders lay against her.

Sean moved closer to the bed until he was only a foot from her, his long hard penis at her head level. She grasped his stalk, gliding her hand back and forth along its length, then cupped his testicles in her hand. As she stroked his penis, Val caressed her nipples.

Marlowe leaned in closer and kissed the tip of Sean's penis, rubbed her lips around its head, then slid down the length with her tongue. It throbbed against her tongue.

"Put it inside your mouth," he whispered. Hesitantly, she slowly put it into her mouth, until her mouth consumed it. He slipped it back and forth, in and out, slowly, never forcing it hard against her.

Sensing the urgency in him growing, her own body started to tremble with excitement. "I want you deep inside me," she whispered.

❖

He sat on the edge of the bed and spread her legs as she came onto his lap, bringing her down onto his hard penis, slipping inside her easily.

The wave of her pleasure spread in her as she sank deeper on his penis. He lay back on the bed, Marlowe on top of him, while Val knelt forward above Sean's face and spread her legs, lowering herself until his tongue found her clit.

Marlowe kissed Val on the lips, harder and harder, as the fire between her legs sent excited bliss throughout her whole body.

❖

25

❖

"It wasn't some goddamn dream, it was the real thing."

She had awakened naked on Sean and Val's bed. There were no tell-tale marks of heavy sex, but there was plenty of soreness in private places. She was alone on the bed when she woke up and realized that she had not fantasized what happened between her and the married couple. It was nearly nine o'clock. That meant Sean had gone off to the university an hour earlier. She heard the toilet flush and Val appeared a moment later, dressed for work.

"You finally wake up, hon?" The woman stopped in front of her vanity and checked her hair.

"You raped me!"

Val slowly turned around and stared at her. "Excuse me?"

"You raped me, you and your husband. You drugged me and raped me."

Val sighed and came over to the bed. Marlowe pulled the covers up to hide her nakedness.

"No one drugged you."

"You gave me LSD—"

"You got a placebo."

"What are you talking about?"

"You think Sean would risk his career and give a young girl LSD at his home?"

"He told me he did."

"He told you he was giving you a pill. What you got was a very mild sedative, something so weak a prescription isn't even needed. It was just to relax you and let your mind do the rest."

"What d'you mean, let my mind do the rest?"

"Sean doesn't believe that psychedelic drugs really cause hallucinations. His theory is that they lower inhibitions, allowing what's already inside a person to be released, that the so-called hallucinations are really fantasies that erupt when inhibition is destroyed."

"I don't understand."

"They're doing experiments at school, some kids get mind-altering drugs and others get placebos. You got a mild sedative so you would think that there was a change in your mental state. You were expected to fall asleep for a short period, then come awake in a sort of twilight dreamy state and let your imagination roam."

"What—what are you saying?"

Val grinned and shook her head. "Hon, you had a lot of built-up sexual inhibitions. When you thought you were drugged, you used that as an excuse to do things you would never have done otherwise."

"You're saying that I—I—"

"You came up here and fucked the pants off me and my husband, something you've probably been fantasizing about for months."

"No way!"

Val leaned down, cupped her chin in her palm, and gave Marlowe a kiss on the lips. "I'm late, hon. Change Adam's diaper and give him his breakfast."

MARLOWE SPOONED SOME SCRAMBLED egg into the baby's mouth. "I'm outta here as soon as they find you another nanny, Adam."

He made a gurgling noise.

"The scene's all too cool for me. When they start playing sexy mind games, it's too much for a girl from Modesto to handle."

❖

26

❖

Two years later, Marlowe was not the same girl who arrived in Baghdad-by-the-Bay green and innocent with central valley dust in her eyes. She had her own place now, a studio apartment in a lower-income building on Polk Street in the government center area, not a fashionable address or even a respectable one, but one she could afford as she waited tables and attended the city's junior college. She had discovered that there was a job with an almost living wage, for a single woman with no skills but good feet and plenty of stamina—waiting tables. Tips were the secret. You didn't get tips working the hat counter at Macy's, and despite the best-laid plans of the IRS, most of her tip money never got reported as income.

She had never communicated with or spoken to her father since she had walked out of the house over two years ago. She heard through a friend that her father had remarried. Her only curiosity about the woman who was technically her stepmother was to wonder if her father beat her.

She finished two years of college with a B-minus average, getting A's in whatever interested her and barely passing courses she found boring. The first two years of college were general education, mostly

❖

making up for the years of high school she barely floated through. She was still technically a high school dropout because it wasn't a California junior college requirement that she finish high school to attend. But the only doors her associate of arts junior college degree opened were out the exit doors of job interviews.

The ink was hardly dry on her diploma when she got a life-altering experience and realized what she wanted to be when she grew up.

She was waiting tables for the lunch group at the Star Chamber, a greasy spoon near the courthouse, walking distance from her apartment, when the realization came to her.

The luncheonette was frequented by lawyers. She heard shop talk every day. Almost by osmosis, she started picking up on the way lawyers thought—and she liked it. "They have a rule of law and the facts of what their client did—they argue back and forth, trying to see if they can get around the law," she told Norma Jean, the counter waitress.

"The only thing they learn in law school is how to send bills," Norma Jean said. "And they're poor tippers."

Marlowe was happy with her tips, but then again, the other woman showed her dislike of lawyers by endlessly chewing on their ears about her two mean-spirited divorces with dicey child custody battles. One of the lawyers she liked told Marlowe, "Most people see a lawyer for a divorce, a drunk driving offense, or when someone dies. And then they have to open their wallets. You can see why a lot of people think Hamlet was right when he said to kill all the lawyers."

There were regulars who came in every day. Usually they were nice. Some were jerks. Like the lawyer who always strained to get a peek down her blouse as she bent over to pour coffee. "You stick your nose too close and you're going to lose it," she told him with a friendly smile. He was a good tipper.

She had learned long ago that clothes didn't change the man. Just because they had professional degrees and wore expensive suits didn't make them any different than the Market Street construction workers who shouted down catcalls to women passing by. Businessmen were just a little more subtle about it—they didn't yell as loud.

She paused as she poured coffee for two lawyers arguing a divorce case. One of them claimed the wife wanted a restraining order because the husband said he was going to kill her and the kids if she divorced him. The other lawyer said, "I've talked to the husband, she's a liar, she just wants his money. The guy has worked for twenty years and now she wants half of everything."

"Of course he said it," Marlowe said. "It's obvious he's threatened her."

The husband's lawyer smirked. "Oh, the jury is in even before there's been any evidence presented. And what makes you think he's a liar?"

She knew two things about the lawyer—his name was Jerry and he was a bad tipper, he had even stiffed her before. "Because she's worried about the kids and he's worried about money. That's why he said it. He doesn't want to kill her because she's leaving him, it's because she wants half."

"Well, honey, you know what these two fighting and calling each other liars does to us? We laugh all the way to the bank."

"Yeah, and what happened to truth, justice, and the American Way?"

"That law firm went bankrupt!" his companion howled.

"If you're so smart, why don't you become a lawyer?" Jerry said.

"Maybe I will. Maybe I will at that. It looks to me like this country needs a few good lawyers."

"Hey, sweetie, if you want to get some legal training, you can get your hands in my briefs anytime."

"That'll be the day," she threw over her shoulder as she went to pick up an order.

"Those ambulance chasers giving you a bad time?" the cook asked.

"Naw, actually they just clued me in on what I want to be when I grow up."

"What?"

"I'm going to be a lawyer."

"How can you become a lawyer? You haven't even finished college."

"I heard you don't have to. Some law schools take you even if you don't have a four-year college degree."

"Where'd you get the idea you can be a lawyer?"

"Those two over there and most of the rest who come in here. They're not any smarter than I am."

❖

The cook shook his head. "It's okay to dream, kid, but be practical. It takes money to be a lawyer. And how many women lawyers have you ever seen? Tell me—after you take the lunch special to table nine."

The notion buzzed in her head for weeks. She confided her ambition to her landlady. "It really comes down to one thing: If they can do it, why can't I? Lawyers come into the café every day for lunch. I hear them talking about their cases. I even go over to the courthouse and watch cases. And you know what? Most lawyers aren't any smarter than me. Some of them that come into the restaurant seem so damn stupid, you wonder how they made it to the courthouse that morning. If they can become lawyers, why can't I?"

"Where would you get the money for law school anyway?"

"I'll work to support myself, and there's student loans. One of the lawyers told me there's a law school in Sacramento that will take anyone, as long as they have the price of tuition. And it doesn't matter where you go to law school. You take the same bar exam that people who graduate from Stanford and Harvard take."

"It's that easy?"

"It's not easy. But if they did it, why can't I?"

❖

27

❖

San Francisco, 1975

Marlowe was nervous. She hadn't felt this nervous since the day she got off the bus in San Francisco, just shy of eighteen years old. That was more than seven years ago. She had just celebrated her twenty-fifth birthday in November.

In the years since she had dusted Modesto off her, she had gotten her junior college degree, spent nearly a year preparing for the Law School Admittance Test, and moved to Sacramento to attend law school. After four years of night school, she had taken the bar exam and waited nearly five months for the results. Slightly less than half of the people who took the California bar, of which seventy-five percent were men, passed the exam on the first attempt. Her school did not attract the best of students and the average pass rate for its students was less than one in five. While her grades had not been exemplary, studying under the disadvantage of working full-time, she had been among the one in five from her school who passed the bar.

It was now January. She had been sworn in at a ceremony conducted by a judge, had her license to practice, and was back in San Francisco. Now all she needed was a job.

To support herself through law school, she had worked as a waitress at a Denny's restaurant in Sacramento during the school year and as a blackjack dealer at Harrah's South Lake Tahoe Casino during summer vacation. She had sent out fifty-two résumés, directed at law firms in the Bay Area. She had chosen the number fifty-two because she had read fifty-two Perry Mason legal thrillers and had hoped for a job in criminal law.

After being turned down by the district attorney's and public defender's offices, and every criminal defense lawyer she contacted, she decided to try for a job at any kind of firm before she went back to dealing blackjack. She had even tried to cold-call the most famous lawyer in town, Melvin Belli, but had been tossed out of his brick building without seeing the King of Torts.

Part of the problem was that she was a woman. One Stone Age lawyer thought it was "cute" that she had gotten a law degree and offered her a job as a secretary. She politely declined.

Her break came from Stella Johnson, a woman she used to serve at the Star Chamber. Stella worked as a clerk for a judge and through her Marlowe got a referral to a prestigious law firm. "These big business firms need female lawyers. They're under pressure from the companies they represent to hire women and minorities before the government comes down on them for discrimination."

She didn't have a strong interest in business law, but her interest in eating and paying her student loans propelled her to the city's Financial District. Most of the business law firms were congregated on and around Montgomery Street, the main artery of the Financial District.

Her interview with the law firm was on one of the upper floors in the Bank of America Building, the tallest building in the city. It was a Big Firm. The named partners were all Ivy League and long dead—both factors added prestige to the firm.

She disliked the interviewer at first sight. Despite the fact that she had not earned her spurs yet in a courtroom, she had a trial lawyer's contempt for lawyers who shuffled papers. This one not only was a paper-shuffler, but he conveyed an attitude that taking time to interview a prospective employee was a waste of his valuable time. The fact that she had lain awake nights worrying over the interview was something he cared little about.

❖

Her résumé was on his desk and he pushed it distastefully away from him with his pen. "I can't say that I'm impressed with your academics," he said.

"I worked full-time," she said.

"Yes, very commendable." He didn't sound sincere. "Pulling yourself up by the bootstraps." He looked up, flashing a grin. "Or we could say panty hose, couldn't we?"

She smiled thinly. *What a jerk.* But she held her temper because Stella had referred her.

"Frankly, even though we need female lawyers, we would never consider hiring someone who wasn't in the top ten percent of her class and in the top ten percent of the schools in the nation."

"Well, that certainly takes me out. But I do appreciate you taking the time to see me." She got up to leave.

"Wait a minute." He waved her back down. "Sit down. There are other considerations besides academics." He tapped the desktop with his pen. "We have a big case, a *very* big case, coming before Judge Bernstein, a matter of utmost importance to the firm. How well do you know the judge?"

"Judge Bernstein?" She blinked. It took a moment for her to make the connection—he was the judge Stella worked for. The interviewer probably thought the judge had referred her to the firm. She smiled and shrugged. "Well, I wouldn't exactly call him family . . ." In her mind it was a very lawyerlike statement, with just enough truth to avoid actual fraud: He certainly wasn't family. In fact, she had never even met the man. Nor did she claim to have met him, no matter what her tone and body language conveyed. *Fraud by omission,* was what her contracts professor would have called it.

"Would you feel comfortable discussing legal matters with him during social occasions, subtly, of course, pillow talk sort of thing? We wouldn't want to leave an impression that we were trying to influence him."

Pillow talk? *Jesus, does this jerk think I'm sleeping with the judge?* She straightened in her chair. Talking to a judge behind the opposing attorney's back was a no-no. "I wouldn't consider speaking to him privately about any matters before his court." She leaned back, smiled

❖

coyly, and shrugged. "Of course, if the matter came up, I would have to address it, wouldn't I? Within the realm of the Rules of Professional Conduct."

He rubbed his hands together and smacked his lips. "Of course, within the rules. We don't do it any other way here at Jones, Hopper and Lewis. Welcome aboard, Marlowe. You'll find we are a close-knit family here."

As she walked toward the elevators, she had a pressing desire to beat it to the courthouse and finagle an introduction to Judge Bernstein from Stella. She had no intention of ever attempting to influence the man for the firm, but she ought to at least know what the man looked like in order to keep up the pretense. Not that she wouldn't consider taking her turn on the proverbial casting room couch—in this case the one in a judge's chamber—to get a job with the most prestigious law firm in town.

Until she got her school loans paid off and knew she had enough in the bank to eat and have a roof over her head for more than three days, she was in the market to make a deal with the devil.

❖

28

❖

"Boring, boring, boring."

Marlowe made the pronouncement as she sat in the Albatross, a Marina District "body exchange"—a phrase that described the bars that singles crowded into after work to swap war stories about their jobs and hope to pick up someone of the opposite sex, though in San Francisco being of the opposite sex was not always a prerequisite.

She was complaining to her friend Deirdre Weiss, who worked at the same firm she did. Like Marlowe, Deirdre was in her twenties and had been with the firm for two years. Both were stuck in lawyer's purgatory—the Law & Motion Department, where they researched and wrote briefs for *other* lawyers to argue.

"Every time I see one of my brilliant briefs heading out the door, on its way to the courthouse to be argued by some schmuck who isn't half as sharp as I am, I want to scream." She leaned closer to her friend and shook her head with wide-eyed frustration. "If those so-called litigators in the Trial Department screw up any more of my finely crafted work, I'm going to leap from the building."

"Sure. And they would wash you off the sidewalk, send your mortal

❖

remains down the drain, and go back to doing what they do best, fucking up other people's work."

Marlowe shook her head. "If there is anything I've learned in my cosmic journey from high school dropout to big-firm lawyer, it's that there's no justice in this world. We're being held back because we are women and we're not rainmakers. It's not fair."

Rainmaker was an old term that described a new profession—people who brought in business to law firms. Unlike smaller law firms, big firms did not operate off of referrals from satisfied clients. Not only was their overhead too high for the capricious nature of referrals, but lawyers had to actually *win* cases to have satisfied clients. The financial wheel of the new age of law practice was the rainmaker, someone who brought to the firm a source of business. Some rainmakers were truth hustlers—and hucksters—who promoted their firm for businesses not unlike Willy Loman and generations of other salesmen. But selling took a talent that few business lawyers had. Most rainmakers had a connection created by marriage or were born into it. The classic example was the lawyer whose uncle was the claims manager at an insurance company. That lawyer, who may never have won a case or even appeared in a courtroom, was more valuable than all the best trial lawyers in the firm put together. Lawyers capable of trying cases could be hired—but having a "connection" was a rare condition that graced only the lucky few.

"We're going to have to do sex change operations before they let us try cases," Deirdre said. "These Neanderthals don't believe women have the gray matter to argue important cases."

"Bullshit," Marlowe said, "they believe it and it scares the hell out of them."

They laughed and toasted each other.

Deirdre said, "I hear you're going down to San Diego with Chunky Chucky for the Weinstock products liability case. Have you ever been there?"

Chunky Chucky was Charles Bellman, the head of the Law & Motion Department. New to the firm and position, he had been head of the unit for six months. Chunky Chucky wasn't a name they called him to his face. He wasn't overweight enough for anyone to castigate his belt line, but he had a fat face that twisted into a scowl whenever he was displeased at a subordinate's work product—which was almost all the time. Chucky was a rainmaker. His father-in-law, a deputy city attorney, directed business his way. It was enough to guarantee him a job as a section chief when he wasn't capable of supervising the maintenance crew.

He was a bureaucratic swine, ruthless and arbitrary to anyone weak, and the only human being that Marlowe regularly prayed would fall under the wheels of the cable car he rode to work on every day down California Street.

"Never been to San Diego, and in answer to your unasked questions, yes, I will hate the place just because he will be there, and no, I'm not willing to sleep with Chucky to get transferred over to the trial unit."

"He's taking Eileen along, too."

"Uh-huh, he's a predator. He knows Eileen will fuck him just because he makes a show of authority."

"Another Margo."

Margo had been a new hire last year. She only lasted three months. After she worked on a case into the evening with a senior partner more than twice her age, he took her to dinner at the Mark Hopkins Hotel. After dinner, he took her by the hand and led her up to a room he had already rented and had sex with her. A couple weeks later, Margo tearfully told Marlowe and Deirdre the story of her "rape." Both of them had listened openmouthed at the tale and offered no sympathy.

"You can't rape a grown woman with a show of executive authority," Marlowe told her. "You should have told him you were out of there when he started for the elevator."

Not getting any sympathy, and angry at herself for letting her boss get into her pants, Margo quit and went back to St. Louis.

Part of Marlowe's lack of sympathy was related to the fact that Margo had asked Marlowe where she had gone to school and had gaped when Marlowe rattled off a junior college and an unaccredited law school.

Marlowe said, "With Eileen, he's playing with fire. She's going through a divorce and she's emotionally distraught and vulnerable.

❖

She's liable to freak out and run down the hallways at work screaming that Chucky's just a little prick."

"And a premature ejaculator!" Deirdre howled.

———————

San Diego was a nightmare. The firm equipped a satellite office at the Desert Princess Hotel near the courthouse to support the products liability trial. Desks and chairs, cases of lawbooks, IBM Selectric typewriters, secretaries, the whole nine yards were there along with Marlowe and Chunky Chucky. Eileen had taken ill with the flu and didn't make it. That left Marlowe having to work side by side with Chucky.

"Someday we'll have business computers as small as travel trunks that will be able to hold dozens of lawbooks," Chucky told her confidently over dinner.

Marlowe smothered a yawn. She personally didn't think a computer was something mobile, and couldn't care less—who could improve upon books and the IBM Selectric?

They had been in town three days and it was the first evening she had to share alone with her boss. The other dinners had been business sessions with the trial attorneys. The case had been settled and they'd be packing up and returning to Frisco in the morning. Marlowe told herself she could stand being alone with Chucky for at least another twenty or thirty minutes before she ran screaming from the hotel's lounge. She had thought she'd be a free woman once dinner was over, but he steered her toward the lounge as soon as they walked out of the adjoining restaurant.

She had to keep reminding herself that he was her boss, and that she now had a condo and a car to support. She ordered a soda and went into a catatonic state, staring at him with glazed-over eyes as he popped down Jack Daniel's on the rocks and told her the utterly boring details of his life. The only saving grace was that the lounge was dark and they were in the dimmest corner, making it unnecessary for her to cringe when people saw her with a man she considered a total loser.

❖

She was tapping the table with the long wooden spear that had pronged the cherry that came with her soda, her mind a million miles away, when she realized that he had changed the subject to career opportunities for her at the firm—and that his hand was up her skirt. It was a hot day and she had shed her panty hose before dinner.

He leaned against her and blew whiskey breath against her neck. "Let's fuck."

She sat perfectly still. Her mind and body were frozen, but she smelled the bad breath he was panting on her and felt the finger that was trying to violate her.

She reacted without thinking, jabbing at his face with the cocktail stick. It caught him in his right nostril. He yelped and grabbed his nose.

He shook with rage as he stopped the bleeding from his nose with a napkin. "You're fired, you fucking bitch."

She was ready for him. "No, I'm not finished, you are. I'm calling the police and having you arrested for rape, then I'm calling your wife and telling her you raped me, then I'm calling your father-in-law. You slimy bastard, you'll be out on the street and selling your ass to chicken hawks in the Tenderloin when I get through with you."

CHUCKY ARRANGED HER TRANSFER to the trial section immediately upon their return to San Francisco.

Marlowe prided herself on the fact that she had not blackmailed him to get the transfer. That would have been unethical, she told herself. However, after tears and pleading on his part, she decided she wouldn't push the matter, rationalizing that she was protecting his wife and kids from his indiscretions.

Back in her condo in the city, she asked herself if it was really right for her to benefit from the incident, whether the world would have been better off had she had him arrested. She decided that, one, it would be a cold day in hell before he ever tried anything with another woman; two, she really did feel sorry for his family; and three, it was a tough world, no one was cutting her any slack, she had to fight for everything she got and had to work twice as hard as everyone else because they all seemed to have the right family or good fortune to have things come easier than they came to her.

She believed in an-eye-for-an-eye justice, that if you lived by the sword, you had to be prepared to die by the sword.

Chucky was just lucky she took the transfer and didn't cut off his dick.

❖

29

❖

"Boring, boring, boring," Marlowe told Deidre. "I've been in Trials for three months and all I've done is carry the briefcase for those bastards."

She and Deidre were in their favorite watering hole again, the Albatross, the neighborhood body exchange. "Those bastards" were the four senior lawyers in the unit.

"Do you know James Stapp, the blond, good-looking guy with the cute southern accent? He's two years older than me and he's been in Trials for four years and has never done a trial. Can you imagine? Four years and has never done a trial. He's only appeared as second chair in small cases and third chair in big cases and he never gets to open his mouth in any case. He has to wait for one of those bastards to die before he'll get a chance to stand up and clear his throat and say 'Your Honor—'" Marlowe emphasized the last two words in a southern accent.

"Stop it, you're killing me," Deirdre moaned. She was laughing so hard she spilled her drink.

"Look at all this talent going to waste," Marlowe said. "I'm at least a hundred and thirty pounds of dynamic lawyer and my talents are being employed to gofer for fossils who probably went to law school with Lincoln."

❖

"Lincoln was a log-cabin type, I'm sure he didn't go to law school."

"Irrelevant, immaterial, inadmissible hearsay. Here's the bottom line: My basic legal education is that I've read fifty-two Perry Mason books. I'm best qualified to represent beautiful people who murder their millionaire spouses and come into my office and lay the smoking gun on my desk when they hire me. I can't get up a passion when Big Corporation A sues Big Corporation B because B is selling widgets that resemble those made by A. Do you know that some idiot in the office has suggested we all wear T-shirts around the office that say BORN TO BILL?"

"That was my suggestion."

"I rest my case."

They were silent for a moment, then Deirdre said, "Look, you'll never be satisfied until you're your own boss. You should become a sole practitioner before you bitch yourself to death."

"Three terrible mistakes keep me from hanging up my own shingle. I don't have parents who would support me while I get a practice going, I don't have a man to support me while I get a practice going, and I already have an overhead to support. It's the trap a steady job snarls you in. A steady paycheck lets you buy things on time, get a cool apartment in the Marina, buy that cute little Mustang convertible I can't live without."

"You're right, we're trapped because we've reached a comfort zone."

As they chatted, Marlowe noticed a young man about her age across the bar. He was interesting on several counts, not the least of which was that he was a new face rather than the same old, same old that came to the place. But she liked everything about him, including the casual, rugged way he dressed in a city where suits and ties were the uniforms of almost any day—khaki pants, a brown leather aviator jacket that had come into vogue, tough hiking boots, plus he was over six feet. His light brown hair complimented light blue eyes, his tush was round and firm, with more shape than most men had.

"Good God, I'm in love."

Deirdre gave him the once-over. "I wouldn't kick him out of bed."

"You're never going to get the chance," Marlowe said. She sat her drink on the bar and went across the room. "Hello."

❖

The man with the aviator jacket grinned at her. "Hi."

"My name is Rockefeller," Marlowe said. "I've got so much money, I can't spend it all. I'm looking for a man to amuse me. The right man will find himself the possessor of wealth and erotic pleasure beyond anything he ever imagined."

"My kind of woman," he said. "Rich, beautiful, totally immoral. Would you like to go someplace quiet and romantic where we can get together for five minutes and learn each other's names before we make love?"

"Sure, but just one thing," Marlowe said with a straight face. "My chauffeur drove away with my purse. Can you pay my bar tab?"

He patted his pockets. "Funny thing, but my valet forgot to give me my wallet. I'm afraid you're going to have to pick up the tab or we'll both be washing beer glasses."

She picked up the tab. It would become a habit.

30

❖

She married Barry Park two weeks later on impulse when they were in South Lake Tahoe gambling.

She hadn't realized how lonely she had been. She had no family to fall back onto and had few friends. Other than casual dates and occasional short-lived love affairs, she had no serious entanglements with men. Barry brought light into her life, filled the voids.

She soon came to realize that she and Barry barely knew each other. They had an intense, almost violently sexual attraction. But they were strangers who had to get to know each other. Their compatibility was entirely in the bedroom.

Barry had rugged good looks, prime-time TV if not movie-star quality. But the genetic lottery that gave him good looks wasn't backed up by the mental qualities of a winner. Barry managed to step into it in almost every aspect of life, but never getting close to succeeding. He got through three years of college, but never went back for the final year and a degree. His doting mother, who was successful herself as an entrepreneur of a small business producing high-end baby clothes, paid for his expensive business school program despite his lackluster college record. He failed to complete that also.

❖

When Marlowe met him, he was working for a Financial District brokerage firm. Good stockbrokers made big money and he boasted he was the best. He certainly looked the part, expensive clothes and cherry-red Corvette convertible, but she discovered the morning after the impromptu wedding that she had to cover his overdrawn checking account and that he was behind in his bills.

His doting mother, whom he had bled for money on a regular basis, was having health and financial problems and was only too happy to turn management of her son over to his new wife. Marlowe paid his back rent and he moved into her Marina condo.

Something had happened at work during their first month together, she wasn't sure what because he wouldn't discuss it with her.

She also discovered that he had a short fuse.

It happened when she suggested they drive over to Sausalito for dinner. Coming down the hill from Highway 101, Barry got angry when a driver behind him honked his horn as Barry came to an almost dead stop on the roadway to point out a house he said he'd like to buy someday. The house was worth more than what she and Barry would earn over the next twenty years, but it was nice wishful thinking.

Marlowe was stunned when Barry slammed on the brakes, nearly causing the other car to rear-end them. He got out of the car and confronted the other driver, grabbing the middle-aged man by the throat.

"Don't fuck with me, asshole."

Marlowe half stood in the convertible Corvette. "Barry! Barry, for God's sake, stop it!"

He came back to the car and they left the scene burning rubber. He was still fuming when they came into town a few minutes later at twice the speed limit. "Slow down, Barry, you're going to get a ticket."

They pulled into the wharfside restaurant and turned over the car to the valet parker. They hadn't spoken about the incident. "There's not a scratch on the car," Barry told the parking attendant. "Bring it back that way."

She grabbed his arm and pulled him aside before they entered. "What happened back there?"

"That prick got on my ass."

❖

"It was just a guy honking his horn because you almost came to a stop on the road."

"It's my fuckin' fault? Some asshole wants to push me around? Fuck you, lady!"

He stomped off. She called his name and stared at his retreating back. She was leaning on a railing, staring at the Golden Gate Bridge, when he came back.

"I'm sorry," he said. He gave her a hug. "I've been told I've got an anger management problem."

Anger management? Back in Modesto, they would have said he was a bully with a bad temper. That's what bothered her the most. Her father was a bully. Her brother had suffered under the blows of bullies. Had the man he grabbed been a husky young guy, Marlowe would not have been as disturbed.

She didn't know what to do. She loved him. He fulfilled a need in her life for family. She was already thinking of babies and a house in the suburbs. But she realized she hardly knew him, that she knew her neighbors and co-workers better than her husband.

A week later she witnessed his anger again. He hit a man in the stomach in an argument over a parking space. The man had pulled a small sports car into a parking space as Barry pulled forward and stopped to back into the space.

They left fast, tires screeching again.

"Why did you do that?"

"I was right, fuckin' right, don't fuck with me!"

He was going so fast he almost hit a woman stepping off a curb.

"Slow down!"

She leaned over in her seat and held her head in her hands.

He reached over and grabbed her by the back of her neck, squeezing hard. "I was right, that parking space was ours!"

"Take your fuckin' hands off me!" He pulled to the curb and they stared at each other, breathless.

"I'm sorry, Jesus, I'm really sorry." He started to sob and beat his head against the steering wheel.

Marlowe collapsed in her seat, her heart racing. "I'm sorry, too."

❖

"You're sorry you married me."

"I didn't say that."

"I heard it in your voice."

She sighed and closed her eyes. "Can we go home? I think I need to throw up and go to bed."

Later, in bed, they made love. For the first time she faked both the desire and her orgasm.

Propped up on a pillow, Marlowe said, "That man may have gotten your license number and called the police."

"Don't worry, that's why I gave him a plex shot."

"A what?"

"I punched him in the solar plexus. When you hit 'em right in the pit of stomach, it's a crippling blow but there's no bruising, they can't prove it."

"I'll have to remember that next time I beat up someone. Why did you hit him?"

He shrugged. "I saw red. He took our parking space."

"But you can't go through life hitting people who do things you don't like."

"Why don't you give the other guy the lecture? I don't need it or deserve it."

"I MARRIED A STRANGER," Marlowe told Deirdre.

"Get a divorce. They're easy now, no fault."

"I can't. It's crazy, but I love him, I really do. Like in the movies, the first time I saw him, bells rang and music played."

"What you heard was the margaritas you drank gurgling between your ears. Get a divorce. It's all just an accounting for the property split now, no emotions involved. And you two haven't really gathered any assets together."

It was more complicated than Deirdre's simple math. She not only loved him, but she felt a need to care for him, to work out his anger problems and the problems that were growing with him. It was the same thing with her brother. She loved him and wanted to protect him. But she didn't want to end up like her mother, a frightened, bullied woman.

❖

She didn't tell Deirdre about the single mother with a fifteen-year-old daughter that looked older who had moved in next door. Both mother and daughter were overly friendly toward Barry and he openly flirted with both of them. "Mrs. Robinson and Lolita," Marlowe called them, after the promiscuous movie females.

"My father always says, you can take a horse to water, but you can't make him drink. You want to reform him. He's the one who has to want to reform before it'll happen," Deirdre told her.

A month passed before she found out Barry had lost his job.

"They're full of shit," he told her. "They never gave me a chance, always directing the good stuff toward other guys."

It wasn't just the loss of a job, but of a career—he admitted to her that it was the second brokerage firm he'd worked for. Stockbrokers were a cottage industry and every one of them would know he had been fired twice.

He talked about going back to school and she encouraged him.

"I don't want a woman to support me," he said.

"It's for both of us. You'd do the same for me."

They'd been married three months when she came home from work before noon feeling nauseated. She thought she might have a touch of the flu or food poisoning. She was surprised to see Barry's car out front. He was supposed to be in school until early afternoon.

He had left his keys in the front door of the condo. In a hurry, she thought. She twisted the key in the lock and stopped, nearly stepping on a pair of pink panties.

Barry was on his back on the floor. His pants were down to his knees. Lolita was on top of him, bouncing up and down, her dress up to her waist. She looked over at Marlowe, her tongue cocked out of her mouth. She smiled and shook her head. "Oh-oh."

Marlowe did something totally unexpected. She calmly walked past them to the bedroom without saying a word. Later, she would realize it wasn't a real surprise, that it was just par for the course with Barry.

She went into the bedroom and began taking Barry's clothes out of the closet. He came to the door. He looked ready to cry. "I'm sorry, shit, I'm really sorry."

❖

She ignored him and began pulling his stuff from a dresser and throwing it on the bed.

He grabbed at her and she spun away. "Keep away from me."

"Please, I need you."

"You need a mother, you fuckin' loser!"

She saw the feral rage in his eyes and stepped back. His fist caught her in the stomach, nearly lifting her off her feet. She collapsed on the floor. He stared at her, gaping. "Oh, my God, I'm sorry. I'm so sorry, I didn't mean to hurt you."

"Get out! You bastard! Get away from me!"

He ran from the room, flying out the front door, coming back to grab his keys and taking the steps two at a time.

She lay on the floor in terrible pain, trying to breathe. Her guts felt like they were on fire. She vomited over and over on the bedroom carpet, unable to even crawl to the bathroom. When she started dry-heaving she realized she was bleeding from her vagina. She crawled to the bedside phone and called 911.

31

❖

Marlowe stared up at the doctor who stood by her hospital bed and repeated what the doctor had told her. "I was pregnant?"

The doctor's statement didn't make much sense to her. They had
brought her in that morning by ambulance. It was late afternoon now
and she had been examined, X-rayed, and put on IV. She had been waiting for the results of a scan. She shook her head. "It can't be, I wasn't
pregnant."

"You were for the last couple months. It's not unusual not to notice,
especially if it's not planned. You had a miscarriage." The expression on
the face of the woman, a gynecologist, was grim. "I'm sorry."

"There's more, isn't there?" Marlowe said.

"You're pretty torn up inside. There's hemorrhaging, a significant
risk of infection. We'll have to operate, we need your permission."

"Do what you have to."

"Marlowe . . ."

The worst was yet to come. She felt like crying.

"We need to do a hysterectomy."

Like *pregnant,* the word had little initial meaning to her. She shook
her head. "No. You can't do that. I won't be able to have children."

❖

"We have to—"

"No! I'd rather die, no, you can't do it." She tried to get up and the doctor gently pushed her back down.

"Marlowe, you will die—"

"No, I don't care, you can't do it, I'll risk it."

The doctor shook her head. "There's nothing left to risk. Your womb was torn, it can't be repaired, we have to take it out. It doesn't matter now, you will never be able to have children."

"No! No! That son-of-a-bitch! No!"

32

❖

Marlowe returned from the courthouse and lay on the bed in her apartment. It had been two months since she had been released from the hospital. She carried home from her hospital stay severe depression, burning anger, and a large scar on her abdomen. She had hardly spoken to anyone, not even returning the phone calls of her friends or answering the door when they came by. She had crawled into herself. It was a cold, dark place.

Barry had been charged with felony assault and battery with great bodily injury for striking her. She had gone to the courthouse that morning because she had been subpoenaed by the district attorney's office. She had had to be subpoenaed rather than showing up voluntarily because she had not cooperated with the prosecutor. The deputy DA in charge of the case against Barry thought she was a typical abused wife, refusing to testify because she was either scared shitless of the bastard who knocked her around or was stupid enough to want the guy back.

"Seventy-five percent of the abused-spouse cases we get, the woman refuses to testify," the deputy told her when she came to the courtroom where Barry was being prosecuted. "We still prosecute if it's serious, and this one is. You have to come to your senses, Ms. James. This guy

❖

really hurt you. He's a danger to you and other women. If you don't care about yourself, then think about the next woman he batters."

Marlowe just stared at him, not speaking. He was wrong, but she didn't tell him that. She wasn't afraid of Barry. She'd refused to go to court because she was so depressed she didn't want to leave the house.

He slammed closed his file. "Fine, be as stupid as you please. You're under subpoena. If you refuse to testify, you'll be held in contempt. If you lie and say he didn't hit you, I'll prosecute you for perjury. You're to stay in our reception area until I tell you we're ready for your testimony."

She was never needed. Barry pled to a misdemeanor battery, was granted probation, fined three hundred dollars, and ordered to perform a hundred hours of community service.

She returned from the courthouse, went back to her bedroom, and crawled back into that dark place in her mind. The light on her answering machine was blinking and she didn't bother answering it. It was probably her boss at work telling her she'd been terminated. She had been granted sick leave without even asking for it, but hadn't communicated with the office since the operation.

The phone rang and the machine went on with the first ring.

"Marlowe."

She felt a stab of pain in her gut.

"Marlowe, it's me. I need to talk to you. Honey, I really need to talk to you, I can't tell you how sorry I am."

Marlowe picked up the receiver and spoke in a whisper. "I'm on."

She heard him take in a deep breath. "Jeez, honey, I'm so sorry, I really am."

She didn't respond.

"I want to thank you, my attorney said they offered me a misdemeanor because you wouldn't cooperate. That means you still love me, baby, I love you, too. I . . . I need to see you."

"Okay," she said.

THE GUN WAS UNDER the bed, still there where Barry had put it after he moved in. He had come back for his things while she was in the hospital, but had forgotten the gun.

❖

She unzipped the leather case and removed the weapon. Turning it in her hands, she stared at it, familiarizing herself with it.

She knew how to point and pull a trigger. Her father had had guns in the house and had taken her and her brother out into the countryside to show them how to use a gun. That had been a 30-30 deer rifle, but her father had two shotguns, and though she'd never fired one, she had seen him shoot them.

Barry called his a duck gun. It was a fancy shotgun with an elegant hardwood stock and silver etchings on the side. His indulgent mother had bought it for him and he had used it only once. But leave it to Barry to screw up—naturally, he left it loaded with even the safety off.

She unlocked the front door and opened it a crack. Then she sat in the living room in a soft chair and waited.

Twenty minutes passed before she heard his hurried footsteps coming up the concrete steps. She got to her feet and held the shotgun at her side, her left hand down the grip, her other hand under with the trigger.

He pushed open the door and stopped in his tracks as he saw her with the gun. His face was flushed, not from the stairway, but from booze. He stared at her holding the gun and burst into a laugh.

"You dumb bitch, give me that."

He stepped forward and she pulled the trigger. The gun jerked in her grasp and she dropped it.

A shotgun blast comes out of the barrel as a tight knot of BB-sized lead pellets, but the wad expands. By the time it reached Barry across the room, the pellets had spread out bigger than a softball. The shot hit him in the groin.

He flew backward with a crazed, violent movement and went down the stairs headfirst.

He mercifully bled to death before an ambulance arrived.

Barry would not have wanted to live as a eunuch.

❖

OLD BAILEY

A quicksand of deceit.

—SHAKESPEARE, *HENRY VI*

33

❖

St. Andrews Hotel

Philip Hall was waiting in the lobby for Marlowe when she stepped out of the elevator. He had come to escort her to the Old Bailey, where her petition to represent the princess would be heard. The press was in full force outside the front doors, with TV cameras ready to beam her image around the globe.

She wondered if people back in Modesto would see it, whether her father would be bragging that that was his daughter. If he was still alive.

She hadn't heard from him since she won the San Francisco jury trial in which she was accused of murdering her husband Barry. He called her soon after the trial was over and she had listened quietly as he spoke. "This is your father, Marlowe. How are you?"

They hadn't spoken for nearly a decade, not since she left Modesto, and his tone sounded as if she had been away for the weekend. In her eyes, it was apropos that her father waited to contact her until after she won the murder case against her for shooting Barry.

"Where were you when I needed you?" she asked, and hung up.

The next day, a woman with a weepy voice on the verge of hysteria called to tell her that she was her stepmother and that her father needed her. He had stomach cancer.

❖

Marlowe listened unsympathetically to her appeal and hung up the phone without replying, and then called the telephone company to change her number to an unlisted one.

She knew what her father wanted—he was facing his Maker and wanted forgiveness and closure. She wasn't willing to give him either. The reason she had been unforgiving was that he had not called for her sake—he had called for his own peace of mind. He could take his guilt and open emotional sores to the grave and toss and turn for eternity.

The sight of the cameras of the Fourth Estate waiting in front of the hotel brought her back to the present.

"Any chance we can sneak out the back rather than face that mob?" she asked Hall.

"'Fraid not. British newspeople can be fair or they can lynch you with printer's ink. We're better off facing the pack than antagonizing them. But Anthony has asked that we limit our interaction with the news media to polite smiles. I've already told the group outside that there will be a news conference later in the day, so all you have to do is give them a nice smile as we wade through."

More of Anthony Trent putting a muzzle on her mouth was her impression, but she didn't have anything she wanted to say to the press. Safely ensconced in the limo, Marlowe said, "I need to ask you something, not specifically about the princess, but the Royals in general. In America, we get cross-signals about the Royals. On the one hand, it appears the British people cherish their royal family, but we hear about people who openly criticize the institution, complain about spending tax money to protect them, and basically want to get rid of the system."

"I think that's a fair assessment of the range of feelings, somewhere between adoration and off with their heads. Most people support the queen."

"Where are you in that equation? And I'm not asking that question of you when you're wearing your hat—or wig—as a lawyer for the princess, but as a person."

Hall pursed his lips with a little disapproval, as if she had asked a question about a family secret. "Where do I stand? I believe the Royals are the very heart of Britain, even more so than Parliament, Westmin-

❖

ster Abbey, the Church of England, and our other assorted monuments and institutions. You Americans have far fewer traditions than we—"

"We're a younger country."

"It's not just that, that excuse doesn't work anymore, America's been around for centuries. I see it differently. Americans don't honor their traditions the way we have. People in your country pride themselves as being irreverent much more than we do. And I think it's because you've never had a central tradition to focus upon. Your presidents come and go, some in disgrace one step ahead of impeachment, some doing tacky telly commercials soon after leaving office—"

"And some work for world peace and lead very distinguished lives."

"Rightly so. But the point is, your heads of state are rarely remembered or revered past their term of office unless they get assassinated. Here in Britain, we have had kings and queens as heads of state, sprouting for centuries from the same family tree. I don't know how the royal genealogical table works, but I would imagine that we've had branches of the same tree going back to the Middle Ages. Unlike many other European countries—France, Germany, Italy—we have not had heads of state and forms of government coming and going and leaving chaos in their wake. And the same goes for other European countries with monarchies—the Dutch, Belgians, Swedes, Danes, Norwegians—all of them have cherished their monarchs and have enjoyed long-term stability."

"What about these Royals, specifically?"

"The only Royals that really matter in terms of the nation are the reigning monarch and heir to the throne. As for the queen, I believe she will go down in our history as one of our most gifted monarchs. She has reigned through the advent of both the atomic age and the computer age, the loss of the colonial empire, the Cold War, the advent of the European Union, and the War Between the Sexes."

"We call that the Sexual Revolution," Marlowe said. "What do you think of the princess? Off the record, in complete confidence." Which was nonsense, of course. How could anything that was said to a lawyer or a reporter be off the record?

"I admire the princess for her courage to stand up for what she believes. She has a good heart, I believe she honestly loves people and has done good with her charities. And she appears to be a caring mother, though one has to wonder how caring it is to kill the boys' father."

"But?"

"Some question whether her immaturity and neurosis killed the heir to the throne. What do you think of her?"

"I haven't reached a conclusion yet. If you had asked me that question before the shooting, I suppose I would have given a response similar to how I imagine many American—and I suppose British—women felt about her. On the one hand, she had married a prince and was to be a queen, that's a fairy-tale romance to us poor unwashed masses. There are many royal weddings, but this one was particularly special because she has that elusive quality called charisma."

"She's quite pretty—"

"No, she's not *that* attractive, and physical beauty has nothing to do with it. Every year at the Miss America and Miss World beauty pageants, there are women who are far more physically beautiful than most of the female actresses in Hollywood. Julia Roberts, for example, would not be a runner-up at a beauty contest. But she has charisma that makes her stand out from the rest. And the princess has some of that mysterious magnetism."

They rode in silence for a moment before Marlowe brought up the subject of the procedure at the courthouse whereby she would be granted permission to appear on the princess's behalf before an English court.

Hall said, "We will meet with the judge and the Crown Prosecutor informally. The right of barristers to act as advocates rests mostly on tradition—theoretically, a judge could allow a solicitor or anyone else to argue a case, but it just isn't done."

"I'm not sure that an American court would permit a barrister not licensed in the state to appear before it. Our courts generally operate by the strict rules of statutory law, not traditions. But we do recognize the similarity between the legal systems. If you came to California from a common-law country like Britain or Canada and wanted to be licensed to practice, you could take the bar exam without going to law school. If you came from continental Europe or almost anywhere else in the world, you would have to go to law school before they permitted you to take the exam."

"Quite so. As Lord Finfall pointed out, both the British and American systems are based upon the same principles, concepts that would be alien to a French, German, Italian, or other continental European attorney. As you well know, the continental system is not based upon attorney adversaries battling before a neutral judge for the favor of a jury, rather it's an inquisitional system, with the judge conducting an interrogation of witnesses. It's called civil law, I believe, as opposed to our system of common law. I seem to recall much of it evolved from the Napoleonic era."

Hall cleaned his glasses with a soft cloth as he went on. "However, don't make the mistake of assuming that there are no differences between your American system and ours. Your legal system tends to be very dynamic, in constant flux and readily adaptable to change. Ours is much more steeped in tradition, but in many ways less structured."

"Really? I would have thought it was much more rigid."

"Not at all. You see, the basic tenet of legal rights under the American criminal justice system is based upon interpretation of a set of written rules."

"The Constitution."

"We don't have a written constitution. More than anything, we have a set of traditions that we honor. The powers of the queen are an example of that. She possesses enormous powers, perhaps even the sort wielded by the proverbial Oriental potentate, but she doesn't utilize them out of a sense of tradition. I was never a student of the political system, but my understanding is that theoretically she could fire the Prime Minister anytime she liked and appoint a new one. The real limitation on her, of course, is common sense and public opinion. If she attempted to use the old-fashioned powers of a monarch, Parliament would strip them from her.

"By the same token, the Crown, meaning the government at large, has the authority to alter the legal system in ways that your structured system would never be able to. The same goes for the entire legal system. It can be altered to protect the nation."

❖

"Protect the nation?"

"We're a small island. America has five times the population, but around thirty or forty times more land area."

"Plus natural resources."

"Exactly, vast resources. We have almost no mineral resources, a few buckets of coal, some barrels of oil sucked with difficulty out of the bottom of the North Sea. That makes us a fragile nation. It wouldn't take much of a natural or military disaster to turn Britain into a third world economy. And everyone knows, we will never completely assimilate into the continental culture or economy. It's not a question of language, there are many languages in Europe. What really separates us is the *law*. We have a system in which the people look up to the law out of respect. On the continent, the law looks down at them and people fear it. The jury system puts justice in the hands of the people, rather than the way the Europeans conduct their cases with a career judge, literally a paid inquisitor, who socially and economically is far removed from the average person. Judges on the continent are not impartial arbiters. In my view they are an extension of the police.

"The essence of the privilege against self-incrimination and separation of the judiciary from the police are to prevent abuses of police power. The system on the continent, where the judiciary and the police work hand in hand and there is no right to refuse to be interrogated, can lead to usurpation of power by the government."

He paused and grinned. "Sorry, I didn't intend to give you a lecture."

"It's okay, I appreciate it, I need to understand your system. More than anything else, I need to know the procedures."

"Then perhaps we should talk about trial procedures. Most of it will be familiar to you, but we don't permit the sort of jury questioning and challenges, voir dire, used in the States. Basically, other than potential jurors who fall into certain exceptions, such as hardships or personal involvement in the matter that would bar them from serving, the jury will be composed of the first twelve called to the box. And verdicts are different, too. We have the same standard, beyond a reasonable doubt, but unlike your American system, the verdicts don't have to be unanimous. If all twelve can't agree upon a verdict, the judge informs them he will accept the will of ten out of twelve."

❖

"That makes it much harder to get a hung jury."

"Exactly. And we will also have to deal with a prosecutorial privilege of vetting prospective jurors."

"What do you mean by vetting?"

"In sensitive cases, prosecutors check the backgrounds of jurors through police, Special Branch, and security services records. They're looking to see if the person has political or social sympathies that would make them unsuitable in cases that could affect the well-being of the nation. Prosecutors have been secretly vetting since 1974, but the practice was only recently exposed."

"What happens if they don't like the person's beliefs?"

"They ask them to stand by for the prosecution. Meaning they are eliminated as jurors."

"That amounts to a preemptory challenge by the prosecution, simply eliminating jurors the prosecution doesn't want, even before they are called to court to be questioned. Do we also have that right?"

"We don't have the right and the vetting information isn't always shared with the defense. Basically, the defense only has the right to whatever the prosecution is willing to turn over. It's a very controversial matter that we barristers are not happy with. In this case, we are making a demand to know if vetting is done, which we know will be done for a certainty. Anthony is planning to make noise if we are not permitted to share information, but there is not a great chance the prosecution will share it with us."

"I'm sorry, but I find that completely undemocratic and unconstitutional. Britain is a cradle of democracy—I'm astonished your courts permit such a thing. How many preemptory challenges does the defense have?"

"None. The use of preemptory challenges by the defense was recently eliminated."

"Holy shit. Excuse my French, but that's a good old-fashioned expression for major frustration," Marlowe said. "I'm getting the impression that we're having the deck stacked against us."

"The princess will be treated the same as other defendants," Hall said stiffly.

She squeezed his arm. "I'm not criticizing your legal system, I just don't find the concept of vetting as just. And I understand the concept of Britain being small and fragile, but maybe the rule should be limited to security issues. Certainly this case isn't shaking the political tree."

"This case is a national issue. You forget that the victim and the killer were the future king and queen."

"I stand corrected. How long have you been a lawyer, Philip?"

"I was called to the law five years ago."

Marlowe smiled. " 'Called to the law' sounds like a religious calling, something like the spiritual beckoning priests and ministers get."

"One of our Briticisms, I'm afraid." He chuckled. "I also had to sit for dinners before I answered the call."

"Okay, what's that?"

"Part of the arcane process of becoming an advocate. Those studying to be barristers belong to an Inn of Court, a gathering of attorneys, and as part of the legal education, the students have to attend dinners at the Inn. As you might expect, legal matters are discussed at these dinners. I had to sit through twenty dinners—not to mention a basic legal education—before I was permitted to answer the call to the bar. Once we become practicing barristers, our procedures are still a bit different than those you're used to. You experienced some of the differences just in the introductions that were made, with Sir Fredic as instructing solicitor."

She nodded and he went on. "You recall that a solicitor is a transactional lawyer, handling paperwork ranging from real estate transactions, to business matters, to domestic situations. But even for us barristers, the solicitor is the first contact with a client. The client goes to a solicitor and explains the problem. With some minor exceptions, if court action such as a trial is necessary, the solicitor will hire a barrister to represent the client in the courtroom and send along a brief."

Marlowe said, "In the States, a brief is a written argument presented to a court."

"We use the word to refer to the instructions and documents the solicitor sends along to the barrister he hires. Traditionally, they arrive bound up with a colored ribbon. In the brief the solicitor will report on the evidence and include statements of witnesses and other pertinent matters of proof. This is the guide the barrister will follow in presenting the client's case before the court."

"So only solicitors can have clients and only barristers can argue in court."

"In a simplistic way, I suppose that's a fair statement. In a significant case, the solicitor will also be in the courtroom, but he or she must remain behind the bar."

"The bar. I'm a member of a bar association but I never gave the expression much thought. It's a railing in the courtroom, isn't it?"

"I've heard the term used a number of ways, as the railing in our Inns of Court that separated students from practitioners, as the railing that the advocate, client, and witnesses stood at when a case was called in old days, and as the railing separating the business conducted in the courtroom from the spectators."

"I recall from the meeting that you, Anthony Trent, and Helen Catters are barristers and Sir Fredic is the instructing solicitor."

"Yes, but Anthony is a silk, Catters and I are juniors."

"A silk?"

"Anthony is a Queen's Counsel, a designation of barristers who are considered distinguished in their profession. Since barristers constitute only about ten percent of the lawyers in the country, the rest being solicitors, and only about ten percent of barristers are made Q.C.s, being given the designation of Queen's Counsel is indeed a rarefied honor. They're called silks because they wear silk robes. We ordinary barristers are called juniors regardless of our age. And we wear a wool material called stuff. As you might expect, a Q.C. can afford silk—they often make in excess of a million pounds a year. Naturally, there are only a small number of silks. And they generally don't appear in court unless accompanied by a junior. While this is no longer an absolute requirement, it is still commonly practiced. In court, I will sit in the bench behind Anthony."

"You're Anthony's partner?"

"No, barristers are forbidden to form partnerships, although they can come together to share a clerk and the expense of a chamber. Anthony has his own chambers."

"It's common for American lawyers to shares offices and secretaries, too."

"A clerk is more of a business and office manager than a secretary. The clerk receives a commission from the fees earned by his barristers. It's not considered good manners for a barrister to negotiate for fees, so it's left up to the clerk to work out a fee from the instructing solicitor. And it's not uncommon for a clerk who works for a number of barristers to make more money than the individual barristers he administers to."

"Wow. American lawyers are forbidden to share fees with non-lawyers."

"Traditionally, the solicitor sends over the brief, with the fee to be paid noted on it. The solicitor is responsible for paying the fee and a barrister cannot sue to obtain it. The solicitor must protect himself by getting advance payment from the client. Obviously, not all the old traditions are still in general use."

"What about female barristers? Any taboos?"

"I'd say female barristers are expected to dress as much as possible like a man, at least from the outside, wearing the wig and robe designed for men and dark, conservative feminine clothing underneath. Barristers do not shake hands with each other because we are all presumed to know one another. Nor do we use first names or make use of a 'Mr.' or 'Mrs.' designation. I am simply 'Hall' and Anthony is 'Trent' in the courthouse hallways. A curious tradition that I believe devolves from the days when the barristers were lads together at public school."

"Public schools being the snooty private boarding schools attended by your country's elite."

He smiled tolerantly at her. "A fair enough characterization—when given by an outspoken woman from the rather uncultured western United States. In the courtroom, a fellow barrister is referred to as 'my learned friend,' while a solicitor is simply 'my friend.'"

"How about the judge?"

"He is generally 'Your Lordship' in groveling, whining terms such as, 'May it please, Your Lordship.'"

They both burst into laughter at his whining intonation.

"Now you have me making fun of our proud traditions," Hall said.

He told her about other requirements for barristers: They must ac-

❖

cept all cases in which a proper professional fee is tendered. "One can't refuse a case for social, political, racial, or other prejudices. We call this the cab-rank principle, as if barristers are lined up at the curb like taxi-cabs, taking the next fare that steps up." By the same token, a barrister ordinarily can't be sued for negligence in his courtroom performance, due to the fact that a barrister is not privileged to refuse to take a case and in some cases he has a duty to the court that transcends the duty to the client.

"There's an interesting aspect to your legal system that we don't have in the States."

"Yes?"

"Class distinctions in a democratic society. I think it was your George Orwell who wrote in *Animal Farm* that all animals are equal, but some are more equal. It isn't just a matter of awarding different levels of professional competency, like your Q.C.s and juniors, but by the way people dress and are positioned in the courtroom—the award-ing of knighthoods and peerages are the most obvious distinctions. All pigs are not equal in America, but we do a better job of pretending that we're completely democratic."

"Titles are awarded for distinguished careers that benefit the na-tion," Hall said, "just as your nation awards civilian medals. There's one other tradition you should know, the most important one," he said. "It's a man's world, this arena of courtroom advocates, and it's not for the faint of heart. Despite all the courteous, old-school-ties veneer, there is nothing a barrister enjoys more than bloodying opposing counsel, just as he once did when they were boys on the soccer field at Eton or Har-row. Women are pushing their way into it, but it's a competitive arena dominated by men and it feeds off of bursts of testosterone."

Marlowe smiled. "Have you ever heard of a monkey trap used to capture monkeys for the cook pot?"

"No, I can't say that I have."

"In the tropics, the natives cut the top off a coconut shell so that the opening is just barely big enough for a monkey to stick its hand into the shell. They fasten the shell on a branch so it can't be removed and put some peanuts inside. A monkey comes along and sticks its hand into the small opening and grabs a fistful of peanuts. When the monkey tries to remove its hand, it can't pull it out because the opening's too small."

"Can't it just let go of the peanuts and remove its hand?"

"It can, but it won't because it's stuck in its ways and won't let go. Instead it struggles frantically to remove its hand, while still clutching the peanuts. It's still holding on to the nuts when the native who set the trap comes back and carts it off to the stew pot." She paused and met Philip Hall's eye. "And that's what happens to men who can't let go of their nuts long enough to realize the world has changed—they get their asses burned."

34

❖

Legal London spreads out from Holborn to near the Thames. The area contains most of the city's barristers and solicitors, the Royal Courts of Justice on the Strand where civil cases and appeals were dealt with, and the Old Bailey, the central criminal court building on Newgate Street.

Marlowe asked, "Why do they call it the Old Bailey?"

"The answer depends upon whom you ask. I've been told it's named after a street that runs nearby. And that the walls of a castle and the inner court were called baileys. I suspect both versions have some merit."

"It's certainly the most famous courthouse in the world."

"It was originally on the site of a prison, Newgate Gaol, one of the most notorious prisons in English history. Commoners were held at Newgate before they were executed. The area of the jail and courthouse was often the scene of hangings and other 'public entertainment.'"

"As opposed to the Tower, where nobility were held?"

"Yes, exactly so. Like so much of our United Kingdom, it is steeped in history, some of it quite bloody, of course. The walls must have some interesting tales to tell, I should say. They tried *Lady Chatterly's Lover* there, you know."

❖

"Really? I thought that was a book, fiction."

"Sorry, an old barrister's joke. Yes, the characters are fictional, but the book went on trial as an offense against public morality back around 1960 or thereabouts. One of my law school instructors had been a clerk who assisted the prosecution of the case. He said they lost the case because defense counsel argued to the jury that it wasn't an immoral book, but badly written, the sort of rubbish that one wouldn't permit one's servants to read."

"That's a wonderful argument. It's something like the one used in another Old Bailey case, the trial of Leonard Voe for the murder of Emily French."

"I'm not familiar with the case. Who was lead counsel?"

"Charles Laughton."

"Laughton? I don't think—" He chuckled. "Touché. *Witness for the Prosecution,* Charles Laughton, the actor, I've heard it's a fine movie."

"You haven't seen it?"

"No, I'm not much for the cinema. My wife saw the play and recommended it."

"Shame on you. The greatest legal thriller ever made, from a play written by Agatha Christie, your country's most famous mystery writer. Laughton did a incredible job as a defense attorney in a case with more twists than a roller coaster. It should be mandatory viewing for every prospective trial lawyer. You should show it the next time law students do dinners at your Inn of Court."

"Ah, Barrister Marlowe James, we come again to the discord between how I view the law and how you view it. I see the courtroom as a place where well-established legal principles are applied to facts in dispute and debated by learned counsel before judges seeped in precedent. You see it as a drama."

"Tell me about some of the other famous Old Bailey cases," she said.

"Well, probably the most famous morality case, even more controversial than *Lady Chatterly's Lover,* was the Oscar Wilde case."

"He was tried for being gay, wasn't he?"

"Actually, he was accused of being what they called in those days a sodomite, but I don't recall if he was tried specifically for that crime or some general offense against public decency."

❖

"It was a sensational trial, wasn't it?"

"Absolutely. I believe the Victorians were titillated by the scandalous references to Mr. Wilde's buggery of young men employed by the telegraph office. The boys would earn a bit more in their free time satisfying the prurient interests of Mr. Wilde and his friends than they did delivering messages during work hours."

He told her about other famous—or infamous—Old Bailey trials:

At a much earlier time, nearly two centuries before Wilde's trial, Daniel Defoe, the author of *Moll Flanders* and *Robinson Crusoe,* experienced the justice system, being tried in Old Bailey and imprisoned at Newgate for political dissent. He later had his immoral Moll Flanders born in the prison.

William Joyce, known during World War II as "Lord Haw-Haw," was tried in Old Bailey and later hanged for his anti-British radio broadcasts for Goebbels, Hitler's propaganda minister.

"Why was he called Lord Haw-Haw?"

"I believe it had to do with the sneering manner of his speech."

Dennis Nielsen, a butcher in the army, was sentenced to life imprisonment after killing fifteen times. Beginning in the late seventies, he picked up young men off the street, often for homosexual activities, and murdered them in his home. Before burying them in his garden, he often dressed the dead bodies up and had sex with them, including oral copulation.

Hall told her the Nielsen story apologetically, a proper Britisher who didn't think a woman should hear about such things, Marlowe thought.

She noticed in his recital of Old Bailey horrors he omitted one of the most notorious, that of Fred and Rosemary West, who together tortured, raped, and murdered about a dozen young women, including their own daughters. She had read about the case. Like Nielsen, the Wests preferred burying the bodies in their own garden. Rosemary, not the nicest of mothers, held down her daughters for their father to rape them. She told her bound-and-gagged eight-year-old as her father raped her that they were only making sure that she would be able to satisfy a husband when she grew up. Another daughter, a teenager, was murdered after she complained to a friend that she was being raped.

❖

Fred hanged himself in jail and Rosemary was sentenced to life imprisonment.

Back in the sixties, the Kray brothers, twins, one of whom was a homosexual, were the two most ruthless gangsters in the country. They were tried and convicted for two gangland killings in the longest murder trial in English history. They were sentenced to life imprisonment.

"Ruth Ellis, on the other hand, had one of the shortest murder trials," Hall said.

Ruth gunned down her lover David Blakely on a London street. Jealous, humiliated by Blakely's treatment after a lifetime of being beaten and betrayed by men, her system fired up from booze, Ruth grabbed a gun, left the house, found Blakely on a street in the Hampstead District, and opened fire, hitting him four or five times.

"I'm afraid that the jury didn't find that Blakely deserved to die for love gone wrong. My best recollection is that the trial lasted only about a day and a half, including jury deliberation, which was all of about twenty minutes. She was hanged just a few weeks later. Justice moved astonishingly quick in the case—it was only about three months from the time she pulled the trigger to the rope around her neck."

"Did her lawyer argue provocation, a heat of passion?"

"To no avail. And to much grumbling around the world. My hazy recollection is that her lawyers tried to argue that Ruth was so consumed by jealousy, she couldn't premeditate. The judge refused the defense, properly so, but did instruct the jury on the difference between murder and manslaughter. It was about ten miles from where she grabbed her gun to where she pulled the trigger. The law then—and *now*"—he gave Marlowe a meaningful look—"is that the time it took her to get to the killing site negated the heat of passion."

"I disagree, of course. I don't believe people are capable of turning on and off their passions like a light switch."

"Worse so, here in chilly old Britain, I'm afraid. As one French paper put it, unless it arises out of cricket or betting, passion to us British is regarded as a shameful disease. The case did, however, bring one good result. There was so much outcry over the execution, Ruth became the last woman hanged in England."

"I'm sure she got great solace from that," Marlowe said.

❖

———

FROM THE STREET, THE famed criminal courts building was impressive, a great, towering monument of gray, with a dome on top that gave the building the look of an American state capitol building, but was capped by a golden statue of Justice holding her scales and sword.

Marlowe wondered what the goddess thought about the way modern media turned celebrity trials into a feeding frenzy. Legions of the press—*a plague of locusts,* Marlowe thought—were waiting at the steps leading into the building. She took a deep breath before she went up the steps with Philip Hall at her side, smiling but not responding to the shouted questions. The police had a roped-off corridor up the steps for people with court business.

As they passed barristers, Marlowe asked, "Will I be expected to wear a wig and robe?"

"No, you are excused from the requirement. I know you must think it's quite old-fashioned."

"Actually, I think it's quite dramatic—a lawyer often deals with life-and-death situations, usually arising from violence, great emotions, and even pathos. The garments emphasize the dramatic nature of their calling, just as a surgeon's mask and smock emphasize medical drama."

They paused at the doors. Hall raised his eyebrows. "You haven't met one of the stars of your drama, yet."

"The judge?"

"Oh, I think you'll find the judge to be a typical character actor, definitely a supporting role, not center stage. The star I'm talking about is the prosecutor. Whether he is a hero or a villain depends upon where you sit in the courtroom."

❖

35

❖

Dutton stood at the window of a second-floor office down the street from the courthouse and watched Marlowe and Hall exit the limo and march up the stairs to the courthouse. The office was a secretarial agency and Dutton had once dated the head stenographer, but like so many of his past romantic entanglements, the relationship had ended with bad feelings and a blood vengeance.

"I should shove you out that window," she told Dutton.

"It's okay, luv, I know you only say that because you are still pining for me. We should get together some night and talk about old times."

"An old cock like you only has one thing on his mind when he wants to get together for old times."

She couldn't have been more than twenty-five. He had less than twenty years on her. "Old cock? Do I strike you as an older man?"

"You strike me as the bastard who stole the notes I took in dictation from that Foreign Office chap and drugged me to get your stick up my dress."

He glanced back at her. "I paid for the notes and you were happy enough to jack up your dress for a bonus."

❖

"That's not what I told my husband." She examined her fingernails. "He has a bad temper, if you get my meaning. Works all night as a bouncer for a club and has to put up with his wife being taken advantage of when he's gone. If he runs into you, he's going to put a cosh across your bone box."

Dutton rubbed his lips. A cosh was a blackjack. A bone box was his mouth. She hadn't been that good a poke to justify getting his teeth knocked out.

He looked back out the window and ignored the woman as she gave him graphic details of the harm her husband did to another man who had "drugged" her.

The more he saw of Marlowe James—and this time he got a bird's-eye view of her in person instead of on the telly—the more he got a little tingling at the back of his neck that told him that she knew something he needed.

He paused by the stenographer's desk on the way out. "I'm on a hot one, Megan. When I cash in on it, I'm going to send you and your hubby to the south of Spain for a whole month. Tell him that."

"We can leave him home and you and I can go."

Yeah, that would work, Dutton thought, as he went out the door and down the corridor. *I'll have to do that the next time I feel suicidal.*

He called his unfaithful editor as soon as he hit the street and started walking, keeping an eye out for a taxi.

"There were parts from four bodies," Cohn said, squealing with delight.

He sounded like an excited little girl, Dutton thought. The bigger the body count, the better. Tabloid editors and funeral directors were cut from the same mold.

"It's all hush-hush, not a word can be printed, the Official Secrets Act has been invoked. But we got the inside dope from the coroner's office. Don't you have a personal contact in the office? Can you—"

"She died," Dutton lied. He had never told Cohn he got his information from Howler because of the no-honor-among-thieves theory of tabloid publishing.

"Four bodies," Dutton muttered, "all dressed up in costume. It's insane."

❖

"It's a signature, you know, the sort of thing that you serial killers use to mark your crimes."

"What'd you say?"

"A signature—"

"You serial killers?'"

"Tony, Tony, you know I love you, but think of the story, you're a professional, think of the story. Four bodies makes it a serial killer. Imagine for a moment that you were the killer, or at least that you didn't deny being the killer for a while. You could be calling in, giving your old friend and editor a blow-by-blow account of your moments as you flee the police, your thoughts, fears, rages—imagine the reader's concern. Will he kill again? Who will be next? It would make the Ripper—"

"I'll give you an inside tip into a killer's mind," Dutton said. "You're going to be next!" He hung up.

He cursed the phone, Cohn, and himself as he went down the street with long angry strides. He had screwed up. He could already see the next *Burn* headline: *Crazed Reporter Vows to Murder Editor.*

Parts from four bodies. Grisly stuff, not for the faint at heart, one had to kill four people and then select the parts. Some nutcase sewing together body parts—to create what? *An exhibit!* Of course, that's what it was, it was a ghastly display piece put together by someone who was used to cutting human flesh and bone. Howler fit the bill nicely not only because of his medical skills, but there was showmanship here and his other source of money to support his drug habit came from Madame Tussauds, the wax museum.

He ducked into the Underground. He'd get there faster and cheaper by tube. Madame Tussauds was a short walk from the Baker Street tube station. It wasn't a far stretch for a talented plastic surgeon like Howler to have done piecework reconstructing stiffs at the morgue and putting a human face on wax dummies for the museum. Madame Tussaud herself probably would have made a great plastic surgeon. And having a chamber of horrors would have come naturally to her—she lived in one during a period of her life.

Early in her life, Tussaud had learned in Paris the art of wax modeling from her uncle who had wax museums. During her thirties, she was an art tutor at Versailles to the king's sister, Princess Elizabeth of France. Elizabeth, like both her English namesakes who became queens, was a woman of courage and loyalty, who refused to flee the country and leave her brother, Louis XVI, and his wife, Marie-Antoinette, to face the wrath of the revolution by themselves. The twenty-eight-year-old princess was imprisoned with her royal relatives by the revolutionaries and went bravely to the guillotine during the Reign of Terror.

Because of her unique skills at creating wax images, Madame Tussaud was given the gruesome job of making death masks from those who lost their heads at the guillotine—frequently, the masks were of her friends, including the tragic young princess.

Tussaud left France and came to England in the early 1800s, touring the country for several decades with her collection of wax models before she purchased a permanent home for them near the site of the present museum on Marylebone Road. Dutton hadn't been in the museum since he was a kid, but he still remembered how awed he was at the "life" wax artists were able to put into historical figures.

Dutton avoided the long line of tourists at the museum entrance by showing his press ID. Inside he talked to Mary Rees, the woman who supervised the "reconstructive surgery" and frequently hired Howler to work his magic on faces, making them lifelike.

"Haven't seen him," Mary said, the words making their way out from a mouthful of ham sandwich.

Dutton followed her as she chewed and checked wax forms being readied for an exhibit that showed the Prince of Wales being shot by his wife at the masquerade party.

"When I see him, I'm going to carve my initials on his arse with one of his scalpels," she said. "He's a master at showing pain and shock—I needed him to put the emotion on the prince's face when he first saw the gun and when the bullet struck him. I should have known he'd run out. He gave me a crazy laugh when I first told him about the job. I even stuck my neck out and got him an advance on the job."

Big mistake, Dutton thought. Giving a drug addict an advance produced about the same result as flushing it down the loo. But the woman

❖

probably had no idea Howler was supporting a habit. He wondered what she'd say if he told her Howler was out of carving wax and into human flesh.

"Haven't heard from him, eh?"

"Not a bleedin' word, hasn't even returned the costume."

Dutton's heart skipped a beat. "Costume?"

"Wanted to borrow it, claimed he needed it for a costume party."

"An Elizabethan costume?"

"It was Henry VIII, it was."

That put the nail on the identification of the Westminster exhibit. Dutton had been convincing himself that the secret to the Tudor costume was to be found in a Shakespeare play, but it was now a certainty that it was the old wife-killer himself.

Confirming the costume was old Henry gave a little hop to his step. He started massacring a Herman's Hermits song as he headed for the door. "I'm Henry the Eighth, I am! Henry the Eighth I am!"

As he came out of the door to the museum, Inspector Bram Archer and Sergeant Lois Kramer were coming in.

Archer grinned at him. "This is my lucky day." In a stage whisper he said, "Make a run for it, Dutton, I'll shoot you in the back and you won't have to stand trial."

"My editor will have your—"

"Your editor says you're a mad-dog killer on the loose." Archer grabbed him by the front of his collar and jerked him close enough to smell the steak and kidney pie he'd had for lunch. "Resist, please, just give me one ounce of resistance."

"Fuck you."

Archer tapped him in the stomach, a little nudge, just enough to knock his wind out and urge the bangers he'd had for lunch to come back up. He fought down the urge to puke the sausages on Archer, out of the clear knowledge the police inspector would have ripped off his head if he had.

Sergeant Kramer's mobile police radio went off and she answered the call as Archer cuffed Dutton and took him to a police car. He shoved Dutton against the car and did a heavy-handed pat-down.

"He didn't kill anyone," Kramer told Archer.

❖

"I'll be damned if he didn't."

"They were all dead, the bodies at the Abbey."

"Of course they were dead, after he hacked their heads off."

"No, really dead, as in past tense, they were stolen from the morgue. They know who did it."

"What are you talking about?"

Dutton had the same question in mind.

Kramer threw up her hands. "They were parts from dead bodies. A morgue employee pinched them."

Archer appeared ready to spontaneously combust. Dutton could read the frustration on the police officer's face, the man wanted so much to add Dutton's head to the Abbey list. The radio went off again. Kramer answered it and handed it to Archer, jerking her head to the side. "Better take it over there."

"Don't let this bugger out of your sight," Archer told her.

"Who's the perpetrator?" Dutton asked Kramer after Archer moved away.

"Official business. You can read about it in the papers when the story's scooped by someone else."

"Do they have him in custody?"

"No comment."

Dutton nodded. They didn't have Howler. "So, what'd this ghoulish character do? Go shopping for body parts in the morgue, pushing a shopping cart along, chopping off a piece here and there?"

She grinned with malice. "Since you know so much about it, looks like you were in on it. We'll hear that story from you, won't we, now? The inspector will want to sweat out the truth from you, why you and your morgue mate stole the body parts. Did you have sex with them?"

"Actually, luv, you were the last dead body I rogered."

She stepped closer and was about to add to Dutton's pain level but stopped on Archer's command. "Take off the cuffs," he told her.

"What? We can still get him on half a dozen charges, breaking and entering, accessory—"

"Uncuff him."

As Kramer took off the cuffs, Archer said politely, "You are free to go, Mr. Dutton. I'm sure you understand why the police have to be

❖

concerned—you were in a national treasure at night, that sort of thing. Have a good day, sir."

Kramer's mouth dropped as far as Dutton's did. Dutton wasted no time putting distance between himself and the two officers.

What the hell was that all about?

The question chased itself in Dutton's head as he hurried toward the tube station. Archer wouldn't be polite to him even if the copper was hanging from the side of Big Ben and needed a hand up.

It was that second police radio message. Archer had been told to stand down from arresting Dutton. There was only one reason he'd get an order like that: *cover-up.*

Arresting him would put the Abbey mystery back on the front pages and open it up for him to insist upon answers. This way they could release an official statement that the matter was "under investigation." But arresting a reporter was sure to put the heat back on.

They obviously didn't have Howler. Howler was two bob short of a quid from long-term drug use, but he still had the clever deviousness of chemically induced paranoia. *Bleedin' clever bastard,* Dutton thought. Howler stole body parts and erected his gruesome display—why? Invited Dutton to it—why? Now he had the government covering his tracks—why?

Why would a mockup of Henry VIII send the powers-that-be into such a titter that the Official Secrets Act was invoked?

Dutton's next stop was Howler's apartment.

"He scurried out like a rat with a dog after it," a wino who fit into the neighborhood told Dutton. The old man had been sitting on the steps nursing a bottle in a paper bag when Dutton arrived. "The Bill came by a couple hours later looking for him."

"Inspector Archer? Big guy, bad temper? Female partner?"

"These coppers were not regulars, you know what I mean."

"Special Branch?"

"I saw guns, they're the only ones that carry 'em, isn't that the truth."

While most officers weren't armed on their regular duties, Dutton knew it was a misconception to think that the London police didn't have access to guns. Special Branch were emergency squads. They carried guns and used them in incidents involving IRA terrorists or other violence. But the timing wasn't right for Archer to have been at the apartment with the officers. He was still back at the Abbey about the time the police came looking under the rug for Howler. From the sounds of it, Howler had been expecting them and left for another rat hole before they arrived.

Interesting, Dutton thought. Howler had expected the police. What did he do, take an ad out in the personals telling the coppers where to look when they needed a suspect for the Abbey job? And he had skipped out and left Dutton to be grilled. *Red herring. The cagey bastard threw me to the police so he'd have more time for his getaway.*

It sounded right to Dutton, but his instincts told him he was still missing pieces about why Howler had brought him into his chamber-of-horrors show. It would have been easier to use one of his brain-dead druggie pals.

Dutton gave the man the price of a bottle. He was walking away when the wino called after him. "Grindstaff, that's a name I heard, one of the coppers was named Grindstaff."

"Did Howler say anything to you about being in trouble?"

The wino shrugged. "The whole world is in trouble. But he did say he was getting a bunch of money for a nice piece of work."

"That's all, just money for work?"

The man thought for a moment. "He said he was going to be rich . . . if he lived."

"If he lived?"

"Isn't that the truth, we'd all be rich if we lived long enough, isn't that the truth."

Dutton left the wino redundantly pondering the mysteries of life on the stoop with his bottle. He walked for ten minutes and popped into a pub, got a pint, and settled into a dark corner with his mobile phone.

He found the notion that the Abbey escapade might have a financial motivation intriguing. Howler had one driving force in his life—money to feed his habit. Years ago, he was caught trying to sell his own kid to feed his real love, the white lady called cocaine, after his marriage broke up.

Dutton called a *Burn* source who worked in the clerical pool at New

❖

Scotland Yard. "Check your computer, luv, I need to know the assignment of an officer named Grindstaff. Probably Special Branch or RPS."

He got his answer in less than a minute and it surprised the hell out of him.

"RPS," was the reply. Royal Protection Service. That tracked with the phone number Howler's mother had. It would fit with the wino's belief that they were armed. Like Special Branch, they carried weapons.

Dutton whistled through his teeth and tapped his phone on the table as he added up the score:

Howler got an invitation to the prince's ball.

Uh-huh.

Howler stuck Henry VIII and the head of one of Henry's wives in the church where monarchs are crowned and not a few buried.

Mondo bizarre.

The Royal Protection coppers came storming after Howler with weapons drawn.

Now, that was just bleedin' nuts and it led to only one conclusion: Howler knew something the Royals wanted to keep under the rug. Laundry dirty enough to keep newspapers and the telly people from disclosing secrets that the government didn't want revealed.

It kept coming back to one thing in Dutton's mind: Howler had a piece of evidence that the Prince of Wales wanted to get rid of his troublesome wife, just as one of his predecessors, old Henry, did. Only she plugged him first.

Dutton looked up at the telly on the wall. A news broadcast during a break in a soccer game showed the scene he'd witnessed earlier, Marlowe James, the hired gun from America, going up the steps of the Old Bailey. It occurred to Dutton that not only was the American attorney the keeper of the secrets, but she probably kept them on the hard drive of her computer.

Dutton toasted her with his pint of brew. "Marlowe, me luv, our stars are about to cross."

❖

36

❖

Old Bailey

"Is this the courtroom we will be in for the trial?" Marlowe asked Philip Hall.

"No, the princess will be tried in a larger one."

They were seated in the gallery above the action on the courtroom floor. A rape case was in progress on the floor of the courtroom below them. A police officer on the stand was being questioned by V. C. Desai, a Crown Prosecutor.

"What do you think of our prosecutor?" Hall whispered.

She couldn't judge the man's legal talents in five minutes of mundane courtroom action—he was asking about Desai's persona.

"Definitely of star quality, much too dynamic to be a character actor. He dominates the stage."

Desai's looks were theatrical. And Marlowe instantly understood Hall's earlier remark that inferred the prosecutor could play hero or villain. He had that much stretch as an actor. The opposing barrister, whom Hall identified as a junior by his robe, was not in Desai's class, either as an advocate or as a movie idol.

Desai was of Indian ancestry. "Both his parents are London-born," Hall said, after they left the gallery when the court went into recess.

❖

Hall went on to explain that the fact that Desai was a third-generation Londoner, bright, well educated, and spoke the queen's language more precisely than a BBC announcer, did not stop an occasional query from strangers as to how long he'd been in the country.

"An elderly barrister from the old school," Hall said, "the school that didn't have people of color in it, once made the mistake of calling Desai a sand nigger, rather rudely, to his face."

"I hope Desai punched his lights out."

"Actually, he did worse. The word was put out that no client of the barrister would get a plea bargain and that Desai would personally try every case the man brought to court and see that the defendant was maxed out at sentencing. Desai is the best advocate in the Crown Prosecutor's Office, he's never lost a case. Since most criminals have overwhelming evidence against them and want an attorney who can get them a good deal, it was a disaster for the barrister. The last I heard, the barrister now works for an insurance company."

Hall told her that the prosecutor had grown up in a poor slum area of London, and that when he first came to work for the Crown Prosecutor's Office there had been rumors that his mother had been a prostitute.

"Desai is sharp, very much so. He came from poor circumstance and had to struggle twice as hard as anyone around him. His left arm is shriveled, a result of a childhood injury that wasn't properly cared for. I'm sure it must remind him of his struggles against the Establishment each morning when he dresses."

"He's anti-Establishment?"

"He's quiet about his feelings, isn't known to really harbor any overt political tendencies, but quite by accident when I was in his office a few months ago, I noticed literature from a socialist party on his desk. One could see why he would be attracted to a political theory that espouses, however falsely, egalitarianism. Hardworking, intelligent, ambitious, he's of a skin color that keeps many doors closed to him, no matter how we pretend that everyone gets an equal opportunity. Desai is no fool, he has to deep down resent the system that holds his humble beginnings and skin color against him. It's the impression of the committee that Desai harbors anti-monarchy feelings and that he may use

❖

the trial to smear and ridicule the princess, and through her the queen herself."

Hall gave her a sideways glance. "I understand you had to work your way though college."

"College and law school, waiting on tables. I guess you can say that I have a few anti-Establishment feelings myself."

Desai was about forty, with a youthful face and prematurely stark-white, silky hair. With his narrow face and thin lips, he reminded Marlowe of a bird of prey, a proud hawk. Bright and ambitious, Hall called him. "He can be unscrupulous when it comes to winning. Very much believes in the advocacy system of justice—the courtroom as a gladiatorial match. I sometimes feel that he seeks redress for whatever wrongs have been done to him by society by winning in the courtroom. Most prosecutors have an attitude that justice must be served and that their job is to put the facts before a jury. If the jury finds for the defendant, justice is still served, and they have performed their duties. My impression of Desai is that he equates winning with justice served, somewhat like playing God."

"Playing God?"

"Rather, in a manner of speaking. I think his view of the advocate is an old-fashioned, medieval view. I'm sure you recall that the adversarial system of justice rose from trial by combat in which guilt or innocence was decided by a test of arms. Clergy, children, women, and persons disabled by age or sickness had the right to nominate champions to fight on their behalf. The theory was that God intervened on the side of the right, that it was the judgment of God that determined the winner. So Desai, in his mind, is the right hand of God."

"He has to be," Marlowe said.

"What do you mean?"

"His left hand is crippled."

37

❖

The princess again greeted Marlowe with a firm handshake, but she was not as vibrant as she had been the first time Marlowe met with her. Her eyes were puffy, either from crying or a lack of sleep, Marlowe thought.

"I need to ask you something," she told Marlowe, as soon as the two were seated and coffee and tea was served. "I want to know what you think of me."

Marlowe stared at the sparkling blue eyes of the princess for a moment. "I haven't really had enough time to get to know you well enough to answer that question."

"We all get first impressions, don't we? After hearing about my undistinguished academic record, I think we can go beyond a first impression."

"Well, I . . . I think that you're not really asking me what I think of you, but rather seeking some kind of approval."

The princess clutched her coffee cup tightly with both hands and looked Marlowe directly in the eye. "Why do you say that?"

"My feeling is that you tend to seek approval from others. I suspect it's related to your belief that you were a disappointment to your

❖

family, starting with that business of not being a boy."

"Do I come across as someone who is buttering up people because I need their pats? Like a puppy dog brushing up against one's leg?"

Marlowe didn't want her answer to be unkind or dishonest, but she also didn't to lie. She chose her words slowly and carefully, not quite sure what the princess's reaction would be. "You come across as someone who is kind and considerate, witty and spirited, with your greatest strength lying in people skills rather than academic skills." She let that sink in for a moment and then added, "But you also come across as someone who is overly concerned about what other people think of you. Now, you can beat yourself with a horsehair whip or we can go on with our discussions about your past."

The princess's jaw worked for a moment as she struggled with an impulse to blow at Marlowe—then she burst into a loud laugh.

"I see why you have Trent and his lot in a tither. You are blunt, aren't you?"

"I have to be, in my profession. Would you prefer I lie?"

"No, that's what they're doing, or if not that, at least not telling me all the truth."

Marlowe wasn't surprised at her answer. She didn't dislike Trent, she hardly knew the man, but she didn't quite trust him, either.

"They think I'm erratic, hiring you and all that. They're worried I might fire them and hire another firm. Wouldn't that take the air out of their tires, being booted off the case?"

"I'm sure it would." She took out the pad of paper with her notes on it. "Let's continue where we left off yesterday. You were eighteen and had moved into your first apartment in London."

"Right. The flat was my coming-of-age present from my parents, physically coming of age, not mentally, of course," she said with a smile. "But anyway, there I was, eighteen and all on my own in London. I was looking forward to it. I invited three of my girlfriends to share my flat with me. I suppose you can say that I had a quiet life in that first year on my own. I didn't smoke or drink and wasn't into partying. Read those romances I get criticized so much for, watched a bit of telly, sat around and talked to friends. The people I related with were pretty much out of the same coop."

❖

"Formal, restrained, rich?" Marlowe asked.

"Yes, but there's also something called breeding. I suppose a psychologist would say we were trained like puppy dogs to all bark alike. We dressed pretty much alike, nothing extravagant unless someone special appeared in our lives, dated the same sort of men, clean-cut, well mannered, although I really wasn't into dating. It was considered to be vulgar to be pretentious or ostentatious."

"What did you do for fun?"

"Girl things, I suppose, maybe even silly things sometimes. We might ring up people with funny names and crack a joke about it or go out and ring doorbells in the dead of night. If a boy let us down by not showing up for a date or not treating us with the respect we demanded, we would throw eggs and flour on his car. You look a bit puzzled. Didn't you do things like this when you were young?"

"Not beyond the age of twelve."

"Is that what I did? Acted like a juvenile? I suppose they were silly things, now that I think about it."

"I'm not judging you, I'm still trying to understand you so I can explain you to a jury. Actually, the things you did sound like harmless fun. They remind me of friends who live in a farm community in Utah and whose children go to barn dances and hay rides. What you described is a joy of innocence you rarely see today among young people. Teenagers nowadays know more about drugs, sex, and rock and roll than naive pranks."

"What did you do when you were eighteen?"

"I was working as a waitress in a greasy spoon."

"Why a waitress?"

"It's a job a woman can get when she doesn't have training for anything else. It's not easy, you're on your feet for eight hours, taking flak from customers and the cook, putting up with people who think their three-dollar special should taste like pheasant under glass, warding off men with wandering hands, letting them know they better keep them in their pockets if they still want to have all their fingers but not so firmly that it kills a tip."

"It sounds perfectly horrid."

"It's survival when you need it."

❖

"When you don't get a three-bedroom flat for your coming-out present, is that what you mean?"

"We came from different backgrounds. If I had your upbringing, I'm sure I would have been one of those girls getting an apartment."

"I was an immature girl doing silly things while I waited to get married and be taken care of for the rest of my life—that's what you're thinking, isn't it?" The princess held up her hands to ward off Marlowe's protest. "I'm sorry, I'll go on. There I was, eighteen, and as my swim instructor would have put it, I was treading water rather than completing laps. But they were happy times, thinking back now, the happiest I've ever had. I even took a cooking class. My mother encouraged it. I suppose it was part of the finishing school I never finished. I learned how to make borscht and yummy chocolates and ended up with a few more pounds on me than when I started."

"Did the added pounds bother you?"

"No, at that time it was just some extra weight, not something that dominated my life."

"Did you have any future plans for life? Any game plan for finding a suitable husband?"

"Not really, I just knew I had to keep myself tidy for what lay ahead."

"What do you mean by that?"

"I had to remain a virgin."

Marlowe cleared her throat. "Well, there's certainly nothing wrong with being a virgin before marriage, though it does sound a bit medieval, the husband showing the wedding guests the bloodstains on the sheets the next morning."

"My God, that's a dreadful thing to say. That isn't at all what I meant."

Marlowe shook her head. "We seem to be constantly on a collision course. I've interviewed dozens of women in cases and I've never acted like an ax murderer, but I seem to bludgeon you every time I open my mouth."

"I feel there is something between us."

"It's just the formality and restraint of being British colliding with my brash Americanism. Sometimes when I'm in a restaurant district back home, like Chinatown or North Beach, I might knock on a café window and with hand signs ask the people sitting at the window table if the food is good. It works there, but when I tried that here last night, the people at the table just gaped at me through the window like I was crazy."

"They probably thought you were a whore soliciting, don't you think?"

"My God, I hope not. Okay, so you said you had to keep yourself tidy for what lay ahead. Did you expect to marry the prince?"

"No, of course not, how would I know he'd be attracted to me?"

"But you say you had to keep yourself tidy for what lay ahead. That's an indication that you did not expect to lead an ordinary life."

"I don't quite agree that being a virgin is as medieval as you believe."

"No, it's not the virgin part I find puzzling, that's just having good old-fashioned values. It's the fact that you saw something out of the ordinary down the road."

"I don't follow you. I don't see what that has to do with the case."

"I've heard criticism that you came into the marriage with the romanticized notion of marrying the prince because of his position rather than for himself and that you became disenchanted when you discovered being married to him was no fairy tale come true. It's a theme that the prosecutor will push, so we need to be prepared to deal with it."

"It's rubbish. It's completely false. I did love him for himself. I may have had idealistic and, yes, even romanticized notions about love and marriage, but not about marrying a prince." She was quiet, then said, "To a young girl reading a fashion magazine, the notion of dating a prince would be titillating. But you have to remember, I spent a lot of time in the sandbox with his two younger brothers."

"But not your husband."

"Obviously not—my husband was an adult when I was a little girl. But my point is that I was not infatuated with the notion of marrying a prince. Marrying a Royal would have been considered a good marriage by women of my background, but not an unheard-of one. The fact that he was the Prince of Wales and that I would be the next queen certainly entered my mind. Marriage is not something I would have entered without love."

❖

It was too great a leap of faith for Marlowe to believe that marrying a prince and becoming a queen wouldn't be an earthshaking experience for any woman. "I don't want to beat a dead horse, but we still have to deal with this issue because the prosecutor definitely will. You said you had to keep yourself tidy. Isn't the implication that you wanted to be chosen as the prince's bride? Why else would you keep yourself a virgin?"

"For my husband, whoever he might turn out to be."

Marlowe finally got it—the innocent heroines in the romance novels that the princess read were *virgins* ravaged by dashing heroes. She wanted a fairy-tale marriage. It also struck her that in terms of the mores in which the princess was raised in, the woman's sense of romance was completely unrealistic, not just old-fashioned but so fantastic, it was hard for Marlowe to comprehend how they got into the head of a young woman growing up during the turmoil and excesses of the sexual revolution. She wondered if the princess had also given thought beyond romance to the practical demands of being married to a prince.

"Were you aware of the responsibilities that came with marrying a prince, what role you would need to play?"

"Of course, yes, but I also thought I would get help from my husband and others in the system. What I wasn't prepared for was all the sudden media attention. It was all very daunting—terrifying, really."

"When did you first start interacting with your future husband?"

"I attended his thirtieth birthday party. I was just seventeen, but my sister had been dating him off and on for a couple of years. Following that, there was another social gathering a few months later. But it was at a barbecue at a country estate when I was turning nineteen that he took notice of me. We were seated on a bale of hay and I told him how forlorn he had looked the prior year when he had attended the funeral of Earl Mountbatten, his great-uncle who had been assassinated by the IRA. I told him that he had looked so lonely that he should have someone looking after him."

"And what was his reaction?"

"Quite strange. He practically leaped on me, talking to me about how he felt about the earl's death. After that, we began to date."

"What was it like to date him?"

She giggled. "I had to call him 'sir.'"

❖

"Sir?"

"Well, you have to remember he was the heir to the throne. Besides being the Heir Apparent, he was Prince of Wales, Duke of Cornwall, Duke of Rothesay, Earl of Carrick, Earl of Chester, Baron of Renfrew, Lord of the Isles, and Great Steward of Scotland. Isn't that a mouthful?"

"Very impressive."

"Even though we were dating, the formalities had to be maintained." The princess cast her eyes downward and then looked up at Marlowe. "If you're wondering whether our romance was fiery, I confess that the formalities had to be maintained there, too. We were not alone very often. He maintained a circle of close friends, there were always servants hovering around, and of course the Royal Protection officers lurk about."

"Tell me about his friends."

"Frankly, I found them intimidating. All of them were older than me, of course. I always had the impression that they had little respect for me as a person, for my opinions. They were better educated than me, but that did not make them better people."

"You didn't like his friends?"

"They didn't accept me as an intellectual equal, they treated me like I was the prince's toy. They would name-drop people and concepts knowing that I wouldn't be familiar with them. It was done very subtly and was humiliating. No, I didn't like them, they were always over the prince like a bad rash and condescending toward me, but they were tame compared to the newshounds.

"The media people—the rat pack, as I call them—were animals, the hounds of hell constantly snapping at my heels. They came at me from all angles, recording my every move. I had no peace. I couldn't leave the house without the camera rolling. They even rented a flat across the street from mine that would give them a view of my bedroom window. I can't tell you what it was like. They got on top of buildings and peered over fences with binoculars, hired helicopters to spy on me when I was on a country estate, hurtled questions at me constantly, shouting them at me every time I stepped outside. One moment I was a nineteen-year-old egg-and-flouring a boy's car for standing me up on a date, and the next I was an international phenomenon. I tried to be nice, answered

❖

questions in the hopes they would leave me alone, but nothing helped. They really didn't want ordinary pictures, what they wanted was to catch me doing something compromising. Even scratching my nose was a sensation."

"You didn't get any help from anyone?

"No, no guidance from anyone, neither in dealing with the news-hounds nor in the Royals' quirky traditions. I was invited to Balmoral, the Queen's castle in Scotland, and I knew nothing about how to act. One poor guest was yelled at just for trying to sit in a chair last sat in by Queen Victoria.

"My husband was not a receptive person toward other people's weaknesses. He had not been brought up to be empathetic. He was strong himself. He had to be, being the crown prince was not an easy job, whether it was some bully at school who wanted to be able to say he knocked him off his feet or an IRA assassin who wanted to put a bullet in his head. I soon found that I was on my own and I didn't know how to handle it.

"Right after the engagement was announced, I went off to Australia for ten days with my mother and stepfather. I pined for him, called him every day, but he never returned the calls. Finally I got exasperated and asked his secretary if I had to make an appointment to speak to my fiancé. When I returned, one of his aides brought me a bouquet of flowers. No note attached."

"This was right after you got engaged?"

"Yes. It made me wonder if I wasn't making a mistake. I spoke to my mother and father and to my friends and the opinion was universal that the prince was very busy and I was being overly sensitive. Do you think I was being too sensitive?"

"You were nineteen years old and in love. I don't think it's being too sensitive to want your fiancé to shower you with love."

"I ended up being the one to apologize for him not calling me. It always came down to that, that he would do something that got me upset and I would show my displeasure and end up begging his forgiveness. I was so confused, I thought that it was just me, that I was immature and didn't understand how more worldly people acted. They stuck me away in Buckingham Palace to prepare for the wedding—you know, select the gown and jewelry and my wardrobe and all that. It would take months of preparation."

"It must have been a very busy and hectic time."

"Yes, it was, but I can't tell you how alone I was there. The place was full of dead energy, like heavy air. It was so depressing. Instead of wild embraces with my lover, I was left alone when I wasn't being measured and sized. I felt like I had been locked up in a museum. I found myself crying at night, lying in bed and feeling sorry for myself. But it all paled in comparison to discovering there were three of us in the marriage."

"Three of you?"

"My husband's first love, and ultimately, I was to discover, his only true love."

"An old girlfriend."

"More than that, his soul mate, if his actions are to be judged. I suppose I was naive in that area. I didn't have any boyfriends, so I had no one to compare him with. The woman is more than a friend, she's his confidante. The fact that I was married to him and that she was married to someone else didn't seem to bother the two of them."

"Are you saying they kept up their relationship even after your marriage?"

"It wasn't just a matter of keeping up their relationship—I don't know when it actually became sexual, if that's what you mean. It was the way she was shoved down my throat right from the beginning. I hadn't twigged on to it before the marriage. I discovered very soon after the ceremony at St. Paul's that my marriage was overcrowded."

She handed Marlowe sheets of paper. "This is what I remember about my honeymoon. Some women would have enjoyed a boat trip with several hundred men, but to me it was the honeymoon from hell."

❖

The Prince took her by the hand and danced with her. He would dance with no other maiden, and never let loose of her hand, and if anyone else came to invite her, he said, "This is my partner."

—*CINDERELLA*

38

❖

In her room, Marlowe read the princess's remembrances.

Royal Yacht *Britannia*

I stood on the deck of the *Britannia* with the wind blowing in my face. It was late afternoon and we were off the warm coast of southern Spain. We had sailed through the Strait of Gibraltar and were not far from that tall rock that rose from the sea and was such a bone of contention between the British and the Spanish. I leaned against the railing and closed my eyes, letting the late afternoon breeze caress me. My marriage was still only days old and this moment with Europe on one side and North Africa on the other was a rare moment when I could be alone with my thoughts since the majestic ceremony at St. Paul's.

So many thoughts swirled in my head, I had a hard time concentrating. I was confused and distraught. My nerves were raw and I knew I showed my anxiety inappropriately, sometimes appearing irritated or even hiding my frayed nerves behind a giggle or loud laugh. I was terribly sick and tired and raw inside. The ap-

❖

prehension that began the day the prince asked me to marry him started as a dull worry and grew into a smothering ball of anxiety.

At first I hid my terrible fright behind nervous giggles with my girlfriends as we laughed in awe over the fact that I was to be the next queen of the Brits. "Oh, God, we're going to have to curtsy to you when you're queen, Duch! How will we keep from laughing!" they howled.

Duch was my nickname among my friends. I told the prince my close friends call me Duch, but he said that wasn't dignified.

After he asked me to marry him, when I moved for a short time into Clarence House to be near the Queen Mother, before I moved into Buckingham Palace to prepare for the wedding, I was suddenly alone with my thoughts—and my fears. There had been no one to share them with. I couldn't speak to the Queen Mother about the silly thoughts and fears swirling around my head. Ancient and revered, she was hardly human to me. Like Westminster and St. Paul's, I thought of the Queen Mum as one of the nation's historical treasures rather than the grandmother of my future husband. A grand lady, born at the turn of the century, for eight decades she had been an exemplary of British motherhood and refined social charm.

Her father was the Earl of Strathmore and Kinghorne and she claimed descent from Robert I, the Bruce, King of Scotland. I thought that because her father, like mine, had been an earl, we would have common ground, with her teaching me about the Royals. But perhaps it was because of her advanced age, or the sixty-year difference in our ages—an eon of difference in terms of culture. The Queen Mum had lived her youth, young womanhood, and entire married life in a different world than I was born into. I was raised in the world of the sexual revolution, the Pill, the Beatles, the rise of feminine consciousness and battle for women's rights. It was a far different world than the one in which the Queen Mum had helped rule Britain. She gave me little guidance as to what my role would be. I suspect that she had spent so much of her life as a Royal, she had hardly known life outside the palace.

My moment of tranquillity was interrupted by a ship's steward.

❖

"His Royal Highness requests your presence in the salon, ma'am," he said. "He would like you to bring your diary."

I tried to smother a sigh, but it slipped out like so many of my emotions, I was so fragile at the time. The summons sounded like my employer asking me to bring my dictation pad. And he literally had. My diary was my schedule of appointments. Before the wedding, it had mostly been filled with parties and hair and nail appointments. Now I would have "official" duties, but it was also scary because I had no idea of how I was to act, what I was to say. I didn't know even how I was to dress for the public.

I knew that I was a puzzlement to the ship's crew. I often went into the royal galley and helped myself to bowls of ice cream and snacks. One time I overheard one of the cook staff ask if I had a tapeworm. It wasn't the first time I had puzzled the servants with my eating habits. *How can you eat so much between meals and still be so slim?* was always the spoken—and more often unspoken—question.

It wasn't possible to tell them that I had my own secret formula for weight loss. I made almost as many trips to the loo to disgorge the food as I did into the kitchen. I had learned that by vomiting out what I consumed, I could temporarily satisfy my urge to eat while remaining slim. I had started a vomiting-after-meals routine several months earlier when the prince said that I was looking a bit thick in the waist. It was a not-too-subtle hint that he wanted me to look the very best for our wedding. It was a wedding that would be beamed around the world by satellite. I knew I had to please him, that he, the queen, and millions of people expected me to look dazzling for the ceremony.

There was nothing wrong with the way I was losing weight, really, but people were funny about such things, so I kept it a secret after I had gotten a strange look from one of my friends when I mentioned that I had discovered a surefire way to keep off the pounds. It certainly worked well, though I found myself bingeing more frequently, needing a quick fix of something sweet and tasty and then depositing my stomach contents in the loo. What people didn't understand was that my body wasn't perfect. If I let up for a moment, I began to look fat and bloated. That made me angry about myself, but I had to keep my wool on and not show my anger to other people.

Food was not my problem, of course, it was something else. I found myself more and more depressed. Gobbling down a bowl of ice cream or a candy bar helped get rid of the feelings, the anxieties, that overwhelmed me. It helped, but soon I felt depressed again. Sometimes I felt like I had no control over my life.

First it was my family. The thing about marrying the prince was a big thing, of course, especially with my father. I wanted to please him. I never really was tops with him—I mean, I know he loves me, but I don't think he really respected my intellect. My friends say that it's the same with their fathers, that it's a male thing, especially with older men, because the society they were raised in only tolerated women maintaining the house and wifely chores in the bedroom. Now that I was a princess, I hoped he was really proud of me.

Crazy thoughts always seemed to creep into my mind. Sometimes I wondered if it was all worth it, you know, trying to please everyone, wanting approval, needing love. A girlfriend at school whose mother killed herself told me that her mother used to say there were worse things than being dead, that at least then she would be able to get some peace.

Horrible. That thought sent me into the kitchen for a quick fix before I got my diary. It had been so hard, these last few months. With all the excitement, all the attention, the newspeople following everywhere I went, people alternately showering attention on me and making demands for my time, sometimes I felt like I was in the middle of a big circle with people walking around me, all of them shouting, "Do this!" "Don't do that!" "Jump this way!" "Jump that way!"

Getting through the marriage ceremony and going on a honeymoon had not brought that big sigh of relief that everyone said it would. I cried my eyes out. This was not the honeymoon I dreamt of during those years after puberty when my hormones suddenly were screaming that I was a young woman with desires and sexual urges. I dreamt of beaching a small sailboat on a paradise isle with my new husband, of running naked on the deserted beach, making love on the warm sand with gentle ocean waves licking at our feet—

After the ceremony, we had brunch at Buckingham Palace, a place as warm and cozy as the British Museum. And as emotional as the mineral exhibit in the museum. The faces around the table were polite and unemotional, welcoming me into the family not with tears and grins but with reserve and courtesy, as if I were a new piece of furniture added to the royal family's collection.

My God, I felt that need to love and be loved right down to my toes. The first three days of the honeymoon were spent at a palatial estate with staff and servants hovering about. Now I was aboard a honeymoon vessel, but rather than a cozy sailboat, it was a royal yacht the size of a battleship and crewed by nearly three hundred men. I would rather have taken a Caribbean cruise ship over the *Britannia*. At least there would have been dancing and entertainment, people to laugh and talk with, a shipboard casino, shops, and tacky little tourist destinations to complain about.

Instead of love on a warm beach or a fun cruise, I felt as if I had been sent on a mission with the Royal Navy. I didn't even have the foresight to bring along anything to read, not even one of those romantic blouse-rippers I enjoy. The prince, however, brought several of his philosophy books along. I wondered why he would want to spend his time with boring books instead of being with me.

Last night, he had wanted to discuss passages from the South African philosopher Van der Post. "Life begins as a quest of the child for the man and ends as a journey by the man to rediscover the child," he said. "What do you suppose he meant by that?"

"I haven't the faintest," I told him. And my tone said I didn't care, either.

He rolled over and read with his back to me. I was angry and humiliated. I wanted to cuddle up to him and have him tell me how much he loved me. Instead, I felt that if I wasn't interested in the Big Questions in life, those found in books by people who sit in front of the fireplace and drink brandy while they discuss endless philosophies of life, that I had no value. There are better things to do and talk about. It's not difficult to fathom that my husband and I walked different paths when it came to subjects like philosophy.

I know I must come across like a silly shopgirl. My new husband is one of the preeminent men in the free world. But I have never pretended to be an intellectual genius. I never pretended to be anything but who I am. I saw women around me trying to please him and gain his attention by focusing in on his interests as if they shared them, women who were bored silly by polo but name-dropped famous players. I was unable to fake it. I am just who I am and it is very discouraging to be constantly made to feel that whatever I am is not good enough, that I have to be someone else. I am perfectly aware that he relates on all levels to his old girlfriend, from polo to the hunt—no doubt she has read the philosopher's books.

I lay in bed after he turned his back on me and fumed. A rage grew in me. Unable to resist an urge to eat, I took a candy bar from where I had them stored in the bottom drawer of the end table. Then I ate another. I had a tremendous urge to rush to the galley and get a big bowl of ice cream, but I smothered it. Feeling bloated after I satisfied myself, I rushed into the bathroom and threw up.

I wanted to storm back into the bedroom and grab him by the throat and tell him that I wasn't stupid, that I was as good as his old girlfriend and the rest of that group that were always all over him like a bad rash.

And, oh, yes, I've been told by my husband that I use the "bad rash" expression too much, but it's the way I talk. I can't help it if it's not found in philosophy books.

This is the only honeymoon I will ever have and I wanted to share it bosom to bosom, soul to soul, with the man who would father the children I bore and be the only lover I would ever know. Instead, I found myself with nearly three hundred sailors, few of whom dared even to smile at me, and a husband who wanted to sit

❖

in the salon and debate the nature of man in between discussions with the captain about the state of the world's navies.

I calmed myself and went to bed. I knew I was wrong, that what was happening was my fault. My new husband is a gentleman, a man of impeccable breeding, well read, well spoken. If the fate of the world was in his hands, I know he would handle the crisis with the skill of a master surgeon at the operating table. He treated me with courtesy and gentleness. But I was immature and silly enough to wish he would at least once lose that calm, collected demeanor and rip off my clothes! That he would confess that he loved me with all the fire and passion his soul could generate.

But it was not just his calm demeanor that was puzzling me. I had seen him around other people. Certainly not the life of the party, but neither was he a wallflower. Although he tended to be reserved and formal toward the people he met as part of his official and social duties, he was comfortable with his intimate friends, the men and women who shared his interest in horses, polo, and the hunt.

And that was the crux of it. My new husband, the man whose bed I expected to share the rest of my life, was not completely relaxed with me. While he didn't treat me as someone who was part of his official regiment, from the very beginning I sensed an invisible shield between us. At first I thought it was nothing more than his own sense of reserve—after all, he is conservative in all his actions. When I told my girlfriends that I sensed a space between us, they told me that it was just his nature, that the reserve would melt once we were intimate. "British men have ice cubes for balls most of the time," one of them said, "but they start rubbing up against you and whimper when they want to get in the pink." I didn't want him horny for me. I wanted him to love me, to need me, and to accept me wholly into his heart and his life.

With my diary in hand, I walked into our private salon.

"My secretary has sent me an update of my schedule on our return to London. You've been scheduled to attend several of the events with me. We need to coordinate our diaries."

❖

He was interrupted by a steward bringing him lemon refresher, his favorite drink, one that he never traveled without. His personal servant always made sure to pack enough of the drink for the duration of his trips. The same was true of his favorite breakfast cereal, bran flakes, and Chocolate Oliver biscuits.

While the prince stepped over to give instructions to the steward concerning cocktails to be served to senior officers that evening, I picked up his diary to inspect the dates. As I lifted the book, a picture fell out. I bent down and picked it up and tossed it on the desk. My heart just broke.

He only stared at me, his features a mask of control, when he came back to retrieve his diary.

"It . . . just fell out. Was there a reason you brought a picture of her with you on our honeymoon?"

"You don't need to concern yourself."

My blood rose and so did my voice. "Excuse me, yes, I do. As your wife, I find it incomprehensible that you would carry a picture of a woman you were rumored to be involved with, on our honeymoon. How can you?"

"Please lower your voice. As I said, it is not your concern. Let's coordinate our diaries before this discussion gets out of hand."

I was speechless. Struck dumb for a moment. "May I ask you something, *sir*?" I said, the sir coming out in a testy voice. "Do you love me?"

He hesitated and looked at the picture he had taken from me. "Of course. Whatever that is. And please don't use that tone of voice with me or be insulting on how you address me."

"Then please flush that bitch's picture down the loo!"

I left the room, shaking. With no place else to find complete privacy, I went into the bathroom and locked the door. I threw up stomach juices that burned my throat. After I brushed my teeth and gargled, I sat on the toilet and stared at the wall. I had turned twenty years old only two weeks earlier and I had hoped I had become a complete woman and left behind any girlish ideals. But now I felt as if the world had been pulled out from under me. My

❖

stomach was in knots. I wanted reassuring words from my new husband that he loved me.

Dinner was a bore. Another night in which the senior officers joined us and the discussion would go to things about the state of the world and ships that had no interest for me.

I put an artificial smile on my face and made every effort to seem interested. Perhaps if I had managed to complete finishing school I would have been better equipped for these times when wives of important men were expected to be stimulating listening posts for male guests. I'd heard that there were tribes in South Pacific islands where it was polite for a man to offer a male guest his wife for the night, and I suppose making the wife listen to endless talk from a male guest was something less provocative and certainly more boring.

My appearance was one of composure, but my insides were still churning and burning from the confrontation with my husband. He had barely spoken to me as we dressed for dinner and escorted me into the dining area. Now as I looked down the table to smile at him, the gesture froze. I stared in shock, not certain my eyes had seen right.

He was wearing matching gold cuff links with intertwined initials on them.

I immediately recognized who they were from.

I couldn't believe my eyes. After my dismay that he carried a picture of her on our honeymoon, instead of appeasing me, his new bride, the bloody bastard was flaunting his old love. *How dare you!* I wanted to scream. My God, did he not have any concern for me? We had been married only days and he was already insulting me, rubbing salt into a wound?

Who did he think he was?

There was no expression on his face as he met my eye, but I realized exactly why he had done it.

He was demonstrating his power—not just the authority of a husband, but the power of a man of worldwide prestige. He would do what he damn well pleased.

❖

As I sat there I felt really low in myself. Had I been chosen as his bride because my breeding made me an uncontroversial place setting at the dinner table? Because I was young and strong and could service him in the bedroom? Because I was expected to produce heirs?

Where did love come into it?

He had put the same sort of thought process into choosing me as his wife as he did in choosing a breeding mare.

I felt ugly and rejected. I felt my body bulging, bloating from the food I had just eaten. It swelled in my stomach. I could taste the acid rising from it into my throat. Unable to resist the terrible urge to throw up, I mumbled an apology and got up from the table.

He threw me a look of disapproval. I'm sure that everyone at the table thought I was having a bout of diarrhea. I guess, as a Royal, if I had the urge to go to the loo, I was supposed to stay seated, keep a stiff upper lip, and shit in my pants.

Love came to Ilona not as a warm, exotic sense of joy, but as an all-consuming fire.

She felt it burn through her until, watching the Prince dancing with Mautya, she wanted to tear the woman from him, to strike her, to do her violent injury, even to murder her.

—BARBARA CARTLAND, *THE PROUD PRINCESS*

The Prisoner of Fear

39

❖

York

While Dutton was trying to unravel the mystery of the Abbey, and Marlowe was sizing up the competition in a British courtroom, Walter Howler, former famed plastic surgeon, reconstructionist of the dead, and a man who could breathe life into wax, was on a train pulling into York. The city, occupied successively by the Romans, Danes, Anglo-Saxons, and the Normans, lay at the confluence of the Rivers Ouse and Foss, about halfway between London and Edinburgh. It wasn't Howler's destination. He planned to stay on the train to the Scottish capital, then make his way by bus into the Highlands, getting as far away from London as his feet could carry him.

His nose dripped and he wiped it with his sleeve. The woman in the facing seat stared at him with undisguised disgust. A stout, large-framed, big-bosomed woman who had the appearance of having worked hard for her living, she had sat rigid in her seat since boarding the crowded train an hour earlier and finding herself forced to sit across from Howler. He certainly did not display confidence in his appearance—disheveled clothes soiled by food and God knows what, hair hanging in dirty oily strands, in need of a shave, a bath, new clothes, and probably louse disinfectant.

❖

The woman hadn't made any movement, as if she expected that the slightest motion would make her a target for whatever might crawl off of him. As the train pulled into the station, she grabbed her bag and rushed to be the first one off.

Howler got up, too, not to disembark but to go into the bathroom and fill a pressing need. Inside the cubbyhole, he was inserting a needle into an arm that showed the track marks of a veteran drug user, the needle scars of a person straddling that thin line between the temporary relief of shooting up and the ultimate mind-exploding experience of a lethal overdose.

The door opened as Howler was inserting the needle. He grinned at the man. "Diabetic."

The man was humorless.

"Mr. Howler, I presume," the man said. "My name is Grindstaff."

40

❖

Oh, what a tangled web we weave, when first we practice to deceive!

The phrase from Sir Walter Scott played in Marlowe's mind as she sat quietly and listened during a meeting of the princess's defense team at Anthony Trent's chambers. Members of the team presented their conclusions in regard to the issues they were assigned as part of the defense.

It was the third meeting she had attended and she had not joined any of the discussions with any enthusiasm. Her refusal to give her all to the committee was based partly on the fact that the sessions always focused on attacks on her position rather than finding ways to support it.

There was little discussion of defenses other than the one she brought to the table. No one supported her belief that she could not only get a jury to mitigate the act from murder down to manslaughter, but that there was a good chance that the jury would find justification and the princess would go free. That justification could only be shown by attacking the acts of the prince, and there was a noticeable silence in the room when she steered the discussion in that direction. There were times when she felt that Lord Finfall could barely constrain himself from bludgeoning her with a conference room chair.

❖

The "tangled web" rhyme came to mind as she realized that the princess did not have a single cohesive defense—there was another system in play, a shadow defense. It wasn't just a matter of planning two different defense strategies for the trial—Marlowe sensed that her heat-of-passion defense was only being given lip service, that the rest of them were focused on an entirely different approach. She could understand their reluctance and doubt of whether her strategy would be successful, but their resistance went beyond that. She had the impression that meetings were taking place and plans were being made that she had no part in, as if an entire backup team was being readied for the moment she was thrown out of the game.

What bothered her most was that she suspected the princess was creating some of the tangled webs. She knew she didn't have a complete grip on the princess's loyalty. The princess had brought her in out of fear that the British attorneys might be compromised, but when it came down to basics, the princess would be much more comfortable with members of the committee, people who shared a similar social background, than with Marlowe.

Marlowe's own attitude was part of the problem. She had a difficult time walking in the princess's shoes. It was the first time she had such difficulty empathizing with a client. Rich or poor, most of the women she had represented in the past were of the same social class as she was—or at least the issue of "social class" never came up.

Deep down she resented the princess, resented the opportunities that she never got herself, the opportunities the princess seemed to have thrown away. And somewhere along the line the princess had picked up on Marlowe's feelings. *That would drive her to Trent,* Marlowe thought.

But she also had to wonder whether the princess was using her simply as a club to keep her other attorneys in line until she could get something she wanted from them.

She suddenly realized Trent was talking to her. "I'm sorry, I was thinking about something."

"We were talking about the news conference coming up today. This will be the first time that you will be directly questioned by reporters on your theory of the princess's defense."

❖

She noted the "your theory" rather than "our theory."

"Our concern is that we don't give away too much of the defense at the news conference, that we save it for the trial."

"I agree," she said, "we shouldn't get into particulars, but the fact that the princess will be pursuing a heat-of-passion defense, a killing in reaction to provocation, isn't a secret. Speculation about it is in the news every day."

"Speculation is where we would like to leave it. I've spoken to the princess and she has agreed that we are to downplay her relationship with the prince at this point."

Marlowe almost laughed. It didn't come as a surprise to her that Trent would meet with the princess behind her back, since she insisted that her own meetings were conducted privately. But once again she sensed tangled webs.

"What exactly are you asking me to do?"

"Don't assassinate the prince's character with cheap shots that will make nasty headlines," Lord Finfall said.

"What his lordship means is, let's save our ammunition for trial," Trent said.

Marlowe nodded. "I agree." She actually did agree with them. The single biggest mistake defense attorneys in high-profile cases made was trying their cases in the news media, giving the prosecution a preview of their strategy. But she also sensed another motive. She said, "Is there any question that at some point we are going to have to drag the prince's name through the mud?" She was deliberately blunt. "If there is, we should deal with it now. You can't have provocation unless there is a bad person doing bad things. We have a client that was driven to bulimia and suicide attempts by verbal abuse from her husband. If we can't portray that abuse as malicious, there's no way a jury will find mitigating circumstances."

"That's something that will be dealt with at the proper time," Lord Finfall said. His tone conveyed that he would be the one deciding when it was the proper time.

Marlowe locked eyes with him. She had come to dislike the old fossil. She couldn't imagine the man dealing with a wife or daughter. She wanted to ask him if his wife had ever had an orgasm.

❖

"It's something that needs to be dealt with now," she said, "before we step into a courtroom and discover we are all pulling in different directions. Is there any question in anyone's mind about putting on a case in which we show the late Prince of Wales as an abusive husband?"

Seven stone faces. She could have been talking to the faces on Mount Rushmore.

Trent gave her the professional smile of a funeral director telling a grieving widow the price of a casket.

"Naturally, we will follow the princess's instructions on that matter."

Now, what the hell did that mean?

Tangled, tangled webs.

All the misery, unhappiness, and loneliness she had felt ever since her wedding-day seemed to flood over her in an agony that was unbearable.

She sank down onto the floor, and still cuddling the doll in her arms bent her head and wept so hard that her whole body shook.

—BARBARA CARTLAND, *THE PROUD PRINCESS*

41

❖

Tower of London

Six months after the wedding, pregnant with my first child, I threw myself downstairs.

I stared at the words I had written and wondered how I could explain to the American lawyer why I threw myself down a set of stairs in an attempt to kill myself when I was pregnant with a future king.

How would I explain it to my son someday? What words do I use to explain to a child that I was so sick, confused, and desperate that I tried to harm myself at a time when my first duty was to protect the child I carried?

In some ways, hiring this attorney was a mistake. I was already seeing that. Unlike my British lawyers, who were too polite to make me take the scabs off my hurts and expose my wounds, she insisted upon making me confront the past. It would be difficult for someone like her, who had worked so hard for success, to understand how being addressed as "Your Royal Highness" was not an instant formula for happiness.

She had asked me before she left our last conference to make a list of the things that occurred during my marriage.

❖

Lonliness. I was surrounded by people but all alone. There was no one I could share my miseries with. No one I could talk to. Family, friends, they all wanted the fairy tale to work, they didn't want to hear that it was a nightmare for me, and so I didn't want to burden them. When I hinted at it, probing for an opening to let them know how terribly lonely I was, they sped right past it and would babble on about how wonderful it must be to be the Princess of Wales and have the world at your feet.

Crying. Behind closed doors I cried my eyes out, wiping my tears and powdering my red nose before showing my face in public. There were days I just couldn't handle, the pressures were phenomenal and I just broke down. I felt a duty to perform and not let people down.

Sick. Physically feeling ill was the worst of it, knowing that there was something the matter with me. And there *was* something wrong. I'm just beginning to realize what damage the bingeing-vomiting cycle did to me, to my body and my mind; it ripped holes in my thinking, my thought processes, holes that aren't filled even now.

What happened after we returned from our honeymoon?

I guess one of the first things was that my bingeing and then bringing it all up came out of the bag—in a manner of speaking. I tried to talk to my husband about it, but he just stared at me. He had heard of such a thing, but had no comprehension that it was done by "normal" people. And his wife, a future queen, had to be "normal." There was no room in his vision of the world, in his entire experience, for his wife to be anything but absolutely normal. Bingeing and vomiting were not in the royal vernacular. Maybe no one had ever been sick before.

One evening when we were dining, after he had been on a hunt, he looked at me as I took a bite of pheasant. "Is that going to reappear later? Pity, my gun handler thought I had brought it down with quite an excellent shot."

"You are a shit!" I exploded. He gaped at me—his server, who was about to place a piece of bread on his bread plate, also gaped at me. In his entire life, no one had raised their voice to him. I swept my dinner plate off the table and stormed out of the room. The moment I was out

❖

of his sight, my anger turned in on me and I raced for the loo to deposit his excellently shot bird.

MY THOUGHTS HERE WERE interrupted by a servant telling me that my American attorney had arrived. As we sat over coffee and tea once again, I told her about the pheasant incident.

"It was the first time I called him a name. He was profoundly shocked, but things got worse after that. He gave me no sympathy, no understanding, not an ounce of compassion for my hurts and fears. Just before the dinner incident, we had been at a public appearance together. We were standing, watching children do a dance, when I suddenly felt faint. I leaned against him and passed out. Later, he was in a fine fit. Rather than having sympathy for the fact I had fainted, he told me I should have done it in private."

Marlowe nodded. "Keep the dirty laundry out of sight?"

"Exactly, show no weaknesses, no emotions, no tears, that stiff-upper-lip thing. Everything in the public eye was to be staged, arranged, like you set up a display of historical objects in a museum."

"You were being treated as an institution rather than a person."

"Yes, exactly that, an institution. And that's how he dealt with me, at arm's length, never really getting in close. At first I responded with fear and was evasive toward him, not wanting him to know I was bingeing and throwing up, keeping my emotions all bottled up, but one day the lid blew off and after that things were increasingly hostile, my outbursts became more frequent."

"He exploded with anger at you, too?"

"I wish he had, I would have been able to deal with it better, but mostly he treated me like a parent would—no, more like a schoolmaster dealing with a rebellious child. He was disapproving rather than sympathetic. He continued on with his own life as if he were still a bachelor, and I'm sure he would have been much happier if he had stayed single. One can't truly understand the frustrations I felt. Even after my . . . my attempts to harm myself, after experiencing a painful labor carrying my first son, my doctor decided labor had to be induced. But the birth was

❖

not done immediately because we had to find a date that would suit my husband's polo schedule. There I was, in great discomfort, emotionally distraught on top of a troubled pregnancy, and we had to schedule the birth of the next heir to the throne to fit my husband's polo practice."

"You became more and more frustrated when you couldn't break down his wall of calm, cool disapproval."

"Yes, that was exactly it. I shouted for understanding, for him to deal with my fears and pains, and his response was to frown and tell me to get myself together, not, 'Is there something I can do?' It was always just, 'Pull yourself together, don't disgrace the family.'"

"Did you tell him you were angry and frustrated at his lack of concern?"

"I shouted it, I begged for understanding. Finally I began to throw things, vases, dishes, anything I could get my hands on. Once I smashed a Ming Dynasty piece. I wanted to wipe that smug frown off his face, but he would just shake his head and tell me I was a child. 'Oh, what is the matter now?' he would ask. Finally, I couldn't take it any longer, I didn't want to live."

"You tried to kill yourself?"

"I don't know what I was doing, my mind was spinning. No matter what I did, he condemned me rather than show any sympathy."

"From what you've told me, your husband's own emotions were lobotomized by his upbringing, hardly being held, trained not to show emotions, trained not to *have* emotions."

"Yes, that was the thing, he was able to smother his feelings, or not to have them, I suppose, but mine stuck out all over me."

"We can take your husband's attitude even a step further. He was indoctrinated that having emotions were defects in character. You were doing things, expressing sentiments and emotions, that were not just alien, not just contrary to how he had been raised to act, but that he had been programmed to view as character flaws."

"Yes, I can see that, that's why he ran back to her, she was more like him, another one of those lobotomized people. Acting out my anger by throwing things and shouting at him, that came later. In the beginning, months following the honeymoon, I kept it all in, all the hurt and pain. I didn't strike out—instead, I cried a lot. I got pregnant and soon dis-

❖

covered that my role in life was to suffer in silence while my husband played polo and enjoyed his friends and lover."

"She was still in his life?"

"She was never out of it. As soon as we were back from our honeymoon, he was getting together with her, inviting her for rides and hunts. I was stunned, shocked. He had flaunted her at me on our honeymoon and kept up his relationship as soon as we were back home. I had terrible nightmares about her. He rejected me, put me into a corner, and told me to stay there until I was needed for the next public appearance. It was duty! duty! duty! smile and be happy before the cameras even if I'm crying inside, while my husband did what he damn well pleased. You understand, it was his father, the Prince Consort to the Queen, who was at fault for my husband's attitude. His father told him before the marriage not to be concerned if he didn't love me, that it was permissible for him to take a lover."

"When was the first incident in which you tried to harm yourself?"

"It was five or six months after we were married. I was pregnant and horribly depressed. I was married to a man I had been raised to idolize, a man I loved, but I was rejected by my husband and made to feel that the only reason he had married me was to be some sort of cow to produce an heir. I can't tell you how I felt, I was suffocating. I felt terribly rejected, my husband bringing another woman into our marriage, I believed everything was my fault, that I was a failure, that I had disappointed my husband as I had once disappointed my parents. I turned it inside and it boiled inside me, the knowledge that I had failed everyone, that there was no reason for me to live."

"So you threw yourself down the stairs while you were pregnant."

"Yes, I did that." She locked eyes with Marlowe. "That bothers you, doesn't it? I understand you lost a child. Are you going to be able to deal with the fact that I was so distraught I risked the life of my unborn child?"

Marlowe's face flushed. "The question isn't whether I can deal with it but how other people will. I'm wondering how women on the jury will react. You didn't just put your own life at risk, you risked the life of the child you were carrying, a child now that is heir to the throne."

"It wasn't like that, it wasn't as if I thought about it and said, *Okay,*

❖

now I'll throw myself down some stairs and kill myself and my child. If you have never been there, to that dark place in your mind where you become lost and you lose your sense of self-worth, you won't understand that you can get to the point where life seems so much more painful and frightening than the peace of death."

"I have to understand," Marlowe said. "We are going to have a jury with men and women on it who have to be told the story in such a way that they won't judge you guilty of your husband's death because they have been prejudiced by other acts."

"Why should that incident upset jurors? My child wasn't harmed."

"Some people have strong religious beliefs or are simply pro-life and would find it morally wrong for a mother to destroy a fetus—"

"Is that what you think I did? That I tried to murder my child?"

"I don't think any—"

"You killed your husband because of that, didn't you? I mean, he hit you and you lost your baby."

"I lost more than my baby. I lost the chance to have any more children."

"Does that prejudice you against me? If you were on the jury, would you think I was a baby killer?" The princess's voice had risen.

Marlowe said calmly and quietly, "You are not a baby killer, your child was born healthy. I hate to use the word *duty,* but I have a duty to question everything so I can come up with the answers we need. You're turning my questions into criticism and value judgments. We have to deal with the fact that you tried to kill yourself when you were pregnant—and the potential effect that will have on jurors."

"I can tell you that I wasn't thinking rationally. I wasn't thinking about hurting my baby, in all honesty, and you will find this hard to believe, but I wasn't even thinking about harming myself." She looked away, staring beyond Marlowe, back at the past. "I was in that dark place in my mind. It was so painful, sad, I wanted to cry and cry, and I did, but there was no relief after I cried, the pain of living was still there, my nerves were raw, I felt so . . . so unnecessary, so confused, life hurt, that's all I can tell you, life hurt and I wanted to stop the pain."

"Did you talk to your husband about your feelings of wanting to kill yourself?"

❖

"I told him how I felt. His contribution to my mental health was to lecture me on how I have to get control of myself. I bawled like a baby that morning and he asked that same question again: 'Oh, what's the matter now?' I told him I didn't want to live. He said I was crying wolf again and went to dress for his ride. I stood at the top of stairs and then . . . then a darkness washed over me and I fell down the stairs."

"Can we say you fainted?"

"No, it would be a lie. I was distraught, confused, but I was conscious when I went down the stairs."

"Were there any other, uh, incidents?"

"You mean did I try to kill myself? No, I didn't go that far, but I did try to hurt myself. Did they tell you about the glass cabinet?"

Marlowe shook her head.

"I threw myself into it, into the glass."

"You threw yourself into glass. Were you hurt?"

"Not seriously, just cut a bit. And then there was the penknife."

I had been keeping my voice level, but I could feel myself slipping now. A tremble had come into my voice.

I looked away, ashamed. "I took his penknife and cut my legs." I gasped for breath. "He just watched, just watched as I cut my legs and the blood ran down. Then he went out to play polo."

The shock on her face turned my stomach. She didn't understand, she was strong, she had never been to that dark place where there was no hope. I felt so stupid, so utterly worthless. My lunch expanded in my stomach and moved into my arms and legs, bloating them. I staggered away, hoping to get to the loo before my lunch made its second journey in my throat.

❖

42

❖

Soho

Dutton got out of a taxi and rang an apartment bell. He identified himself when the query came over the speaker and said, "Tell Lady Grey I'm here."

She came out ten minutes later, a sexy woman, perhaps in her thirties, dressed provocatively, too much breast showing, too much leg—thigh—showing, whorish-red lipstick sparkling with glitter, all perfect for a night out on the town.

"Get your tush back upstairs, Henry," Dutton told Lady Grey. "Get a coat to put over what little there is of your dress."

"You told me to dress sexy."

"I said sexy, not lewd. I want to get into a hotel room, not a jail cell. They're not going to let us into a respectable hotel with your boobs hanging out and your dress up to your . . . whatever it is you have under that dress. Do you still have a bat and balls, or did they get chopped when you got the boob job?"

"You're so coarse." Lady Grey shook a finger in his face. "You promised me a full-page spread in *Burn* for my services. I'm playing the new La Cage show. I need coverage."

❖

"Would I lie to you?" Dutton was happy the transvestite didn't think too much about the question as Lady Grey went back up to get a coat.

He checked his watch as the taxi dropped them off in front of Marlowe's hotel. The news conference the princess's defense team was holding was scheduled to take place in an hour. Add a half hour for the conference and another half hour for the American lawyer to bail out and get back to the hotel, and that gave him at least two hours.

Plenty of time for a leisurely search of her room.

"Mr. and Mrs. John Grey," Dutton told the check-in clerk.

"Lord and Lady Grey," Henry said.

"Welcome to our hotel, Lady Grey."

Lady Grey gave the clerk a grin and lewdly licked her lip. Dutton was tempted to stick the pen he was using to sign with in her eye.

"We want Mike the Bellman to show us up to our room."

"Mike has been sent on an errand for a guest. We can have one of our other bellmen take you up."

"We'll wait for Mike. When will he be back?"

"Sir, we—"

"We'll wait for Mike. It's an old superstition I have."

"We came here on our honeymoon," Lady Grey interjected. Her tone and expression left no doubt that the honeymoon had been a threesome and Mike had been the third.

"When will Mike be back?" Dutton snapped.

"In about an hour."

"We'll wait in the lounge."

He grabbed his "wife" by the arm and marched her toward the lounge, checking his watch on the way. An hour's wait still left him plenty of time.

Mike the Bellman had provided tidbits about the extracurricular activities of celebrities and government bigwigs over the years. Permitting Dutton to use a hotel master key to get into the American attorney's room was beyond the realm of what Mike would do for money. But Dutton had learned long ago that what people wouldn't do for money, they would for sex. And Mike had a special prurient interest that Lady Grey could satisfy.

❖

———————

AN HOUR AND FIFTEEN minutes later, Dutton left Mike and Lady Grey alone to pursue whatever piqued their interest, with Mike's pants coming down even before Dutton reached the door.

He entered Marlowe's room, took one look around, and shook his head with admiration. The American attorney was no fool—she had a rented safe in the room. It was too big to carry away and would take serious explosives to blow it open. No snoopy reporter was going to stick his nose into her files. However, her notebook computer was on the room desk. A security chain from the computer to the desk kept one from walking off with the computer without a bolt cutter. But not from using it.

"Should have put your computer in the safe," he told the absent Marlowe.

He opened the computer and turned it on. It stopped booting up as a menu came on that demanded a password.

"Son-of-a-bitch." That was why she didn't bother putting it in the safe. That might stop the maid from snooping, and even put the skids under your average reporter, but *Burn* reporters were a special breed of felon.

He called the office and got the tech on the line whose payroll description was computer maintenance but who spent a good portion of his time hacking into other people's computers for the tabloid.

"Cohn the Barbarian said you'd been fired," Hacker told Dutton.

"Not a bit of it! That's a cover story, lad, Cohn got me working undercover on something bigger than the royal killing."

"There's nothing bigger than that."

"Help me crack the code for this computer and you'll have your place in history."

❖

43

❖

Tower of London

Philip Hall was waiting with the limo to take Marlowe to the news conference to be held outside Trent's office when she came out of her meeting with the princess. She got into the back and stared straight ahead as the limo made its way out of the tower compound.

"Are you okay?" he asked.

"Yes—no. I'm disturbed about my meeting with the princess. I'm having a hard time seeing the forest for the trees." She didn't want to discuss it, didn't want him to know that the princess had become emotional and rushed out of the room. A few minutes later a stone-faced servant told her that the princess would be indisposed for the rest of the day.

"Anything I can help with?"

"I'm afraid I'm a lost cause at the moment. It's the time that bothers me, it all happened so quickly. She's chosen as the bride for the prince, they're engaged, married, she's pregnant and throwing herself down stairs and into glass cases, all in a very short period of time, only about six months from the stunning wedding until the first attempt on her own life. People don't usually descend to hell that quickly."

"Unless they were already there at the beginning."

❖

"That's the question, isn't it? Did she bring a lot of emotional baggage into the marriage?"

He shrugged. "How else do you explain how we go from A to Z in less time than it takes most married people to get to B or C?"

"Maybe he just pushed her harder, and maybe she was just a more vulnerable victim."

"Which is it?"

"I don't know, but I do know that I'm not ready for a news conference. Drop me off at my hotel."

"Anthony will—"

"Be delighted. He and that fossil Lord Bluenose will get along fine with the newspeople. They'd prefer I wasn't there, anyway."

She smiled sourly at Hall. "As far as that goes, I'm sure they'd prefer I fell off the end of the earth."

44

❖

"It's not working!" Dutton gave the little computer a hit with the phone receiver just in case that might do it. He put the phone back to his ear as Hacker spoke.

"You have to bring it in, it will take hours to break into it, she isn't using the manufacturer's code program, she's got something custom."

"I can't bring it in, it's chained."

"Break the chain."

"With my teeth?"

He hung up and thought fast. Maybe he could get Mike the Bellman to borrow a plumber's tool that cuts pipe. He checked his watch—he'd killed another twenty minutes, but was sure he still had another half hour, yet there was little chance of getting a pipe cutter in that time—he didn't even know if there was one in the hotel. He'd have to find Mike, too—the assignation with Lady Grey would be over and the transvestite on her way back to theaterland. And he'd have to figure out a way to convince the bellman to risk his job again, only this time just for filthy lucre.

The security chain was held together by a simple key lock. He grabbed a letter opener and started working on the lock. His phone rang.

❖

"She's on her way up!"

"What!"

"I saw her get in the elevator a minute ago, but the manager called me over and asked—"

Dutton didn't wait to find out what the manager had asked. He knocked over the desk chair as he shot up and raced for the room door. He heard the lock click before he reached it. Panicked, he pressed himself against the wall where the door would cover him as it opened.

Marlowe stepped in and swung the door closed behind her. She saw her computer open and on. "What the—"

He grabbed her from behind, putting his hand over her mouth, clutching her around the waist with the other hand. She struggled and he exclaimed, "Stop! I won't hurt you!"

She didn't stop, but back-kicked his shin. He howled and loosened his grip enough for her to twist out of his grasp. She let out the start of a scream before he threw himself at her, clutching at her mouth as he forced her toward the bed and lay atop her.

"Stop! I'm a reporter!" He glared down at her. "Stop, damn it."

She stopped struggling. He had one hand on her mouth and another on her breast, holding her down.

"Now, look, I'll let you go if you promise not to scream. You promise?" She nodded.

"I'm serious, damn it. I'm a reporter, not a rapist." She nodded.

He let her go. She jerked up and butted him in the nose with her forehead. He staggered back, holding his face, and she reared back on the bed and kicked him in the groin.

He screamed and ran from the room, wounded and in pain.

She locked the door behind her and called the police.

45

❖

"I'm well aware of the perversions of this man," Inspector Bram Archer told Marlowe. "He is known to have sex with the dead."

Behind him, Sergeant Lois Kramer rolled her eyes.

The three of them were standing in Marlowe's room.

"Does he kill them first?" Marlowe asked.

"That's under investigation."

More eye-rolling.

"I have a special interest in this subject, that's why I was called when the report came in that he had attacked you." He pulled a picture out of a leather folder. "Is this the man who attacked you?"

"That's him." She hesitated, then said, "I don't know if you police people here do it the same as back in the States, but I'm used to a photo lineup where witnesses get a six-pack, six pictures of suspects. It usually isn't legal if the witness is only shown one." She smiled. "I'm a criminal defense lawyer."

"Oh, we have the same procedure." Archer pulled out five more pictures. "Recognize any of these?"

"Uh, yeah, all six are of this man Dutton."

❖

Lois Kramer was standing behind Archer. She caught Marlowe's eye and shrugged.

Archer said, "Sergeant Kramer will take down your statement. I'm going to question the hotel staff. There was a lapse in security somewhere, for this maniac to have gotten into your room."

After he was gone, Marlowe said, "I've never seen a photo six pack with six pictures of the same suspect."

"Neither have I. You have to excuse Archer, he's getting close to retirement, his wife is divorcing him rather than face having him around the house twenty-four/seven, and Dutton cost him a promotion that reduces his pension. It seems to have all come and dropped on his head. He's not been himself."

"Who is this Dutton character?"

"He's works for *Burn,* the tabloid—it's the most outrageous paper in the city. Actually, I think he's freelance."

"Does he really sleep with the dead?"

"Actually, he said I was the last dead body he gave a poke to."

"Oh."

"I'm going to burn his ass for that one, but Archer's gone around the bend, focusing on Dutton as the cause of all his problems. Dutton's a first-class bastard, not above a little breaking and entering for a story, but there's nothing kooky about his sexual appetites. He can still come three times in a night, not bad for a chap past the four-oh."

"Thanks for sharing," Marlowe murmured.

"At one time Dutton was a top reporter, the real kind, an investigative journalist who got a prize for bringing down the government when he uncovered the fact that they were sitting on another one of those MI6 double-agent scandals."

"How'd he go from bringing down governments to peeking through keyholes for a tabloid?"

"He wrote a story that got his girlfriend killed. Shit happens, doesn't it?" Sergeant Kramer grinned. "I heard that one in a movie."

SHE HAD JUST GOTTEN rid of the police when the phone rang.

"Yes."

❖

"Why did you call the police?"

She took the receiver away from her ear and stared at it for a moment before putting it back.

"Inspector Archer is very interested in talking to you. Why don't you give yourself up? I think he's going to take you dead or dead."

"He's a nutcase, isn't he?"

"*He's* a nutcase? He wasn't the one who burglarized my room and attacked me."

"I didn't attack you, luv, it was all self-defense. I got the worse of it, didn't I?"

"You didn't get half of what you deserve. If there's anything I plan on accomplishing in my stay in this country, it will be to see you in jail."

"Been there, done that, but you're not going to do that, anyway. I'm the best friend you have."

"You are a sneaky, slimy, repulsive—"

"Self-defense, it was."

"What was?"

"That's why she shot him."

"What are you talking about?"

"I'm talking about your husband-killing client, the one who put a bullet in the heart of the heir apparent before an audience of millions. It was self-defense. I can give you the goods on it, and in return, you give me the inside line on every major development that comes up. Tic for tac.

"What kind of tabloid bullshit are you trying to sell me?"

"Have a drink with me and I'll tell you why it was self-defense."

"Sure, we'll make it a threesome: you, me, and Inspector Archer."

"Tsk-tsk, don't be catty, luv, not to your knight in shining armor. You heard what Sergeant Kramer told you: I'm a great reporter hiding in tabloid clothing—and I hold my ejaculations."

She stared at the receiver. "You have my room bugged!"

"Not at all, luv." The adjoining-room door opened and Dutton stepped in with a portable phone to his ear. The adjoining room door was near the door to the hallway. He grinned at her.

She gaped. "How—"

He shrugged and tried to look modest. "There are few limits to my

❖

abilities. Now that we're old friends, let's have a drink together and I'll tell you my theory of your case and you can give me a headline."

Someone knocked on her room door.

She grinned at Dutton. "We'll need a table for four if your police friends are coming." She spoke to his retreating back.

Dutton quickly stepped back into his room, closing and locking the door behind him.

She opened her door to find the hotel manager and the head of hotel security, not Archer and Kramer.

She listened to two minutes of apologies before she cut him off. "The person who broke into my room had the adjoining room, but my side was locked when I left. Someone had to unlock it. That makes it an inside job with your employees."

A quick look into the adjoining room by the security officer revealed Lord and Lady Grey had gone on the lam.

She got rid of the hotel management, letting them know that she was leaning toward a lawsuit but could be diverted from legal action if her hotel bill went away.

After they were gone, she sat on her bed and stared at the now-locked door to the adjoining room. She thought about what Dutton had said about self-defense being the motive behind the shooting. She shook her head. No way, it was the man's tabloid-rotted brain searching for a headline. She was glad she hadn't discussed the charge with him. She didn't need a lamebrained defense like that to appear in the papers with her seal of approval.

There was a fundamental problem with the reporter's self-defense theory: The princess shot an unarmed man.

❖

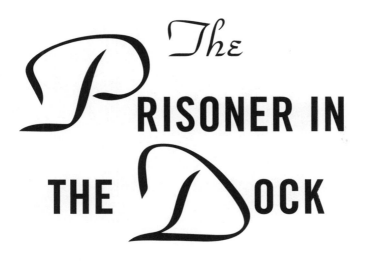

The Prisoner in the Dock

Why may not that be the skull of a lawyer?
Where be his quiddities now, his quillets,
his cases, his tenures, and his tricks?

—SHAKESPEARE, *HAMLET*

46

❖

DEFEND THE CHILDREN OF THE POOR & PUNISH THE WRONGDOER

Marlowe read the inscription carved in Old Bailey's stone. Noble words, a noble goal. *They usually don't put inspirational inscriptions on build- ings anymore,* she thought. *But they don't build them intending to last centuries, either.* The building appeared old and hallowed even though it was a mere babe in a country that still had vestiges of Roman walls.

High above, standing on a globe atop a great dome, stood golden Justice, a set of scales in one hand, a sword in the other. She liked the representation of Justice as a fighter. She didn't care for the statues of the goddess that showed the goddess blind. If she had had her way, she'd show Justice with a sword in one hand and an Uzi in another— she knew from her own experience and that of the people she defended that you couldn't rely upon justice to be blindly handed down, it was something that had to be fought for. Courts are places of law, not fairness—sometimes the Children of the Poor are screwed and Wrong- doers are rewarded.

She recalled that in one of her early trials she had told a judge the case against her client was "not fair." The judge went volcanic and

❖

nearly blew her out of the courtroom, yelling that Marlowe was required to cite legal authority, not value judgments.

MARLOWE WALKED DOWN A corridor in the courthouse. It was early—the bewigged barristers, suited solicitors, and nervous clients had not yet made their appearance. She had come early to "acclimatize" herself to the hallowed environment in the heart of the English criminal justice system. As she walked down the deserted corridor, she imagined she could hear the murmurings of the great cases that had been decided in the courtrooms—Oscar Wilde, huge beast that he was, pompous, contemptuous, brilliant, and utterly without street smarts, flaunting his homosexuality in an era when it was a hangable offense; Lord Haw-Haw, Nazi, traitor, affecting a proper British accent as he haughtily informed the court it had no authority over him—even as the gallows were being prepared.

Her heels on the hard floor made a hollow sound that bounced off the walls. A numbness gripped her. There were no complex thoughts about the case flying around her head. The numbness froze them.

It was always the same for her on the first day of trial—no obvious nervousness showed, but it wasn't because she had steel nerves. Her state of icy calm was a defense mechanism that kicked in so she wouldn't expose her raw nerves. For days, her nerves had been on fire, she thought of nothing other than the case, reading, worrying, thinking, working each piece of evidence, each witness over and over in her mind, seeing if it all added up to a victory for her client—the law was not about what one knew, but what could be proven.

She had played the case over and over in her mind as a movie, imagining it scene by scene. In an out-of-body view, she saw herself giving an opening statement, looking at herself standing at a podium, moving over to talk face-to-face with jurors, questioning witnesses, watching a movie of them responding to her questions. It was how she always prepared, running the movie in her mind, seeing the trial before she faced it in court.

She built the movie from scenes but left some of it on her mind's cutting room floor when she realized that she would not be able to

❖

move around the courtroom as she commonly did in the States. There were three rows of wooden bench seats for attorneys in the courtroom: the first row for senior counsel, behind them the juniors, while the instructing solicitor occupied the third row. Besides the bench to sit on, in front of the seated attorney was a flat area to use as a writing desk. Because the senior counsels and senior prosecutor would rise to address the court, jurors, and witnesses, they had a small wooden podium to place their papers on. The podium sat atop the flat desk area.

The seniors had to rise from the bench where they sat and speak with the podium immediately in front of them. Marlowe had already discovered that the desktop podium blocked her view and made her claustrophobic. She'd had it removed, but she still was permitted only to stand up and talk without moving away from her bench seat. She hated the lack of mobility. She thought better on her feet, feet that were in motion, not cemented to the floor. But she planned for the lack of movement, the mental movie she used for prep had her addressing the judge and jury with her feet planted. It also had her seated closest to the jury. As a California defense attorney, she was used to the prosecutor being seated closest to the jury, but the English courtroom had a different rule.

Her frozen nerves would thaw the first time she rose to challenge the prosecutor in a verbal debate over a point of law or spoke directly to the jury with her opening statement. Her voice would be shaky—for a moment. Then adrenaline would kick in. Her frozen nerves and shaky voice would melt in the baptism of fire in the courtroom.

She had never met a good trial attorney who wasn't nervous before a trial. An actor once told her that most actors were nervous when they had to speak their lines. And the dividing line between actors and trial attorneys was often vague.

She entered the courtroom and paused. The only person in the room was the bailiff. He nodded at her and continued reading a newspaper.

She went to her bench seat behind the rail and looked around at the courtroom. She loved the dramatic soul, the aura of old-fashioned justice, of the Old Bailey courtroom. It was unlike any courtroom she had been in, more dramatic theater than legal forum, a place that

❖

reeked with the intense conflicts and powerful emotions that had exploded against its aged walls. Conflict was the basis of great fiction—and great courtroom drama. It was a courtroom where attorneys Abe Lincoln, Clarence Darrow, and Gary Spence (not to mention screen lawyers Charles Laughton, Paul Newman, and barrister Rumpole) would have felt comfortable speaking their lines.

American courtrooms were built like auditoriums, with only the moderator—the judge—facing the audience. But the Old Bailey courtroom was built like a theater, with a viewing gallery, "box seats," above the dramatic action on the courtroom floor, permitting the audience to watch the dramatic tension on the floor below with a bird's-eye view.

There were even theatrical costumes for the judge and attorneys, wigs out of fashion for centuries and gowns that separated the "classes" of lawyers by rank and distinction.

Adding to the dramatic tension, the sense of tragedy and impending conflict, was "the prisoner in the dock." The defendant did not sit next to her attorneys, but was in the "dock," a square, elevated box that displayed the prisoner dramatically as the center of attention. The dock in the courtroom was a large box-shaped compartment that the defendant shared with two bailiffs. At the top was an ornamental iron trim of spearheads, the original purpose of which was to keep the prisoner from climbing over and lunging for the judge.

In an American courtroom the defendants sat at the counsel table with their lawyers and usually had to be pointed out for the jury to realize which person sitting at the table was on trial. Putting prisoners in a display box with guards nearby made the defendant the focus of attention—there was no question of who the accused was and little possibility of the prisoner hiding emotions except behind a dull stare that itself bespoke guilt.

As in any hallowed theater, there was said to be a house ghost in Old Bailey, an innocent person who had been unfairly condemned and was hanged.

Marlowe hoped that the ghost was on her side.

She thought about the wheels of justice that were to begin spinning. It would play out almost exactly like a boxing match—a judge

❖

would act as a referee between competing combatants, with the jury deciding who won the fight.

Throughout the trial, the judge would constantly be making ruling on "quiddities" and "quillets," those esoteric points of law that Prince Hamlet complained were a lawyer's weapons. "Rules of evidence" were lawyers' swords and pikes, which they used to jab each other as they fought to get their evidence in and their opponent's excluded. In the European system, where judges decided guilt or innocence, there was no need for elaborate rules for admitting evidence because the judge was presumed to be a professional who could separate the wheat from the chaff. But under the Anglo-American system, jurors walked into a courtroom and had months and even years of complex trial preparation by experts thrown at them in hours. Untrained and unprepared to know the difference between reliable and unreliable evidence, the jury had to have the evidence strained for them by the judge.

The net result was that the jurors didn't necessarily hear all evidence, nor all the truth—the cases were decided upon only on the facts the judge let them hear.

One of the most common questions asked of an attorney during a social gathering is, "How can you defend someone you know is guilty?" The answer isn't that a defendant is presumed innocent—the truth is that the adversarial system of justice the British invented requires that even the known guilty be defended because prosecutors are not neutral parties, but combatants whose duty it is to champion only the police view.

She knew that she had a fault, one that made her a good attorney but also sometimes blindsided her—she had too much empathy for her clients. You couldn't be a good doctor unless you could stand the sight of blood—and it was inevitable that patients would die. If you weren't able to accept those deaths, you had to find another profession. The same was true of attorneys who defended people in courtrooms—sometimes blood was spilled, the innocent went to prison, the guilty went free. If you couldn't keep your professional life in a box separated from your emotions, if you had too much feeling, trials became an emotional roller coaster. And she couldn't separate her personal emotions—

she felt fear and pain for the client, often even more than the clients themselves appeared to feel.

Marlowe didn't have a connection with organized religion in the sense of being a churchgoer, but at these moments when there was an uncanny silence in the courtroom before the bloody battle began, she was always reminded of the old soldier's truth: There are no atheists in the foxhole.

She was wondering if there was a prayer for lawyers on the day a trial began when the other players started entering the theater.

SHE TOOK HER SEAT in the first row. Trent was on her right, and farther down, at the other end of the bench, was where the prosecutor would sit. Neither the prosecutor nor his junior had arrived.

Philip Hall sat behind her and Trent in the row for juniors. In the row behind Hall, Sir Fredic, the instructing solicitor, sat.

Marlowe thought the arrangement of counsel in rows like benches at a train station was inefficient. The setup made it difficult for senior counsel to communicate with the junior without making it very obvious and even more difficult to communicate with the solicitor except by passing down notes or whispers through the junior.

Tradition got in the way of communication even worse when it came to the defendant. Marlowe spoke to the princess before the proceedings, but her client would be in the dock during the trial rather than beside her.

She felt conspicuous, a fly in a sugar bowl. The barristers were in dark robes and gray wigs, as were the prosecutors.

She had met Desai when she appeared before the judge to be granted permission to represent the princess. She thought about what Hall told her about the prosecutor. In the days when trial was by combat, the king or queen had a champion with lance and armor, and who threw down the gauntlet and challenged anyone who denied the monarch's right to rule. Today, the Crown Prosecutor in wig and gown with a sharp pencil was the champion.

❖

V. C. DESAI CAME INTO THE courtroom. Along with his glowing brown predatory features and silver hair, the wig and robe gave him an even more dramatic appearance than the other barristers. It was also the way he carried himself, she thought: He didn't just walk, he marched.

He paused in front of her, leaning across the front rail, and recited:

> "And thus I clothe my naked villainy
> With old odd ends, stolen out of holy writ;
> And seem a saint . . ."

He leaned closer, bending over the rail down toward her, whispering, "When most I play the devil."

He bowed. "Good morning, Miss James, Trent."

Trent said to Marlowe, "A poor rendition of *Richard III.*"

"Did he prosecute him, too?" Marlowe asked.

❖

47

❖

Marlowe smiled encouragement up to the princess in the dock. The princess nodded down at her without smiling. She wore a calm mask, but Marlowe knew how forlorn the woman felt, how frightened and alone it was to be center stage in a murder trial.

The jury was seated with minor quibbling, none of it in front of them.

The previous day Trent had made a demand for the results of the prosecution's investigation and elimination of potential jurors, and the prosecutor had refused to provide the information—or even admit that vetting had occurred. The judge backed up the prosecutor's position on the grounds of national security, a term Marlowe decided the British government seemed to employ to its advantage.

Seven women, five men, no one too rich, too old, or too young, eleven white, one black—it was a reasonable cross-section of people in the city who weren't able to avoid jury service on one excuse or another, only in this case no one wanted to avoid it. It occurred to her that the people on the jury were a good representation of solid middle-class British values. That was the kind of jury prosecutors sought—and that made her wonder whether it had been stacked. Defendants sought younger people,

❖

poor minorities, people with liberal educations, people with indications that they had counterculture values—bottom line, people who were more inclined to question authority and would not automatically take the word of a police officer as the gospel. The only minority on the jury, a bank officer of African descent, looked too successful to Marlowe for her to believe that he questioned authority. Most minorities suffered a degree of prejudice almost every day of their lives, but it bounced off the backs of some of them and angered others. The bank officer didn't seem the angry type.

The jurors took an oath of fairness: *I swear by the Almighty God I will faithfully try the defendant and give a true verdict according to the evidence.*

That's how it was in the courtroom, nearly everyone took—or had previously taken—an oath to serve justice. Attorneys took an oath before they got their license to practice, judges when they were appointed to the bench, people called to the witness box swore to state "the truth, the whole truth, and nothing but the truth."

The judge, Lord Bennington, was rigid, the type who ran a courtroom as a tight ship. He had a thin, humorless smile that seemed permanently etched on his face, and a sharp, dry, sarcastic wit that was seldom used but left nasty cuts when it was.

"Eminently qualified," Hall had told her earlier about the judge. "Tends to lean toward the conservative side of legal issues, but he's reasonably fair. We could have done better, but we also could have drawn much worse."

Her own take on the judge was that he was the type to give you enough rope when he wanted to hang you. He had been extremely condescending when she had met with him prior to trial. The fact that an American trial attorney—a woman, no less—was appearing as trial counsel obviously frayed his ingrained sense of the reserve and propriety of his elitist concept of British jurisprudence. *One is supposed to reply kindly, Yes, milord, No, milord, as he puts the rope around your neck,* Marlowe thought. She had assumed initially that she would give lip service to the courtroom decorum by also addressing him as "Your Lordship," but after he told her that he expected her to dress "ladylike"

❖

rather than the fashionable feminine suit of pants and jacket she wore to the courtroom, she decided a simple "Your Honor" would do and that she would dress as she damn well pleased.

She wasn't stupid enough to piss off a judge—it was always a no-win scenario for a lawyer. But when anyone stepped out of line and gave her a push, she pushed back. The judge wasn't happy about her representing the princess and might have been less critical had she been a male trial lawyer. Her instinct was to push back. If she didn't, she felt she would risk having the judge prejudice the jury against her. Judges did it subtly, not so much by a choice of words but a slight difference in tone that subliminally conveyed lesser respect for one attorney than another. When she pushed back and showed a judge she had teeth, most jurists became cautious and neutral. And if nothing else, it showed the jury that she believed in her client and had the courage to stand and fight.

"Mr. Desai," the judge said, nodding at the prosecutor, signaling him to present his opening statement to the jury, to "open the case for the prosecution," as Philip Hall had put it.

"Your Lordship." Desai, five or six feet down the bench from her, stood and faced the jury to make his opening statement.

"As you have been told, I am the Crown Prosecutor in this matter. I have, along with my junior, Mr. Timmings, the official duty to place before you the physical evidence and sworn testimony that the crown has gathered from witnesses, police, and forensic experts. To fulfill that duty, at this time it is my privilege to introduce you to the particulars of the offense and a summary of the evidence that will be presented. You have before you a copy of the indictment. As you can see, the crown alleges the killing of a human being in a premeditated manner with deliberation, in cold blood, if you will.

"As you all know, as the whole world I am sure knows, this trial revolves around the death of a man, not an ordinary man, but a person of great eminence and importance, but also a man who is capable of suffering and bleeding as any of us."

Bastard, Marlowe thought. There was no evidence of "suffering" and Desai knew it. But she kept her mouth shut—Hall had told her that objections were tolerated but only when absolutely necessary.

❖

"I do believe that I will be bearing false witness if I tell you that the case will not revolve around who killed him—the shooting was televised and watched by many millions—but why the shooting occurred. The 'why' will become obvious as you hear the evidence.

"The evidence will show that the killer is a neurotic, immature woman, a compulsive reader of silly romance novels in which beautiful virginal young women and handsome dashing young men with powerful loins come together in fiery embrace.

"She is a woman who has never performed a day's work in her life—born and raised in the lap of luxury, she is very much the spoiled girl in 'The Princess and the Pea' who thought of herself as so delicate, she felt a single pea hidden beneath twenty mattresses.

"She has exceeded at nothing, but was chosen to marry a prince and be a presumptive future queen because of her social position and physical attractiveness. She came into the marriage not as a mature woman with realistic ideals about what marriage entailed, but with juvenile notions.

"Nurtured on romantic drivel, from early in life she saw herself not as an ordinary person who must work and play and marry within the bounds of our society, but as someone *chosen* by the gods to be a queen. The prince was taken by her and lured into marriage by her. But he soon found that he had not married a responsible young woman, but a demanding girl with impossible romantic notions, and who wanted him at her feet day and night.

"The prince was a man of moderation and impeccable manners. He respected tradition and was dedicated to the tasks the nation assigned to him. He found relief from the tremendous pressures of his official duties in reading matters of intellectual concern—often issues of moral and social significance—and in sports activities with a small circle of friends.

"However, this life pattern was not one that the princess wanted. She expected the prince to give up his social activities, his pleasures of polo and the hunt, and provide her with the attention she craved—*and demanded*!

"When her neurotic demands for his fullest attention were not heeded, she tried to capture his attention with staged, melodramatic

❖

attempts to hurt herself. When she became pregnant with the prince heir to the throne, and was again denied the absolute attention she sought, she brought these theatrical dramas to an almost tragic conclusion by throwing herself down a stairway in an attempt to *murder* the baby in her womb!"

"Objection!" Marlowe snapped, getting to her feet. "That statement is outrageous, it's a lie and outrageous, and the prosecutor knows it! He's deliberately trying to prejudice the jury. I want the statement struck and the prosecutor sanctioned."

"Please take your seat, Miss James," the judge told her. He was agitated, but controlled it as he sent the jurors out of the courtroom.

Trent rose after the last juror had filed out. "Our apologies, Your Lordship. Miss James is not familiar with the decorum of our system. But I must say that my learned friend, Mr. Desai, has stepped beyond the bounds of tempered advocacy."

"He's prejudiced this jury with an outrageous remark," Marlowe said.

The judge stared down at her. It was the first time she had seen his thin smile gone. He spoke calmly but firmly. "Miss James, you are permitted to make objections. Shouting them in a loud, argumentative voice is not part of our procedures. Perhaps that is the way of the American system, but we abide by a different courtroom etiquette."

She faced him without flinching. "I apologize, Your Honor, but I was caught completely by surprise. I expected the courtroom etiquette to be on a much higher level. It came as a shock to hear the prosecutor take a cheap shot at the defendant, accusing her of a heinous crime without proof, the sort of underhanded tactic that I wouldn't expect from a prosecutor anywhere in the free world. I'm making a motion for a mistrial. This jury should be excused and a new one impaneled."

The judge looked like he was going to have a coronary. He was speechless, probably for the first time in his professional life. He gained control of himself and spoke in a calm, deliberate manner. "Please resume your seat. Mr. Desai, you will deal with the evidence in the matter before the court and not bring in collateral matters."

"Yes, Your Lordship."

❖

"This is an unusual case in all aspects, but let us remember that we have—*that most of us have*—been trained to observe proprieties and protocols that do not include attempting to inflame the jury with matters not supported by the evidence."

With the jury back in the courtroom, Desai continued his opening.

"When the defendant discovered that she had driven away the prince and she believed he had taken refuge in the arms of another woman, hate and anger consumed her. She was a woman with violent jealous tendencies, capable of sitting in front of her husband and cutting herself with a blade. The fact that she had been rejected festered in her, inflaming her thoughts, her very marrow.

"In order to understand why the crime was committed, why the life of an innocent person bled out of a gunshot wound, you have to understand how the prisoner in the dock thought of herself.

"In each case of that romantic drivel she read, the handsome prince casts aside the attentions of shrews and vixens and takes into his arms and his heart the deserving young heroine."

Desai's voice grew low, deliberately. Jurors and the judge leaned forward to catch his words.

"But you see, she had not won the love of the prince. After her childish antics from the beginning of the marriage, her irrationality, endless demands for attention, she had lost his passion—his ardor had gone to another woman.

"To her shock, she realized she was the vixen in the story, the ugly stepsister, an ill-tempered, malicious shrew who would act out her rage at the truth with murder. . . ."

He paused and met the eye of each juror in turn. "I used an interesting phrase earlier, 'in cold blood.' By that I am referring to the fact that the crime was committed deliberately and premeditatedly, that it was not a result of a sudden rush of anger.

"This scorned woman calculated, deliberated, and premeditated, finally—in her own twisted mind—arriving at a scheme to get revenge for what she considered to be a slight to the self-image she had created for herself out of silly stories of romantic fantasies.

"All she needed was a gun.

"And an audience of millions. . . ."

❖

———

DURING THE NOON BREAK, Marlowe joined the princess in a clerk's office that had been converted into a holding area for the princess when she wasn't in the courtroom.

"What a dreadful person," the princess said.

Marlowe said, "What a bastard."

"No, not the prosecutor, *me*. The person he described, the malicious shrew who murdered because she was rejected."

"That's not you, that's a straw man the prosecutor created to blow away in front of the jury. He does it not by portraying you as you really are, but by casting you in a false light, taking bits and pieces of the truth, blowing them out of proportion, and inferring motives from them that you never harbored."

But Marlowe knew she was in trouble. After she left the princess, she said to Hall, "I've never seen a prosecutor with an imagination. Every one I've been up against has been like Joe Friday in the old *Dragnet* series, sticking to the facts, just the facts, often boring the jury with them. This one has the imagination of Barbara Cartland and Danielle Steel. I'll bet he's read a few romance novels himself."

"Trent asked me—"

"I know, he's a little pushed out of shape about my attack on his learned pal, the prosecutor. But he's too damn reserved and well mannered to talk to me about it directly, so he asks you to do his dirty work. Is that about the size of it?"

Hall's jaw visibly tightened and she laughed from nervous tension. She grabbed his arm and squeezed. "I'll be a good girl, but I'm not going to let Desai walk all over our client. Maybe Trent should be more miffed at the prosecutor who took a cheap shot at her. That baby-murder allegation got to the jury and will be in big black headlines tonight, but at least the damage is mitigated by the fact that I threw it back in Desai's face. And he's on notice that I'm not an old-school chum—he won't step out of line again because he knows I will go after him. I'll play this learned-friend stuff only when the other person considers me an equal. Neither Desai nor Trent give a damn about me—they'd both like to see

❖

me fall on my face." She held up her hand. "I don't expect a reply to my accusation about your learned friends."

Hall nodded and pursed his lips, struggling with a reply. Finally he gave her a reluctant grin. "I will admit you gave Desai tit for tat—titfer, as the Cockneys say. But perhaps we can at least try not to antagonize the judge—or Trent."

"I won't antagonize the judge, at least not deliberately. But I won't take any more cheap shots from the prosecutor. I believe in doing unto others as they do unto you."

"Don't you mean doing unto others as you would want them to do unto you?"

"No, my courtroom God is the fire-and-brimstone deity of the Old Testament, not turn-the-other-cheek. When my client's life is at stake, it's an eye for an eye, a tooth for a tooth, war to the knife, and the last person standing wins."

❖

48

❖

Desai presented his case in chronological order, calling the prince's assistant who had organized the party and playing the videotape of the killing itself. No doubt each juror had seen the shooting a dozen times on TV before being picked as a juror. His first significant witness was General Sir Henry Percy, a retired army officer and senior member of the Establishment. He was at the party and saw the shooting. He testified that the princess was calm and collected, that she was so composed, he thought it was a joke.

The reason for calling Percy was to defuse the anticipated heat-of-passion defense, to rebut the contention that the princess's demeanor was one of sudden anger, but instead was calm, controlled, and determined. While the shooting was caught on film, the cameras were not positioned for a view of the princess's face.

Marlowe realized that Desai was not just going to put on his own case, but at the same time was going to attack hers. Since he would have a chance at the end of the defense case to put on rebutting evidence, this gave him two chances to attack her case, to really drill his version into the minds of the jurors.

❖

"Sir Henry, besides your military experiences, have you had prior experience in a situation in which someone was killed in a social context?"

"Unfortunately, I have."

"Would you tell us about that matter?"

"I was a friend and fellow soldier with Robert Rhenford, the 4ᵗʰ Earl of Rhenford. Many in this courtroom are too young to recall the case, but it was quite sensational in its day, about thirty years ago. The earl, believing his wife to be unfaithful, killed her. He made rather a mess of it. He observed her being flirtatious during a social gathering at his estate. I was in attendance and saw that she had had a bit too much to drink and was getting too familiar with another man. In a moment of intense anger, the earl rushed into his library, where he kept a gun in his desk drawer, and came running back into the room. He shot her before any of us could intervene."

"Really, not unlike the shooting of the prince, would you say?"

Marlowe knew what he would say and had a number of reasons to object but kept her seat—this was going to be one of a number of witnesses who testified about the princess's composure at the time she pulled the trigger.

"Actually," the general said, "it was quite unlike the current situation. The earl was in quite distress, his anger was obvious, he had lost total control of himself, letting his passions take the driver's seat."

When it came time for cross-examination, Marlowe asked the general, "You were a close friend of the earl's, isn't that correct?"

"Yes, Bobby and I were at Eton together."

"And you shared many experiences with him—attended his wedding, the christening of his children, shared many glasses of brandy and quite a number of cigars, isn't that right?" She smiled and nodded at a cigar poking out of his pocket. Her information came from a profile prepared by Trent's staff.

"Yes, we were chums." The general's voice cracked with emotion, but he immediately gained control of it. "Until the killing of his wife, of course—that was quite unforgivable. He avoided the rope because of heat of passion, provocation, that sort of thing. He died soon after in an auto accident."

❖

"An accident in which he had been drinking?"

"Yes, as a matter of fact, there was alcohol involved."

"And he had been drinking heavily the night he shot his wife?"

"Yes, that's true."

"Now, in regard to the prince, you were an acquaintance of his prior to his marriage to the princess, is that correct?"

"Yes."

"In fact, you never even met the princess until after the wedding?"

"I believe I met her at a polo match a few months after the wedding."

"You've never seen the princess drunk, have you?"

"Drunk? Of course not."

"Never saw her when she appeared angry or hurt? Never saw her when she was so desperate and distraught she was suicidal. Isn't that true?"

"I don't know what you are getting at."

"What I am getting at is a response to my question. The truth is, you have never been around the princess enough to be able to gauge her emotional state, nor are you a mind-reader. The truth is that you don't know what turmoil was going on in her head the night of the shooting, do you?"

"I saw her face clearly before she pulled the trigger."

"Have you ever heard of the expression *shell shock,* General?"

"Of course I've heard the expression, I've been a career officer."

"It comes in different manifestations, doesn't it? Some soldiers who have been traumatized react overtly violently and others appear to go into a catatonic state?"

"As I have testified, I have a previous experience with a killing that gives me great insight into the mental processes of a person who kills. The princess was not a victim of battlefield trauma."

"What traumas has the princess experienced?"

"Excuse me?"

"I asked you about the traumas the princess experienced."

"I—well, I don't know the answer to that. I know she had a very fine life and an excellent husband."

"Do you? What was their married life like? What did they say to each other in the privacy of their bedroom? Was there any violence in their marriage?"

"My lord," Desai said.

"Yes, Miss James, restrict yourself to a single question and wait for an answer."

"Yes, thank you. Now, General, even though you have hardly spoken to the princess in your life, you claim to know personal things about her. Did you get your information from the tabloids?"

"My lord!" Desai shot up from his seat.

The judge frowned down at Marlowe. "General Sir Henry Percy is well known to this court as a distinguished gentleman and soldier."

"He's also an opinionated, adverse witness to my client who has been permitted to testify about matters he has no knowledge of. May I proceed, Your Honor?"

"Proceed," the judge whispered.

"You spent your entire adult life in the army, isn't that correct?"

"Yes."

"And besides your friend Bobby, you have seen many men under stress during your military career?"

"Yes, of course."

"For many reasons, not just military ones, but domestic problems? Would you say that you've dealt with hundreds of men with problems over the decades?"

He grinned. "Perhaps thousands."

"Thousands of men?"

"Yes."

"Would you consider yourself a man who enjoys the type of things that are typically male-oriented, things like sports, guns, hunting, horses, that sort of thing?"

"I have never gotten into crochet or knitting."

Laughter exploded in the courtroom.

Marlowe didn't smile. "In fact, General, other than a short marriage—your wife passed away early in the marriage, I understand—you have spent your entire life surrounded by men and dealing with men, isn't that correct?"

❖

"I suppose that's a correct statement. It's the way of career military men."

"For most of your active duty time, women were not in uniform other than in those few positions allotted to females?"

"Correct."

"Men are sometimes quick to anger, aren't they? You've seen men having a beer one minute while talking about soccer or rugby, and the next throwing punches at each other, haven't you?"

"Many times."

"But you don't see it that often with a woman, do you? It's more unusual for a woman to resort to physical violence?"

"Yes, I suppose that's been my experience. Men are more likely to fly off the handle and get physical."

"And women tend to hold in their emotions, correct?"

"My lord," Desai said, "we are getting into areas of psychology that are best left for those in that field."

"I don't agree," Marlowe said. "This gentleman has testified about the emotional state of my client. I'm entitled to discover his qualifications for making his judgment of her character."

"Proceed."

"I saw a calm, collected woman in complete control of her emotions," the general said.

"Actually, I never asked you a question, but thank you for volunteering the information. I don't doubt that's what you *thought* you saw, but you don't have the experience to judge a young woman's emotions, do you? As you pointed out, you've spent your entire career surrounded by men."

"I have had experiences with women, thank you."

"But not on the same level as men, that's what you've testified to, most of your adult life you have been in a position to judge the emotional responses of men."

"You're making a speech, not asking a question. Go to your next question," the judge said.

"In this case, you judged the princess as you would a man, isn't that a fact?"

"No. I—"

❖

"In fact, General, you don't have the foggiest notion of what was going on at the time of the incident in the mind, heart, and soul of the young woman you're testifying against, do you?"

"I know what I saw. She was calm and collected." His jaw was tight.

"You are not used to having your opinions challenged, are you, General? Especially by a woman, isn't that true?"

"Your Lordship," Desai said in a pained tone.

"Are you finished with this witness?" the judge asked her.

"No. Alcohol is a disinhibitor, isn't it?" she asked the general.

"We all know that alcohol will make one less inhibited."

"And isn't it true that what you experienced thirty years ago was your drunken friend losing control under the effect of alcohol and shooting his wife because of who she was talking to? Isn't that why his emotions were so obvious—he was a lush who couldn't hold his liquor?"

General Sir Henry Percy pressed his lips together and didn't respond. Marlowe went on.

"In fact, isn't it true that the accident that took his life also killed a young mother and two children, an accident your old school chum caused when his car went over the dividing line because he was dead drunk?"

"I am not here to be badgered."

"I believe you're here to testify, and it's still my turn to ask the questions. You don't like the princess, do you?"

"No, I have a prejudice against people who kill the Crown Prince of my country."

"It's more than that, isn't it? You've never liked her, have you? She was never part of the polo and hunt crowd, was she?"

"I'm sure I can't tell you exactly what the woman did with her spare time."

"Isn't it true that you came into this court to condemn a woman whose suffering you know nothing about and have your voice crack with emotion over the fate of a damn lush who killed an innocent woman and children with his car?"

"My—my lord!" Desai stammered.

"You found nothing wrong with your drunken friend killing his wife

❖

and innocent people, but you are aghast that a woman could strike back—"

The judge shot up. "You are out of order! This court is in recess!"

TWENTY MINUTES LATER MARLOWE left the judge's office with Philip Hall at her side. Desai and Trent had both left ahead of her in a proper British huff. The judge had mostly sat and stared at her. He appeared confused and in a quandary, as if he wanted desperately to hold her in contempt but knew it wouldn't play well in the news media.

"I don't think they know what to do with you," Philip said.

"Who? Trent and his learned friend?"

"Everyone—Desai, Trent, Sir Fredic, the judge."

"Because I'm a woman in their territory."

"Oh, no, a fossil like General Sir Henry may still believe that women aren't the intellectual equal of men, but there are too many fine female lawyers for anyone involved with the law to have that Stone Age notion. Besides, British women are every bit as tough to handle as you are. The judge who gets respect all day in court goes home at night to have his wife take him down a notch or two because he forgot her birthday. No, it's something completely different."

He paused in the hallway and met her eye.

"I really suspect that their problem is not because you're a woman, but because you're such a damn fine lawyer."

49

❖

Desai's next witnesses was a twenty-year staff member of the royal household. He was the servant who offered to announce the princess as she entered the main hall where the party was being held. That put him in a position to observe the princess close up immediately before the shooting. He testified that the princess had been calm and collected when she walked by him.

"In your twenty years in a royal household, have you ever seen a Royal present anything but restraint toward the public?" Marlowe asked on cross.

He admitted that he had not.

Another member of the household, a woman who assisted the princess as a maid the night of the shooting, followed with the same theme, that the princess was calm.

Marlowe asked her, "I notice you told the police that the princess could have swift mood changes—what did you mean?"

"Oh, she's quite famous for going from one place to another with her moods. She'd be calm one moment, then blow at us, and then laugh hysterically the next. But she was calm that night, she was."

❖

"At that precise moment you did not observe anger in her face, is that what you mean?"

"She was calm when she killed the prince," the woman said stubbornly.

"You didn't see her kill the prince, did you?"

"No, but—"

"And you just testified that she had swift mood changes, didn't you?"

The woman's eyes narrowed. "I saw what I saw."

"You don't like the princess, do you? I mean, even before the shooting, you didn't like her, did you?"

The woman shrugged. "She wasn't well liked by some staff members."

"By the staff members who supported the prince in his marital disputes with his wife, you mean."

"We saw how he suffered from her constant mood swings."

"Did you see how she suffered from the treatment she got from him? Or did the fact you were getting a paycheck signed by the prince blind you to her pain?"

The maid was followed by a police officer. Chief Inspector Arthur Field supervised the crime scene investigation and had taken the princess into custody. He spoke briefly with her after she waived her rights. His theme was the same as the others', that the princess was calm and collected.

When Desai paused in the questioning to peruse his notes, a bailiff handed Marlowe a folded note with a page attached. The note was a scribble that read, *Sold to the tabs by an informed source.* It was signed, *Your pal Dutton.*

She looked up at the spectators' gallery. Dutton grinned down at her.

The attachment was a poor photocopy of a page from a Preliminary Investigation Report. The page had been filled in by hand. In the block that called for the officer to describe the suspect's demeanor, the word *hysterical* was written. At the bottom of the page were the initials *AF.*

"Your witness," the judge told her.

Marlowe took a deep breath and stood up, placing the page on her podium.

❖

"I was given a document by the prosecutor, Chief Inspector, called the Final Investigation Report. You were the author of that report?"

"Yes, ma'am."

"And in that report you describe the princess's demeanor at the time you questioned her as calm?"

"Yes, ma'am."

"And you wrote that report . . . when? About a week after the incident?"

"Yes, ma'am, that's correct."

"And in that report you described the princess's demeanor following the shooting as calm?"

"Yes, ma'am."

"Now, there was another report, wasn't there? An earlier one?"

The officer visibly tensed.

"Isn't that correct?"

"Yes, ma'am."

"And in that report, the Preliminary Investigation Report you wrote within hours of the incident, you described the princess's demeanor as hysterical?"

"What I meant was—"

"What did you write in the report?"

"My lord," Desai said.

"Give the witness a chance to respond, Miss James," the judge said.

"Thank you. Chief Inspector, you described her demeanor as hysterical in the earlier report, yes or no?"

"You see—"

"Yes or no, did you describe her as hysterical?"

"Yes, ma'am."

"Now please turn to the jury and tell them who instructed you to criminally and fraudulently conceal this fact—"

"My lord!"

"Was it the prosecutor?" Marlowe shouted on the heel of Desai's plea to the judge.

The judge surprised Marlowe by calling a recess and leaving the bench—without instructing the attorneys to present themselves in his office.

"I thought for sure he'd have me in chains," Marlowe told Hall.

"He's disgusted," Philip Hall told her, "he realizes Desai withheld the original report."

"Knows it and isn't going to do anything about it. How the hell do you have a system in which a prosecutor can get away with that? And don't give me that national security crap."

He shook his head. "You can't judge a legal system based upon a trial that is extraordinary."

She was only pretending shock at the fact that the police and prosecution had buried a report. It was not an uncommon practice in American cases. It was rare for a major case to go to trial in the States where accusations weren't made that critical information was being concealed from the defense.

"What's left of Desai's case?" she asked. "I can't believe that he's only going to call the medical examiner and rest."

"That's what he told us."

She looked at the autopsy photos that had been turned over. They showed the entry round of the bullet in the chest area but not the prince's face. "In terms of the ghastly photos jurors are often shown in murder cases, these are really tame. We don't even get to see suffering on the prince's face."

"I suppose there has been an effort to keep the prince's face out of the pictures, not show a Royal in a horrid death pose, that sort of thing."

"Something's wrong," she said. She looked up at the gallery. Dutton was gone. Probably not sure she wouldn't sic the police on him, she thought.

"What do you mean?"

"It's been too easy. The prosecution's case has been too tame. I've jerked Desai's leash a few times, but overall, he's too damn smug. Something's wrong, I can feel it in my bones. The other shoe hasn't dropped yet."

50

❖

After court, Dutton hung around the courthouse, hoping to catch sight of Marlowe James and maybe let her show her gratitude by buying him a drink and giving him a story. He didn't see Marlowe come out, but he spotted another familiar face—Keith Willard, the prince's armorer, the servant who cared for the prince's gun collection. Willard was one of a long line of "an unnamed but well-placed source inside the palace" who sold tidbits to *Burn* and other trash publications.

He had never really gotten anything really juicy out of the gun handler, but it piqued his interest to see the man at the courthouse, because he wasn't mentioned in the police reports and wasn't on the witness list that the prosecution had disclosed.

When Desai came out of the courtroom with Chief Inspector Field, Willard started to approach them. Desai gave him a warning look and a slight shake of his head and kept walking. Willard took the hint and stopped.

Dutton caught the fact that Field said something in an aside to Willard as the police inspector veered over to a drinking fountain.

Willard nodded, spun on his heel, and started for the exit out of the Old Bailey.

❖

What's that all about? Dutton asked himself, as he followed Willard. It came as no surprise that Willard would testify—he was the person who took care of the prince's guns, including the pistol the princess had used to blow a hole in her husband. One would expect that he would be called to the stand to identify the gun as belonging to the prince. But he hadn't testified for the prosecution so far. And now he was skulking around the courthouse playing at intrigue with the Crown Prosecutor.

"What's it all about, Alfie?" Dutton sang as he exited the courthouse. He let Willard get halfway to the Underground station before he came up behind him.

"Hello, Keith, haven't seen you in a long time."

Concern flashed on Willard's face. "Piss off, I'm not supposed to talk to reporters."

"That makes two of us avoiding reporters. I'm on my own now, writing a novel. Say, we should talk—you knew a lot about the prince, didn't you? You were his executive assistant, eh?"

"I was his armorer and I'm not supposed to talk to reporters."

"I'm a novelist, don't you know, and the book won't come out for a year or two—won't make much difference then, will it?" He grabbed Willard's arm and steered him toward a pub. "I need to wet my throat before I hit the tube. You know, Willard, a man like you who was close to the prince should consider a book, too. I could introduce you to my publisher. I'm buying myself a place on the Costa del Sol. You've been to the south of Spain? Bet your old lady is crazy about it, all that sun, and it's not a bad place for men, is it, the women wear nothing but a little sand at those beaches. With your insider information about the prince, I'll bet you could buy a bloody villa, eh?"

51

❖

"You're being sandbagged," Dutton told Marlowe.

She had no sooner entered her room than the phone rang. And Dutton had the ability to catch her by surprise. "The hotel operator is supposed to screen my calls."

"I told her I was Anthony Trent."

"I should call the police."

"And turn in your friend? Your only *friend.*"

"You are a slimy reporter for a scandal rag."

"I'm the guy who tipped you off about the police report, remember?"

"Mr. Dutton, I know who you are and what you are, and for certain you don't do favors without getting blood in return. I appreciate your tip today, it repays me for burglarizing my room and assaulting me. Now let's just call ourselves even before I yell for the police again."

"Tsk-tsk, it's going to be that way, is it? I just thought you might be interested in knowing when you were being had, but I guess you'll have to read about it after you fall on your face."

She gripped the phone tighter. The bastard thought he could manipulate her. And he could, she was that desperate. "All right, you tell me what you have and I'll tell you if it's worth anything to me."

❖

"Now, that's a hell of a deal—I give, you take, I get lost. I thought perhaps we could get together and get to know each other better—"

"I'd rather cuddle up to a snake."

"And pass information back and forth, give and take, tit for tat, buy and sell."

"You have nothing I want or need."

"You're a smarter girl than that, aren't you? Did you hear the part where I said you were being sandbagged? Again."

She sighed. "Talking to you is like having a conversation with the devil. It's all very tempting, but I know in the end you will want nothing less than my soul. Tell me what you have. If it's any good, I'll give you an exclusive first chance I get. You'll have to trust me."

He chuckled. "I know Shakespeare's philosophy about lawyers, but I admit I do have a place in my heart for street lawyers. I'll be in the hotel lounge. You'll recognize me, I'm the handsome devil who was feeling you up the other day."

"How did you get into the hotel?"

"A police officer investigating the attack in your hotel room is always welcomed by the more-than-cooperative hotel personnel."

SHE FOUND HIM IN the lounge. "I'm glad you chose a dark corner."

"I could learn to love you in the dark, luv. In fact, I already do. I've always had a fatal weakness for women who get right down to it and let me know that I am worthless and despicable."

"What are you trying to sell me, Mr. Dutton?"

"Tony."

"Let's get on with this, Mr. Dutton. What do you have?"

"You don't really understand. I take this personal."

"Really? I wouldn't think a tabloid reporter had feelings."

"Oh, I'm not talking about your insults, those are just defense mechanisms to protect yourself. You are captivated by my sensuous male charisma and are—"

"My God, you're delusional."

"But let's put aside our differences, because we both have the same exact motivation about the princess's case."

❖

"Which is?"

"We both want to win. I have something for you. I will put you on your honor as a lawyer for the people and not the muckety-mucks that you will repay me when you can with an exclusive. I want to build a bond of trust between us. I believe that there should be trust besides sex with the woman in my life."

"Would you mind getting to the point before they come to cart you off?"

"The point is Keith Willard."

"All right, I'll bite, who's Keith Willard?"

He nodded. "I didn't think you knew. Interesting, very interesting. You have a gun in your case, right? The smoking one the princess used to shoot her husband with."

"I think you, me, and five billion other people are aware of that."

"You understand that the prince had a gun collection, that between what he inherited, got as gifts, and bought, his collection was probably the size of the armaments of some small nations."

"Okay, he had a lot of guns."

"He didn't just have a lot of guns, he had a collection valued at a king's ransom."

"And Keith Willard had something to do with that collection?"

"When most of us think of a woman grabbing her husband's gun and ventilating him with it, the image of a weapon that was stored in a bedroom end table or closet comes to mind, perhaps even a desk in a home office. But the prince didn't own a gun or even a bunch of guns, he had hundreds of them. Willard is—was—the prince's armorer, the person who cared for the guns, cleaning them, repairing them, keeping them from rusting, whatever you do to guns. Most of the weapons are kept under lock and key in display cases."

"The princess got the gun from Willard?"

"Indirectly. She got the key to the display case from him."

It hit her, a revelation from hell. She saw it coming, but kept her features frozen. "I take it Willard has some recollection of when she checked the gun out."

"He kept a log. She didn't sign out the gun, but he saw her take it and noted it in the log."

❖

She nodded. Her throat was dry. "And?"

"The media briefing from Trent's office says the princess got the gun three hours before the shooting, then drove to Cragthorpe and used it."

"What does the log say?"

"She got it the day before. Twenty-seven hours before."

Twenty-seven hours. Not even Slow Trigger James could sell a jury on a heat-of-passion defense in which the shooter got prepared the day before—then drove a couple hundred miles to pull the trigger.

It was one thing to spend years building up provocation, but another to plan the killing one day, sleep on it, and execute it the next day.

Especially after the world's been told that she had gotten the gun a few hours before.

52

❖

"It's prejudicial misconduct of the most egregious nature," Marlowe told the judge. "The prosecutor has sandbagged the defense every step of the way. This latest obstruction of justice denies the defendant the fundamental right to a fair trial. It was deliberate, malicious, prejudicial, and irreparable."

She spoke calmly, with deliberation. The judge listened to her quietly. Trent and Hall had arrived in the room only seconds before. She had stormed the judge's office and demanded he call in the prosecutor.

When she was finished, the judge said, "Mr. Desai?"

"As usual, Miss James makes accusations beyond the limits of sound legal precedent. It's true that we did not reveal the armorer's exact knowledge. However, that information was in the hands of the defense, wasn't it? The princess knew how and when she got the gun—it's not the fault of the prosecution if their client lied to them. We planned to use the evidence during rebuttal and would have notified the defense once that phase of the trial began."

"Miss James?"

"The defendant doesn't have a duty to reveal information. It's the prosecution that has the burden of coming forth with evidence to prove

❖

the allegations—and to reveal that information to the defense. The duty of disclosure includes witnesses and physical evidence. The princess didn't tell us about the armorer because she didn't know he had observed her, if in fact he did, and didn't know he made an entry in the log, if in fact he did. . . . As we know, it wouldn't be the first time that evidence was tampered with in this case by the police."

The judge flushed. "Miss James, I have tried to give you as much free rein as possible because you are not used to our legal system, but I will not permit a catty remark to be made that defames a Crown Prosecutor."

"Judge, I did not make a *catty* remark and I find your statement that I did as being chauvinistic—I don't think you would refer to a man's comment in those terms. I spoke the truth, and once again you have come down on me. You have just heard that the prosecutor did not turn over critical evidence and earlier had tampered with a police report, you have been in the courtroom when the prosecutor made a prejudicial, inadmissible statement to the jury calling the defendant a child murderer, and I have yet to hear you sanction the prosecutor. What I do hear is continuous remarks on my character and I want that to stop. If you can't handle this trial with an even hand, I suggest you disqualify yourself and let's get another judge."

The judge turned so purple he appeared on the verge of a coronary. She was certain he had stopped breathing. There was frozen silence in the room until Trent spoke.

"My lord, I apologize on behalf of the princess and her defense team. May we be excused?"

Without waiting for a response, Trent got up and she and Philip Hall followed him out.

"What exactly do you think you're doing?" he demanded in the outer chamber.

"Something you're not doing—defending the client. Why didn't you know about the armorer?"

"We knew about the armorer, we knew about the log."

"How did you—"

"We spoke to the armorer's supervisor."

"Why didn't you tell me?"

"You never asked. You never bothered to tell us before you confronted the judge with it."

"Desai thought he was sandbagging me, but it turns out that it was my cocounsels who were doing it. How did you plan to deal with the armorer's testimony when he brought him on rebuttal?"

"We had prepared a legal argument to keep him out."

"The judge won't keep him out."

"We understand that, but our duty is to make the argument, not guarantee results. You are deliberately antagonizing the judge. You have to go back in there and offer a sincere apology."

She took a deep breath to calm her voice. "I understand that you have to live with the man after this trial and I don't. I respect judges, but I also know when I'm being torpedoed by one. This one is out to sink me. I'm not going to apologize. You can offer your apologies and tell him for me that if he comes down on me again when he should be on the prosecutor's back, I'm going to put his prejudicial conduct on the front pages of every paper in the country. And if I find out that you are withholding critical evidence from me, I'm going to put you next to him on the front pages."

Trent gaped. "You—you're insane." He backed away from her, then fled back into the judge's office, his silk robes flying.

Hall stared at her for a moment, started after Trent, and stopped when Marlowe called his name.

"Tell the judge I want an order for this armorer to appear in court tomorrow. He's going to be the first witness I call."

It was Hall's turn to gape. *"What?"*

"We have to, for damage control. We bring it out and make it part of our case, reshaping our defense. We can't hide it, so we have to use it."

"How do you plan to use it?"

"I don't know yet, I need to talk to the princess. But I'm reminded of an expression they had in my hometown when I was a kid—if you're being run out of town, get to the front of the mob and pretend it's a parade."

She gave a great sigh. "Let's hope it doesn't rain on our parade."

❖

A STUFFED MANILA ENVELOPE was waiting for Marlowe at the front desk when she got back to the hotel. She had asked Hall to have a background check done on Tony Dutton. Opening the envelope in her room, she found a series of articles from a newspaper morgue going back a dozen years. The note attached to the articles called them a "sampling" and indicated there were others available if she wanted more information.

Sergeant Kramer, who was impressed by Dutton's virility, had been correct when she said he had been a prizewinning investigative reporter. During his time in "respectable journalism," he had written exposés about the government, industry, and crime.

"A man after my own heart," Marlowe murmured as she read articles in which he crusaded against injustices against women, minorities, and poor working stiffs. The last series of articles was a crime exposé before a two-year hiatus in reporting. After the break in writing, he began to crank out hack tabloid contributions.

She read the crime exposé first with growing interest and then horror.

It started with Dutton being offered a line of cocaine at a party. It gave him the idea to follow the "tracks" of the drug back as far as he could. He got the name of the small-time supplier who sold the cocaine to his host, and he was off and running. From the street supplier, who never bought more than a pound of cocaine at a time and sold it to consumers in grams and ounces, he followed the crooked road to the district "distributor," who bought and sold kilos to a "wholesaler," who dealt in hundred-kilo units. He kept digging until he followed the trail back to Liverpool, where a "bent copper," which from the context Marlowe realized was a crooked cop, was providing cover for shipments that came into the port from ships sailing out of Colombia.

The investigation had taken Dutton a year. Along the way he met and began a romantic relationship with a woman in the Colombian embassy. She was a commercial attaché for her country and she fed him information on what ships she suspected were carrying contraband.

Dutton had been careful to disguise his source in his stories, but the dopers had also been smart: They stole his phone bill out of his mailbox. It had the calls made to the woman.

❖

He received a message from her to meet her at her apartment. When he arrived, her door was slightly ajar. He pushed it open—and stood in shock.

The woman was tied up, with her mouth taped. She was sitting on five gallons of gasoline.

And pushing open the door ignited the fuse.

The explosion mercifully killed her.

Marlowe felt sick as she read the account of the murder. What beasts there were in this world. Her hands shook as she stuffed the articles back in the envelope.

She had picked up one more piece of information from the news accounts. Dutton had received burns on his legs and chest from the fire. The plastic surgeon who treated him was Walter Howler.

53

❖

The prisoner of the Tower stood at a window and watched the Thames go by. She was melancholy and the deep, dark, slow waters did nothing to raise her spirits.

A message had arrived that her American lawyer was coming for another conference. She hated having to relive the past and dreaded that she might actually be called to testify. She had been told it was usually best that a defendant didn't take the witness stand, that she would only be asked to testify if it was a last-ditch hope, but that was what her whole life had seemed to come down to, a last-ditch hope.

She thought about the tales of other princesses held prisoner in towers and the knights in shining armor who rescued them. The one that stuck with her was a story about a romantic rescue at the Tower of London.

It concerned the Earl of Nithsdale, a rebellious young Scottish nobleman who was captured in battle with the English and taken to the Tower to await execution with two other nobles in 1716. They were sentenced to death and scheduled to be executed in two weeks. When word of the execution sentence reached Nithsdale's beautiful twenty-four-year-old wife in Scotland, the country had been covered with snow and

❖

travel in stagecoaches canceled. With no time to spare, the brave young woman road horseback nearly four hundred miles to London in brutal winter weather.

Arriving two days before the execution, she went straight to the king and threw herself at his feet, begging for the life of her husband. The poor king dragged her across the room with her hanging on to his long coat until his guards grabbed her. Swooning in the arms of the guards, she got thrown out of the palace rather than tossed in the dungeon.

She could not get into the Tower to see her husband without written permission. She lied to the guards, telling them that the king had promised a reprieve, and bribed them into letting her see her husband. Alone with her husband, she told him she would find a way to save him.

She took lodging in the city for her and her maid, and by the next day had come up with a plan, enlisting her maid, the landlady at the lodging, and a friend of the landlady into the plan.

With only hours to spare before the execution, she returned to the Tower with the three women. Lady Nithsdale again bribed the guards, but was only allowed to bring in one lady at a time. She took in the landlady's friend first, a woman named Mrs. Hilton. Inside the room, Mrs. Hilton took off extra woman's clothing she had brought for the earl. Lady Nithsdale escorted Mrs. Hilton and brought back Mrs. Mills, her landlady. Using a wig for her husband's hair, and makeup for his dark eyebrows, she rouged his cheeks to hide the stubbles of his beard.

She then escorted her husband out, with him dressed as a woman and holding a handkerchief in front of his face to hide weeping. Seeing him to the Tower gates, she returned to his room and pretended to carry on a conversation with him in the room to give him a chance to get away.

Her husband escaped out of the city while his two codefendants were being executed. She joined him later in Italy.

The princess had never heard the reason why Lady Nithsdale was never punished for her crime, but she imagined that her romantic daring brought admiration rather than scorn from the men of the era.

The Nithsdales lived a long life together in Italy . . . happily ever after.

Lord Nithsdale was lucky, the princess thought. He had a woman who loved him more than life itself.

❖

What sort of feeling was love that burned as bright as life itself?

What kind of courage and imagination did it take to escape from a life that you hated?

To run off to Italy and live happily ever after with the man you loved?

❖

54

❖

"Why did you take the gun from your husband's collection a full day before you used it?" Marlowe asked.

The princess shook her head. "There are things that can't be explained."

Marlowe paced in the Tower room, her adrenaline high.

"That answer won't do. When they have you under the microscope—
and that's what's happening, not just the jury but the whole world is
watching this trial—you have to fill in all the blanks. We can't leave
anything unanswered—if we do, the prosecution will provide a conclusion we don't want. I'm not even sure the judge will permit us to argue
heat of passion when you got the gun the day before. You have to tell me
the truth."

"I was afraid."

"Afraid of who? What?"

"Everything, everybody."

"Be more specific—why did you take the gun?"

"To protect myself." She shook her head. "I can't explain. I was
frightened, I took the gun."

"What were you frightened of?"

❖

"I told you: everything. I wanted the pain to go away."

"You planned to kill yourself?"

"Yes, that's right, I planned to use the gun on myself."

Marlowe shut her eyes. The princess's statement that she planned to use the gun on herself resounded in her mind. And it rang false. She opened her eyes and said, "I don't believe you. But more importantly, the jury won't believe you."

"Well, they will have to believe me, it's the truth. I was going to kill myself and at the last moment I decided to kill my husband instead. I—I had the gun already, to use on myself. But at the party, I went suddenly into a rage and used it on him instead. That still makes it sudden provocation, doesn't it?"

"If I thought you could sell that story to a jury, I'd say run with it, but it's not ringing true to me. If it's true, you should have told me and we could have built a defense around it. Now that we know you got the gun a day ahead of the shooting, you either got it as part of a premeditated plan to kill your husband . . . or you got it for another reason. It's going to sound contrived when we suddenly come up with a suicide theory."

"As my advocate, isn't it your duty to sponsor my story? That's how it was explained to me, that you tell your barrister what happened and they explain it to the judge and jury. Well, I want you to say that I took the gun because I planned to kill myself and changed my mind when I was provoked by my husband."

"My job as an attorney is to represent you to the best of my ability, within the scope of what I have to work with. But that doesn't include helping you concoct a story. I don't have to believe in your story to advocate it, but I'm not a robot, either. What I saw in this room was you latching on to a version I suggested, that you took the gun to use it on yourself.

"Let's get down to the bottom line. I don't care where you got your story, you're the only person on earth who really knows why you pulled that trigger. I'm not your judge or jury, I'm here to persuade them. My only concern is whether a jury will buy it. My instincts are that the story sounds contrived, a tap dance around the truth. And it gets

❖

worse—the only way to get before the jury is for you to testify. I don't think you can do it convincingly."

"I don't want to testify."

"No defense lawyer wants a defendant to testify, but if it's the only way to avoid a conviction, you will have to do it."

The princess turned away from her and Marlowe spoke to her back.

"I'm getting a gut feeling that you have lied to me about exactly what brought you to the point where you pulled the trigger and killed your husband."

She turned around to face Marlowe. "You have lost faith in me."

"That's not true. Trials aren't based upon faith, trust, loyalty, or any other fine moral stance. They're not even based upon the truth—they're based upon the evidence that gets admitted. And that evidence has to be credible. Despite anything you've heard or read, juries are not easily fooled. When you get twelve people from different walks of life listening to the same evidence, there's always going to be one or more who see through bullshit. When you lose credibility with a jury on one issue, you might as well pack it up, because they will not believe anything you say. Once a liar, always a liar, that's how juries judge lawyers and their clients. If they think they're getting a snow job at any time, you'll lose them."

"And you think they will believe I am snowing them, as you put it."

"I think there's something you're holding back. You've talked about your fears in general, but I also get the impression that you were actually frightened about something specific, but that you won't tell me what it is."

The princess got up and stood by the window, looking out at the Thames. After a moment she turned back to Marlowe.

"I'm afraid that I have said all I plan to say about the subject."

Marlowe sighed. She checked her watch. "We're due back in court in an hour. I will be giving my opening statement." She met the princess's eye. "All right: As they say, you're a big girl and it's your life. But if there are any more surprises, you had better let me in on them now."

The princess turned back to the window for a long moment. Without turning, she asked Marlowe, "Have they told you I once took a lover?"

❖

"No one's told me about a lover."

"He was a man much like my husband, very well bred, he reminded me of my husband."

"You loved him? Had an affair?"

"Loved him, had an affair. Later, I heard that he had told others about it."

"Do you still love him?"

"I'm not sure I know what love is anymore. I was lonely and needed him. I'm certain about one thing, though. Men are bastards."

55

❖

The judge called upon Marlowe to open her case.

She stood up and placed her notes on the small podium that sat atop the bench table. She always had copious notes on hand when she began her opening and closing statements and examinations of witnesses—and rarely relied on them. It was a security blanket, but one she didn't need because she had performed the three vital tasks any lawyer had to do prior to trial: preparation, preparation, preparation.

"Mr. Desai was wrong when he described to you the plight of a princess as a fairy tale. As you will learn during the trial, it was a horror story, a story of torment and abuse, of a young woman swept into a nightmare, spiraling down further and further in a dark hell until she ended the abuse by striking back at her tormentor.

"It is a tale of a marriage that was a fraud, of a domineering bridegroom who took a picture of his lover along on his honeymoon.

"The princess was an ordinary young woman. She had been born into an old family that had money and position, but she was raised in that conservative British fashion where young ladies who take skiing vacations to the Swiss Alps also learn how to darn socks and cook plum pudding.

❖

"Before she entered into the royal marriage, there wasn't much that distinguished her from most other young women in her late teens. She was something of a dreamer, a romantic dreamer whose ambitions were not in the direction of academics. She was more inclined to read a tale of love than dissect a frog.

"That is a key thing that you have to realize about her. Her goal was to find a man who would love her and take care of her. Unlike many young women in her late teens in this day and age, she did not even experiment with sex. She was saving her virginity to give it to the man she loved.

"The man who came into her life was not an ordinary person but a prince, a real one, one of the richest and most powerful men on earth, the scion of the First Family of the entire English-speaking world. Heir to the throne of a world power. A person of rank and privilege that is unimaginable to ordinary people.

"This prince of princes pointed at the young woman and literally picked her out of a crowd and asked her to be his wife.

"The future princess is an impressionable, inexperienced, naive, rather immature eighteen-year-old when the prince first gives attention to her. Her only experiences in life are those of a schoolgirl.

"He is thirteen years her senior, a symbol of world power and privilege, worldly, well traveled, a veteran of the military. He has spent his entire life in the public eye. Instilled in him are centuries of both supreme privilege and a sense of duty.

"He reaches out and asks the young girl to marry him, to become a real-life princess, to someday become the queen of a world power, a position of unparalleled power, privilege, and prestige. It meant someday she would assume an ancient throne and have the adulation of hundreds of millions of people.

"When the news is made public, a media storm the like of which the world has never seen ignited like the burst of a supernova. And that media explosion knocks the young woman off her feet. In one fell swoop, she goes from being a rather ordinary teenage girl, living in an apartment and doing odd jobs, to being the focus of world attention.

"To say that it was a mind-blowing experience for her would be a gross understatement. It went beyond the impossible and unbelievable,

❖

it was a *soul-wrenching* experience—an experience she had no training or background to deal with."

Marlowe's eyes slowly swept the jurors. "It was an unimaginable turn of events. An average teenage girl was overnight turned into a worldwide media sensation—and no one offered assistance or advice on how to handle the sudden explosion of interest.

"The world acclaimed her as their fairy-tale princess. *It was not a position she sought.* She was not a young woman who lacked a good sense of reality. She did not think of herself as a fairy-tale princess. *It was how the world thought of her.*"

She paused to take a drink of water and let what she had said sink into the minds of the jurors. Her eyes traveled slowly from juror to juror as she continued, making sure she made direct eye-to-eye contact with each.

"If there is anything about the princess that dominated her emotions, it was the need to not disappoint people. She felt she had been rejected by her own parents when she was a child, that she had disappointed them, and that experience resulted in a need not just to be accepted, but to be loved. And she thought she had found that love and acceptance.

"But while the public would find her marriage to be a fairy tale come true, she would soon discover that it was a living nightmare, a horror story.

"She had been waiting for love. Like many of us women, she was waiting for the knight in shining armor to ride up and carry her away. When the prince gave her attention, she adored him. By the time he asked for her hand, she was hopelessly in love with him.

"You have to keep in mind, this was no ordinary man who was asking for her hand. Like millions of other young girls, she had been raised to respect and admire the man who was heir to the throne of their country.

"She is a woman of infinite passion, a woman who had held her passions in check, waiting for the right man and the right time. And when he came along, she was willing and eager to share her fire with the man she loved.

"But that sharing was never to happen.

❖

"You see, the fairy-tale marriage was a fraud. It was a loveless, emotionally brutal *institution* of a marriage, a pro forma arrangement by a man who used and abused his power and privileges in his treatment of his bride.

"He did not marry the princess for love.

"He married her out of a sense of duty to his royal mother and the country, out of a need to fulfill his duty to father a child that would follow him on the throne."

She spoke slowly. *"He did not marry for love.* That fact needs to be repeated, because if he married her for any other reason, the marriage contract was a fraud."

She paused again and pretended to peruse papers, letting her comments sink in some more.

"Regretfully for both of them, the woman he deceived was a diehard romantic, a woman who gave him her heart and soul, who had married for only one reason—*true love.*"

Marlowe deliberately slapped her hand on the podium.

"He deceived her and cheated her of love because the marriage was a sham and a fraud from the beginning. As the princess would later put it, the marriage was rather crowded because there were three of them in it from the beginning.

"The other woman was not a ghost in the marriage, the memory of a premarital fling. Many men and women have had prior love affairs before marriage, and marriage doesn't wipe clean memories of love past.

"But this was a perverse one, because the prince didn't just carry on a relationship with the other woman after marriage, but from the very beginning made her part of the marriage, right from the time of the honeymoon, when he took along mementos of the woman.

"Honeymoon. It's an unusual combination of two words, isn't it? I suppose the word grew out of the belief that the first month of marriage is the sweetest. But it wasn't, in this royal marriage. There was strychnine on the honeymoon, not sweetness.

"You need to understand what was happening to this teenage girl. She was the fairy-tale bride in the marriage of the century. But thrown into a media frenzy, into the preparations for the wedding of the century, isolated and alone, by the time of the wedding she was sick, physically ill, suffering from bulimia, a terrible, violent reaction to stress and depression that caused her to vomit out much of what she ate, leaving her to waste away.

"Rather than a romantic, relaxing, passionate honeymoon, the virginal bride is taken to a relative's estate for a few days where there are other people in residence. They then go on board the royal yacht with a crew of several hundred.

"It was not a passionate honeymoon because the prince had not married the woman he really loved. He married a girl he considered to be little more than a breeding animal to provide a royal heir.

"Throughout the marriage, the princess asked him to be honest with her about his feelings about her and this other woman. He refused to discuss the matter. He refused to discuss it on their honeymoon and continued to refuse to discuss it as the marriage began to unravel and he renewed his relationship with the other woman.

Marlowe paused and met the eye of every juror.

"*Who the hell did he think he was?* What gave him the right to grind his young bride's dreams and passions under his heel? Where did he get the audacity to do what he damn well pleased when he had entered into a marriage?

"Flaunting the other woman, not into the face of a person he had been married to for years . . . *but on their honeymoon.*"

Marlowe shook her head and lifted her arms in frustration. She painted a picture for the jury of the scene aboard the honeymoon ship when the prince wore to dinner the cuff links given to him by the other woman.

"Through his actions, the prince flaunted in the bride's face that he had not married her out of love, but out of duty. And that, like some Oriental potentate with a new woman in his harem, she would have no voice in the marriage."

She could feel Trent's discomfort beside her. He stared straight ahead, his features blank. She sneaked a glance up at the princess. Her head was down, her cheeks streaked with tears.

Marlowe felt empathy and fear for her. For a moment, she lost her place in her thoughts and had to fumble through her papers to get back on track.

❖

She forced herself back into eye contact with the jury.

"We have to keep in mind the nature of the man she was dealing with . . . a man of unparalleled power and privilege . . . a man who spent his entire life surrounded by servants and cronies . . . who had never bought a pair of socks or walked down a public street without creating a national sensation.

"And in truth, a man with a great sense of duty to his country . . . but little to his young bride.

"In his own mind, he had taken a girl literally off the street and made her a royal princess.

"In his mind, she was to be eternally grateful to him for what he did for her.

"He had spent his entire life being bowed to. He had no understanding of his duty to his emotional young bride because the only duty he ever had was to perpetuate the royal image.

"He didn't understand what he was doing to the young woman. And he didn't care because *he never appreciated the fact that she loved him.* He was used to being loved and admired. The fact that another impressionable young girl was doe-eyed when she looked at him was not important. To him, she was just another object in the royal possessions.

"But it should have been important. She is a caring, loving, and passionate young woman, who needs to love and be loved.

"Less than five months after the honeymoon of the century, this passionate young woman threw herself down stairs at a time when she was pregnant.

"My God!" Marlowe shook her head and stared at the jurors. "It was a shocking, unimaginable act of desperation . . . by a tormented woman who could no longer live a lie . . . an act of self-abuse, yet an abuse that was guided by an unfaithful husband who had humiliated her and deceived her until she had lost her sense of *self.*

"The world hailed her, worshipped her, as the fairy-tale princess. But in her husband's cold palace, she was treated as little more than a valuable piece of furniture, a breeding animal of great value, but not someone deserving of respect.

"She knew her life had become a fraud. She knew she had been tricked into a marriage, trapped into a royal marriage, that left her a

❖

prisoner in a gilt cage. Her husband could do what he liked, enjoying his hunting and fishing, his polo and his brandy with his hangers-on and his girlfriend.

"But she had been cheated out of true love, out of a marriage made in heaven. She had saved herself for a man who took her in bed only to create an heir for his kingdom.

"She began to crumble under the pressures of the public demands on her and the pretension of the lies she had to live.

"As she began to unravel emotionally, instead of giving her understanding and psychological support, he belittled her, humiliated her, isolating her from her friends and surrounding her with his hangers-ons, his cronies, restricting her access even to the staff, and ultimately even turning the staff against her by leaving the impression there was no cause for her behavior other than her own neurosis.

"She was never encouraged to seek treatment for her bulimia, pregnancy blues, and postnatal depression. Instead, she was criticized and discouraged.

"And then another factor came into the equation, an unexpected one: jealousy on the prince's part. Even if her husband didn't love her, the world fell in love with the Princess of Wales. The public adored her. Everywhere the couple went, the crowds ignored him and shouted for her. The public recognized something in her, she had *charisma* that ignited adulation.

"A prince who had spent his entire life being the center of attention and exaltation, suddenly found that he was taking the back seat in the public eye to the young woman he treated in private with little more than contempt.

"He responded to the reaction of the crowds to her by increasing his criticism of her, repeatedly showing his disapproval of the way she walked, talked, and dressed. Nothing about her pleased him. She couldn't even faint from exhaustion in a manner to please him.

"The anger and criticisms, the humiliations and degradation, ate at her. And she began to abuse herself. *Physically*. She alternately binged and starved herself, spiraling down emotionally and physically as bulimia and anorexia ravaged her body.

"But the originator of that physical abuse was not herself, but her

❖

husband. It was her hands, but he drove her to it by tormenting her, crushing her spirit under his heel, exploiting her weaknesses.

"As she grew more emotional, crying out for help, he became more critical, colder, and more distant.

"When she was crumbling under the pressure, he pushed her over the edge.

"He abused his power in vicious and insidious ways.

"He betrayed her love."

She paused and pretended to shuffle her papers as she fought back tears. She got control of herself and turned back to the jury.

"Finally, he delivered a blow that put her into a heat of passion, a heat of anger and frustration so powerful, she lost her own will and ability to control her rage.

"Operating under the years of provocation, overwhelmed by a rage that erupted as he committed one final act of humiliation, one last act of torment, she lashed out.

"The physical and mental abuse that she had suffered for years in their relationship came full circle.

"She picked up a gun and used it to stop the abuse."

She paused and once again looked at each juror in turn, connecting with each momentarily, making a bond with them.

"Most of the women alive today were raised in a man's world, a world dominated by and governed by men. During the course of this trial you will learn that much of your deliberation will center around whether the princess acted *reasonably*.

"During the course of the trial you will hear about how a *reasonable* man would have acted in her shoes. Now, the law tries to accommodate women by stating that what the law really means is how a reasonable person, male or female, would have acted. But we will prove that the psychological and legal rules that the prosecution attempts to have you judge the princess by were rules *made by and intended for men*."

Desai stood up. "My lord, Miss James is arguing her case rather than simply opening it."

"Quite so. I assume you have finished your opening?" the judge asked Marlowe. She nodded. "Then we will recess until tomorrow, when you will call your first witness."

"Thank you, milord." She smiled to herself as she gathered up her papers. She had wanted just once to have used the phrase.

Her first witness would be the armorer. She also had to have other witnesses standing by. She needed to meet with her main psychiatric expert. The psychiatrist was going to explain Marlowe's theory that a woman cannot be judged the same way men are judged when it comes to reacting to provocation, that just as women react to sexual stimuli differently than men, they are less likely to suddenly blow and commit an act of violence. Instead, the arousal to violence of a "reasonable woman" was a slow buildup rather than an abrupt snap. She also needed to run by the psychiatrist the princess's story about obtaining the gun for a suicide attempt. There might be a way the story could be made credible with expert testimony.

She followed Philip Hall out of the courtroom, hurrying a little to try and catch him in the hallway. He usually walked out with her to run interference with the mob of reporters waiting outside the building, but this time he had disappeared by the time she came out of the court-room. She assumed that they would have lunch together and discuss the case.

When she came to the front doors of the building, Trent was facing a mob of newspeople. He turned to her as she approached.

With a blank face and great solemnity, he handed her a small enve-lope.

"What's this?" she asked.

"An instruction from the princess. She has fired you."

❖

56

❖

Dutton made peace with Cohn the Barbarian and showed up at the *Burn* office to get Hacker to conduct an electronic search. He chose a time when Cohn was out so he'd avoid having the editor looking over his shoulder.

"We won't find anything under his own name," he told Hacker. "Start with the Royal Protection Service. Can you get into their accounting records? Good. The Royals are all in town, so look for an expense out of town, gas receipts, train fare, hotels, pubs, anything that would indicate there are officers on an assignment outside London, maybe even across the Channel."

He decided to concentrate on outside the city for two reasons—the expenses incurred inside the city would be too numerous to provide any meaning, and it seemed logical that Howler would have made a run for it, maybe even across the Channel to continental countries.

It didn't take long for Hacker to make a hit. "York mean anything?"

"What about York?"

"Quite a bit, actually. Authorizations for car, train, inn, pub food."

"Any agents named?"

Hacker scrolled down through a list. "Four agents: McKinzie, Miller, Grindstaff—"

"Grindstaff! That's it."

"There's four altogether. The other's Tucker."

"That has to be it. Unless they're holding a bleedin' convention, there's no reason for four, and Grindstaff tops it off. What else is there?"

"From the dates on the expenses, I'd say they all lead to a village in the West Yorkshire area, more or less northwest of the city of York. They have expenses authorized there until further notice."

"What's the name of the inn?"

"They're staying at a pub that rents rooms, the Fallen Sparrow."

"Give me a minute."

Dutton called information and got the inn's number and placed a call to it. "This is the *Sunday Travel News*," he told the clerk who answered. He went on to explain that the Sunday supplement travel guide wanted to do a story about the pub and the region. "Are there any notable noble manor houses, royal palaces, castles, that sort of thing nearby?"

There were none. But the clerk told him that there was a rather prestigious medical facility.

"Bingo," Dutton told Hacker. "There's a mental hospital close by. Howler's a genuine nutcase and he has a serious drug problem. They couldn't just grab him and hold him anywhere, he'd go into shock if he didn't get medications to take the place of the drugs. I can't just call up and ask them if he's there. Any chance you can tap into their system?"

"Not much, not unless the hospital is part of a larger organization or they hire out their accounting. If it is, they'd likely be on line for their accounting services. Medical billing is a paperwork nightmare—many facilities send it out to accounting jobbers who specialize in paperwork required by insurance companies and the government."

"How long will it take you to find out if they're online?"

"Minutes. You know how many times I've been asked to check a mental facility to find out whether a VIP, a spouse, child, or girlfriend is in for a cure? Abortions and STDs are other treatments Cohn has me frequently check for."

Hacker slowly laid out the information for Dutton. "By coordinating the date the RPS officers checked into the inn with the patient admissions into the facility, I came up with one man who fits your profile, right down to sex, diagnosis, and date of birth. One John Smith."

"These coppers are original thinkers, aren't they? Mr. Smith has been admitted for what?"

"Substance abuse. And his security rating requires twenty-four/seven lockdown."

Dutton was so elated, he almost hopped up and down.

"What's with this Howler character?" Hacker asked. "Cohn will ask me the minute you're out of here."

"He's the prime minister's lover," Dutton said.

"No bleedin' way. What a story. Watch yourself, Cohn will steal it."

"I've got a lock on it," Dutton said. "I've got pictures of unnatural acts *in flagrante delicto.* One more thing: Does the Royal Protection group keep a copy of their officers' photo IDs in their computer system?"

"Probably."

"See if you can print one out for me, make it a handsome devil, about my age, hair color."

Hacker gave him a look. "I'll see if I can find one as homely-looking as you."

He got out of the *Burn* offices before Cohn found him and made a demand for the fictitious pictures of sex and the prime minister.

57

❖

Marlowe sat in her room and sobbed as she poured herself another apple martini and watched herself on TV. She had ordered up a pitcher of the apple-flavored booze to drown her sorrows in. She sobbed because the TV cameras had caught her looking utterly shocked and dumbfounded when Trent handed her the note and told her the princess had fired her. Actually, the note didn't use that ugly word, *fired,* or even the more ominous-sounding *terminated.* Rather, it stated in polite but firm terms that her services were no longer needed on behalf of the princess, expressed great gratitude for her "outstanding services," and assured her that all monies promised would be faithfully tendered.

But the saccharine coating didn't diminish the fact that she had been canned, sacked, dumped, and given the boot.

"Fuck you!" Marlowe threw the remote at the TV. Her aim was too good—it hit the screen with a crack, there was a flash of light, and the TV went dark.

"Son-of-a-bitch!" Watching the TV had been company, even if it depressed her. Now she had to drink alone. It wasn't the first time she had been fired by a client. Clients came in all shapes and mental states, sometimes they were just too crazy to deal with. But her previous fir-

❖

ings had all occurred during mutual recriminations with raised voices. This was the first time she was fired by a client with whom she'd thought she was working well—and the firing was broadcast around the world.

Now what would they think of her in Modesto?

She called the front desk and told them to have another TV brought up. "Mine is broken—no, I don't want someone to check, it's terminal, just send a damn TV up. You people have no problem sending murderers and rapists to my room, I'm sure you can manage a TV."

She slammed down the phone. Then picked up it again and ordered another pitcher of apple martini.

"How the hell did it happen?" she asked herself. How did Trent and his "learned friends" get the drop on her? And pull the rug out, sending her crashing onto her tush? She had her problems with the princess, there was a clash of cultures, of attitudes, but she thought she had the situation under control. She thought she set exactly the right tone with her opening statement, making the princess the victim of an uncaring, self-centered bastard.

The phone rang and she grabbed it. "Bring that damn TV up!"

After a slight pause, a voice she recognized said, "I'm afraid the pub owner and the dozen patrons watching it might object."

"Dutton, I don't want to speak to you, hear from you, talk to you. You are a great big zero."

"It's coming over the telly now. It's quite a stunning development, totally unexpected."

She cringed. "What's so unexpected about a lawyer getting fired? Happens every day."

"That's not what I'm talking about, luv. Aren't you watching the telly?"

"My telly had a nervous breakdown."

"Why did she do it?"

"Who? The princess? Because I'm a shit attorney, that's why."

"Why'd she plead?"

"Plead?"

"Are you drunk?"

"Not anymore. The princess has pled guilty?"

❖

"She's copping an insanity plea."

"What! That's crazy, it's the last thing she wanted to do." She thought for a second. "I guess it's an easy way out. She can get some psych help and in six months be back on the street."

"Won't happen, she's taking a section 41 commitment."

"What's that?"

"You must have been really out of the loop if you didn't know this was coming down. A Section 41 commitment isn't something that a defendant agrees to on the spur of the moment—it would have been planned and negotiated, with psychiatric exams underlying it. I'm getting the idea that they really had you sandbagged."

"What exactly is it?"

"My understanding is that it gives the judge the right to lock her up and throw away the key."

"That's insane!"

"No, she's the one who's admitting to be insane. Maybe you better come down here—I'm at a pub two blocks from your hotel. You can probably walk out the front door of the hotel without being hassled by reporters. I hate to break it to you, luv, but you're yesterday's news."

SHE SAT IN THE pub with Dutton and watched a forensic psychologist and a barrister who specialized in criminal law being interviewed on TV about the princess's plea agreement.

"It amounts to a complete capitulation to the prosecution's charges," the barrister said. "If a person is committed under Section 41 of the Mental Health Act, the commitment order from the court is without limit of time."

"You mean life imprisonment?"

"It's not imprisonment in a jail . . . she will be held in a mental health facility—a hospital, if you please—that specializes in treatment and confinement of mentally disturbed persons who are a danger. If the court makes a finding that there's a risk that the person will commit further offenses or that there is a need for protection of the public from serious harm, he orders the person confined without a release date. It's

❖

not a sentence of imprisonment, but what the law calls a restriction or-der, the power of the higher court to prevent discharge."

"And how does the princess get out once she is put under this re-striction order?" the commentator asked.

The psychiatrist said, "That's the rub, isn't it? The princess has agreed to the order, but it's not in her power to undo it. As long as the court finds that she presents a danger, she will be kept in. If she is con-sidered a danger for the rest of her life, she will be kept in custody."

"This is utter bunk," Marlowe told Dutton. "The very nature of a killing of one spouse by another in a heat of passion is that the perpe-trator rarely commits another crime. Juries and the law are forgiving toward these offenses because the perpetrators are not a danger to so-ciety, the crimes arise from the unique relationships between the par-ties. This Section 41 stuff is for criminals who are schizoid."

"That's all good and well, but she's not pleading to manslaughter, she's saying she was crazy when she popped her husband and that she's still crazy, dangerously so."

"I can't tell you how little sense this makes. This is exactly why I was hired: The princess was afraid that her lawyers would sell her out, that she'd end up confined forever, being stuck away as a nutcase. I'm sure she would rather be dead than in a mental ward. Why would she change her mind?"

"What did she say when she fired you?"

"Nothing. I was just handed my walking papers by Trent, a thank-you and the check's in the mail." Marlowe shook her head. "I just don't understand it, things were going well in the trial, I had just given my opening statement. The armorer's testimony wasn't going to be as dam-aging as the prosecution thought, I was going to neutralize it. I had everything set to turn the case around, portraying the princess as the victim and the prince as the aggressor. I even had a good theory on how to get around the fact that there was no actual physical abuse, showing that he drove her to physically abuse herself."

"And what did she say to that?"

Marlowe shrugged. "She would have liked to win the case without smearing her husband's name. She wanted to know if we could do the case without attacking his character. I told her it wasn't possible, we

❖

had to make the jury understand that he was the bad guy and she was the victim, that his royal upbringing had created a thoughtless, self-centered bastard who had no understanding of his young wife's needs."

"I see." He nodded. "Yes, you walked right into it."

"What did I walk into?"

"Tradition. As an American, you wouldn't have understood. The princess would not have let you assassinate her husband's reputation."

"Excuse me, the princess assassinated her husband's life."

"That's different, people kill each other all the time. But Britain has had monarchs for all of recorded history, save a few years when Cromwell was running the country. The tradition of the monarchy is ingrained in the blood of all of us. These people aren't rock stars that rise and fall, they were there when we were born and will be there when we die."

"There are people who oppose the monarchy and tabloid slimes like you who constantly attack it."

"There are people who murder, rape, kill, and steal, too, but they're not in the majority or running the country. You have to stop thinking like an American and think like the princess. From her earliest memories, on the telly, newspapers, magazines, table talk, in school, work, and play, the queen and the Prince of Wales were honored and revered."

"But she still killed him."

"She attacked the man, *not the institution*. She believes in the monarchy. She might strike out at her husband as a man who she thinks wronged her, but she's no more capable of attacking the monarchy than Pavlov's dog was of keeping a dry mouth. Don't you understand? She's part of the monarchy, by birth, by upbringing. What would you say was the most important thing in her life, the thing she loved the most?"

"Her children—she's devoted to her children, determined that they will have happy lives."

"Exactly, and her firstborn is now the Prince of Wales and future king. Do you think she's capable of sabotaging her son's birthright?"

"No way, that would be the last thing she would do. You're starting to make sense. It must be the booze." She stared at the glass of beer in front of her. The barmaid had just stared at her when Marlowe asked if they could whip up an apple martini.

❖

"Or love," Dutton said. If you recall, we got a head start on a roll in the hay in your hotel room, just before you savagely attacked me."

"Don't get yourself worked up. I'd rather make love to a monkey than a tabloid reporter, though I'm not sure there's much difference. But I'm beginning to think you're on to something. She's no longer in the fog she'd been in when she struck at the prince and reached across the ocean for me. She's thinking clearer now, less panicked, more apt to listen to those around her. You can bet that each time after I left the Tower, Trent and his learned friends snuck in and worked on her, telling her that she was going to destroy the monarchy, that she would cause her son to lose his birthright."

"The insanity plea works out nicely," Dutton said. "It's no reflection on the monarchy that the princess was crazy—she was royalty only by marriage, and by pleading out, the whole issue of the prince's behavior is avoided."

"Nice for everyone except the princess—and me. I go home in disgrace and she ends up with a life-sized commitment to a loony bin. Fine advocate I turned out to be. I thought these stuffy British lawyers were a pushover. Now I know how you arrogant bastards managed to rule half of the world: It was done with an olive leaf in one hand—and a club to bash people with when they reached for the peace offering."

"If you go home now, you'll miss solving the mystery."

"What mystery?"

"The biggest mystery of all: why the princess shot her husband."

"Where have you been, on another planet while your news media friends covered the story from every possible—and impossible—angle? What's your theory, Mr. Tabloid Trash Reporter? Aliens took control of the princess's mind as part of a plot to kill off the royal family and take over the government? I think the rest of the world pretty well knows that she killed him because he mentally abused her and wronged her with another woman."

He took a sip of beer, slowly, meeting her eyes over the rim of the glass. "Oh, you believe that public relations propaganda the princess has been selling to the press and people like you. No, luv, I'm talking about the *real* reason she put a bullet in the heart of her husband."

Marlowe's heart pumped like a steam hammer. He had hit upon a suspicion that had been lurking in her mind, one that she had been suppressing, refusing to face because it fell outside the purview of her defense of her client. "You're not trying to tell me that I was sold a bill of goods, that the princess's defense was a lie, are you? What is this, some kind of tabloid bullshit? You need a story, so you're going to make it up as you go along?"

"Look me in the eye and tell me that the whole thing doesn't stink to you."

She looked him in the eye. "I believe every word the princess told me. She could not have made up that story—I'd know." She saluted him with her beer. "And as we say back in Modesto, fuck you and the horse you rode in on."

"I don't know about the horse, but we'll be going more into the subject of coitus before the evening's out. But getting back to whether you were lied to, she lied to you about when she got the gun."

"She didn't, actually—all right, she misled me, or let me mislead myself."

"She lied. Now, here's how I see it. The life of the princess and the prince is well documented up to the time she decided to kill him. There were servants around when she threw herself down the stairs, doctors who treated her for bulimia and depression, and so forth. But where the story goes askew is the murder plot."

"Heat of passion."

"That, too. The first curious thing is that she decided to strike back instead of just getting out of the relationship."

"There's nothing strange about that. It's an almost universal behavior pattern in these abused-spouse cases that the woman believed she was trapped and that killing her tormentor was the only way out."

"But it wasn't that kind of torment, was it, luv? You can do all your fancy lawyer dance steps for the jury about how he was verbally abusing her into abusing herself physically, but this old reporter knows that's bunk. And I don't buy the notion that she was crazy, any more than you do. The princess is a woman who went through her own private hell, a naive girl who entered a fairy-tale marriage only to find out

❖

it was a nightmare, but she doesn't have it in her to commit a cold-blooded murder."

"Heat of—"

"There is only one thing that would have driven her to pick up that gun and shoot her husband. It's something that is in every one of us, rich and poor, the good, the bad, and the ugly."

"Which is?"

"*Self-preservation.*"

They drank on it and watched more television discussion as legal and psychiatric experts took on the insanity plea.

Marlowe licked beer suds from her lips and nodded. "Okay, we are back to your self-defense theory. There is a very serious flaw in your theory—you can't shoot an unarmed person in cold blood and call it self-defense. And there is no evidence that he had a weapon or reached for something that looked like a weapon. So your theory stinks."

"Bear with me, I get less smelly as you get to know me better. What if the princess *thought* she was in danger—what if she killed her husband because she thought he was going to kill her?"

Marlowe kept her eyes on the TV, but her mind was flying, analyzing his question. "If she thought she was in danger? Okay, let's deal with that. It can't be self defense, you have to actually be in harm's way, you can't just believe you're in danger. But there is a doctrine of law called *imperfect self-defense.* I'm sure you have it here, we probably got it from your courts, anyway. It works this way: It's an allowable defense if you have a reasonable belief that you were in imminent danger of being harmed by that person—even though you were wrong. A classic example would be that people told you that Joe was going to shoot you, you see Joe coming toward you with a rifle, you pull out your long-barreled .44 revolver—we're assuming you live in Texas—and you blow Joe away."

"Joe didn't have a rifle."

"Exactly, it was a toy gun. But if the jury finds that you had a reasonable belief that Joe was going to plug you, they can find you not guilty based on an imperfect self-defense theory. In the princess's case, a jury would have to find that she had a reasonable belief that she was in imminent danger from her husband."

❖

Dutton said, "What if there was hard evidence that the princess had a genuine belief that her husband planned to have her killed? How would that have affected her case?"

"She could raise an imperfect self-defense and get off—if the danger was imminent. From a practical point of view, if jurors thought the princess had a reasonable belief she was going to be harmed, they would care little about the fine points of law. Jurors are more influenced by common sense than legal technicalities. But it's all moot now—she's taking a plea."

"She's agreed to a plea, but the news reports are that the plea won't be entered until next week."

Marlowe shook her head. "It doesn't matter, she's still going to plead. She never brought up the subject of being afraid for her life, probably for exactly the reason you've mentioned before, that it would show real malice on his part and put the monarchy in jeopardy."

Dutton put his hand on the top of her thigh and kissed her ear as he whispered, "Ah, but luv, what if you had the evidence and were able to put such a scare into the government that they offered the princess a heat-of-passion plea and probation? Or even dismissed the charges?"

Indeed, if she had the evidence and was able to pull it off, then what would they think of her in Modesto?

She gave him an appraising look. "How did you get so smart about people?"

"Osmosis working for a tabloid. Tabloid reporters, criminal defense lawyers, and morticians all have something in common—they see only the worst side of life. No news is good news, there's a dead body in most bad news, and pretty soon there's a lawyer. When you see enough of man's inhumanity to man, you come to understand that there is a violent nature in humans, cruelty that goes beyond our animal instinct. Animals kill for food, we do it for sport. Sometimes we kill each other just for fun."

"I'm impressed, quite a philosopher—"

"For a slimy tabloid hound."

"For a prizewinning journalist. According to the last dead body you had sex with."

He saluted her with his mug of beer. "Ah, you've uncovered my secret, that I had a veneer of respectability before The Fall. Like Satan

❖

and his Dark Angels, I was cast out of heaven and I've been floundering in a purgatory of sex, lies, and mediocrity ever since. But that's beside the point. We have to work with the hand we've been dealt. We need to deal with the two matters at hand."

He told her about tracking down Howler. "He's being held by the Royal Protection Service, the bill's being picked up by the palace gang. Now, what does that tell you?"

"A cover-up."

"Bigger, a Royalgate. There was a message in that macabre presentation Howler created at Westminster."

"A man in Tudor-era dress with a woman's head on his lap."

"But not just any man, but bloody old Henry VIII, the wife killer himself. Shortly before Columbus sailed the ocean blue, Henry VII beat Richard III and became the first of the House of Tudor to reign. He was followed by his son Henry VIII, who sired the great Elizabeth I. He repaid Elizabeth's mother for not giving him a future king by having her head chopped off."

"Obviously, you think the message is that the Prince of Wales was going to be a wife killer, too. Tell me some more about the display at the Abbey."

"I found out from Tussauds that the costume Howler ripped off was designed for Henry VIII. Add the woman's head on bloody old Henry's lap, and you have Anne Boleyn or Catherine Howard. Henry was a brutal bastard, nuttier than a Christmas cake. He fell in love with Anne Boleyn when she was just twenty. He divorced his wife and cut England off from the Catholic Church when the pope refused to grant an annulment from the wife. Not that it did Anne much good—Henry soon bored of her, threw her in the Tower on trumped-up charges, and had her head chopped off."

"What were the charges?"

"Witchcraft, adultery, and incest with her brother. It's all pretty well documented that they were contrived by Henry to get rid of her. She lost her head when she was less than thirty, but she has a connection to two world-shattering events—a Church of England separate from the church in Rome, and birthing a daughter, Elizabeth, who would one day lead England to greatness.

❖

"He was especially cruel to Anne because the charges were false. He also had his wife Catherine Howard beheaded. That was a bit unfair, too. She was accused of adultery, but it's probable that her love affairs occurred before she married Henry. She did compound her error, though, by appointing a former lover as her personal secretary. Along with his wives, he had the heads of a bunch of others separated from their bodies."

She said, "Henry was a real charmer. By today's standards, he would probably qualify as a serial killer."

"You can bet today's Royals have wet dreams about the good old days when kings could get rid of troublesome wives and dissenters with a wave of their hand."

"The problem with your friend Howler's art piece, Henry holding the head of one of his wives in his lap, is that in our case, it wasn't the wife who died but the husband."

"True, but consider this about Howler—he's smart, real smart, book smart, street smart, and at this stage of his life when he's lost a few trillion brain cells from addiction, he's crazy smart. He graduated first in his class from university and medical school and he was the best plastic surgeon in the country before the white and brown ladies stole his soul."

"Which ladies?"

"Crack cocaine and tar heroin, his lovers of choice. Look, I'm certain Howler is on to something big about the prince, princess, and the killing. There has always been a rumor of a letter that the princess is supposed to have written in which she charged that the prince and his cohorts wanted to kill her because she was such a bother."

"Who did she write it to?"

"I don't know, no one's come forward with it, but it fits in with her paranoia. You know she once claimed she'd been shot at while jogging at Kensington Park?"

"A car backfired?"

He shrugged. "Who knows? But we do know that she was hated and feared by the prince's entourage. First she fought them because she felt they worked against her, prejudicing her husband about her, then they feared her because she couldn't be managed, wasn't a starter, as they

❖

thought of it. The point is, maybe the people around the prince had a lot to lose, or might strike at her out of a sense of loyalty."

"You think Howler has this letter?"

I believe he has the letter, that the Abbey horror and having a tabloid reporter show up were signals to the palace that he meant business and wants those millions he's been telling people he's coming into. It's just too coincidental for Howler to have a connection to the prince just before the prince is killed, and then gets picked up by the Royals and hidden away in a mental ward. It bears looking into."

Marlowe found herself torn between running to the airport and back to the States, back to her apartment, where she would barricade the door and hide her head under the blankets . . . and tackling the mystery that Dutton believed he was on to. In her heart of hearts, she felt that she had let the princess down, that the woman was sacrificing herself because the only path Marlowe had found for a defense was one that the princess could not abide by.

Dutton said, "My proposal is this: Help me track down Howler and get the truth from him. He won't talk without money. You have it, I don't."

"You said there were two things that needed to be taken care of."

"Sex. We need to take care of that right away. I've been horny for you since the first time I jumped on your bones and got a feel."

As THEY STEPPED THROUGH Marlowe's room door, Dutton let the door swing shut behind them and pulled her to him. She moved out of his arms. "I have to freshen up," she said, then went into the bathroom and shut the door behind her.

She'd told him she busted her telly, but the one in her room wasn't damaged. He turned it on with the remote and sat on the end of the bed. Another news story about the princess's plea came on and he turned off the set. He hesitated a moment and then went to the bathroom door and opened it a crack. The shower was running.

He took off his clothes, went into the bathroom, and opened the shower door. He was surprised at her body. A woman who was not naturally thin or slender, her flesh was creamy and lush, her hips and behind generously rounded.

Her back was to him, with the shower spray coming down on her. He stepped into the shower and pulled the door closed. He touched her back, letting his hand slide down the curve of her spine, feeling the smoothness of her well-rounded buttocks.

"You have a beautiful body," he said. "I've wanted to be with you since the first moment I saw you on the telly."

He reached around her and cupped both her breasts with his hands. They were firm and full, the strawberrylike nipples getting hard beneath his fingers. His hands slipped down and touched her dark pubic mound.

He suddenly realized she was sobbing. He leaned closer, pulling her tightly against him.

"What's the matter?"

She shook her head and twisted so he couldn't see the tears.

"What is it?"

"I don't want to just have sex," she said, "I want to make love, not be jumped and humped."

He drew back. "I'm sorry."

She turned and pulled him back to her. "It's not you, it's the goddamn booze and memories. I was thinking about my husband, about the good times, the good sex at first, but when we started having troubles he'd grab me and ram it in like I was a piece of meat to beat. It's been a long time since I've been with a man who didn't think the longest time in the world was the time between coming and going."

"Coming and—" Then he got it.

The tears came again and she sobbed, "I'm sorry, I didn't want you to see me cry. It's not you. I've been lonely for so long, not so much for sex, there's always some guy who wants to knock off a piece, but for love. I'm so stupid, I'm just like the princess, I'm lonely and I've been waiting for a knight to pick me up and carry me off."

"I'm no knight," he said.

She put her arms around him and pulled him close, pressing his nakedness against hers. "Yes, you are, you're my knight." She put her

❖

hand around his penis and lowered her eyes at the swollen red glans. Her hand slid back and forth, stroking it gently.

She kissed him on the lips, the shower spray coming down on them.

"You must be a knight," she whispered. "You have a long lance."

He cupped both her breasts. He kissed the hard nipples, licking them with his tongue. She leaned back against the wall of the shower as his lips slid down her stomach, kissing and nibbling her flesh. Kneeling, he reached her pubic bush of hair and traced the hairline with his tongue, running the tip of his tongue along her bare skin.

Using the shower wall for support, she bent her knees and spread her legs. He placed his head between her thighs, pressing his mouth against the lips of her vulva. He kissed her fleshy lips, savoring them several times, then pushed his tongue into the opening.

The sexual hunger in her body was growing as his tongue found her sensitive clit and she squirmed with delight as he began to bring her to an ecstasy she hadn't experienced in a long time. She tried to push his head away from her electrified organ, but he pushed back, keeping up the pressure until she dropped to her knees. She hugged him and ravished him with kisses.

"That was nirvana," she told him, kissing him again.

Still being caressed by the shower spray, she kissed his nipples, surprised at how firm and hard they grew under her tongue as her hand went down, grasping his stalk until she had his stone-hard testicles in the palm of her hand.

She kissed his ear and whispered, "It's your turn."

Still cupping his balls, she kissed the tip of his penis, then traced it with her tongue. She pulled it slowly into her mouth at first, then sucking it harder as she moved it in and out, masturbating it with her mouth.

After a moment he pulled her from him. "I want to be inside you."

They stood and stepped out of the shower, leaving it running behind them as they went into the bedroom. She lay on the bed on her back and pulled him toward her.

"Fuck me hard," she said.

"You wanted love, not—"

She stopped him with a kiss, her mouth chewing impatiently at his

❖

lips. "I wanted love a minute ago, now I want to be fucked." She pulled him down on her, spreading her legs, directing his penis into her. "It's a woman's right," she whispered. "Sometimes we're a princess and sometimes the slut in us comes out."

58

❖

The next morning they hired a car for their trip to the mental hospital in the York region to find Howler. Dutton drove. Leaving London, Marlowe was silent.

"You look like you're mulling over serious affairs of state," Dutton said.

"I'm still trying to grasp this puzzle in an enigma. Tell me about the prince."

"What do you want to know?"

"Everything. I want to understand him."

"Then you should start with the fact that he didn't choose his life—and that it hasn't been an easy one. I know it's hard for people who pulled themselves up by the bootstraps to understand"—he gave her a sideways grin—"but it's not easy to meet the demands the nation puts on the queen and the Prince of Wales. The rest of the Royals are a bunch of freeloaders, but the woman on the throne and the guy next in line earn their bread."

"The princess told me he was barely held by his mother when he was a baby, something like thirty minutes a day."

"Maybe so, though that was probably in the morning—I think he

❖

got another hug in the evening. So what does that tell you? Do you think his mum, the queen, lacks maternal instincts? Is that it . . . or did she realize from day one that the last thing her son needed was to be a touchy-feely kind of guy, that she had to toughen him up straight from the womb so that he would survive in this cold, cruel world? You really have no idea what he went through, do you? As a kid, a teenager, a young man."

"I know what I had to go through, and it didn't include being raised in a palace and pampered by servants. Pardon me if I have a hard time sympathizing with people who never had to work a day in their lives because they were born rich." She sighed. "Okay, I see that you're determined to bring me to tears, so tell me what he went through."

"When you went to school, were you expected to be a brilliant student? A dynamite athlete? A natural-born leader?"

"Lots of kids are pushed by their parents to succeed."

"He wasn't just pushed by his parents, there were sixty million Brits and a billion other former British subjects around the world watching him, judging him, evaluating him, every moment of every day. Any slipup, any screwup, the slightest hint that he had human frailties, appeared on the front pages. Boarding school was hell for him, even sleeping in a dorm was a terror. If he snored at night he'd not just get hit by a flying shoe, but it would become a school joke and make it into the papers. When he was out on the playing field participating in sporting events, the boys took turns knocking him down and getting in a punch, so someday they could brag that they bowled over the king and put an elbow in his ribs.

"He was tested every day, in every way. If he was sensitive, if he couldn't roll with the punches, he wouldn't have lasted a week at boarding school or in the military. He had to take the punishment, keep—"

"A stiff upper lip."

"And maintain a stoic countenance to the world. How could the princess expect him to show emotion toward her? He'd never been permitted to show anger, hate, love, or anything more than mild interest in anything or anyone—and God help him if he showed the wrong sort of interest." He grinned at her. "Have you ever farted in public or picked your nose while driving? Front-page stuff if he did it. Taken a shower with a bunch of other school chums who bragged that their dick was bigger than yours?"

"Not lately."

"He'd never done it, because if he did, some slime publication would put it on the front pages. At sixteen he flunked his O levels in math. The press tore him apart. Can you imagine what they would have done if he had had a premature ejaculation? The prince lived under a microscope from the moment he was born. He walked, talked, loved, and acted like an institution because *he was one.* This was a guy who'd probably never bought a pair of socks, didn't carry money because he paid for nothing, wouldn't know how to tip in a restaurant because he'd never picked up a check. If he went into a store to buy a jock strap, a large crowd would gather, the police would have to set up barricades and the Royal Protection Service would be sweating it because anyone within range could put a knife into their charge, and the papers would have twelve theories as to why he needed his balls tucked up.

"Think of it, luv, this was a guy who didn't even dress himself. He changed several times a day, more if he was on tour. He had something like fifty suitcases when he traveled because he might have to change five or six times in a day. It's easy to see why he got into polo and the hunt. They're both games for the privileged few—and no one got to knock him on his arse.

"Can you imagine going through your entire life under a microscope, in which your every move was watched and evaluated and even criticized? It wasn't until he was out of the military and into his twenties that he could even sleep alone with the knowledge that he could snore if he wanted to."

"So you think it's all a downside, this bit about being a prince."

"Oh, no, the other Royals have it made. They get all the benefits and little of the flack that goes with the job. Like I told you, it's only the Prince of Wales and his mum who face the firing line twenty-four hours a day, whose lives are dictated by duty, duty, duty to all of us unwashed Brits. And yes, luv, it's a job I wouldn't like. Would I change places with the guy? you ask. Hell, yes, if I could do it knowing what I know today, but not if it meant being switched at birth. My dick's my own business and I don't need the guys in the shower room sizing it up."

❖

"That's a very intelligent way to think of it."

"It is a very intelligent way to think of it, and you're not getting it because you're thinking of the prince as an institution and forgetting the person. The things you do naturally, being a mall rat, going to a movie, buying a new sweater, he couldn't do any of it. Movie stars can't do those things, either, but most of them had a normal childhood and they chose their fate, busting their buns to get the fame because they wanted it."

They drove in silence for a while, then he asked, "Well, do you understand the prince now? Do you see why the queen had to raise him tough, for his own protection and for the sake of the nation?"

"Sure, I'm real sorry that I was lucky enough to be born poor while your prince had to lick his silver spoon. I feel bad that I had to work for everything I ever had, that I had to wait tables and get my ass pinched in a casino lounge in order to get through school instead of playing soccer at a school for spoiled, privileged kids."

He shook his head. "Didn't hear a word I said."

"I heard the part about duty, duty, duty, the princess was overwhelmed by her duties. I'll give you this much about the two of them, the prince and the princess, they were a couple of birds who got their wings clipped at an early age and were put on display in a gilded cage."

59

❖

Marlowe and Dutton sat in the car in the dark parking lot in front of the mental institution where they expected to find Howler and a royal secret. It was a four-story building, built of dull gray concrete and sitting at the far end of an oversized parking lot.

"There will be only one Royal Protection officer on duty," Dutton said.

"Why?"

"There's only four of them assigned to cover twenty-four hours a day. The other three will be sleeping, resting, or playing pool at that pub down the road."

"What if you're wrong?"

"We go to Plan B."

"Which is?"

"We go back to London and have three days of kinky sex before you fly back to the States and I go back to making up stories about alien rape."

"You really know how to make a woman feel needed for something besides sexual gratification."

"That's the police car in front."

❖

Marlowe squinted at the car parked in front of the main entrance. "How do you know? There's no markings on it."

"It's in the no-parking fire zone. There's a security guard at a desk right inside the front door. See him?"

"Yes."

"He'd make the driver move it if it wasn't a coppers' car. I'll be just around the corner to the right. When you create the diversion, I'll walk in."

Marlowe was ready to bite her fingernails. "I don't like this. We could get arrested."

He patted her knee. "Not to worry, luv, I'm here to protect you."

"That's what's got me most worried."

He got out of the car and made his way through the dark parking lot to the side of the building. When he got to the corner of the building, he waved.

She started the car and took a deep breath. "Why me, Lord, why didn't I stay in Modesto and be a farmer's wife?"

She let up on the clutch and the car jerked, jumped, and shimmied to a stop. "Damn." The best-laid plan had a flaw—her American driving skills in a British car. She had to sit on the wrong side, to steer from the wrong side, which was doable without practice because she was in a parking lot, but she was used to driving an automatic transmission. The car had a typical center-mounted stick shift. She had to use her left hand to shift gears and her left foot on the clutch while keeping her right foot on the gas and somewhere along the line have a foot for the brake.

She got the car moving across the parking lot. "An accident waiting to happen," she said aloud. That fit in nicely with the plan.

When her car was near the front entrance, she stopped. Trying to force the gearshift into reverse caused a grinding that make her nerves raw. She saw the security guard inside the door look up at the sound. He got up and came around his desk to look out. The gear suddenly went into reverse and she popped the clutch. The car lurched back, hitting the side door of the police car with a bang.

That was the plan, but it didn't include making enough noise to wake the dead.

She put her head down on the steering wheel. "Jesus."

The security officer hurried up to her open window. "You okay?"

"Yes, uh, I messed up. Can you find the car's owner?"

"Bad luck for you, it's a copper's car. Don't go anywhere." He started back inside, but spun around and came back and wrote down the license plate number. He smiled and waved his notebook at her and disappeared back inside.

She stuck her head out the window and got a look at Dutton at the corner of the building. He made a gesture, it looked like he gave her the finger, but it was too dark to see and she concluded he probably gave her an "OK" sign.

She got out the driver's license Dutton had prepared for her. "A real license," he had told her, "except that the picture belongs to the woman who owns the car. If they check, it's all up and up." She resisted the temptation to add up the number of crimes she was committing or was an accessory to. She knew she had passed the grounds for disbarment.

When the security guard returned with a man hurrying toward her, Dutton started for the front doors.

DUTTON NODDED AND FLASHED his RPS ID card at the woman on the phone behind the reception desk as he headed for the elevator. "Going up," he said.

She put her hand over the phone receiver. "What's happening outside?"

"Woman backed into one of our cars."

He took the elevator to the fourth floor and flashed his ID at the nurses' station.

"Here for Mr. Smith, are you? Haven't seen you before. What happened to McKinzie?"

"Be back up, little fender bender with the car."

Howler was held in a room at the end of the corridor. A comfy chair, TV, and table with coffee and magazines was set out in front of it for the Royal Protection officer on duty. He had assured Marlowe that there

❖

would be only one on duty at a time, but had held his breath until he confirmed it.

He opened the door and walked in. Walter Howler, aka John Smith, was on the bed in the room, wide wake, watching the telly.

"Hello, How-ee, how the bleedin' hell are you?"

Howler stared at him. "Do I know you?"

"Off your medicine? Don't recognize your old pal, the one you set up for that chamber of horrors you created at the Abbey?"

He squinted at Dutton. "You're that arse of a reporter."

Dutton moved next to the bed. "I'm your savior, your old school pal come to make you healthy and wealthy."

"Fuck you, you ain't got nothing I want, you don't have a pot to piss in. I'm selling my story for millions."

"And who do you plan to sell it to? Those coppers who have you imprisoned here? I can get you out of here and see that you have a villa on the Costa del Sol—"

Howler laughed hysterically. "A piece of shit like that? You measly little man, I'm going to have a palace, not a house." He got off the bed and stood up, still bending over laughing. "The prince is going to pay me ten million pounds, that's my demand, ten million—and maybe a baronage or an earldom, too, take it from his estates in Cornwall."

"For a letter that says what?"

Howler blinked at him. "Letter?"

"The letter, you have the princess's letter, the one in which she says her husband's going to do her in."

Howler stared at him wild-eyed. "Bing-bing, wrong answer, bing-bing, wrong answer. You lose, you lose."

"What are you talking about?" Dutton grabbed him by the front of his hospital pajamas. "What do you know about the killing?"

"I sent a letter, but I'm not going to tell you about it, it's under the rose, you have to look under the rose. Here." He kneed Dutton in the groin. The blow didn't connect well, but it made Dutton let go of Howler's collar and go off balance. Howler gave him a shove that knocked him off his feet and flew out of the room.

❖

Dutton scrambled to his feet and raced after him. As Dutton came out the door, Howler was running down the corridor, flying by the nurses' station. "Stop him!" she yelled. Dutton went by her as Howler ran past a door marked STAIRWAY and into a room. Dutton heard the door lock as he got to it.

"He's locked it," Dutton told the nurse. "But at least he didn't get away."

"He doesn't want to get away, that's where the drugs are kept."

She banged on the door. "Open this door immediately, Mr. Smith! Open it right now!"

Dutton heard the elevator chime that it had reached the fourth floor. Without waiting to see if it contained an RPS officer, he ducked through the door marked STAIRWAY.

❖

60

❖

They were in the car on their way out of the parking lot when Marlowe looked back. "Someone's out on a ledge."

Dutton slammed on the brakes and stuck his head out the window. A male figure in white pajamas had climbed out a fourth-floor window. "It's Howler."

With his back to the building, the man scooted sideways along the ledge. Another man, the RPS duty officer, stuck his head and shoulders out the window. He reached over for Howler's pants leg. And Howler stepped off the ledge.

"Oh, my God!" Marlowe cried.

Dutton got the car moving. "We'll go to York and leave the car at a car park, I'll arrange to have it driven back later. We can take the train back to London."

"That man, he has to be dead."

Dutton shrugged. "Best thing that ever happened to him. His mind was dead long ago."

"We're in trouble—"

"Not a bit of it," Dutton said. "You've been a lawyer too long. We haven't violated any laws. Howler was being held illegally by the Roy-

❖

als, kidnapped and imprisoned. They're probably happy he's out of the way. They certainly aren't going to place charges against us, are they? What did we do? Visited an old friend in hospital, that's the only thing we did."

"I—"

"Just relax, luv. You're used to dealing with laws and courts and everything by the book. The world doesn't run that way, does it? Howler was a death waiting to happen, he was a miserable bastard who mutilated people he operated on while under drugs and tried to sell one of his own kids for a hit. He brought his death on himself and the world's better without him."

"You're right," she said, "and now I can go home, way back home, back to Modesto and see if there's still a Denny's in town that's hiring waitresses."

"There you go again, Miss Pessimistic, with you the glass isn't just only half full, it's strychnine, not water. You're a world-famous lawyer."

"I got fired."

"What does that matter? How many world-famous lawyers can you think of who actually won a case? It's not whether you win or lose anymore, you have celebrity status."

"I don't want to talk about it."

They were on the train on their way back to London before Marlowe asked about Howler. "When you got into the car, you said it was all a fiasco, that he wouldn't tell you about the letter. What exactly did he tell you?"

"He said the only letter was the one he sent, that he was demanding ten million pounds and for the prince to make him a Cornish noble."

"What prince?"

"The one your client killed. He didn't name him, but mentioned estates in Cornwall. The Prince of Wales is also the Duke of Cornwall and gets a big chunk of his income from there."

"It makes no sense."

"Sure it does. When your brain's been fried, things look different."

"Didn't he say anything else? Nothing about the princess's letter?"

"Nothing about it. When I asked him about the letter he sent, he said you had to look under the rose."

❖

"Under the rose? What'd he mean?"

"It's a phrase from Roman times, maybe earlier. In ancient times they put roses on the ceilings of dining rooms to remind guests that anything said under the influence of wine was confidential. 'Under the rose' came to mean it was a secret. I think old Henry VIII used the phrase, too. They used to hang a rose over a discussion they wanted kept secret."

"None of this is computing," Marlowe said.

"You have to have a scrambled brain for it all to make sense. It made perfect sense to Howler."

61

❖

Tower of London

As she cut off strands of her hair, the princess thought about her marriage. "No chance at all," she told the mirror. Neither one of them—the man who would be king or the bride he chose—had had a chance to make a go of it. A thousand years of ingrained traditions had doomed their romance and turned their marriage into a quagmire of recriminations.

She stared at her reflection in the mirror and wondered how she could have done the strange things that happened in her marriage. Throwing herself down the stairs just months after the honeymoon, while she was pregnant. "Did you really do that?" she asked her reflection.

It had been an act of desperation. She had felt abandoned and betrayed—and useless. As time went on, the hurt had turned to hate.

She chopped off more hair. She was bringing it down to about an inch, all the way around. Her hairdresser would be driven mad if she saw what a mess she made of giving herself a haircut.

She had been the spoiler, the nonstarter who upset things. She had emotions and imagination, two things that had been bred out of the Royals. As she sat in front of the mirror and chopped off more hair, she understood why the Royals had been lobotomized emotionally. There

❖

was no room for tears or fears, for strong emotions like love and hate in their world. There was duty, honor, country.

If she had understood that she was entering into an institution instead of a romance, would she have fled before a Cinderella coach arrived to carry her to St. Paul's and the wedding of the century?

An honest appraisal of the situation would have made history different. Instead, she had entered into a cold marriage. And her husband made a cruel mistake by not recognizing her needs, isolating her instead and letting her paranoia run rampant. . . .

But he was even more a Prisoner of Wales than she was. He had been born into it and had never known anything different.

Her maid knocked on her door. She had it locked from the inside. She answered without opening it. "Yes?"

"Your sons are here, ma'am."

"I'll be with them in a moment. You may leave now. I don't need you for the rest of the day."

"Thank you, ma'am."

When she came out a few minutes later, her two sons got out of their chairs and hugged her. The younger one said, "Mum, you look funny with your hair so short."

His older brother shook his head. "Bad cut, looks like you put a bowl over your head and trimmed around it."

"Fine, then you two hair critics can finish cutting it for me. Did you bring the things I asked for?"

The older boy nodded. "Under our clothes."

"You know why I have to do this, don't you?"

They both nodded.

Tears welled inside her. She hugged both of them. "You know I love you both, don't you?"

IT WAS EARLY EVENING when the governor of the Tower entered the princess's quarters. Not all of the expense of housing the princess in the Tower was being borne by the government. He had invoices to be signed for personal items that would be presented to her accounting firm for payment.

❖

He was surprised to find her older son in the living room reading a book. The boy, a handsome young man, would soon officially be installed as Prince of Wales and would someday be king. Fortunately, he had gotten his looks from his mother and thus avoided the ears his father was famous for possessing.

"I didn't expect to see you here, young man. I was told you and your brother left earlier."

"No, sir, as you can see, I am still here."

"Well, I suppose we can bend the rules we've set up for your mother's visitors this once. Where is the princess?"

"You mean my mum?"

"Well, I don't know of any other princess that resides here in the Tower, do you?"

The boy shook his head.

"Well, please call her for me."

"I can't do that, sir."

"And why can't you do that? Do you know who I am?"

"Yes, sir, but I still can't call my mum." The boy put aside his book and stared at the man gravely.

The governor frowned. Future king or not, the young man was being impertinent.

"Perhaps you would like to tell me why you won't call her?"

The boy set aside his book, stood up, and faced the Tower governor.

"I'm afraid I can't, sir. My mum's escaped."

62

❖

Marlowe and Dutton sat in bed in Dutton's apartment and watched the stunning news about the princess's escape. She had left the Tower in the company of her younger son—and dressed in the clothes of her older boy, who was about the same height as her.

The boys had smuggled in clothes for the older brother to dress in after he gave up the ones the guards had seen him wear for his visit with his mother.

Dutton left the bed for a few moments and came back with two glasses of beer. "Called my editor," he said. "They'll be running a story in the morning that an unnamed source had witnessed the princess being beamed up to an alien space ship."

Marlowe choked on her beer. "Who came up with that nonsense?"

Dutton shrugged and grinned modestly. "I did. Great times bring out the best in my writing."

"He's not dead," Marlowe said.

"Of course he's not. She's disappeared, but her younger son arrived safely home by taxi. Both boys deny knowing where their mum's flown off to."

"I'm talking about their father."

❖

He stared at her. "You've got your own inside scoop on alien abduction, do you?"

"He's not dead. That's the secret under the rose."

He took a long sip of beer and stared at the telly. He clicked it off and turned to her. "All right, luv, spill it."

"Howler's letter was a blackmail letter to the prince. You said to think like Howler, didn't you? You always said Howler was smart crazy, not *crazy* crazy. And he had magic hands at bringing life back to dead bodies. A body reconstructionist, you said."

"He was a wizard at plastic surgery, with flesh or wax, that I give you."

"That's what the message was all about. Those body parts you found at the Abbey, those are the leftovers."

"Leftovers from what?"

"From creating a body to be buried as the Prince of Wales."

"You're crazy. Damp old England has made mold grow in your brain."

"Don't you see? You were right when you said it was a message, you just had the wrong message. He re-created the Abbey horror just to show the prince that he was going to expose him. When you talked to him, he kept referring to the prince as being alive, kept thinking that he'd blackmail him. Well, guess what, he is blackmailing him, or trying to."

"You're telling me that you think the Royals hired Howler to make a dummy body to be buried? What about the real body?"

"I don't think it was the Royals who hired Howler, not the queen for sure. There was no real body. You know what really did it for me? I suddenly realized that in this homicide investigation, the coroner's office had not taken pictures of the prince's body in a way that made him identifiable. The pictures turned over to me from the coroner's office didn't show his face."

"I'm still not getting it."

"I'm just getting it. I think I know what has bothered me the most about the princess—she was truly a nice person. There simply wasn't the malice in her that permits one to kill. To the contrary, in the past, she turned the violence on herself. Even abused women usually don't

❖

attempt to hurt themselves repeatedly before they finally blow and kill their husbands.

"What I'm seeing is a plot, not by the queen or the government, but by two star-crossed lovers who found themselves in a terrible situation—a bad marriage and the whole world spying on them, paparazzi watching their every move, driving them crazy, constantly embarrassing them. What if these two just sat down one day and said the hell with it, let's get out of this? What if they decided one day that what they really wanted to do with their lives is be normal, be able to walk into a store and buy a pair of socks without causing a sensation? These people have vast amounts of money and friends around the world. It wouldn't be hard for them to do a vanishing act."

"I don't know—"

"Yes, you do, I hear it in your voice. The prince has powerful friends who could set the whole thing up and make sure the local authorities don't look too closely into the shooting. The gun she shoots him with is loaded with a blank instead of a real bullet. One of his close friends is his doctor, he was there and was the person who had the prince removed to inside the palace. They would have arranged at an earlier time for Howler to create a look-alike from spare body parts. Hell, with ears like the Prince of Wales had, it wouldn't be hard to fool a casual onlooker. And there wouldn't be that many casual onlookers because you're talking about a man and his close intimates who have enormous power and influence. They can dictate exactly who gets to see the body, even during a police investigation.

"The one flaw was Howler. They needed him, but he was uncontrollable. The Royal Protection officers guarding him may be in on the plot, or the government has stumbled on to it and is working to cover it up, to do damage control."

"My God, this is better than my alien abduction story."

"Don't you dare try to get it printed—I'll hound you to the grave if you do. You know, I really do like her. I'm just beginning to realize how much I have in common with her. Neither of us cared for school or did well at it, we're both essentially high school dropouts whose first job was babysitting. We came out of dysfunctional families, ruled by domi-

❖

nant fathers. But in our own ways, we both became a success. She had little education, but she had love for people, especially for the underdog, and the whole world recognized it. And hell, she wasn't that overboard in the romance department. There aren't many women on this planet who haven't dreamt of Prince Charming sweeping them off their feet and riding off into the sunset.

"I've never met the prince, but I've come to have a lot of empathy for him even if he was born in a palace. In a strange way, she was right when she said, I was lucky to have been born poor. But she needed to add a caveat—I was lucky to have been born poor and had the good fortune to have wanted to better myself and the luck and drive to make it. They never had a chance. I started at the bottom and reached for the sky, they started at the top and had nowhere to go but down. Even my marriage was different than hers. I got into a bad marriage, but at least I never fooled myself into thinking that it was a fairy tale."

"That's the mistake, isn't it? Fairy tales usually are horror stories."

"What do you mean?"

"Have you ever read Cinderella? Not the modern children's-book version or the Hollywood version, but the original tale?"

"I don't know, I read whatever small children read, or maybe it was a Walt Disney movie I remember."

"Then you're in for a surprise if you read the original fairy tale, because it's a real horror story. You know the business about Cinderella leaving her glass slipper at the ball and the prince coming to her house to see if it fits any of the girls? Well, the two stepsisters were members of a dysfunctional family—they had a mother that belonged with Howler, locked up in a ward for the criminally insane.

"When the prince gave the first stepsister the slipper to try on, the mother took her into another room. The girl's foot was too long, so they cut off the girl's big toe so her foot would slip into it. Seeing the girl's foot in the shoe, the prince thought she was the girl he'd danced with at the ball. But as he rode away with her on his horse, he saw blood dripping from the shoe and caught on to the fact her toe had been hacked off."

"My God, that's horrible."

"Gets worse. He brings that sister back to the house and gives the

❖

slipper for the other stepsister to try on. The mother takes her into the other room to fit it and it turns out that she couldn't get her heel into it."

"You're not going to tell me . . ."

"Right! She cut off the girl's heel. Then the same thing happens, the prince takes her away and discovers the bleeding foot."

"What happens next?"

"Cinderella lives happily ever after, but her two sisters didn't."

"What happened to them?"

"If I tell you, you'll never believe in another fairy tale. I can tell you this—it's worse than cutting off a toe."

"Is there a moral to all this? Or did you just tell it to get me sick?"

"The moral, luv, is that there are no fairy tales, but life doesn't have to be a horror story. They made their lives into a mess themselves. The prince and the princess were mere mortals, just like the rest of us. They didn't want to show it, because when they did, they would disappoint us. We want them to be special, but they put their pants on one leg at a time like the rest of us. They should have just been honest with each other and the world, done their thing, and told the rest of the world to screw off."

Marlowe kissed him long and hard. "Dutton, when it comes to philosophy about the mysteries of life, I think you should stick to alien abduction theories."

❖

When the wedding with the King's son was to be celebrated, the two false sisters came and wanted to get into favor with Cinderella and share her good fortune.

When the betrothed couple went to church, the elder was at the right side and the younger at the left, and the pigeons pecked out one eye from each of them.

Afterwards as they came back, the elder was at the left, and the younger at the right, and then the pigeons pecked out the other eye from each.

And thus, for their wickedness and falsehood, they were punished with blindness all their days.

— CINDERELLA

63

❖

Rome

Two young women, sales clerks in a department store in the Eternal City, huddled together near a cash register and whispered to each other.

"What a strange man that foreigner is over there at the sock rack."

"What's so strange about him?"

"He's buying a pair of socks, but he's taking forever to do it. He doesn't know his size or that one size fits most men, can't make up his mind about the colors. He asked me whether he was supposed to coordinate the color of socks with his shoes or with his clothes. All this for buying a pair of socks. I wanted to ask him, is your mama still dressing you?"

"He *is* a little odd. He's looking at the price tag like he's trying to figure out what it means. Did you notice his ears, too?"

"Aren't they strange? Both are bandaged, like he's just been operated on."

❖

She felt Aladár's fingers undoing her gown, and as it fell to the floor he lifted her in his arms.

With his mouth holding her captive, he carried her away into a glorious secret kingdom of their own where there was no pride . . . only a fiery, uncontrolled, ecstatic love.

—BARBARA CARTLAND, *THE PROUD PRINCESS*